LOUISE,
Soccer
Star?

LOUISE, Soccer, Star?

by STEPHEN KRENSKY

pictures by SUSANNA NATTI

DIAL BOOKS FOR YOUNG READERS

New York

Published by Dial Books for Young Readers
A division of Penguin Putnam Inc.
345 Hudson Street
New York, New York 10014

Designed by Kimi Weart
The text for this book was set in Caslon 540.
Printed in the U.S.A. on acid-free paper
3 5 7 9 10 8 6 4 2

Library of Congress Cataloging in Publication Data
Krensky, Stephen.
Louise, soccer star?/by Stephen Krensky; pictures by Susanna Natti.
p. cm.
Summary: Louise's love of soccer and her high hopes
for the new season are tested when she feels overshadowed
by a talented new player.
ISBN 0-8037-2495-0 (hc trade)
[1. Soccer—Fiction.] I. Natti, Susanna, ill. II. Title.
PZ7.K883 Lmk 2000
[Fic]—dc21   99-048535

*For all the keepers, sweepers, midfielders,
wings, forwards, and strikers in
Lexington Youth Soccer*
S. K.

To Aunt Betty and Uncle Teddy
S. N.

CHAPTER 1

"Go! Go! Go!"

The words rang through Louise Page's head as she sprinted down the soccer field, dribbling the ball expertly through a clutch of midfielders—left, right, left, right. . . . The ball never strayed more than a few inches from her foot.

Suddenly, the fullbacks charged. Louise dodged one, then another. Ahead, the defending sweeper was moving forward, trying to contain her.

Just a little closer, thought Louise. That's *it*. . . .

As the sweeper closed in, Louise threw a quick head fake and blew by her.

The crowd in the stands rose to its feet.

"LOU-ISE! LOU-ISE!"

Though she couldn't help hearing her name, Louise remained focused. She looked around quickly to pass. Assist or goal, it made no difference to her. Unfortunately, her blazing speed had left her teammates far behind.

"Oh, well," she murmured, "they're trying their best. But it's time for action—and I *won't* let them down."

Just then, the stopper tried to force her to the outside. Louise did a quick stutter step and a spinning reverse cut. The stopper tried to keep up but, dazzled by Louise's deft moves, she tripped over her own feet.

"LOU-ISE!"

She was now in the goal area. Just ahead, she could see the goalie sweating, nervously shifting her weight from one foot to the other.

Cool and collected, Louise smiled. At this

distance, her aim was deadly.

The crowd was shouting again.

"LOU-ISE! LOU-ISE!"

Eyes glued to the goal, Louise focused on the far post. She pulled back her foot, prepared to strike.

"LOU-ISE! How many times do I have to call you?"

Louise sighed. She opened her eyes and looked up from her bed. The crowd, the soccer field, and her soon-to-be goal all faded away.

"What is it, Mother?"

Mrs. Page was standing in the doorway. "Are you ready?"

"I just have to put on my cleats."

"Your soccer practice starts in ten minutes. We don't want to be late."

Louise reached forward and pulled on her shin guards. She smiled up at the wall, where a poster of the Women's U.S.A. World Cup champions beamed back at her.

Her younger brother, Lionel, appeared at the door.

"Still not ready? You know, Louise, you're taking a big chance."

"I am? How come?"

"By not getting to your practice early. All the lucky uniform numbers will be taken before you get there."

Louise held up her hand. "I'm not worried. Everybody knows I like number 7. That's always been my number. Nobody else will take it."

"You can't be so sure what some people will do," Lionel insisted. "So just remember, I warned you."

Louise waved off his concern. She had been preparing for this day all summer. What could possibly go wrong?

CHAPTER 2

It was only a short ride to the soccer field, but Louise spent the whole time drumming her fingers on the armrest.

"Can't we go any faster?" she asked.

"*Now* you're in a hurry," said her mother.

"I guess I am."

Mrs. Page smiled. "You've really been looking forward to this season, haven't you?"

Louise nodded. Last year she had been among the younger players on her team. It had been hard to keep up with the bigger, faster girls.

But this year would be different. This year

Louise and her friends would be the bigger, faster kids.

As they reached the town soccer fields, they saw three team practices going on.

"Which one is yours?" asked Mrs. Page.

"Over there. To the right. I see Emily and Megan. Um, can you let me out here?"

"Afraid I'll embarrass you?" Her mother sighed. "And here I went to the trouble of removing the spinach from between my teeth."

Louise rolled her eyes. "See you later, Mother."

She ran over to join her friends. Megan was busy computing the odds of scoring from midfield. She was very good with numbers and could make an equation out of almost any situation.

"I suppose wind velocity would play a part," she said. "Not to mention the barometric pressure."

"If you say so," said Emily. "Hey, Louise, we were beginning to wonder. The uniforms are over there." She pointed to a box on the grass.

Louise rummaged through it. "Number 7 is gone!"

"Don't look at me," said Emily. "I've got 9."

"Mine's 13," said Megan.

Louise looked around. "There it is—on some new girl."

"That's Trelawney Hunt," said Emily. "She just moved into town."

"Tre-hooey?"

"Tre-lawn-ey," Emily repeated. "It's a British name. Which makes sense because Trelawney is from England."

"Well, then, I guess she couldn't know about me and my number 7. I'd better go talk to her about it."

This new girl was bouncing a soccer ball from one knee to the other and then down to her foot.

Louise watched in awe. Trelawney made it look so easy. Louise always felt like a jerky wind-up toy when she tried it herself.

"Excuse me," she said. "I think you took my shirt by accident."

Trelawney trapped the ball. "I did?"

"You see, number 7 is special to me. Good luck, you might say."

Trelawney bounced the ball on her right foot. Once, twice, three times. "I didn't realize you could reserve a certain number."

"You can't, exactly," Louise admitted. She hesitated. How could she put what she was feeling into words?

"Never mind," Trelawney went on. "I'll let you have it. My name's Trelawney, by the way. Trelawney Hunt. My mum just got transferred over here to the States."

"Hi. I'm Louise Page. Um, welcome to America. And never mind about the shirt."

"Really, you can have it."

Now that Trelawney was offering the shirt, Louise felt funny about taking it. The shirt would probably like being with Trelawney because she was such a good player. "No thanks. I couldn't take it now," she said.

"Why not? I've only just put it on. It isn't even sweaty yet."

"I know, but it's, um, bonded with you already. It would be bad luck to change things now."

"I've never heard of that. Is it an American custom?"

Actually, it was only Louise's custom, but she didn't want to explain that. It was hard enough to accept that the soccer season had barely begun—and she was already starting off on the wrong foot.

CHAPTER 3

"Rats! Rats! And more rats!"

Emily laughed. "Sounds like a plague to me. Come on, now, Louise, it wasn't *that* bad."

They were standing with Megan after school. That morning Mr. Hathaway had asked Louise to give Trelawney a tour of the school. Then he sat the two of them at adjoining desks.

"Your face is all red, Louise," Emily added.

Megan agreed. "I estimate your blood pressure is up 20%. You should try to calm down."

Louise continued to pace. "Calm down? Hah! Did you see the coach actually rubbing

18

her hands together? She was so pleased. *'Trelawney can show us'* this and *'Trelawney can show us'* that."

"But that wasn't Trelawney's fault, and she actually looked pretty uncomfortable about the whole thing."

"I guess. But remember last year, when *we* were smaller than all the older kids in the league? Well, this is supposed to be *our* big chance."

"I remember you wanted to play center forward," said Emily.

Louise nodded. "That's right! And I would if it weren't for her. First she takes my number, then my soccer position."

"Or *football* position, as she probably calls it," Megan added. "Actually, it's called football or *futbol* in almost every country in the world. It's just here in the United States that we insist on—"

"Megan, that's not the point," Louise went on. "I just want to know why this had to happen to *me*."

"It didn't exactly happen to you," Megan reminded her. "I mean, Trelawney didn't single you out."

Louise sighed. "That's easy for you to say. Trelawney isn't a goalie, like you are."

"Well, if it makes you feel any better, Trelawney won't be here forever."

"She won't?"

"Uh-uh. She told me that her mother's company only transferred her here for five years."

Louise gasped. "Five years! I'm supposed to feel better because Trelawney Hunt will *only* be here until we're in high school?"

Emily shook her head. "Oh, Louise, things aren't that bad. Besides, it's exciting to have such a good player on the team. We might even win a few games."

Louise snorted. "Well, Coach always says winning isn't everything."

"True," Emily admitted, "but it could make for a nice change."

Louise just bit her lip. "And do you know what's even worse?" she said, sighing.

"No, what?"

"She's *nice*. I mean, the whole time I was taking her around, she was *so* friendly. Why couldn't she be all mean or snobby?"

Megan looked quickly in both directions. "It must be part of a master plan to ruin your life."

"Yes," Louise said firmly, "that *must* be it."

CHAPTER 4

The first game of the season always made Louise feel funny. Somehow these official games seemed so different from the ones played at recess. There was this feeling of being in the spotlight, of having everyone watching you. Of course, that made the game more exciting too.

Louise's parents and Lionel were all at the game. On the one hand, Louise liked to have her family cheering for her. On the other hand, there was always the very real danger of being embarrassed—like once when her father had shouted, "Totally awesome, Louise!" after she had just made a simple pass up the line. Of course, what made it even worse was hearing words like *totally* and *awesome* coming out of her parents' mouths.

"Come on, Lou-ise!" her mother yelled as the referee blew the whistle to start the game.

For the first few minutes, neither team had a shot on goal. The ball just ping-ponged back and forth on the field.

Then a long goal kick bounced toward Louise at midfield. As she trapped it, Trelawney broke toward the middle. Louise considered a quick cross, but hesitated.

Thunnnk!

A defender kicked the ball out from between her legs.

Her teammates groaned.

"Shake it off, Louise!"

"Keep your head in the game."

Twweeeet!

The whistle sounded the end of the first half with the score still 0–0. The coach huddled the team together.

"I know it's early in the season," she said, "but we need to look out for each other a bit more. Remember what Benjamin Franklin said: 'If we don't hang together, then surely we will all hang separately.'"

Louise turned to Trelawney. "He said that right before the American Revolution."

Trelawney laughed. "Just a little before my time."

In the second half Trelawney unloaded one strong shot. Then another. And a third. But each time, the opposing goalie managed to block the shot.

"Try to contain them!" the coach yelled. "Don't let them get by you."

Things would be different if I were center forward, Louise thought. She was so ready to charge down the field, to dart fearlessly in and out and head the ball into the goal. But that was the center forward's job—Trelawney's job. So instead Louise shuffled up and down the field until she was taken out for a rest.

The game ended in a 1–1 tie. Both teams seemed relieved to have escaped without a loss.

"That new player is really something," said Mr. Page as they drove off. "What's that tricky thing she does?"

"It's called a *rainbow*," Lionel explained. "You have to kick the ball with your heels so that it comes back over your head. No one else in the whole school can do it. And did you see the way she headed in the tying goal? She's amazing."

"Do we have to talk about this now?" Louise asked.

Her mother frowned. "You're a little grumpy, aren't you? After all, a tie isn't so bad."

Mr. Page rubbed his forehead. "Heading the ball always looks like it hurts. Anyway, Lionel, no one player wins the game alone. Or ties it either. It's a team effort. Right, Louise?"

Louise had scrunched herself up in the

backseat. "I guess," she said. Louise knew teamwork was important, but she wanted to stand out at the same time.

So far, she hadn't even come close.

CHAPTER 5

The next morning at school Louise found herself approaching the back of a large crowd.

"What's going on?" she asked. "Was there an accident? Is somebody hurt?"

Emily turned around. "Jasper made a bet with Trelawney that she couldn't bounce a soccer ball off her knees twenty times before it hit the ground."

"How's she doing?" asked Louise. Even with hours of practice, her personal record was only eight.

"Let's go and see," said Emily. Both girls squirmed forward for a better look.

"Eighteen, nineteen, twenty," Trelawney said. She caught the ball in her hands.

"I can't believe it," said Jasper. "On the first try too. You're sure you're not a professional?"

Trelawney smiled. "Just an amateur in good standing."

More than good standing, thought Louise. Twenty was *very* impressive.

"Do you think you could show me how to do that?" Jasper asked.

"Sure. Start like this. . . ."

Emily put her hand on Louise's shoulder.

"Louise, are you feeling okay? You look a little pale."

Louise smiled weakly. "I'll be fine. Hey, do you want to come over after school today? I've got the new issue of *Soccer Monthly*. We could take another look at that World Cup video, you know, for pointers."

"Sorry," said Emily. "Trelawney invited me over." She paused. "But you could probably come too. I'll ask—"

"No, no," said Louise. "You go ahead."

In class, Mr. Hathaway began a lesson on the Greek myths. It turned out to be a subject Trelawney had already studied. When Mr. Hathaway asked for impressions of life on Mt. Olympus, she rattled off descriptions of the gods and goddesses without pausing for breath. She even worked in a joke about Zeus' lightning bolts of inspiration.

At lunch, Trelawney joined the girls at their usual table.

"Are castles as cold as they look?" Megan asked, taking a bite from her sandwich.

Trelawney shivered. "Worse," she said. "And damp too. Not to mention all those chamber pots." She held up her milk carton. "A toast to modern plumbing."

"Hear, hear," said Emily.

"There's something I've always wanted to know," Louise broke in. "Does steak-and-kidney pie have real kidney in it?"

"Of course," said Trelawney. "It's a key ingredient."

"I think there was some kidney in yesterday's mystery glop," said Megan.

Louise looked down at her sandwich, which she was relieved to see was good old peanut butter and jelly.

But even peanut butter and jelly didn't seem to help Louise much during the afternoon soccer practice. The coach played her in different positions, but in each one Louise just shuffled along.

If I were center forward, things would be different, thought Louise. I'd be a blur, a flash, a gust—

The coach blew her whistle.

"Louise, where are you going?"

Louise looked puzzled. "I was just dribbling down the wing."

"But, Louise, you're going the wrong way!"

Louise felt her face turning bright red.

Some of the other girls laughed, but most kept their eyes on the ground.

"Enough, enough," the coach warned them. "Louise, unturn yourself and get into the game."

Louise nodded. But she couldn't help feeling a little lost. Everything seemed to be going downhill lately. Enough, she decided, was definitely enough.

It was time to bounce back.

CHAPTER 6

The front door of the Pages' house slammed shut.

"Is that you, Louise?" Mrs. Page called out.

Louise grunted.

"Hmmm," her mother went on. "An after-school grunt. Definitely not a good sign. Can we talk about it?"

Louise grunted again. Twice.

"I'll take that as a no. But let me know if you change your mind."

Louise made herself a snack. Then she plopped down in front of the computer to play Trek, her favorite adventure game. Usually she could forget about the real world while maneuvering through Trek's tricky terrain. But today even successfully passing through the Forest of Terrifying Trees didn't help.

She closed down the game and turned on the TV instead.

"*Welcome to* The Muscle Hustle. *Our guest today is going to demonstrate new ways to build muscles and increase coordination.*"

"*That's right, Biff. Instead of joining an expensive health club or buying fancy equipment, why not integrate household activities into an effective strength-and-conditioning program?*"

Louise sat up. Now this sounded interesting. If she could build up her muscles and endurance, the team would have to make room for more than one star. She grabbed a pen and started taking notes.

A short while later Louise stood in her driveway checking off the items on her list—a hose, a bucket of soapy water, a backpack full of books.

She started sponging the car's hood in a circular motion. The backpack weighed her down, making it harder to move. But when she returned to the soccer field, her muscles would be primed for action.

"Wow!"

Lionel was standing at the edge of the driveway. "What did you do?" he went on.

Louise put down the hose. "What do you mean?"

"It must have been something really terrible to get such a punishment."

"Lionel, I'm not being punished."

Her brother laughed. "Oh, I suppose it was *your* idea to wash the car?"

"That's right."

Lionel took a step back. "Is this some kind of weird disease?"

"I'm not sick, Lionel. I'm building up my cardiovascular system."

"Is that dangerous?"

"No, Lionel. It just means I'm creatively increasing my endurance."

"But you're still washing the car, right?" Lionel squinted at her. "Are you *sure* you're the real Louise?"

"Yes, Lionel, I'm the real Louise, the one who's getting tired of all these silly questions."

"That still doesn't—"

"Enough, Lionel! Just stay out of my way. Unless, of course," she added darkly, picking up the hose, "you feel like being washed too."

CHAPTER 7

"You might think," Mr. Hathaway was saying, "that given their many powers the Greek gods and goddesses would have been happy and easygoing. But the gods were all too human in their loves and hates, in their strengths and weaknesses. None of them were very forgiving, and revenge was ultimately their favorite sport. Zeus, after all, had come to power by betraying and imprisoning his own father. So it wasn't surprising that they all spent so much time looking over their shoulders. Yes, Emily?"

"I know that some gods didn't get along at all. Which ones were they?"

Mr. Hathaway laughed. "It's a long list. As the god of war, Ares was always very touchy and loved to start fights. But jealousy between gods was the biggest problem. For example, Hera was Zeus' wife and the mother of many other gods and goddesses. But Athena simply sprang from Zeus' forehead one day. So Hera couldn't claim any credit for her. Her sudden arrival caught Hera by surprise."

Louise stole a look at Trelawney. She knew what that felt like.

* * *

41

At lunch Emily, Megan, Trelawney, and Louise were still discussing the different myths.

"I'd like to be one of those Titans," said Emily. "Can you see me as a giant walking the earth?"

"Yes," said Louise. "Stepping on the rest of us and squashing us like bugs."

Emily considered this. "What would be the odds of stepping on someone, Megan?"

Megan considered the problem. "Maybe 38%. Of course, we'd have some warning, considering the Titans' shadows and the vibrations they made as they walked. So maybe we could avoid getting squished."

"Things didn't work out that way in *Rex on the Rampage*," Louise reminded them.

Megan groaned.

Emily shook her head.

"I loved that movie!" said Trelawney.

Louise was surprised. "You did?"

"Oh, yes. I especially liked the first part, when the Tyrannosaurus destroys Tokyo."

"No, no," said Louise. "First the dinosaur trashes New York. Then Tokyo."

Trelawney shook her head. "I don't think so."

"Trelawney, I've seen this movie five times. I know which city gets flattened—"

"Wait a minute, Louise," said Emily. "I think Tokyo *is* destroyed first."

"That's right," said Megan. "Because after Tokyo the dinosaur has a giant metal splinter

43

in his paw. And it gets knocked out against the Empire State Building."

Louise blinked. She had forgotten about that splinter. Trelawney was right and she was wrong—again.

"I guess," she said abruptly, and was very quiet after that.

Louise went home alone that afternoon. Emily had offered to play, but Louise had told her that she had errands to do.

After consulting her notes, Louise started on the next phase of her conditioning.

"Louise, what's going on?"

"What does it look like, Lionel?"

"It looks like you're cleaning the house."

"Wrong again, Lionel. This is a muscle-conditioning follow-up."

"I guess that explains why you filled your pockets with sand."

"How did you . . ." She looked around. "Oh, I guess I am leaking a little. . . ."

Lionel backed away. "First the car and now

this. Whatever you're infected with, I hope *I* don't catch it!"

Louise ignored him. "I am Hera," she told herself, huffing and puffing as she went up and down the stairs. "And when I get done, all of Olympus, especially Athena, will know my power!"

CHAPTER 8

The leaf caught Louise's eye as it fluttered to the ground.

Wait . . . wait . . .

At the last second Louise swung out with her foot, trying to kick the leaf with her big toe. It was the next step of her program—*practicing her conditioning in an unfamiliar environment.*

"Louise goes for the loose ball. . . ."

The leaf caught the edge of her sneaker.

"She fights off a defender to chip toward midfield. . . ."

Louise took another swing. *Missed!*

"Rats!" she muttered. That was twelve misses in a row!

The grass was covered with leaves that had fallen earlier. Starting in one corner, Louise began pushing them around. She did several sweeps with her right foot, then an equal number with her left.

"Hey, Louise!"

Megan came running up to her. "Your mother

said you were back here. What are you doing?"

Louise folded her arms. "It's kind of like yard work, but not exactly."

Megan looked at the scattered line of leaves. "Hmmmm. It almost looks like you're raking. Of course, it might help if you were actually holding a rake."

Louise knew she had to say something. "Oh, sure, I could use a rake," she said. "But this way it's more like soccer practice. I'm swinging my foot a lot."

Megan smiled. "Does that really help?"

"It's an experiment, really. If you want to practice too, there's plenty of leaves to go around."

Megan shook her head. "Thanks, but no thanks. I mean, don't get me wrong, Louise. I like soccer. I just don't love it like you do. Anyway, I came over to see if you wanted to go downtown."

Louise surveyed the leaf-covered lawn.

"Thanks. But I've still got lots more practicing to do."

"Okay. Well, I'll see you later. Hi, Mr. Page."

"Hello yourself, Megan," said Louise's father, coming around the corner. "Any good odds to report today?"

"Not yet. But it's early. There's an 83% chance of a prediction before nightfall. Bye."

Mr. Page waited till Megan was out of sight. Then he spoke up.

"Louise, I think we need to talk."

Louise looked up at her father's face. She knew what his *we-need-to-talk* voice meant. She wasn't in trouble exactly, but he was bothered by something she was doing, something that should be changed.

"Couldn't we talk later?" she asked. "I'm kind of in the middle of things."

"No excuses, Louise," said Mr. Page. "It's about your behavior lately. Now, don't get me wrong. The house has never looked better."

Louise kept sweeping, but her foot slowed a little.

"It's the reason behind all this that I'm concerned about."

"What did Lionel tell you?" she asked.

"Enough. And I'm glad he did. You know, Louise, I usually think you tackle your problems constructively. But here you seem to be a little, um, over-sensitive—"

"I am not!" Louise snapped. "I just thought

this season was going to be my chance to show what I could do. And then along comes Trelawney to mess things up."

Mr. Page frowned. "Hold on a minute, Louise. Just because Trelawney's a good player doesn't mean you can't be too. I'm sure the team can use as many good players as possible."

"I still think *my* friends should take *my* side."

Her father smiled. "Louise, I'll bet they don't even know they haven't. Adding a new friend doesn't have to mean getting rid of old ones. And put yourself in Trelawney's place—new town, new classmates, new country. That must be pretty hard."

Louise opened her mouth to speak, but no words came out. She knew her father was right, but knowing it and admitting it were not the same thing.

"It just doesn't seem fair," she said finally.

"I can understand that," her father said.

"Please don't agree with me," said Louise. "I can't argue with you if you agree with me."

Her father smiled. "I know. That's one of the best strategies in *The Father's Handbook*."

Louise folded her arms. "You're always mentioning that book. I'd like to see it sometime."

Mr. Page shook his head. "Not allowed. Definitely not allowed."

"Well, that's not fair either."

"Maybe. Or maybe it all depends on how you look at it. Most things are that way."

"Yes," Louise agreed reluctantly. They definitely were.

CHAPTER 9

Louise stood amid the swirl of clouds at mid-field. All around her, the gods and goddesses were warming up for the game. Zeus and Hera were the opposing coaches. The three Fates were the referees, which made sense since they were the only ones who didn't fear Zeus and his thunderbolts.

Louise had been invited to participate because the gods had decided that she was just too good to play with mere mortals. Off to the left she saw Hermes, the messenger, lapping the field on his winged feet. Poseidon, god of the sea, was in goal. All that swimming had given him arms that seemed

to be everywhere—she had heard his teammates call him "the octopus."

"Hey, Louise!"

Louise blinked—and the gods and goddesses faded away.

Emily was standing over her.

"Didn't you hear the coach? We're supposed to do a warm-up lap before the game
starts."

As Louise sprinted around the field, she imagined herself having the speed of Hermes and the strength of Hercules. That would surely impress the other mortals—uh, players. Of course, running around in a toga and sandals would be tricky. . . .

Louise could have used those Olympian skills right then. Neither team made any big mistakes in the first half, and the ball zigged and zagged back and forth.

At the start of the fourth quarter, Louise stood on the sidelines. This was only her second substitution. Normally by this point she was running out of steam. But after two weeks of car washing, vacuuming, and basement cleaning, she was not even breathing hard.

As the ball went out of bounds, the coach called for substitutions.

"All right," she said, "we're down by one, but there's still plenty of time. Louise, go back in at right midfield. And take the throw-in."

"What about forward, Coach? I'm not tired at all."

"That's why I need you to clog up the middle."

Clog up the middle? She hadn't been doing all those chores—um, training—just to be a clog. What was the matter with the coach?

Couldn't she tell that Louise had become a sleek and powerful soccer weapon? All she needed was a chance.

"But—"

"Louise, who's the coach here? Now take the throw-in!"

Louise was so flustered that she lifted her back foot on the throw-in—and the other team got the ball. But she quickly made up for her mistake, forcing a turnover.

"Over here, Louise!"

Louise heard Megan—and chipped the ball to her on the wing. Then she sprinted down-field, receiving Megan's kick back on the give-and-go. As the defense converged on Louise, Trelawney was left alone near the goal. She waved frantically to Louise, trying to get her attention without alerting the other team.

But Louise kept her head down. Think goal, she told herself, and nothing else.

Darting past the sweeper, she dodged one fullback and spun past the other. As the goalie

charged at her, Louise chipped the ball up just beyond her reach.

GOAL!

Louise pumped her hands in the air as the crowd cheered.

On the way home, Mr. Page stole a glance at Louise in the rear-view mirror. She was staring out the window.

"You're awfully quiet, Louise," her father commented. "Wait till you tell Lionel you scored the tying goal. He'll be impressed."

"I suppose."

"I would have thought you'd be more excited than that."

Louise sighed. "Well, I wanted to be. But it's hard to be excited when your team isn't excited with you."

"The crowd cheered," her father reminded her.

"Yeah, but the crowd doesn't know that much. They're just happy to see a goal."

"And what did your team see differently?" asked Mr. Page.

Louise hesitated. She knew the answer—she just wasn't sure she wanted to say it out loud.

"Louise?"

"Well," she said slowly, "I didn't look for any help. I was kind of a ball hog." Louise sighed.

"Ah," said Mr. Page. He didn't say anything more. He didn't have to.

Louise knew what he was thinking.

CHAPTER 10

Louise hesitated as she and her mother entered the mall.

"Mother, once we're inside, do we have to walk together?"

Mrs. Page drummed her fingers on her arm. "How far apart did you have in mind? Three feet? Six? What if I just walk ten steps behind you?"

Louise considered it. "I suppose that would be all right. Thanks."

"If you're embarrassed to be seen with me," said her mother, "imagine how I feel."

"What do you mean?"

"My daughter is walking through the mall

carrying a backpack full of books. Does she
need the books at the mall? No. Are they
heavy? Yes."

"It's all part of my training," Louise
explained.

"Don't get me wrong," said her mother. "I
love our spotless garage and weeded back-
yard. I just think you're overdoing it a little."

"Not at all," said Louise, adjusting one of
the straps weighing down her shoulder. "I
feel fine."

"Just remember, we could have gone to the library. They have lots of classic books on gods and goddesses."

"No, no, this has to be a new book, something that contains new information, new insights, new . . ."

"You mean something no one else in the class already knows."

Louise smiled. "I suppose you could put it like that. I prefer to think of it as part of my never-ending search for knowledge."

Her mother smiled back.

They parted inside the bookstore, promising to meet again in a few minutes. Louise was headed for the section labeled Myths & Legends when she heard one of the clerks talking to a customer.

"It *is* a tough level. You get out on the cliff and there doesn't seem to be anywhere to go."

Even from that brief description, Louise knew exactly what he was talking about.

"I haven't seen any guides for Trek published yet."

The girl he was talking to had her back turned, but Louise could see her nodding.

"Excuse me," said Louise. "But I know Trek and I've gotten past that point. You just have to . . ."

The clerk and the customer had turned toward her. The clerk looked a little bored, but the customer . . .

"Oh. It's you, Trelawney."

She nodded. "Hi, Louise."

"Ah," said the clerk, "you two know each other? Great. See if you can put your heads together."

He moved on to help someone else.

Louise knew that while this wasn't the *most* awkward moment in her life, it was certainly awkward enough.

Aware that her cheeks were beginning to flush, Louise was surprised to see that Trelawney also looked embarrassed.

"I had no idea," said Louise.

Trelawney looked around. "About what?"

"About you and Trek. I mean, I never pictured you playing computer games."

"Oh, yes," said Trelawney. "Back home I spent hours fairly glued to the screen."

"Really? What level are you on?"

Trelawney shrugged. "Only Level 4. I keep falling off the cliff."

Louise nodded. "I was stuck there for a while too. Then I realized you have to step back and take a running leap across the Conjurer's Chasm."

"I've tried jumping off," said Trelawney. "I always end up crushed on the rocks below."

"That's because they make you think it's a dead end," Louise explained. "But actually, if you start back and leap across, the screen scrolls forward to another cliff just out of view."

"Did you figure that out yourself?"

"I guess so." Louise grinned. "Of course, I ended up on the rocks myself a few times."

Trelawney blinked. "You're terribly clever, Louise."

Louise felt her face reddening again, but this time she didn't mind at all.

CHAPTER 11

"I don't get it."

Lionel was standing outside Louise's room. Louise was lying on her bed, reading *Soccer Monthly*.

"I said, 'I DON'T GET IT'!"

Louise lowered her magazine. "You don't get what, Lionel? You have to be more specific. After all, there are many things you don't get."

"I'm talking about Trelawney."

"What about her?"

"All of a sudden you're spending lots of time with her."

"So?"

"So I thought you didn't like her."

Louise smiled at him. "That just shows how little you know me, Lionel."

Lionel folded his arms. "Come on, Louise, tell the truth. What's your master plan? I'll bet it's something really sneaky."

"Sorry, Lionel. Go fish. I'm not planning—"

"Louise!" Mrs. Page called out from downstairs. "Trelawney's here!"

"Here!" Lionel gasped.

Louise ignored him and got up to greet her guest.

"Flee!" cried Lionel. "Run for your lives!"

"That's my little brother," Louise explained. "Say good-bye, Lionel."

"Good-bye, Lionel. I should tell you, though," he added to Trelawney. "I don't usually talk to myself like this."

Trelawney nodded. "That's good."

"Welcome to my world," said Louise. "How about a snack? I think we have some triple fudge ice cream."

"Scrumptious," said Trelawney. "We never had more than single fudge at home." She blinked suddenly.

Louise knew that look. It was the same one she had seen in the mirror after her first week at sleepaway camp.

"I guess it's hard settling in a new place," Louise said softly.

After polishing off their ice cream, the two girls sat down to play Trek on the computer.

Louise watched as Trelawney entered the Forbidden Swamp.

"That's perfect," said Louise. "Now pay attention around this next corner. One of the crocodiles is waiting there. Look closely, you can see his shadow."

Trelawney nodded, her eyes scanning across the screen.

"Now dart to the right and stop short. See the crocodile following you? He can't turn as fast as you can. So he keeps going—straight into the quicksand."

"Hurrah!" cried Trelawney, beaming. "I can't tell you how many times that croc did me in."

"It's all about timing," Louise explained. "You have to wait for the, um, *croc* to react before you make your move."

Trelawney nodded. "I never quite thought of it that way. It's really rather like how I think during a football match." She grinned. "I mean, a soccer game. You know, Louise, if you took the same sense of timing you showed here and put it on the soccer field, you could be amazing."

Louise blushed. "Really?"

"Oh, yes. You already have the moves. And you're obviously well trained. All you have to do is think beyond yourself. Just imagine the field as a giant computer screen with pieces moving around."

"Hmmm . . ."

"You just have to anticipate different moves. With a little practice, I think you could definitely surprise people."

Louise nodded. "I'd like that. People are always accusing me of being too predictable."

"Me too. 'We can always see you coming, Trelawney,' they say. 'You're as clear as glass.'"

Louise nodded. "Who do they think they are?"

"Quite right."

"Well, maybe if we work together, and practiced some plays, we could *both* surprise the team."

Trelawney smiled. "*I'd* like that," she said.

CHAPTER 12

It was late in the second half, and Louise couldn't help feeling that she had played this game before. The moves, the action—it all seemed so familiar.

Of course! This was almost exactly like her dream, the one where she was all alone and ready to score. But this was no dream. Her parents really were on the sidelines cheering, and her teammates were rushing into position.

"Shoot, Louise!" Megan screamed at her.

Louise had a shot, she could see that.

"Louise, come on! Time's running out!"

This came from Emily.

Louise waited. She knew she had a shot, but it wasn't a great one. But if she could just wait for the defense to collapse on her . . .

Imagine the field as a giant computer screen.

"Louise, watch out!"

But Louise *was* watching. As the sweeper bore down on her, cutting her angle to the goal, her chance to shoot vanished. But shooting wasn't what Louise had in mind.

"You snooze, you lose," said the sweeper, creeping closer.

Louise opened her arms to shrug—and chipped the ball gently toward the middle.

The startled sweeper leapt up, but the ball sailed just out of reach . . . and fell to where Trelawney was waiting.

The two girls had practiced this play for hours and hours. Trelawney had helped Louise understand that it was just like in Trek where you had to lure the gremlins into the pit so you could jump over them to safety. And Louise had helped her make that jump.

As the ball hit the ground, Trelawney trapped it neatly. Then she whirled around—and fired.

GOAL!

The whole team erupted in a giant cheer, and Louise joined in loudly. Hera and Athena, she thought, couldn't have done any better.

Tweeeet!

The referee blew her whistle—and the game was over.

The Pages rushed over from the sidelines to congratulate the winning team.

"Louise looked great out there," Megan's father said to Mr. Page.

"Thanks. I've been giving her pointers."

Mrs. Page laughed.

Louise was glad to see them, even Lionel. But his expression puzzled her.

"What's the matter, Lionel? You look disappointed."

"Gee, Louise," said Lionel, "I'm glad you

won and everything. But I thought you were going to do a rainbow or something."

"Well, Lionel," Louise said with a smile, "I guess that's just the way the ball bounces—and bounces back!"

And with that, she sprinted off to join the victory celebration.

EZRA POUND AMONG THE POETS

EZRA POUND
AMONG the POETS

HOMERHOMERHOMEI
OVIDOVIDOVIDOV
PO LI PO LI PO LI PO LIP
DANTEDANTEDANTE
WHITMANWHIT
BROWNINGBROW
YEATSYEATSYEATSY
WILLIAMSWILLI
ELIOTELIOTELIOTE

Edited by GEORGE BORNSTEIN

The University of Chicago Press   Chicago and London

The University of Chicago Press, Chicago 60637
The University of Chicago Press, Ltd., London

© 1985 by The University of Chicago
All rights reserved. Published 1985
Printed in the United States of America

94 93 92 91 90 89 88 87 86 85   5 4 3 2 1

Library of Congress Cataloging in Publication Data
Main entry under title:

Ezra Pound among the poets.

   Includes bibliographical references and index.
   1. Pound, Ezra, 1885–1972—Knowledge—Literature—
Addresses, essays, lectures.   2. Pound, Ezra, 1885–1972—
Influence—Addresses, essays, lectures.   3. Poetry—
History and criticism—Addresses, essays, lectures.
I. Bornstein, George.
PS3531.O82Z623   1985   811'.52   85-1076
ISBN 0-226-06640-1

For Jane

Contents

Acknowledgments

Shorter versions of these papers were delivered in a lecture series sponsored by the University of Michigan during the 1983/84 academic year. Vice-President Alfred S. Sussman continuously supported and encouraged this project in his capacity as dean of the Horace Rackham School of Graduate Study; so, too, did Provost B. E. Frye, Vice-President Charles G. Overberger, and the chairman of the Department of English, Professor John R. Knott, Jr. Ms. Gloria Parsons, Ms. Marjorie Howes, and Ms. Anna Battigelli provided capable support services. The students, faculty, and community of the University of Michigan offered enthusiastic and sensitive responses which sharpened the final form of these essays.

Introduction

George Bornstein

"In my university I found various men interested (or uninterested) in their subjects but, I think, no man with a view of literature as a whole, or with any idea whatsoever of the relation of the part he himself taught to any other part," recalled the iconoclastic Ezra Pound in an essay entitled "How to Read" (1929).[1] Pound's complaint has ironically come to be true even of some of his own modern defenders. Impressed by the rich erudition of Pound's work and thrown into a defensive posture by the controversies surrounding his wartime activities, his commentators have often aimed their labors chiefly at other Pound enthusiasts. The result has been a body of useful, learned, and often loving scholarship which has remained more isolated than it might from general literary consciousness. Poets have often taken what they needed from Pound piecemeal, but except for some welcome recent guidebooks the general reader—even the general academic reader—has remained about where he or she was thirty-five years ago.

Celebration of the centenary of Pound's birth this year offers a good time to rectify the situation. With Pound's achievement secure, if still not widely understood, Pound studies can turn outward again toward that genuinely comparative stance which his work invites. They can integrate that achievement with "a view of literature as a whole," or at least with the relation of Pound's poetry to that of other great poets. For finally, it is as a poet that Pound matters. In that belief, ten leading American scholars have come together to offer appreciations of Pound's relation to those poetic forerunners and contemporaries most important

to him—Homer, Ovid, Dante, Li Po, Whitman, Browning, Yeats, Eliot, and Williams—and to suggest something of his importance to writers today. For a poet as assimilative as Pound, the list could be extended almost indefinitely, but it does represent Pound's most important encounters with the literature of Greece, Rome, China, Tuscany, England, and America. Chronologically arranged, the ten essays offer a condensed curriculum for understanding a major line of modernist art. Those on Homer, Ovid, Whitman, Eliot, and Williams offer a synoptic view of Pound's lifelong involvement with those poets; the discussions of Li Po, Dante, Browning, and Yeats focus more on the crucial decade and a half stretching from Pound's graduate student days through the publication of the *Mauberley* sequence (1920); and the treatment of his influence necessarily draws on his entire career. As a group they raise important questions about the nature of literary influence, the constitution of the canon of major writers, and the relation between tradition and originality.

Pound held firm views on literary influence. "Be influenced by as many great artists as you can, but have the decency either to acknowledge the debt outright, or to try to conceal it," he advised in "A Retrospect." "Don't allow 'influence' to mean merely that you mop up the particular decorative vocabulary of some one or two poets whom you happen to admire" (*LE* 5). Certainly, Pound followed his own advice in opening himself to an extraordinary range of writers and in learning far more from them than mere tricks of decorative vocabulary. In so doing he displayed little of the anxiety posited by some contemporary influence theory; instead, he adhered to a more classical conception of influence as benign and strengthening. His elevation of craftsmanship, ideogrammic conception of literary history, and international allegiance helped to protect him from the fearfulness of the postmiltonic line of English poetry. For the first five essays in this volume, influence runs in one direction, from the earlier poets to Pound; in the last five, however, influence begins to run the other way as well, with Pound's impact on others increasingly outstripping their impact on him.

Fully half the essays extend Pound's canon by drawing heavily on previously unpublished materials. They remind us how difficult Pound found it to get his work into print, how much of his work remains unpublished or uncollected, and, hence, how partial a picture even the efforts of Faber in England and of New Directions in America present.

The case of Pound epitomizes that of modernist literature generally. Only recently have we come to realize that the problems of inaccurate texts and unpublished manuscript material so familiar in studies of earlier literature apply to high modernist works as well. Publication of the *Waste Land* manuscripts in 1971 provided the most spectacular recent example of how such research can reshape our view of the modernist achievement, and the new Cornell Yeats promises analogous results. Pound studies lag somewhat behind here, but new collections and editions do continue to appear sporadically and may achieve greater coherence in future. The present essays show what may be gained by scrutinizing the notes from which Pound worked in translating Li Po, considering his early effort at a Dantesque epic, pondering the Browningesque view of poetic influence in his student journal, analyzing the remarks on Yeats in letters to his wife, or examining unpublished portions of the Pound-Williams correspondence.

While all the essays study Pound's relation to other poets, they seek neither to diminish nor exalt him unfairly. At times, indeed, Pound by his own admission and the reader's testimony fails to equal the achievement of his great precursors. At other times, though, he succeeds in his great endeavor to "make it new" and thus to render the past vital for our time and to enable the achievements of the future. Such was always his aim. "My pawing over the ancients and semi-ancients has been one struggle to find out what has been done, once for all, better than it can ever be done again, and to find out what remains for us to do," he wrote (*LE* 11). It is our good fortune that Pound succeeded so often as poet, and that when he failed he instructed us even by his example. That legacy represents his continuing gift to us on this centenary occasion.

Notes

1. *Literary Essays of Ezra Pound*, ed. T. S. Eliot (New York: New Directions, 1968), p. 15. Hereafter cited in the text as *LE* followed by page number.

[OMERHOMERHOME]

Pound and Homer

Hugh Kenner

No exertion spent upon any of the great classics of the world, and attended with any amount of real result, is really thrown away. It is better to write one word upon the rock, than a thousand on the water or the sand.

—W. E. Gladstone, *Studies on Homer and the Homeric Age*

Homer is the West's six trillion dollar man. For two millennia and a half at least we have kept him alive and vigorous with an increasingly complex and costly life-support system that from earliest times has drawn on all the technology around. To make papyrus in Egypt, then construct and navigate a ship to take it to Athens, entailed most of the chemistry, the metallurgy, the carpentry, and the mathematics accessible to Mediterranean men of the fifth century B.C. What Athenians did with papyrus was, of course, write out on it the two big books of Homer.

Parchment came later, and parchment Homers were precious spoil from Byzantium, 1453. Renaissance architects designed libraries that housed handmade copies; blacksmiths forged chains to keep them where they belonged. As soon as there were printing presses in Italy, there was a folio Homer, two volumes, printed in Florence about 1480. The next need was for a Homer you could carry around. That meant both smaller sheets and smaller type. Pound's Canto 30 shows us Francesco da Bologna incising dies with the Greek letters they'd need for the pocket Aldine Homer.[1] To aid comprehension scholars made Latin versions,

1

their printings embellished by the newly designed Italic characters. Readers of Canto 1 will remember one such version of the *Odyssey*, Divus's, dated 1538. And all over Europe lens-grinders were enabling presbyopic and myopic eyes to scan Homer's lines.

Our own silicon technology stores Homer and retrieves him, catalogs his words and cross-references them, relying on magnetic disks, on air conditioners, on central processing units, on central generating stations, and also on toil and ingenuity in California and Japan, to keep alive an old poet whose very existence has been repeatedly questioned. We have no such continuous record of commitment to any other part of our heritage save the Bible. The six trillion dollars I hazarded was rhetorical; what eighty generations have invested in Homer, directly and indirectly, eludes computation and nearly defies comprehension.

For we've not even settled what the Homeric poems *are*; something more than Bronze-Age entertainments, surely? Our efforts to assure ourselves that we know what we're valuing have constituted much of the history of our thought. At one time the *Iliad* and *Odyssey* were esteemed as a comprehensive curriculum in grammar, rhetoric, history, geography, navigation, strategy, even medicine. But by the mid-nineteenth century A.D. they no longer seemed to contain real information of any kind at all. Had there ever been a Trojan War? Scholars inclined to think not, much as connoisseurs of the West's other main book were doubting that there had been a Garden of Eden with an apple tree, or that planks of an Ark might have rotted atop Mount Ararat. Both books got rescued by identical stratagems; the Bible was turned into Literature, and so was Homer. That entailed redefining Literature, as something that is good for us, however unfactual. That in turn meant Nobility, and also Style. It also required that Longinus supplant Aristotle as the prince of ancient critics, and that Matthew Arnold become the Longinus of Christian England. He said that Homer was rapid and plain and noble: by Longinian standards, Sublime. Those were the qualities a translator should reach for, in part to sweep us past mere awkward nonfact. The Bible in the same way was edifying if you knew how to go about not believing it.

In 1861, while British ink was drying on printed copies of Arnold's three lectures on translating Homer, Heinrich Schliemann was nourishing a dream. He had dreamed it since boyhood. He was going to find Troy! By 1870 he had found it, yes he had, at a place the maps called

2

Hissarlik, found traces, too, of the great burning, and he photographed his wife Sophie wearing what he thought were Helen's jewels. (A photograph, no light undertaking in 1870, was merely the most recent of the technologies mankind's Homeric enterprise keeps conscripting.)

The story, as so often, now slips out of synch. Andrew Lang, the folklorist, published with one collaborator an English *Odyssey* in 1879, with two others an English *Iliad* in 1883. These, for various reasons not excluding the fine print of copyright law, remained the standard English versions as late as the mid twentieth century—even the Modern Library used to offer them—and they were already obsolete when they appeared. For Lang and Butcher, Lang, and Leaf and Myers had fetched their working principle from pre-Schliemann times. The way to translate Homer, they thought, was to make him sound like the King James Bible, the idiom of which has great power to ward off questions about what details mean. But what details mean—in particular what many nouns meant—was being settled year by year as men with spades ransacked Troy and Mycenae for such cups and golden safety pins as Helen and Hector knew.

Ezra Pound was born in 1885, just two years after the Butcher and Lang *Odyssey*. One unforgotten day when he was twelve or so, enrolled at the Cheltenham Military Academy in Pennsylvania, a teacher chanted some Homer for his special benefit. After four dozen years, from amid the wreckage of Europe, the man's name merited preserving:

> and it was old Spencer (, H.) who first declaimed me the Odyssey
> with a head built like Bill Shepard's
> on the quais of what Siracusa?
> or what tennis court
> near what pine trees?

> (C 512)

It was from "Bill Shepard" at Hamilton that he'd picked up his first Provençal enthusiasm, so the heads of these two instigators made a fit rhyme. And hearing Homer declaimed, he testified, was "worth more than grammar."[2] Though all his life a great connoisseur of detail, he was never easy with schoolmasters' grammar. It screened out what he thought crucial, the tang of voices.

That would have been about 1897, when it was just beginning to look as though the wanderings of Odysseus, too, might mirror an

3

order of factuality analogous to that of the new historic Troy. In 1902
Schliemann's architectural adviser, Wilhelm Dörpfeld, explained the
topography of Ithaka; in the same year, Victor Berard published the
book Joyce was to use so copiously, about the origins of the *Odyssey* in
Phoenician *periploi*, a noun Pound was to gloss:

> periplum, not as land looks on a map
> but as sea bord seen by men sailing.

> (C 324)

Those are arguably the most important lines in the *Cantos*. It is characteristic of the poem's way of working that we find them embedded in a
narrative about seventeenth-century China. And the word on which
they turn came from the edges of the new Homeric scholarship.

The *periplous* (a Greek noun Pound transmuted into an unre-
corded Latin form, *periplum*) registers the lay of the land the way it
looks now, from here.

> Olive grey in the near,
> far, smoke grey of the rock-slide,
> . . . .
> The tower like a one-eyed great goose
> cranes up out of the olive-grove.

> (C 10)

That is an Imagist detail, also "sea bord seen by men sailing": a detail
from some imagined *periplous*. If you were sailing in the track of that
skipper you might not find the color useful—light shifts day by day—
but "the tower like a one-eyed great goose" would help you be sure of
your position: such an apparition is not easy to mistake for some other
tower. Likewise the Homer we encounter in the first canto is not to be
taken for Pope's or Lattimore's. Homer mutates down the centuries; we
can only begin to savor the mutations when translators begin to record
what they can of them.

And translators only began their notes on the *periplous* past Homeric
capes and shoals when they had Homer's text to translate, some time
after Byzantine scholars had carried the precious manuscripts to Italy.
The first canto reminds us just what Andreas Divus did: he mapped the
words in blind fidelity. The canto's resonant "And then went down to
the ship" follows Divus's "At postquam ad navem descendimus," which

in turn follows Homer's "Autar epei hr' epi nea katelthomen": *Autar*, and; *epei*, then; *epi nea*, to the ship; *katelthomen*, we went down. In placing "descendimus" where he did, Divus even kept the order of Homer's words, putting the Greek into Latin, as he says, *ad verbum*, the way one inflected language can map another. With his page-by-page, line-by-line, often word-by-word fidelity, Divus was making a crib a student in the sixteenth century could lay open beside the Aldine Greek, to get guidance you and I might seek in a dictionary. When Ezra Pound thought his Latin "even singable," he was suggesting what much later he would suggest of a fiddle rendition of Clement Janequin's *Canzone degli ucelli*, that sheer note-by-note fidelity had kept the song audible.[3]

Can sheer blind fidelity be faithful to so much? We have come to something fundamental. A while ago we were talking of fact, the order of Homeric fact archaeologists were producing, to supplant the circumlocutions of the lexicons. Pound yielded to no one in his respect for fact, but for him the "fact" was apt to be whatever he could find right there on the page: whatever Dante might have meant by "the literal sense": mere letters, queer sounds, or even just lexicon entries. Letters, sounds, tagmemes: from the 1930s till he died he would love the Chinese character out of conviction that alone among the scripts of civilized men it collapsed all of these, shape, sound, and referent, into a sole inscrutable polysemous sign. The Chinese ideogram for "man" is a picture of a man; the Chinese spoken word for "cat" is what all cats say, "mao." If you say that "with a Greek inflection," you are saying the Greek for a catly thing, "I am eager." That's a detail we find in Canto 98 (C 686); in the late cantos especially we see words *exhibited*: isolated words, including a few of Homer's words, set off on the page by white space. Such words, though no taller than a printed line, are aspiring to the status of the ideogram. They are centers of radiance. We may think of them as opportunisms, like Shakespeare's when he rhymed "dust" with "must," mortality with necessity.

Such opportunisms irradiate the "Seafarer" of 1911. "Blaed is genaeged" says, word by word, "glory is humbled." Pound looked at "blaed," saw a sword-blade, and wrote "The blade is laid low." There's no arguing with that, and no justifying either. Nor can we argue when, in Canto 1, by a triumph of the literal, English words map Divus's words which map Homer's words and the whole goes to "Seafarer" cadences.

He is following Divus because for one thing, he wants to celebrate the occasion when, thanks partly to Aldus and Divus, Homer was recovered for the West; for another because he was himself a man of the Renaissance in having been well-taught his Latin and ill-taught his Greek. Latin, even Latin verse, Pound could read at sight. Greek, even Homer's, he'd pick at, with a crib. Divus might have labored with Ezra Pound in mind. No one in four hundred years has owed him so much.

Now though Divus intended a drudgelike fidelity, still he, too, invented a Homer: whether by sheer human exuberance, or by inadvertence, or via textual error we can't always say. Now and then his Homer is not the Greek scholars' Homer. For listen:

> And then went down to the ship,
> Set keel to breakers, forth on the godly sea and
> We set up mast and sail on that swart ship. . . .
>
> (C 3)

"On the godly sea?" Yes, it's alive with gods. But any modern crib, for instance, the Loeb, says, "on the *bright* sea," and for the good reason that the Greek word is "dian," a form of "dios," one of Homer's favorite epithets, especially for the sea you push a ship into. "Eis hala dian," reads *Odyssey* 11.2: "into the bright sea." It's a formulaic phrase at the *Odyssey*'s numerous launchings.[4]

But what does Divus have? He has "in mare divum," as if he were distracting us by a play on his own name. *Divus*, says the Latin lexicon, "of or belonging to a divinity; divine." A contracted neuter form would be *dium*, perhaps close enough to *dian* to have caused confusion in a shaky time for classical understanding. How did someone, in those days before lexicons, collect equivalences between Greek and Latin words? About Divus we seem to know nothing save that he may have come from East Asia Minor, a better place for Greek than for Latin. But however *divum* arrived on Divus's page, Ezra Pound followed him faithfully, and wrote "the godly sea":

> periplum, not as land looks on a map
> but as sea bord seen by men sailing

—here, as seen by a man who sailed four centuries agone, and whose compass was not wholly reliable. It is an interesting rule, that in the

presence of a textual crux Ezra Pound is apt to be utterly literal. Those
are just the places where credentialled scholars guess. But Pound would
only guess when the text was foolproof. When he didn't understand the
words, or when they diverged from convention, then he'd presuppose
someone else who'd known better than he; as Divus had, in prompting
him to write "godly."

"Of Homer," Pound wrote as long ago as 1918, "two qualities remain untranslated: the magnificent onomatopoeia, as of the rush of the
waves on the sea-beach and their recession in

para thina poluphloisboio thalasses

untranslated and untranslatable; and, secondly, the authentic cadence
of speech; the absolute conviction that the words used, let us say by
Achilles to the 'dog-faced' chicken-hearted Agamemnon, are in the actual swing of words spoken."[5] When men speak, not by the book but as
they are moved to, uncounterfeitable rhythm asserts itself—"the actual
swing." It eludes the dictionary, eludes mappings of "meaning": the
translator has to leap for it, with his own time's live speech in his ears.
Only if he makes that leap has he a chance of making us hear.

Hughes Salel, 1545, called Odysseus "ce ruse personage":[6] that is
one French way to look at *polytropos*, the Odyssey's first epithet, and
from our own century we might use "that tricky bastard" as a sightline
on Salel. (Yes, "bastard" is extreme, but it's part of an idiom.) Andreas
Divus, 1538, has "multiscium," much-knowing, as it were "savvy."
Thereafter the reality fades, and the renderings decline. Butcher and
Lang, 1879, offer "so ready at need," like a detail from a hymn. A. T.
Murray in the 1919 Loeb tries "man of many devices," and Liddell and
Scott in their lexicon make a stereophonic mumble, "of many counsels
or expedients." "That man skilled in all ways of contending," says the
often admirable Robert Fitzgerald, here smothering perception with po-
etic dignity. Nobody speaks phrases like those.

You cannot cut such a knot with a trick of idiom, not even one as
stolidly idiomatic as W. H. D. Rouse's "never at a loss." The problem
goes far too deep. It has been hard for many centuries to imagine what
Odysseus was really being commended for. We have all inherited the
Roman distrust for quick Greek intelligence—we associate it with huck-
stering—and translators, being men of literary cultivation, have addi-

7

tionally been infected with the changed attitude to our hero that set in when his name became Ulixes ("Ulysses") and he got tarred with the brush of fatal deviousness.[7] Dante did much to propagate the tricky Ulysses. We need not blame Dante. Though he placed Ulysses in the hell of the false counselors, he had the excuse of never having read Homer. He had read Dictys and Dares, second-century popularizers who turned the designer of the wooden horse and vanquisher of the Cyclops into (says W. B. Stanford) "an anti-hero."[8]

Pound read Homer's Greek slowly, Dante's Italian fluently, and it is unsurprising that the way he conceives Odysseus owes as much to Dante as it does to Homer. Luckily, he was also misreading Dante, to the extent that he was thrilling to the eloquent speech and disregarding the great flame in which the evil counselor is imprisoned. So he stressed what the speech stresses, an urgent thirst after novelty, and read it back into Homer where it is not to be found. It is Dante, not Homer, whose Ulysses grows bored in Ithaca, where no amenity, no, not the bed of Penelope,

> Could conquer the inward hunger that I had
>> To master the earth's experience, and to attain
>> Knowledge of man's mind, both the good and bad.[9]

That was where Tennyson had found a Ulysses

> . . . yearning in desire
> To follow knowledge like a sinking star
> Beyond the utmost bound of human thought,

and that is what Pound is echoing in his own way:

>> Knowledge the shade of a shade,
> Yet must thou sail after knowledge.

> (C 236)

In its place in the *Cantos* that is a doom laid on Odysseus, spoken in the regretful voice of Circe. In making it a doom Pound is faithful to one aspect of Homer, whose Odysseus thought nothing was worse for mortal man than wandering and for whom no place was sweeter than home.[10] That is Pound's way of compromising Homer as little as possible, all the while he is handling the hero's need to sail after knowledge, weaving it right back into a scene in Homer's tenth book, where the Greek is inno-

cent of any such motif. Odysseus is pleading with Circe in her bedroom to be let go to continue his voyage home, and in Canto 39 the crucial six lines of her response [11] are reproduced in the Greek, word for word and accent for accent (a printer lost one line, but Pound gives the line numbers, and they show what he intended). No other passage of Homer gets transcribed in full anywhere in the long poem.

Possible English for what her Greek says might run: "But first you must complete another journey, to the house of Hades and dread Persephone, to seek the shade of Tiresias of Thebes, the blind seer, whose mind stays firm. To him in death Persephone has given mind, he alone unimpaired while the rest flit about as shades." That is exactly all, and in Canto 39 we see it on the page in Homer's very words. But eight cantos later we encounter it again, memorably paraphrased and amplified:

Who even dead, yet hath his mind entire!
    This sound came in the dark
    First must thou go the road
                to hell
And to the bower of Ceres' daughter Proserpine,
Through overhanging dark, to see Tiresias,
Eyeless that was, a shade, that is in hell
So full of knowing that the beefy men know less than he,
Ere thou come to thy road's end.
             Knowledge the shade of a shade,
Yet must thou sail after knowledge
Knowing less than drugged beasts.

                                  (C 236)

That seems to make sailing after knowledge a theme of the *Odyssey*, as it was certainly a theme for Ezra Pound. It has been recognizably a theme for Americans, in a country whose Enlightenment heritage sets knowing anything at all above not knowing it. (Never mind knowing what; there is an American book on how to win at Pac Man.) Quoting, in another connection, "Who even dead, yet hath his mind entire!" Pound hoped he had done sufficient homage to the Greek veneration of intelligence above brute force (GK 146).

Let us concede, though, that there is intelligence and intelligence,

and credit Pound with having intended more than bric-à-brac knowing-ness. "Who even dead, yet hath his mind entire!" That resonant line is drawn from five words of Homer's, where "mind" is *phrenes*, the whole central part of the body, where you know that you are yourself and not a shade, and "entire" is *empedoi*, meaning firm on the foot, not slipping. Both are body-words: the midriff, the foot. The intelligence is in the body the way the meaning is in the ideogram: intrinsic and manifested, independent of lexicons, not deconstructible. To have merely one's "mind" entire is a later and less substantial concept. Pound lends it body as best he can with a weight of monosyllables and a stark contrast with how it is to be dead. Homer's word for how the dead flit about, *aissousin*, held his attention; it is a word he places on show twice in the *Thrones* cantos (C 675, 730). Disembodied, they have no minds; they flutter. If intelligence is in them, it is in the way it is in dictionaries. ("The trouble with the dictionary," Louis Zukofsky liked to say, "is that it keeps chang-ing the subject.") A flitting, a fluttering: that was the Greek sense of dis-embodiment, and it fascinated Pound, and it was not intelligence. ("Butterflying around all the time," he said once, of aimless specula-tion. He was speaking of Richard of St. Victor's *cogitatio*, to be distin-guished from *meditatio* and the highest thing, *contemplatio*.)[12]

So we are learning how to take the stark physicality of the rites in the first canto, in particular how to take the need of the shades for blood. They need blood to get what is peculiar to the body, hence to the *phrenes*, the totally embodied intelligence. Without blood, the shades cannot so much as speak. Canto 1 draws on the part of the *Odyssey* Pound judged "older than the rest":[13] Ronald Bush suggests he may have been following Cambridge anthropology here—the tradition of studies that, following on *The Golden Bough*, made Greek intuitions seem so much less cerebral than they had been for Flaxman and Arnold.[14] Or—since I don't know whether he so much as read such a book as Jane Harrison's *Themis*—it is conceivable that in ascribing the underworld journey to "fore-time" he was trusting sheer intuition. It implies, anyhow, the Homeric sense of "intelligence," of "knowledge," something so remote from "ideas"—a word whose Greek credentials are post-Homeric— as to have drawn the snort, "Damn ideas, anyhow . . . poor two-dimensional stuff, a scant, scratch covering."[15]

To sail after knowledge, then, is to seek what cannot be found in

10

libraries, no, a wholeness of experience. I hope I have suggested that in weaving that phrase back from Dante into Homer, Pound was embellishing less than we may have thought. And it brought him to the superbly colloquial words of Zeus, who, admiring Odysseus, says (in Ezra Pound's English), "With a mind like that he is one of us" (C 512).[16] That consorts with a fact that has given scandal but need not, that Homer's gods are superbly physical, embodied. Odysseus, for such a god, is "one of us," precisely in having not a Ph.D. but *phrenes*: "the embodiment," said Pound's classmate Bill Williams, "of knowledge."[17]

Having sailed a long circuit after the colloquial, we will not need a second for the other thing Pound wanted, "the magnificent onomatopoeia." Though "untranslated and untranslatable,"

para thina poluphloisboio thalasses

may serve as our terminal emblem: not boom rattle and buzz but the rare identity of words with whatever they signify, achieved with the signifying sound the way Chinese calligraphers achieved it with a signifying outline. Pound listened and heard the wave break, and in the sibilants of *thalasses* heard "the scutter of receding pebbles" (L 274): that whole mighty recurrent phenomenon incarnated in a few syllables represented by a few marks. The way into understanding this is like the way into understanding Homeric intelligence, something only there when it is embodied. So meanings are only there when the words embody them; otherwise, like the dead, they flutter, *aissousin*. And we are back, in a circle, to "the actual swing of words spoken," the other stamp that can authenticate language. Pound first encountered Homer through a man speaking: Mr. Spencer, at the Cheltenham Military Academy, the man "who first declaimed me the *Odyssey*," and was remembered for that after forty years.

Scholars now imagine an "oral-formulaic" Homer, a poet continually speaking, but speaking with the aid of formulae to fill out the meter. When Pound, aged eighty-four, heard an exposition of that, he responded that it did not explain "why Homer is so much better than everybody else." That was very nearly all that he said that day. Why Homer is so much better than everybody else is a thing there's no way to explain; nor why, having sailed after knowledge and turned astray, Ezra Pound should have fulfilled Dante's image with such precision: trans-

muted after so much eloquence into a tongue of flame, and a tongue that went silent.

Notes

1. *The Cantos of Ezra Pound* (New York: New Directions, 1970), p. 148. Hereafter cited in the text as C followed by page number.

2. *Guide to Kulchur* (New York: New Directions, 1968), p. 145. Hereafter cited as GK followed by page number.

3. See the *Cantos*, pp. 450–51; also Murray Schafer, ed., *Ezra Pound and Music* (New York: New Directions, 1977), p. 434, where we see Pound commencing a 1938 article by citing his own sentences of 1934: "Clement Janequin wrote a chorus . . . when Francesco da Milano reduced it for the lute, the birds were still with the music. And when Münch transcribed it for modern instruments, the birds were still there."

4. R. J. Cunliffe's useful *Lexicon of the Homeric Dialect* (1924; Norman: University of Oklahoma Press, 1963), s.v. *dios*, reports too many instances to enumerate.

5. "Translators of Greek" (1918), in *Literary Essays of Ezra Pound*, ed. T. S. Eliot (New York: New Directions, 1968), p. 250.

6. Pound attributes this phrase to Salel in *Polite Essays* (London: Faber & Faber, 1937), p. 126.

7. W. B. Stanford and J. V. Luce, *The Quest for Ulysses* (New York: Praeger, 1974), p. 168.

8. Ibid., p. 171.

9. From Laurence Binyon's 1933 translation of *Inferno* 27.

10. *Odyssey* 15.343 and 9.28, cited by Stanford and Luce, p. 60.

11. *Cantos*, p. 194; *Odyssey* 10.490–95.

12. Viva voce, at St. Elizabeths Hospital, 1956.

13. Letter (23 May 1935) to W. H. D. Rouse, in D. D. Paige, ed., *The Selected Letters of Ezra Pound* (New York: New Directions, 1971), p. 274. Hereafter cited in the text as L followed by page number.

14. Ronald Bush, *The Genesis of Ezra Pound's Cantos* (Princeton: Princeton University Press, 1976), pp. 125–34.

15. "Translators of Greek," in *Literary Essays*, p. 267.

16. See Pound's comment in GK, p. 146. The source is *Odyssey* 1.65; here W. H. D. Rouse's translation has Zeus say "He is almost one of us."

17. That is the title of a posthumous book by Williams, who also liked to say, "No ideas but in things."

IDOVIDOVIDOVIDOV

Pound and Ovid

Lillian Feder

In *Guide to Kulchur,* first published in 1938, Ezra Pound evaluates Kung and Ovid as precursors of modern anthropologists. Having praised Kung as "modern in his interest in folk-lore," and the research of Frazer and Frobenius as "Confucian," he observes that, although Ovid was concerned with "these matters," there is no evidence that his "interest" was as "sober" as theirs. This judgment is followed by a statement that seems unrelated to it: "Ovid, I keep repeating from one decade to another, is one of the most interesting of all enigmas—if you grant that he was an enigma at all." [1] Although Pound had praised Ovid many times in his essays and letters and had used Ovidian myths and techniques in his poetry, he had not—for publication at least—referred to him repeatedly as a puzzling figure. To the implied question in Pound's conditional clause, I would respond that I consider Ovid no more an enigma than any other poet, especially an ancient one. There are, of course, unanswered questions about his life, particularly the cause of his sentence of exile, as well as about his work, for example, how seriously he intends the Pythagorean speech of *Metamorphoses* 15 to be taken, but there is no evidence to suggest that it is to such specific issues that Pound refers. It seems rather that Pound is projecting on Ovid, as he does on many other figures—long dead or contemporary—his own literary and personal inclinations. A summary of some of Pound's comments on Ovid in his essays and letters suggests some of the reasons Pound may have had for considering him enigmatic, but one must al-

13

ways be aware that this is Pound's Ovid, not necessarily the poet one discovers in the body of his work.

In *The Spirit of Romance*, which appeared in 1910, Pound describes Ovid as "urbane, sceptical, a Roman of the city." After quoting the line: "Convenit esse deos et ergo credemus," which he translates: "It is convenient to have Gods, and therefore we believe they exist," Pound remarks that for a "sceptical age," longing for the "definite, . . . something it can pretend to believe," Ovid makes the supernatural "plausible." His gods are "humanized," his heroes seem to be family acquaintances. In his poetry the "mood, the play is everything; the facts are nothing. Ovid, before Browning, raises the dead and dissects their mental processes." [2] Some nine years later he says in a letter that he has fused something of Ovid with his portrait of Propertius as "the young man of the Augustan Age, hating rhetoric and undeceived by imperial hog-wash." [3]

Subsequent comments indicate that this skeptical Ovid, pretending "scientific accuracy" (*SR* 15), is also a religious influence. Pound says, in a letter written in 1922, that he regards "the Writings of Confucius" and "Ovid's *Metamorphoses*" as "the only safe guides in religion" and the *Metamorphoses* as "a sacred book" (*L* 183). In his essay "Cavalcanti," he suggests that the reader and he "might grant that Ovid had in him more divine wisdom than all the Fathers of the Church put together." [4] And in *Guide to Kulchur*, not many pages after he has compared Ovid's interest in folklore rather unfavorably with Frazer's, Frobenius's, and Kung's, he asserts his belief "that a great treasure of verity exists for mankind in Ovid and in the subject matter of Ovid's long poem, and that only in this form could it be registered" (*GK* 299).

As Pound's view of Ovid emerges even from these brief comments, we begin to understand why he regarded him as an enigma: he is a political and religious skeptic who considers the gods merely convenient and portrays them as human beings, yet this poet, whose own attitude toward the mythology he has helped to preserve [5] is not particularly "sober," has nonetheless provided a "sacred book," an enduring source of religious belief. Still, it seems to me that the enigma, although it has to do with these apparent contradictions, is more fundamental.

The chief subject of Ovid's "long poem" is continuous flux, metamorphosis, which is also the poetic technique that paradoxically bestows coherence and permanence on ceaseless change. Pound's aim in the *Cantos* was to produce an epic, and to create for it his own meta-

morphic language and structure. Ovid cites Pythagoras as his philosopher of flux; Pound quotes Heraclitus. Rejecting orthodox religion, he sought the "verity" he projected on Ovid, a religious conception of human nature and society, in traditional myths and legends. The fundamental reason that Pound regarded Ovid as enigmatic, I believe, is that the *Metamorphoses*, while serving as a model for his "bust thru . . . into 'divine or permanent world'" (*L* 210), provided neither the conception of deity nor the ideological framework that he required for converting metamorphosis into the religious and social process which the *Cantos* promulgate. Pound found other sources to supply these needs— chiefly Confucian and Neoplatonic—whose ideas and values he conveyed through Ovidian transformations. In so doing he created his own variety of metamorphosis.

Pound's adaptations of Ovid are more extensive than actual allusions would indicate. These appear in two major ways: in his versions of the relationship between the divine and the human, and in his narrative, thematic, and stylistic conception of the process of metamorphosis. Of course, Pound's references to pagan gods in his prose and poetry are not always to those in Ovid. They also evoke Homer, Aeschylus, Bion, Catullus, and other ancient poets. But it is the capacity of Ovid's deities to transform themselves, nature, and human beings that is fundamental to the divine presences—named and unnamed—that pervade the *Cantos*, however Pound converted them to his own conception.

In the *Metamorphoses*, Ovid's gods and goddesses reveal human needs, desires, and weaknesses. They also enact forms of wrath and vengeance beyond the capacities of mortals, which nonetheless convey human situations. Love makes his deities most vulnerable, the victims of other gods, especially Cupid and Venus, and the suppliants of the mortals they desire. Filled with "saeva ira" against Apollo, Cupid takes vengeance by making him fall in love with Daphne and ensuring her rejection of the god. Once Apollo is smitten, not only the reader but the god himself is aware of the disparity between the great powers he possesses as an immortal and his all too human weakness: he contrasts his reputation as "opifer," help-bringer, with his helplessness before his own passion. After Daphne has been transformed into a laurel, the two aspects of the god merge in a moving passage in which Apollo embraces and kisses the branches and cries out: "Since you cannot be my wife, you will certainly be my tree." As the god, like any spurned lover, clings to a

mere remnant of his beloved, he restores his own dignity by bestowing on the laurel a civic function: it will stand on Augustus' doorposts, a faithful guardian, protecting the crown of oak which hangs there. Like Apollo, with his "young head with its unshorn hair," Daphne will have the "perpetual honor" of her "leaves." As the laurel responds to this continuous relationship by waving its branches and nodding its top, like a head (1.452–567), Apollo's divine powers seem more than a mere consolation for his loss and frustration; he has imposed continuity on metamorphosis and, at least in some form, gained the assent of the nymph.[6]

Other gods in love are equally touching in their yearning and disappointment. But if Pan, Jupiter, and Venus, for example, also seem more human than divine in their emotional transformations, they ultimately restore a measure of their divinity by compensating for their frustration in love with metamorphic powers. Pan, deprived of the nymph Syrinx, who is transformed into marsh reeds as he finally clasps her, discovers that his sighs of disappointed love become music when they stir the reeds. His expression of failure, like Apollo's, is also his divine compensation: "This union with you will endure for me," he says to Syrinx as he invents the reed pipe (1.682–712). These are only two examples out of many in which the disappointment and pain of frustrated love are transmuted into lasting creations of beauty and productivity.

Jupiter's various passions reduce his stature as he fears Juno, lies to her, and also deceives the objects of his love. Just before the god takes the form of a bull in order to capture Europa, Ovid says explicitly: "Majesty and love do not fit well together and do not remain long in the same place" (2.846–47). Yet the god's ingenuity and power to change himself and others into marvelous creatures and natural forces offset this loss of majesty. Ovid is equally explicit about Venus: "caelo praefertur Adonis" (10.532), "she prefers Adonis to the heavens." She cannot prevent his death, but she can, as she says, deprive fate of some of its power by transforming his blood into the anemone, short-lived but recurrent.

For the most part, Ovid's gods are appealing in their loves, but their vengeance is harsh. The tale of Venus' love for Adonis is interrupted by her account to him of her punishment of Hippomenes, who slighted the goddess after she had helped him to win the love of Atalanta, who also becomes her victim. Metamorphosis, although not always a punishment, is often used in this way by the gods, especially against mortals

16

involved in an illicit love affair. Ovid's "avenging gods," says Brooks Otis, "are to an appreciable extent images of arbitrary power very like that which he saw in the Augustan state."[7] Otis is convinced that Ovid's "distaste for his gods and their almost diabolical cruelty" expresses his strong objections to "the mercilessness of absolute power" and "is certainly an implicit criticism of Augustan ideology and practice." Acknowledging that the dire effects of the gods' wrath are intrinsic to the myths Ovid tells, Otis admits that it is difficult to give precise evidence of their connection with the injustices of "Augustus and his court." He is entirely convincing, however, in his view that "There is . . . a deliberate refusal" on Ovid's part "to take theodicy seriously, to acknowledge the reality of divine justice and goodness."[8]

Ovid's gods are indeed often cruel, but in the *Metamorphoses* and other poems they can also be benevolent to ordinary human beings, heroes, and poets. In the *Fasti*, which was written during the same period as the *Metamorphoses*, just prior to his exile, there are several passages that reveal the poet's special relationship with the gods. For readers of Pound, the following example is particularly interesting:

> est deus in nobis; agitante calescimus illo:
> impetus hic sacrae semina mentis habet.
> fas mihi praecipue voltus vidisse deorum
> vel quia sum vates, vel quia sacra cano.
>
> (6.5–8)
>
> There is a god in us; he, stirring us, we grow warm. This impulse contains the seeds of inspiration. I especially have a right to behold the faces of the gods, either because I am a poet or because I sing of sacred subjects.[9]

Here and elsewhere in his poetry, Ovid adapts the traditional conception of the "vates" to a personal expression of belief in his own gifts, which give him insight into the nature of divinity. In *Tristia*, which he wrote during the long journey into exile, there is a striking contrast between the gods of the Palatine Hill and other clear equations of Augustus with Jupiter[10] and the gods who favor poets. On the one hand, deity is political tyranny; on the other, it is the poetic gift that is his only salvation. Of all the deities, it is the Muse on whom Ovid most relies in hope and in despair. In *Tristia* 2, assuming that it was the *Ars Amatoria* that at least in part caused Augustus' wrath, he treats poetry and the Muse as one in expressing his hope that "the very object that wounds

17

will heal" him and "the Muse who aroused the anger will also mitigate it" (ll. 20–21). Defending himself as a poet of love in this poem, Ovid provides a long list of Greek and Latin poets and dramatists from Homer to his contemporaries who wrote on this subject. It is a defense not only of himself but of "teneros amores" (l. 361) as a theme of literature.

Love is certainly a dominant motif in Ovid's poetry, not only in the *Ars Amatoria*, the *Amores*, and the *Heroides*, but in the *Metamorphoses* as well. Otis refers to Ovid's "high valuation of *love as such*" in this poem, and there is much evidence to support this view, but he emphasizes "conjugal" love in contrast with what he calls "the blind sexual urge" that often has dire consequences.[11] Yet even when perverted love drives Ovid's mythical characters to deceit and irrationality, they are generally touching in their conflict and suffering. Their metamorphoses, moreover, are ambiguous: even when they are punished for immoderate or unlawful desire, as they take on its symbolic form, they are relieved of its human anguish and often attain a new and perennial existence in their transformations.

Recent commentaries on the *Metamorphoses* generally dismiss the importance of the Pythagoras speech on flux in the last book, and one can only agree that it does not represent a philosophical commitment on Ovid's part. It seems rather his way of explicating and thus extending the organizing principle of his poem, metamorphosis, as a process of life itself. "Believe me, nothing in the universe dies; it merely changes and renews its form" (15.254–55). As gods take on animal forms, to which they sometimes reduce human beings, as young women become trees or birds or animals, connections between the interchanged forms are disclosed and they are shown to partake of each other's nature. Divinity is reduced to an extension of the human and animal species; men, women, animals, and inanimate nature emerge as infinitely varied in their changing forms.

Describing Arachne's tapestry, Ovid says you would think her portrait of Europa deceived by Jupiter in the form of a bull to be "true" (6.103–7); the bull, the waves, the young woman all seem real. But art does not merely disclose the metamorphic quality of experience; it is part of the process itself, clarifying reality by transforming it. It can, moreover, bestow immortality upon its human creator. This metamorphosis, which exceeds all others, follows and contrasts with the mythical deification of Augustus. Ovid ends the *Metamorphoses* with

18

the prophecy that "neither the wrath of Jove, nor fire, nor sword, nor greedy time can destroy" his work; his poetry is his assurance of immortality, a conviction he holds to firmly even in *Tristia* (3.3, 77–80; 4.10, 129–32) after he has experienced the wrath of Jove in the pain of exile.

Although in the *Cantos* external nature, mythical and historical figures, and the poet himself are also involved with divinity through metamorphosis, Pound has a very different conception of the process itself. In fact, his "bust thru[s]" into the "divine or permanent world" generally reverse Ovid's essential scheme. Whereas Ovid's gods are all too human in their desires, limits, indulgences, and anger, in the *Cantos*, chosen human beings are allowed the prerogatives of gods. In the *Metamorphoses*, most transformations are from divine or human forms of life into lower ones. As Otis points out, "The only great exception to this rule is that of the deified hero, the man who becomes a god, and this (save for the preparatory Hercules episodes) is reserved for the concluding part of the poem," where the deifications are surely ironic.[12] Even when Pound adapts specific Ovidian metamorphoses, he does not disclose human weakness, yearning, suffering, or transcendence in love, nature, or art; instead he creates "magic moment[s]" (*L* 210) of divine revelation or superhuman omnipotence. Pound's conversion of Ovid into a guide in religion results in his extension of metamorphosis far beyond Ovid's original conception. For Pound metamorphosis is continual religious experience in which he participates, at once discovering and creating divinity in external and human nature, which includes the various personae of the *Cantos* who move between Hades, earth, and Paradise. It is also the method by which he can reveal the superhuman forces in society and history.

Comparing Ovid's (*Metamorphoses* 3.582–691) and Pound's[13] versions of Acoetes' account of the sailors' attempt to deceive Bacchus, Edgar Glenn notes the different emphases of the two poets: Ovid's on the transformation of the sailors into fish and Pound's on the appearance of Bacchus' animals. His explanation is that "Pound is interested in the spiritual or divine as it becomes perceptible, in other words, in the religious and in the numinous as it interpenetrates phenomena. Ovid is more concerned about the human and its modification, the change of material being into other material being."[14] These differences do exist but, in oversimplifying Ovid's purpose, Glenn ignores more important ones.

19

The Acoetes episode in the *Metamorphoses* occurs within a long narrative about Bacchus' appearance in Thebes and Pentheus' rejection of the god. In this context, the metamorphosis of the sailors into fish, as Ovid describes it, is far more than a mere "change of material being into other material being." Like all who reject the god, the sailors feel his influence. As one by one they are transformed into fish, "they leap about everywhere" in the sea, "producing much spray." Like a Bacchic "chorus of dancers, they play and toss their wanton bodies about." Their metamorphosis, though a punishment, is also an affirmation of the Bacchic fertility and pleasure inherent in natural and human life which, unwittingly, they now acknowledge with their transformed bodies. The importance of their change lies less in its material properties than in its evocation of the ethical and psychological implications of Bacchic worship. This group of grown men who had planned "to deceive a boy" must now express his influence as a force of nature.

Pound omits the description of the dancing fish and concentrates instead on the manifestation of the god's presence in the appearance of his animals. Ovid describes these as "simulacra inania," empty images or likenesses of the beasts, a point Pound makes four times:

> And, out of nothing, a breathing,
> hot breath on my ankles,
> Beasts like shadows in glass,
> a furred tail upon nothingness.
>
> . . . .
> Rustle of airy sheaths,
> dry forms in the *aether*.
>
> . . . .
> Lifeless air become sinewed,
> feline leisure of panthers.

(C 8)

This emphasis on the god's creation of beasts out of "nothingness," out of "lifeless air," sets up a dichotomy between nature and the numinous presences that appear within it and give form and power to what is otherwise empty. In Ovid, myth is merged with nature, human and inanimate; "deus et melior . . . natura" create order out of chaos (*Metamorphoses* 1.21). In the *Cantos* mythical beings transform nature to reflect their presence.

This is one of the most important ways in which Pound alters Ovidian metamorphosis. It accounts for some of his most original and haunting evocations of external nature, and it is fundamental to his reversal of the process itself. In Canto 2, after the metamorphosis of the sailors, he extends the mythicized sea to fuse past and present time:

> And of a later year,
>> pale in the wine-red algae,
> If you will lean over the rock,
>> the coral face under wave-tinge,
> Rose-paleness under water-shift,
>> Ileuthyeria, fair Dafne of sea-bords,
> The swimmer's arms turned to branches,
> Who will say in what year,
>> fleeing what band of tritons,
> The smooth brows, seen, and half seen,
>> now ivory stillness.

> (C 9)

Here Pound connects the Acoetes episode with a story he invents about a sea nymph, Ileuthyeria. Perhaps inspired by Ovid's description of Daphne's appeal to her father, the sea god Peneus, to help her "si flumina numen habetis" (if you rivers have divinity, *Metamorphoses* 1.545), he makes her "fair Dafne of sea-bords," a swimmer whose "arms turned to branches" when she fled a "band of tritons." Pound's comment on his departure from Ovid calls attention to important differences in the two poets' use of metamorphosis: "a theme of Ovid— Dafne, my own myth, not changed into a laurel but into coral." [15] The metamorphosis of Ovid's Daphne is preceded by a long description of Apollo's love for her and her fear of love itself, the god's typically human frustration and suffering and the nymph's desperation. The motivation for the flight of Pound's Ileuthyeria is vague: "Who will say in what year, / fleeing what band of tritons." Daniel Pearlman suggests that her "metamorphosis saves her from rape" by the pursuing tritons, certainly a possible interpretation, but his view of the meaning of the passage is, to say the least, questionable. He contrasts the "punitive metamorphosis" of those who would metaphorically "rape"—his term—Dionysus with the effects of the attempted rape of the nymph, which "brings down no vindictive metamorphosis upon the would-be rapists; it results rather in the

transformation of the nymph herself—into the rich permanence of coral. Where love is the motivating force," he goes on to say, "the transformation appears to be a positive one." [16] The contrast he suggests seems forced, since even metaphorical rape is hardly applicable to the sailors' plans for the god, and actual rape is at most implied in "fleeing what band of tritons." Furthermore, there is no evidence in the passage to suggest an equation of rape with love, surely a distorted view of that emotion. In fact, one of the great differences between Ovid's adaptation of a traditional myth and Pound's invented one is that Pound is not concerned here with love at all but with the numinous inherent in the sea. He does not, like Ovid, reveal the human emotions projected on divinity but rather converts metamorphosis into a deification of natural phenomena.

This difference emerges also in the two poets' use of metamorphosis to suggest continuity. In the *Metamorphoses*, as I pointed out earlier, the laurel as a perennial natural product and as a symbol of protection both expresses and compensates for the god's, and by extension, human beings' limitations. But Pound is concerned chiefly with the continuity of the process itself as he imposes mythical time on nature. The time of Ileuthyeria's metamorphosis is indefinite. It takes place in "a later year," in "Who will say in what year," and it is manifest in the present.

All the metamorphoses in this canto are involved with the sea, however remotely. Even Atalanta, whose "voice" Pound, in another bit of mythmaking, relates to the "doom" of Eleanor and Helen, was metamorphosed into a lion as a result of her love for Hippomenes, the great-grandson of Neptune. [17] But neither Atalanta's nor Tyro's love concerns Pound here; they appear, like Proteus, with whom the canto ends, as part of the continuous process of merging and transformation through which the natural and the divine become indistinguishable.

In the next canto, this god-invested atmosphere is extended to the air and the woods, and it reappears throughout the *Cantos*, lending superhuman authority to the speaker who merges historical periods and events and who invests human nature with godlike attributes. The numinous may be "splintered" and "jagged," as Michael Bernstein points out, [18] "but the Divine Mind is abundant / unceasing / *improvisatore* / Omniformis / unstill" (C 620) and its presence manifests itself everywhere, in daily life, in history, and in culture, with a promise

of the Neoplatonic oneness that Pound fused with the ideology of Kung and the method of Ovid.

Bernstein observes that "'Le Paradis' is always potentially available, but to mortals its manifestations are inherently unstable, and its existence provides no secure framework within which the other moments of purely historical and contingent existence can be rendered comprehensible, or by which an extended poem can be structured. Pound's poem, that is, exhibits what may be called a mythic consciousness, but it does not rely on a coherent mythic structure to create its form." [19] This is no doubt true, but it is also clear that Pound attempts to create his own syncretic structure through a metamorphic process which continually transforms both myth and history. [20] I can only agree with Bernstein's view that Pound's "insight into magic moments . . . cannot . . . adequately engage historical reality on its own terms," [21] but I do not think that Pound's two major "codes," the historical and the mythical, are as often "mutually exclusive" in the *Cantos* as he believes they are, however Pound's union of the two may discredit him as an interpreter of history.

One of the techniques Pound uses in attempting to combine history and myth is the adaptation of metamorphosis to the ideogrammic method. Bernstein regards these two methods as "logically" different, and in some respects they are, but the difference that he posits is not a valid one. "Metamorphosis," he says, "implies some universal *forma*, some constant element which finds expression in a multitude of changing guises, as Aphrodite can appear to the poet in a wide range of incarnations from the traditional terrible goddess to the barefoot girl of Pisa. . . . With the ideogrammic juxtaposition, on the other hand, the emphasis resides in the new insight that emerges from the combination of two or more apparently unrelated elements." [22] The type of metamorphosis Bernstein describes here is characteristic of the gods in Ovid, but it surely does not apply to the nymphs and mortals who are the objects of their love or wrath. Daphne, Syrinx, Atalanta, Hippomenes, and a host of others who are changed into new forms do not represent a "constant element which finds expression in a multitude of changing guises." They are transformed from the condition of human life into that of tree, plant, or animal, in which form they take on new and lasting attributes. The juxtapositions of their two states are both similar to

23

and different from those produced by the ideogrammic method. From the combination of elements—a head and a tree top, sailors and leaping fish, disdain for love and sighing marsh reeds—new insights do emerge (as they do in the transformations of the gods) into the nature of divinity, mortality, and the relationship between them.

It is not the absence of insight through juxtaposition that distinguishes the metamorphic from the ideogrammic method but rather the fact that metamorphosis entails a change from one state of existence to another, implying connections among the natural, human, and divine, whereas the ideogram does not necessarily include such juxtapositions and often, especially in Pound's versions, alludes to many other conditions and events—historical, economic, and aesthetic. Another important difference is that metamorphosis is intrinsically narrative in method, the ideogram pictorial and associative. Pound exploits these differences as well as the common capacity of both methods to make "things . . . become other things by swift and unanalysable process" (*LE* 431) by fusing the two in a unique type of metamorphic ideogram, one of his chief vehicles for conveying his mythical view of history. [23]

Ronald Bush points out that in Pound's "collected and uncollected prose, no programmatic use of the term 'ideogram' or 'ideograph' appears until 1927." Referring to Pound's "ambivalence" regarding "Cocteau's 'ideographic' style in 1921," he suggests that "it is highly unlikely that he thought of himself as using such a technique in 1919, when Canto IV was published." [24] Bush is no doubt correct in concluding that Pound had not yet developed his own ideogrammic method, but it is also evident that Canto 4 foreshadows his later more complex and more extensive use of the technique.

In lines 3 and 4 of this canto (C 13), Pound uses ideogrammic juxtapositions as an invocation. Walter Baumann observes that, in the juxtaposition of "ANAXIFORMINGES!" with "Aurunculeia!" in line 3, "Pindar and his lyre are dismissed from the *Cantos* once and for all," and the name of the bride indicates that "Pound's subject here is above all that of Sappho, Catullus, Propertius, and Ovid: the ways of love and woman." [25] It seems to me that in the next line Pound adds a third element to the juxtaposition: "Cadmus of Golden Prows!" which, together with the other two, establishes a much broader thematic structure for the canto. Pound juxtaposes Pindar, the aristocratic Theban, so proud of his birth, with Cadmus who, as founder of Thebes, represents the city

24

that rose to the music of Amphion's lyre, a city that contrasts with the destruction of Troy with which the canto begins. In "Hugh Selwyn Mauberley," which appeared in 1920, Pound mocks the line in Pindar's second Olympian, "What god, what hero, what man shall we praise?" which follows "Anaxiforminges hymnoi." In this canto, to assert the superiority of his own concept of deity, heroism, and poetry over Pindar's, he juxtaposes the Theban Cadmus, who "established a city granted by the oracle of Phoebus" (*Metamorphoses* 3.130), with the Theban Pindar as ancient models. Whereas the lyre of Pindar merely confirms orthodoxy, Cadmus is associated with the lyre of Amphion, which moved rocks to create a new realm. "Cadmus of Golden Prows" identifies the poet's function with that of the god-inspired builder of an ideal city. Vinia Aurunculeia, moreover, conveys more than the "serene life" that Baumann suggests;[26] she represents a principle of love and fertility which Catullus' epithalamion celebrates and which rules a city built in accordance with a divine plan.

Most of Canto 4 consists of myths and legends in abbreviated or extended form, or sometimes in both. In this respect it resembles a book of the *Metamorphoses*, as one myth leads to another, and earlier tales are sometimes resumed. But the resemblance is only superficial; for the most part the Ovidian narrative is omitted, and there is no sequential development. Ovidian metamorphoses are also juxtaposed with later myths, legends, and beliefs, for example, Itys with Cabestan, Actaeon with Vidal, who evokes Ovid as he mutters the names of three pools associated with transformations in the *Metamorphoses*, and Danaë with the Chinese poet Sō-Gyoku's notion of the "king's wind," which is identified with Zeus' "golden rain" as she becomes "the god's bride" in the idealized city of Ecbatan. All these transformations are evoked as part of a historical process which encompasses love, violence, and death, measured against an ideal of order: first Thebes, then Ecbatan, the perfect city, an image of "paradiso terrestre."

This "vision" (C 17) assumes various forms as historical figures and events increasingly "become other things" in metamorphic ideograms. Using mythical figures that appear in the *Metamorphoses* and other ancient works, Pound relies on this unique adaptation of metamorphosis to interpret history by standards he imposes on myth. Transforming historical figures such as Malatesta or Jefferson into versions of Odysseus ultimately equated with a Confucian ideal of order, or Eleanor of Aqui-

taine into a medieval Helen, or Elizabeth I into both Helen and Artemis, he creates ideograms as historical exempla.

When, in one line, Malatesta is "Poliorcetes" (taker of cities) and, in the next, "a bit too POLUMETIS" (C 36), the juxtaposition transforms a Renaissance despot into both a Macedonian deified king and a mythical hero who is also the chief persona of the *Cantos*. Among the characteristics of "the *polumetis*," according to Pound, was "the carriage of the man who knew how to rule, who had been everywhere, Weltmensch, with 'ruling caste' stamped all over him. . . . And as Zeus said: 'A chap with a mind like THAT! the fellow is one of us. One of US" (GK 146). Neither Odysseus nor Demetrius is named in the passage in Canto 9 referred to above; they are evoked not as figures but as godlike qualities in a new incarnation. Despite his shortcomings and failures, Malatesta, as ruler, warrior, and patron of the arts, emerges in the *Cantos* as one of many historical figures to whom Pound assigns divine attributes and with whom the poet shares a vision of an earthly paradise. This paradisiacal state is authoritarian, hierarchical, and controlled by ritual, which produces renewal through metamorphosis.

No matter how far Pound seems to stray from Ovid—and there are fewer specific references to his poetry in the later cantos than in the early ones—he continues to adapt metamorphosis to the ideology of Kung fused with a Neoplatonic conception of reality. Demeter's and Persephone's metamorphic powers of regeneration, which he evokes throughout the *Cantos*, are explicitly equated with ancient Chinese ritual in the juxtaposition of the two models in "Between KUNG and ELEUSIS" (C 258) and their union in "Kung and Eleusis / to catechumen alone" (C 272). In Canto 74, Persephone appears "under Taishan," the sacred mountain of China which occurs frequently in the *Cantos* in connection with the "building of the Ideal City."[27] At the beginning of Canto 106, the Ovidian Persephone's powers over the fertility of the soil are combined with the decrees of the *Kuan-tzu*, which is identified by Massimo Bacigalupo as "an 'economic' work compiled around the third century B.C. and attributed to the semi-legendary Kuan Chung."[28] Bacigalupo suggests that for Pound "the *Kuan-tzu* is not sufficient" to attain "the promised land; . . . what we need is a shawl or a bikini, or a cup of white-gold modeled upon the breast of Helen. The road to ROMA lies through AMOR, the love of the Cruel Fair, who calls here for the last time in the poem."[29] Persephone, in this canto,

appears "in the cotton fields," she is identified with the just emperors Yao and Shun who "ruled by jade," the most magical of stones, "That the goddess turn crystal within her," and in this role she is also "grain rite." As a fertility goddess, she is connected with Circe, Artemis, and Aphrodite, to whom she ultimately gives way. Persephone's role in the *Cantos* is the principle and process of metamorphosis itself. In "grain rite" her story is compressed into a metamorphic ideogram for Pound's adaptation of metamorphosis as the seminal process that converts nature and history into myth, and society into a ritualized paradise in which order, fertility, and love become one.

Much has been written about the role of love in the *Cantos* and its connection with death, fertility, and renewal. As in the *Metamorphoses*, Aphrodite appears in the poem in her dual capacities as the nourishing and fearful goddess. But there are essential differences between Ovid's and Pound's treatment of love. Obsessed by passion, Ovid's gods move from the "divine . . . world" into the quotidian. His human figures endure fear and conflict and are often punished for passions they cannot control. Love takes many forms in the *Cantos* but none that resemble these.

In Pound's most personal references to love in *The Pisan Cantos*, it is a memory trace that he hopes can preserve and heal him in a literal hell. Here and elsewhere it is the "true heritage" that ultimately leads far beyond individual experience. It is mainly an impersonal force,[30] lending divine sanction to nature and history. In Canto 90, even the story of Ovid's most humble and loving pair, Baucis and Philemon, is transformed into a mythical paradigm for a Neoplatonic conception of the unity of all creation.

Ovid (*Metamorphoses* 8.618–724) tells of how, in exchange for their hospitality to Jupiter and Mercury, the old man and woman are granted their wish to die together and are changed into two trees, an oak and a linden, that grow from a double trunk. The hero Lelex, who tells the story, says that he saw garlands hanging from its branches and that he placed fresh ones there to honor this couple whom the gods cared for: "Let those who worshipped be worshipped."

In the large demands Pound makes on this story, the tenderness and piety of this human pair, which Ovid narrates so lovingly, are lost. The epigraph to Canto 90, a quotation from Richard of St. Victor, which says in part that "the human soul is not love, but love proceeds from it,"

27

announces Pound's transformation of Ovid's metamorphic depiction of human love recognized and commemorated by the gods in nature. To Pound the old couple are:

> Beatific spirits welding together
>> as in one ash-tree in Ygdrasail.
>> Baucis, Philemon.

Associated with the ash which, according to Norse mythology, unites earth, heaven, and hell through its roots and branches, Baucis and Philemon now exemplify the force of divine love permeating and unifying all of creation, with which the poet identifies. The lines that follow the allusion to Baucis and Philemon:

> Castalia is the name of that fount in the hill's fold,
>> the sea below,
>>> narrow beach.
> Templum aedificans, not yet marble,
>> "Amphion!"

join the spring on Mt. Parnassus, which is sacred to Apollo and the Muses, with Amphion, the magical builder, and, as Bacigalupo points out, "the temple is the very poem that Pound is in the process ('aedificans') of constructing," thus "'not yet [of] marble.'"[31]

The epigraph from Richard of St. Victor, his declaration, "Ubi amor, ibi oculus" (Where love is there also is the eye), which appears twice in this canto, and his belief, quoted in Latin, that the "image of the divine is to be found in us" support Pound's use of Baucis and Philemon, Aretheusa—whose metamorphosis Ovid also relates—and various other pagan deities to establish the poet's participation in the divine capacity to manifest itself "omniformis" in history and culture.

Among the quotations from Richard of St. Victor that Pound selected and translated for publication in 1956 is the sentence: "Ignis quidquid in nobis est." He translates the line: "There is a certain fire within us," and then adds: "OVID: . . . est Deus in nobis, agitante calescemus [sic] illo."[32] This statement which, as I pointed out above, expresses Ovid's faith in poetic inspiration, was important to Pound, who alludes to it several times in the *Cantos*. As always, however, he extends its meaning as he changes its context. In Canto 98 he uses "Est deus in nobis" twice as a general statement summarizing a series of meta-

morphic unions and identifications. Thus, the Odysseus persona's attendant sea-goddess, Leucothea, with whose magic powers he is identified (see especially Canto 100), and Ovid's Leucothoe, who "rose as an incense bush," become one object of worship. Leucothea, "being of Cadmus line" (i.e., Ino, the daughter of Cadmus), we are led back to Cadmus, founder of Thebes, and once again (through references to Plotinus and Gemisto) to Neoplatonic oneness combined with the Confucian-Eleusinian concept of fertility and order in the ideal society.

In his last cantos, Pound, still clinging to his vision of uniting Ovidian metamorphosis with Neoplatonic philosophy and Confucian ideology, acknowledges the failure of his scheme. Once again, in Canto 104, combining ancient Chinese ritual with his concept of the metamorphic "bust thru," he assigns to the vegetation rite Muan-bpo the power of moving the god within:

> and there is
> > > no glow such as of pine-needles burning
> Without muan   bpo
> > > no reality
> Wind over snow-slope   agitante
> > > > nos otros
> > > > > > calescimus
> Against jade
> > > calescimus,
> > > and the jade weathers dust-swirl.

> > > > > > > > (C 739)

The words "agitante" and "calescimus" recall Ovid, but the god Pound evokes stirs and warms the initiates in a ritual that transforms and sanctifies physical reality. As I observed earlier, he is still at this late stage summoning Persephone and other Ovidian gods in similar "grain rites." In these last cantos, the name Sulmona (C 754, 794), Ovid's birthplace, appears like a nostalgic memory. But it is apparent that he wavers in his faith in the capacity of the self-created god within to grant either the paradisiacal community or the coherent epic.

Acknowledging his "errors and wrecks," Pound admits: "And I am not a demigod, / I cannot make it cohere. / If love be not in the house there is nothing" (C 796). Later in the same canto, however, he returns to his vision of paradise:

29

again is all "paradiso"
    a nice quiet paradise
        over the shambles,
and some climbing
    before the take-off,
to "see again,"
the verb is "see," not "walk on"
i.e. it coheres all right
        even if my notes do not cohere.

                                 (C 796–97)

And the canto ends with the hope for "a little light, like a rushlight / to lead back to splendour" (C 797). According to Michael Bernstein, these lines can be understood only in connection with Pound's reliance on Plotinus throughout the *Cantos*. He places special importance on Plotinus' use of "the word ἀγλαΐα ('splendour') in a highly personal way to describe the primary Intellect to which man must rise, the source of all good and goal of all efforts (*Enneads*, VI.9.4)." In some detail, he convincingly relates "this entire section of *The Enneads*" to "Pound's conviction that there is a primal truth which remains valid, irrespective of our failure to attain, or to describe adequately, its plenitude." Bernstein also indicates the similarity between the endings of the *Enneads* and the *Cantos*: Pound, saying "it coheres all right / even if my notes do not cohere," seems to be echoing Plotinus, who "points to the failure of his discourse to encompass the *splendour* of the One, while still affirming the value of his work as an instigation, an aid on an arduous journey."[33]

But there is another work that also helps to clarify Pound's simultaneous acknowledgment of his inability to "make it cohere" and his insistence that coherence and "splendour" do indeed still exist for him, and that is Pound's own version of Sophocles' *Trachiniae*. Near the end of the tragedy, Heracles realizes that the prophecy of his release from his labors meant not the happiness he first imagined it did, but his death. Just before asking his son Hyllus' aid in fulfilling this prophecy, Sophocles' Heracles says (l. 1174, literally translated): "since at all events these things which are coming to pass are clear." Pound translates the line:

           . . . what
SPLENDOUR,
        IT ALL COHERES.[34]

The word λαμπρά, which, in the context of the oracular voice that Heracles heard, undoubtedly means "clear," can also be translated as "bright" or "splendid," but this variety of possible meanings cannot justify Pound's interpretation of the line. His translation and his statement in a footnote[35] that this "is the key phrase, for which the play exists," indicate that he believes Heracles has recognized a final order and unity in his life and work and that his death is a transcendence of mortality. Neither this line nor the events that follow in the drama justify such an interpretation. Although Heracles arranges for his own funeral pyre on a peak of Mt. Oeta, Sophocles does not include the apotheosis, which is part of his myth. Heracles' life ends in pain and despair, and the play concludes with Hyllus' comments on the cruelty of the gods and Zeus' responsibility for his father's tragic death. Pound's imposition of Plotinus' "splendour" on Heracles' bitter recognition that his hopes will not be realized converts disappointment into exaltation. In Canto 116, having renounced the role of "demigod," he claims for himself the same consolation that he projects on Heracles.

There is one more ending that should be considered in connection with that of the *Cantos*. In the last lines of the *Metamorphoses* Ovid expresses his certainty of the immortality of his art; it was the only metamorphosis he sought for himself. Pound, in contrast, still clinging to his messianic vision of creating a "paradiso terrestre," ends by acknowledging that his demands on metamorphosis, love, and poetry have exceeded his human limits.

Notes

1. *Guide to Kulchur* (New York: New Directions, 1968), p. 272; hereafter cited as GK followed by page number. T. S. Eliot had earlier observed that Ovid was interesting in this respect. Quoting from the *Metamorphoses* in his note on Tiresias in *The Waste Land*, he says: "The whole passage is of great anthropological interest."

2. *The Spirit of Romance* (New York: New Directions, 1968), pp. 15–16; hereafter cited as SR followed by page number.

3. *The Selected Letters of Ezra Pound, 1907–1941*, ed. D. D. Paige (New York: New Directions, 1971), p. 150; hereafter cited as L followed by page number.

4. *Literary Essays of Ezra Pound*, ed. T. S. Eliot (New York: New Directions, 1968), p. 179; hereafter cited as *LE* followed by page number.

5. Ezra Pound, *ABC of Reading* (Norfolk, Conn.: New Directions, n.d.), p. 48.

6. Unless otherwise noted, all translations from Ovid are mine.

In *Ovid as an Epic Poet*, 2d ed. (London: Cambridge University Press, 1970), Brooks Otis considers Apollo's "situation . . . the most ridiculous possible" and regards his humanization as comic (pp. 103–4), a view with which I obviously disagree. Apart from the pathos of the situation, the emphasis on continuity, it seems to me, indicates a more serious meaning than Otis perceives. This is one of several episodes in the *Metamorphoses* in which a god must accept the loss of a beloved who is transformed into a natural phenomenon. The story of Pan's love for Syrinx, which appears soon after that of Apollo's love for Daphne (see text below) also follows this pattern. If the first is intended as comic, the second must also be so regarded. Such repetition in close proximity does not strike me as a technique likely to produce humor.

7. Otis, *Ovid*, p. 133.

8. Ibid., pp. 144–45.

9. See also *Fasti* 1.95 ff., 3.167 ff., and *Epistulae ex Ponto* 3.3, 13 ff.

10. *Tristia* 1.1, 69–82; see also the prayer to Jupiter in 5.2, and *Epistulae ex Ponto*, especially 1.4, 43–44.

11. Otis, *Ovid*, pp. 270–71.

12. Ibid., p. 262 and chap. 9.

13. *The Cantos of Ezra Pound* (New York: New Directions, 1971), pp. 7–9; hereafter cited as *C* followed by page number.

14. Edgar Glenn, "Pound and Ovid," *Paideuma* 10 (Winter 1981): 630. For Pound's "development of the usury theme" through metamorphosis in this episode, see Sister M. Bernetta Quinn, *The Metamorphic Tradition in Modern Poetry* (New Brunswick, N.J.: Rutgers University Press, 1955), pp. 32–33.

15. Quoted by Mary de Rachewiltz, *Discretions* (Boston: Little, Brown, 1971), p. 159.

16. Daniel Pearlman, *The Barb of Time* (New York: Oxford University Press, 1969), p. 49.

17. Hippomenes says of himself, "pronepos ego regis aquarum" (*Metamorphoses* 10.606) and Venus, who tells his story, describes him twice as "proles Neptunia" (10.639, 665).

18. Michael Bernstein, *The Tale of the Tribe: Ezra Pound and the Modern Verse Epic* (Princeton: Princeton University Press, 1980), p. 76.

19. Ibid.

20. Bernstein refers to Pound's "awareness of metamorphosis as a specific

kind of mythological thinking" (p. 98), but he does not explore its essential functions in Pound's efforts to fuse myth and history.

21. Ibid.

22. Ibid., p. 43 n.

23. I discuss this subject more extensively in "Ezra Pound: The Messianic Vision," *Ancient Myth in Modern Poetry* (Princeton: Princeton University Press, 1971), pp. 293–307.

24. Ronald Bush, *The Genesis of Ezra Pound's Cantos* (Princeton: Princeton University Press, 1976), pp. 10–11. For an effective analysis of Pound's early use of the ideogram, see "The Poundian Ideogram," chap. 3 of Laszlo Géfin, *Ideogram: History of a Poetic Method* (Austin: University of Texas Press, 1982).

25. Walter Baumann, *The Rose in the Steel Dust: An Examination of the Cantos of Ezra Pound* (Bern: Francke Verlag, 1967), p. 22.

26. Ibid., p. 22.

27. Ibid., p. 97.

28. Massimo Bacigalupo, *The Forméd Trace: The Later Poetry of Ezra Pound* (New York: Columbia University Press, 1980), p. 427.

29. Ibid., pp. 429–30.

30. Pound's references to love in the *Cantos* are generally statements of an ideological position rather than the expression of individual feeling. His many avowals of love, moreover, are constantly refuted by his harsh attacks on historical figures or groups in lines that convey a rage and contempt more deeply felt than the professed love. In the very canto (91) in which love, identified with light and creation, is the mover and object of the poet, democracies, Jews, and others of whom Pound disapproves are equated with filth:

> *Democracies electing their sewage*
> *till there is no clear thought about holiness*
> *a dung flow from 1913*
> *and, in this, their kikery functioned, Marx, Freud*
> *   and the american beaneries*
> *Filth under filth,*
> *   Maritain, Hutchins,*
> *or as Benda remarked: "La trahison"*

(C 613–14)

As Bacigalupo points out: "the eight lines of italicized abuse Pound plants at the very center of canto 91 lack moral authority and only succeed in exposing 'mean hate' (c. 81) as the actual core of the 'love' he makes so much of" (p. 295).

31. Ibid., p. 266.

32. *Selected Prose, 1909–1965*, ed. William Cookson (New York: New Directions, 1973), p. 72.

33. Bernstein, *Tale of the Tribe*, pp. 89–90.

34. *Sophokles' Women of Trachis: A Version by Ezra Pound* (New York: New Directions, 1957), p. 50.

35. Ibid., p. 50.

POLIPOLIPOLIPOLIP

Pound and Li Po
What Becomes a Man

Ronald Bush

SO-SHU dreamed,
    And having dreamed that he was a bird, a bee,
and a butterfly,
    He was uncertain why he should try to feel like
anything else,

Hence, his contentment.
  —Ezra Pound, "Ancient Wisdom, Rather Cosmic" (after Li Po)

"Mr. Vetch . . . had always, even into the shabbiness of his old age,
kept that mark of English good-breeding (which is composed of some
such odd elements) that there was a shyness, an aversion to possible
phrase-making, in his manner of expressing gratitude for favours, and
that in spite of this cursory tone his acknowledgement had ever the accent of sincerity."
  —Henry James, *The Princess Casamassima*

Camerado, this is no book,
Who touches this touches a man.
  —Walt Whitman, "So Long"

    Pound and Homer. Pound and Ovid. The names call up an Ameri-
can in a small room in London haunted by antique cadences ringing in
his ears and antique places vivid in his mind's eye. The case of Pound

and Li Po is different. As Pound read Fenollosa's literal translations from the Chinese of Li Po, not only was the personality of the man behind the old poems dim and fluid, but so was his language and culture. Instead of a meeting of two strong presences, the encounter recalls what happens in a psychiatrist's office when a patient invests a companionable stranger's voice with part of his own identity. Released from the insistent otherness of the external world, in revery the patient weaves what he hears into a drama of his own making and suddenly finds himself thrown into focus. Which is very much what happened to Pound when, after pondering Fenollosa's nearly illegible notebooks in late 1914, he burst through into translation.[1] Pound once confessed that the masks he donned in his early poetry helped him say "'I am' this, that, or the other, and with the words scarcely uttered" cease to be that thing (GB 85). But translating from an alien tongue, he said, did more.[2] To quote the one western poem he printed with his Chinese translations, it let him his "own self song's truth reckon."[3] And as he had made over the Anglo-Saxon "Seafarer," so he made over Li Po's poems—into his own image. The question remains: what was that apparition's local habitation and its name?

Thanks to Hugh Kenner, we are reasonably certain at least of one thing. Like the book of translations he published in 1915, "for the most part from the Chinese of Rihaku [Li Po]" (P 126), the self Pound realized within it was covered in khaki. As Kenner observes, the war poems Pound included obliquely mirror World War I and the entire suite speaks of a "sensibility responsive to torn Belgium and disrupted London."[4] But Kenner, it now appears, might have said more. An unpublished letter at Harvard and the Fenollosa notebooks at Yale tell us that Cathay, though in 1915 very much a reflection of the war, did not start out that way nor did it remain so for long. Pound, for example, had not included two of its three battle pieces in his first plans, and as early as 1916, when he revised the sequence for collection, had already altered its emphasis.[5] Confirming a contemporary intuition of Ford Madox Ford, this evidence suggests the wartime loneliness that echoes through the 1915 suite was but one expression of something deeper. Ford had spoken of the poem, "Lament of the Frontier Guard," in a postpublication review and asked the rhetorical question: what more beautiful rendering could be found of the feelings "of one of those lonely watchers, in the outposts of progress, whether it be Ovid in Hyrcania, a Roman

sentinel upon the Great Wall of [England], or merely ourselves, in the lonely recesses of our minds . . . ?"[6] And by making the military outpost in the "Lament" a figure for the advance guard of our minds, Ford called attention to the suite's fundamental preoccupations: first with the recesses of poetic sensation—with the places where feelings are at once most authentic and most difficult to put into words—and then with the dedicated artist's courage as he advances into those regions. In Ford's view, Li Po's poetry represented yet one more link in the "Apostolic Succession" of sensibilities that Ford himself had taught Pound to revere.[7]

Nor, looking back, is it surprising that Pound's encounter with Li Po should have been so colored by turn-of-the-century romanticism. Its sponsor, after all, had been Ernest Fenollosa, the nineteenth-century scholar-vagabond par excellence. Starting as a devotee of Emerson, Fenollosa took a B.A. in philosophy from Harvard and finished two and a half years of graduate and divinity school before he withdrew in 1877 to study painting at the Boston Museum of Fine Arts. At that point, neither philosopher nor artist, he might have drifted indefinitely had not a Salem neighbor, Edward Morse, recruited him to fill one of a handful of unprecedented faculty openings for westerners at Tokyo University. Less than ten years later, due largely to his Emersonian penchant for finding the universal in the local, he had championed the value of Japanese artistic traditions and had been rewarded with the position of Japanese Imperial Commissioner of Fine Arts. With no previous formal training in the field, Fenollosa found himself the West's leading critic of Japanese art. Along the way he had been initiated into a family guild of traditional painters, had been ordained a Buddhist priest, and had conducted archaeological expeditions into the provinces of Japan. He had also had the pleasure of welcoming American dignitaries such as Henry Adams and had won financial security by selling off his private collection of oriental art. In 1890 he returned to Boston and the MFA as the curator of his own collection, only to toss position and respectability aside when he divorced to marry his bohemian assistant, Mary McNeil Scott. It was the sometime novelist Mary Fenollosa, accompanying her new husband back to Japan, who encouraged him to study the Chinese classics and who, after his death, passed on his notes to Ezra Pound. (Her story was that Pound, infatuated with China, pursued her at a literary gathering; his that she had read his work and recognized "the interpreter whom her husband would have wished.")[8]

37

Entering western literature in the salons of bohemia and under the eyes of three quintessentially American figures, Li Po was bound to emerge as an even more striking figure than he is in Chinese tradition, and as the Yale notebooks make clear, he did. The account of Li Po Fenollosa construed from his instructor, Professor Mori, highlights those sections of the canonical lives that tell of the Chinese poet's drinking, swordsmanship, and love of travel,[9] and it relates how the precocious Li Po disappointed his elders by refusing to become a Confucian scholar and by cultivating an unprecedented liberty of literary expression. Mori's account stresses other things as well: the poet's intuitive insight into character and his ability to mimic the styles of earlier poets at will.[10] Combining all this with a description of how Li Po got inside the Confucian tradition and made it new, the commentary could only confirm some of Pound's most deep-seated ambitions. To those familiar with Pound's career, there is no need to point up the resonance of a passage in which Li Po repeats Confucius's "My interest lies in compilation," nor is there need to underscore Mori's comment that for the Chinese compilation or selecting what is alive in a tradition is more "creative" than "creating anew."[11]

But it would be as deceptive to simplify the way Pound turned Li Po into a heroic version of himself as it would be to do the same to his treatment of, say, Villon, and for similar reasons. For Pound, the adolescent gesture of adopting a hero's mask was often a way of addressing moods of isolation and loss, moods that lay very near the center of his mature sensibility. The stratagem also helped him get at a corollary theme, which Ford broached in his review of *Cathay*. Speaking of "Lament of the Frontier Guard," Ford had directed Pound's readers toward the feelings of a lonely watcher and suggested the near impossibility of articulating these feelings. "Man is to mankind," he said, "a wolf . . . largely because the means of communication between man and man are very limited."[12] Thus conceived, the great question of literature is the one raised to unique prominence in a particular strain of Chinese poetry culminating in the work of the isolated wanderer Li Po: whether it is the nature of language to break down just when we need it most— when it might join our hearts and end our loneliness.

This question, as a remarkable student of mine demonstrated several years ago, not only gives *Cathay* its thematic coherence, but is a

constant in Pound's earlier work.[13] In Pound's early poetry and translations, situations of exile, confusion, and loss consistently correspond to
the theme of a painful separation of language from experience. The
theme is resonant in the *Cantos'* version of the eleventh book of the
Odyssey, where Odysseus, far from home, pours the sacrificial blood of
experience so that Tiresias might provide him authentic speech and end
his wanderings. But the theme also appears in certain canzoni of Arnaut
Daniel which Pound translated in *The Spirit of Romance*—canzoni
which speak of the need of the heart to speak "out his hiddenness"
and which lament "the bitter air" that "holdeth dumb and stuttering the
birds' glad mouths" just as separation enforces the troubadour's "struggle
to speak" (pp. 27–29). And if anything the theme is even stronger in
Pound's translation of the Anglo-Saxon "Seafarer," where a longing to
"fare forth" and "seek out a foreign fastness" corresponds to a resistance
to easy talk so painful that the seafarer's heart must "burst" from his
"breastlock" for him to say anything at all (*P* 64–65).

Together these three translations voice Pound's insistent sense of
the fragility of authentic feeling and authentic speech. In *Patria Mia*,
drafted a year before he received the Fenollosa papers, he had written
that he found

> in "The Seafarer" and in "The Wanderer" trace of what I should call the
> English national chemical. In those early Anglo-Saxon poems I find ex-
> pression of that quality which seems to me to have transformed the suc-
> cessive arts of poetry that have been brought to England from the South.
> For the art has come mostly from the south, and it has found on the island
> something in the temper of the race which has strengthened it and given it
> fibre. And this is hardly more than a race conviction that words scarcely
> become a man. (*PM* 45)

Soon afterwards, the remarks became a credo. Asserting that words
"scarcely become a man" because they commonly arise from inauthen-
tic experience, they also suggest that only authentic speech can overcome the alienation we habitually suffer from our inner lives.

Nor did Pound consider this attitude merely the English national
chemical. According to *Patria Mia*, it was "our American keynote" as
well—the keynote sounded by Walt Whitman when he wrote: "Camerado, this is no book, / Who reads this, touches a man." For this au-

thenticity and for this alone, Pound added, the true artist "is ready to endure personally a strain which his craftsmanship would scarcely endure" (PM 46).

We understand the poems of *Cathay* better, I think, when we discover that Pound originally considered printing them with the Tiresias episode of the *Odyssey* and the Daniel canzoni, and that he actually did print them with "The Seafarer."[14] These juxtapositions, illuminated by Pound's remarks in *Patria Mia*, explain why Cathay's opening poem, which portrays frontier troops eating fern-shoots, ends portentously by having the troops ask whether anyone will ever "know" of their "grief." The same grouping also suggests why Pound chose a centerpiece, the "Exile's Letter," which arrives at the question, "What is the use of talking . . . ?" and why the suite itself, at least in the enlarged version Pound included in his collected poems, ends as birds lament that however they "long to speak," even the most sympathetic man "can not know" of their "sorrow." The heart of Pound's sequence lies in its progression from a desperate suspicion to a melancholy acknowledgment that shared experience is beyond the power of language to effect. And within the order framed by that opening question and that disconsolate conclusion, we find a series of impeded journeys and blocked reunions which figure man's inarticulate heart and his inevitable isolation. Thus in "The Beautiful Toilet" a lone and silent woman is reduced to the synechdoche of extending a slender hand at the threshold of a door she does not open. And in "Taking Leave of a Friend" a parting that might have been a moment of shared feeling shows us two men standing silent as a river road winds to the far side of a looming mountain. As in most of the poems of *Cathay*, there is as much of their inability to voice their love in that road as there is prefiguration of the miles that will soon rise between them.

But the present occasion requires me to concentrate on those poems in *Cathay* Pound translated from Li Po. And by far the best way to do that is to speak of the suite's two masterpieces.

About the poem that Pound called "The River-Merchant's Wife: A Letter," Fenollosa's Professor Mori remarked that it beautifully presents the wife's unspoken feeling "not logical or straight but trailing here and there."[15] Few of us, I think, would disagree. Which only makes more interesting the fact that Pound, maintaining the beautiful indirection of the poem, transformed its subject. As a Sinologist has recently

pointed out, the river merchant of the poem would have been under-stood by Li Po's contemporary readers as the poet himself, and the poem read as "a love-poem to his wife but written as if from her to him, which was a common Chinese practice at the time."[16] The implied emotional drama of the poem, therefore, is one of love maturing before our eyes. The wife remembers herself as a little girl, recalls a time when she entered into an arranged marriage without much feeling, and then, spurred by the pain her husband's departure has provoked, slowly real-izes how much she cares for him. Li Po's poem swells to maximum feel-ing twice. At its center, moved by the river merchant's prolonged ab-sence, the wife recalls her fifteenth year, when she realized what love was and first desired her "dust to be mingled with" his, "forever and forever and forever." Then at the end of the poem she dreams of his returning and achieves a poignant reunion by traveling a considerable distance in her imagination to meet him halfway.

In Pound's hands, this poem becomes a dark reflection of its Chi-nese self and a recognizable cousin to the poems of blocked expression in the suite around it. Recalling Mori's remark that the wife belatedly discovers her own 'ignorance' after her husband leaves home,[17] Pound tuned his ear to a line near the beginning of the poem in which the wife recognizes that she and her lord were once "Two small people, without dislike or suspicion"—a line that unmistakably announces those feel-ings have arrived. The emotional curve Pound conveys is accordingly more complicated and more problematic than Li Po's. In Pound's poem, to affirm her love for her husband (that is, to deliver her letter), the wife must overcome not only the miles between them but also her own fugitive feelings of betrayal. Consequently, near the beginning of her monologue we detect nostalgia not only for the time when she first met her husband, but for an innocence before and beyond that, for a time when she was a child and her hair was "*still* cut straight across [her] forehead." The word "still" here is Pound's invention and not Li Po's. In Fenollosa's notes, as in his Chinese original, the line reads: when her hair was "first" cut across her forehead, and speaks of a cheerful mem-ory of the beginning of youth.[18] In Pound's version it implies a world of disappointment in what has followed.

In "The River-Merchant's Wife," moreover, this is only the first hint of suppressed ambivalence. Another involves the wife's worries about the route her husband must take on his journey home. In Fenol-

41

losa, the wife thinks of him passing through a notoriously dangerous group of river narrows.[19] In "The River-Merchant's Wife," the same narrows become more figure than fact. Beyond worrying about her husband's return, Pound's wife reveals reservations about whether her domestic happiness will ever be restored, and she telescopes the river narrows with the dark passages of her heart. In *her* unfolding vision, the merchant passes through a "river of swirling eddies" of her own conflicted feelings to a region where monkeys echo her own sorrow, only to then negotiate his return through the "narrows" of her suspicion. At that point, though, the completed fellow feeling figured by his return seems as unlikely as the possibility in "South-Folk in Cold Country" that China might acknowledge a fallen hero. Li Po's poem had ended with the wife crying out that she does not care about the great distance, she will travel to meet him to far Cho-fu-sa. But Pound deliberately alters what he found in Fenollosa and allows his syntax to overpower a geography none of his readers would be likely to guess. Fenollosa had translated the poem's last lines "For I will go out to meet [you], not caring that the way be far. / And will directly come to Chofusa."[20] Pound, shifting the feeling, has *his* wife aver that if her husband lets her know beforehand, she will come out to meet him *"as far as* Cho-Fu-Sa," with the implication (it is the culmination of her ambivalence) that she will come so far and no farther.

As rich a poem as "The River-Merchant's Wife" is, though, in *Cathay* it is outshone by the "Exile's Letter," which Pound said was one "of the finest things in all literature."[21] This is the piece that in 1920, along with "The Seafarer" and "Homage to Sextus Propertius" he called one of his "major personae,"[22] and which, in the first version of *Cathay*, he printed side by side with "The Seafarer." Both the "Exile's Letter" and "The Seafarer," he noted, give "not just the whole man, and his whole life-course, but [also] the age."[23] And not surprisingly, as he had done with "The Seafarer," he turned his translation of its counterpart into an excoriation of a bourgeois age.[24]

Comparing the "Exile's Letter" to the notes on which it is based, we notice first that Pound exaggerated Li Po's nostalgia for a past when poets were joined in true fellowship. In the fourth and fifth lines, without authority Pound introduces the pronoun "we" into the story of the poet's club, and in the seventh, ninth, and tenth lines he transforms Li Po's praise of a special friend into a celebration of a group of poets in a

halcyon time. In Fenollosa, the poet addresses "you," Chancellor Gen. But Pound broadens the address beyond "you" and I to include "they," with whom "There was nothing at cross purpose," explaining that

> *they* made nothing of sea-crossing or of
> mountain crossing,
> If only *they* could be of that fellowship [my italics].

The result is that in his poem something extraordinary is created not by a single friendship but by a poetic community that disdains gold and has forgotten kings and princes. It is this unique fellowship that allows the poets—almost a miracle in Pound's world—for once to speak out their "hearts and minds . . . without regret."

But as in the circumstances of Pound's other "major personae" such a state cannot last, and so we encounter the first of the poem's four separations. Remaking Fenollosa's confused verse about laurel trees, Pound evokes the quick of his own experience. Whether or not we allow western associations to remind us of the golden cage of those who wear the laurel crown, the phrase, "smothered in laurel groves" suggests what happens to the psyche when deprived of genuine speech. As in "Homage to Sextus Propertius," where a diminished speech and a diminished life make Pound think of "vacant dust" (P 219), here he feels a drying up of spirit, a lack of breath, as well as a disruption of his ease in what the *Cantos* would call the "green world" (C 521).

The rest of the poem, moreover, picks up that unease to flesh out the meaning of isolation and silence. We find, for example, that the reunion that follows the two friends' first separation involves a serpentine journey "Through all the thirty-six folds of the turning and twisting waters." This journey, it is true, ultimately opens out to a moment where the voices of man and nature—the mouth-organ and the phoenix cries—are in harmony. After a second separation, though, we are shown a second reunion even more vivid because it must be so much harder won. This time, as in "The River-Merchant's Wife," coming together is a matter of navigating the heart's narrows—in this case of traveling "over roads twisted like sheep's guts" in the "cutting wind," "late in the year." These disorders of the natural world are figures for psychic alienation, and together they represent a dislocation that may be overcome only at the cost of labor and suffering. In this vein the friend's last

43

separation, which cannot be overcome, makes the speaker remember a crowd breaking up and feel

> like the flowers falling at Spring's end
> Confused, whirled in a tangle.

Against these feelings, of course, the poem contains glorious moments in which the poet's being and voice as well as his place in the green world are restored. And it is worth noting that these cases of fulfillment are repeated in the structure of *Cathay*. To my mind, the most compelling of them begins with line 47:

> And you would walk out with me to the western corner of the castle,
> To the dynastic temple, with water about it clear as blue jade,
> With boats floating, and the sound of mouth-organs and drums,
> With ripples like dragon-scales, going grass green on the water,
> Pleasure lasting, with courtezans, going and coming without hindrance,
> With the willow flakes falling like snow,
> And the vermillioned girls getting drunk about sunset,
> And the water, a hundred feet deep, reflecting green eyebrows
> —Eyebrows painted green are a fine sight in young moonlight,
> Gracefully painted—
> And the girls singing back at each other,
> Dancing in transparent brocade,
> And the wind lifting the song, and interrupting it,
> Tossing it up under the clouds.

Here, nature and art are held in a harmony that feels eternal, presenting us with an epiphany like the one in "Poem by the Bridge at Ten-Shin," where fallen petals are momentarily preserved by a river current before "evening drives them on the eastward-flowing waters," and where the great Han-rei, "his own skiffsman" in the timelessness of his heroic moment, rescues his mistress, her hair forever "unbound."[25]

Pound was obviously moved by this section of the "Exile's Letter" and gave to it some of his finest inventions. For instance, he subtracted agents and agency from Fenollosa's line, "we floated a boat and played with the water." Through a series of present participles, Pound's lines convey a privileged moment in which, the "pleasure lasting," all remains in suspension. In this moment, the human world and the world of the landscape reflect each other, and the equilibrium suggests the

permanent ministry of poetry. Thus, whereas Fenollosa mentions that the "water grass was green" and juxtaposes it with scalelike ripples, Pound's ripples "go grass green on the water," telescoping the greening power of nature with the metamorphic power of poetic vision. And whereas Fenollosa gives us beautiful green eyebrows that shine "like" the new moon, Pound, dispensing with simile, has eyebrows transfigure the light into "young moonlight."

By the end of this sequence, the "girls singing back at each other, / Dancing in transparent brocade" have become an emblem for the way poetry, nature's consort, lets us feel the energy that moves through all things. And so secure is Pound in his authority that at the end of the sequence he takes liberties that, even when we are made aware of them, seem inevitable. In his lines, the wind itself lifts the burden of the song, and interrupts the song according to its own measure.

Contemplating the lines just discussed it can appear that an antique master of the romantic mood has found his reincarnation. And yet as soon as we look for further evidence of this kind of thing, we realize the generalization will not hold. Consider the conclusion of the poem's first reunion scene, which in Fenollosa's paraphrase reads:

> At this entertainment I felt as if my spiritedness
> permeated all through the 9 heavens
> (But) before the end of the day (before evening) we
> had to disperse with stars and rain.

The sense here is that after their moment of happiness the two friends were separated as rain clouds separate the stars, and in his note Professor Mori remarks that the line demonstrates Li Po's great skill at transitions.[26] In a few words, that is, the poet brings to bear an extraordinary concatenation of natural process and links the parting of the two friends with the forces of night and winter. One would think that of all people Pound would have appreciated the beautiful economy of the verse and would have done his best to make his translation worthy of its original. Instead, almost as if repelled, he threw the line away, and compounded his insensitivity by ignoring an image of a nesting bird in the next line but one. Most grievous of all, he cut the sequence short, truncating the last three lines of the separation into two.

The truth of the matter is that Pound was far from sanguine about

the Wordsworthian side of Li Po. More like Coleridge rather, he seeks companionable forms in nature but only to validate his own echoing spirit. In the "Exile's Letter," when he chooses to revise a phrase it is usually to highlight the poem's brooding speaker rather than to call attention to some glory the speaker has perceived. This is especially clear from the places where Pound breaks a line into two, dramatizing by the resultant hesitation a movement of the mind and necessarily reminding us of the speaker's self-consciousness. An example of this occurs in lines seven and eight, where Pound's interjected pause suggests the sudden weight of years:

> And with them, and with you especially
> There *was* nothing [as there presumably now is] at
>   cross purpose.

Lines 36–37 and 42–43 are equally effective. In the first pair we over-hear the exile suddenly realize how unique and special a thing it was

> one May . . . [for you to] send for me,
>   *despite the long distance.*

And in the second, his sense of:

> how little you cared for the cost,
>   and [of] you caring enough to pay it.

But the handful of times Pound breaks a line only reinforces his smaller interventions, which from the beginning build up a sense of the speaker's melancholy, of what he has lost between there and here, past and present, fellowship and isolation:

> (l.2) *Now* I remember that you built me a special tavern
> (l.11) And we all *spoke* out [then, not now] our hearts and minds. . . .
> (l.46) And I was drunk, and had [then, not now] no thought of returning.

Through such small emphases, Pound prepares us for the somber-ness of his conclusion. Li Po's coda, Mori had remarked, reiterates his opening word ("to recollect") and sums up the poem's history.[27] Even in Fenollosa the four lines are bleak:

> Words cannot be exhausted
> Nor can the feeling be fathomed.

So calling upon my son, I make him sit on the ground for a long time,
    and write to my dictation these words . . .
And, sending them to you over 1,000 miles, we think of each other at a
    distance.

In Pound, they are bleaker still:

What is the use of talking, and there is no end of talking,
There is no end of things in the heart.
I call in the boy,
Have him sit on his knees here
    To seal this,
And send it a thousand miles, thinking.

Here, instead of two friends thinking of each other, there is only a
solitary who speaks of his son as "the boy," who is a thousand miles from
solace and who confirms his isolation by "thinking." And there is no
longer mention of a letter sent, only (as the pronounced pause of an
added line brings home) a letter "sealed"—sealed up, interred. Nor
need we wonder about the reason why. It would be bad enough, as
Fenollosa's notes suggest, if words could never be exhausted and if the
last bit of our affection could never be expressed. But it is worse than
that. In the "Exile's Letter," there is no "use" in talking because, as the
idiomatic tone of the words tells us, talk is only blather—there "is no
end of" it. Or so at least, in his most moving pronouncement, says the
composite author we may call "Li Pound."

But perhaps it would be better to leave the last word to the unaug-
mented voice of Ezra in one of his testier moods. The verses of "The
Seafarer," Pound wrote in 1916,

> were made for no man's entertainment, but because a man believing in
> silence found himself unable to withold himself from speaking. And that
> more uneven poem, *The Wanderer*, is like to this, a broken man speak-
> ing . . . an apology for speaking at all. . . .
>   Such poems are not made for after-dinner speakers, nor was the elev-
> enth book of the Odyssey. Still it flatters the mob to tell them that their
> importance is so great that the solace of lonely men, and the lordliest of the
> arts, was created for their amusement.[28]

47

Appendix 1

A Transcript of Fenollosa's Notes for the "Exile's Letter," not Including Transliterations

[Title]

recollecting past pleasure- write to name district family council bar
        old   making   name   title

Remembering former play write to chancellor Gen of Sho district
                                (epistle)

[Text]

recollect   ancient   Rakuyo   to   so   Kiu   (=Kasu)
                              name   lit. name
                              of family   husk-hill
                                        what remains after wine is extracted

I now remember that it was To-so Kiu of Rakuyo

For   me   ten   shin   bridge   south   make   wine   storied
               heaven port   build   house

(Who) for me specially built a tavern to the South of the Tenshin bridge

yellow   gold   white   jewel   buy   songs   laughter

(Where) buying song and laughter with gold and jewels

one   drink   successive   months   disdain   kings(+)princes
once drunk

(And) once drunk for months together I despised Kings + princes

sea   interior   wise   great   blue   could   guest

From all parts of the Empire came flocking wise and great
     guests in prosperous court life (to me while I was there)

take   middle   with   lord   mind   not   ran counter
 "especially"   you   oppose

And amongst them it was with you especially that our minds had
     nothing running counter.

to make   Mt.   to make   sea   not   make   hard
  roll   turn   consider

(You) considering it nothing even if you had to roll over mts
        and turn back the oceans for me, (determined to gather hardships
        for my sake)

????   emotion   invest   mind   not   what   lament
"make incline"   give entirely to   will   regret
pour into = here,   (upset?)
"tip"

And pour out all your emotion + will, without regret (devote your
        mind for me)

I   facing   name of river   south   climb up   [name] laurel   leaves

I facing the region south of the Wai, climbed the laurel
        trees (they are abundant there and there is a poem of ????
        empire by old king of ????) and a poetical way of saying he had
        to go there.

lord   remaining   name of   north   feeling-seeing   dream   thought
you   water

And you remained North of the Raku wan, so that we had to undergo of
        thinking of each other in dream land

not   forbear   separate

And as we could not forbear being separated

again   mutually   follow

We again came together.

mutually   following   far-far   visit   sennin fortress
                                    very   name of mt.

And accompanying each other we travelled far into the Sengo Mts

36   fold   bent   water   twining   bent toward
                                                                      twist

Where the 36 fold bending waters twine + twist.

one   valley   first   entered   1000   flowers   bright
    (watery valley)

On entering the first valley (one already sees the scene to be entirely
    changed) there being 1000 different bright flowers

10000   valleys   pass through   lit. = "spent"   pine   wind   voice
    (rocky valleys)   entirely

And after passing through innumerable rocky valleys one comes to a
    calm region where one hears nothing but the voice of the pine
    winds.

silver   harness   gold   semi   bow prostrate   flat   ground
        saddle   lit. = "inverted"
                          "upside down"

(Presently) comes the governor [in Fenollosa's hand, this word looks
    much like 'foreman'] of the East of the Kan to

Kan   to   grand guard   come   mutually   meet
Han River   East   governor

Meet us riding (on horses) of silver saddle + gold reins, and
    prostrating himself on the flat ground.

Shi   yo   shi   true man
Purple yang   's   sennin
name of mt.

There also came the sennin of Shiyo to meet me

Coming to meet   me   play   jewel   mouth organ
Playing a jewelled mouth organ

San   ka   storied   one   more   sennin   music
feast mist   house
    name

In Sanka storied house they gave us entertainment of sennin music

loud symphonic   adj. ending   exactly   resemble   young   ho   singing
sounds of many   —like   phoenix   crying
    notes

Whose loud symphony resembled the crying of young + old *ho* (phoenix)
    birds singing

50

sleeves	long	(by)pipe	becoming	waits to	light(ly)	rise
		tribe of	excited	about to		
		the sho				

The governor of Kanchu, drunk, stands and

Kan	middle	great defender	drunk	stand up	dance
water		guard			

Prince dances, because his long sleeves, excited by the pipes,
    could not but rise lightly of its own accord

hand	holding	brocade	upper garment	cover	my	body
						self

I, drunk, lay down, with my head pillowed on his thigh

I	drunk	horizontal	sleep	pillow	its	thigh
		laying down		(rest)	his	

And he with his brocade garment in hand covered me.

This day	lit "carpet"	will	spirit	prevail	9	sky
occasion	dinner	state of mind				
	entertainment					

At this entertainment I felt as if my spiritedness permeated all
    through the 9 heavens

stars	separate	rain	disperse	not	end	morning-day

(but) before the end of the day (before evening) we had to disperse
    with stars and rain.

separate	fly	so	Kan	Mt	water	far off
		name of place				
		So's fortress gate				

I had to fly apart toward the So frontier, and Mts. + waters put us far
    apart.

I	already return	Mt.	ask after	old	nest
			search		

I already returned to the Mt and had to search for my old nest.

lord	also	return	home	pass over	name of river	bridge
you						

And you, going home, would have passed over the 4 bridges

2nd part of poem

lord's	house	strict-lord	brave	leopard	tiger
you		your father			

Your father "brave like leopards and tigers" (used in Shokiu classic of
general)

????	governor	hei	shu	put down	barba-	prisoners
having become		name of province	province		rians	hordes

Having become the governor of Heishu, was occupied in putting down the
barbarian hordes.

five	month	mutually	calling	pass over	tai	ko
					great	journey
						= march

In May he caused you to call me, (travelling) across Taiko (a name of
a Mt.)

break	wheel	not	say	sheep	intestines	difficulty =
						hardship

Where, although wheels be broken, I will not say the hardship of
travelling through Mountains winding like sheep's intestines
[illegible comment]

go	come	north	cool	year	month	deep

Going (continual travelling), I come, and where the North wind's
already cold, being advanced in year

feel	lord's	noble	faithful to	despise	yellow	gold
	you		friends	disdain		

I was struck by your esteem of faithfulness and disdain of gold

red gems	cup	beautiful	food	blue	jade enamel	stand
jewels		(of clothes)				

Red jade cup and fine colored food, placed on blue jewelled table

make	me	drunk	full	no	return	mind

then made me drunk and satisfied, and forgetful of returning.

time time	go out	face	castle	west	corner (or two
					meanings

From time to time you took me out towards western corner of the city

shin	temple	flow	water	is like	deep blue	jade
dynastic	shrine					

Where (as I remember) around the Shin Shrine, is surrounded by running
   water, clear as blue gems

making-	boat	play	water	mouth	dream	sing
float		with		organ		play out,
						make noise

Then we floated a boat, and played with the water (in hand), sounding
   our flutes and drums.

faint	waves	dragon	scales	water-floating	grass	green
ripples						

The small ripples resembled the scales of dragons, and the water grass
   was green.

rise or	come,	bring	courtezan	free of	pass	pass
raise	coming	with		one's will		
pleasure						

At the height of pleasure, we took with us courtezans, and passed
   along (parts of water) in utter liberty.

What	like	willow	flowers	resemble	snow	how!
How						

What shall I do with the willow flowers falling like snow (It's to
   be regretted that willow flowers fall—expression of
   separateness)

crimson or   paint   want to   drink   had better   incline   sun
vermillion   (on face)

The red painted girls about to be drunk, are appropriate to the
    inclining sun (look beautiful with glow of sun very fine in
    color) the *red* here refers to all 3, all girls red—also,
    drink, also sun—

hundred   feet   prove   deep   copy   green   eyebrow
                                           reflect

Where the hundred feet deep clear water are reflected their green
    eyebrows (the girls.) [illegible comment]

green   eyebrow   beautiful   early   moon   shine
                    (of lady's face)

The green eyebrows are graceful and beautiful, (^and like) the new moon
    ^shines shining.
(The beauty of the line lies in there being no like—2 assertions, but
    likeness implied).

beautiful   persons   one another   sing   dance   brocade   clothing
women   transparent

The beauties sing to one another, and some dance with trans. brocade
    clothes. (like no dresses)

Pure   wind   blow against   poetry   enter   space   go away
                               song   vanish

The clear wind, blowing against the song, rises with it into the sky,
    (the voice seems to ascend with the wind).

song   melody   of itself   wind in—   going   cloud   fly
                              involve   passing

And the songs and music by themselves fly around the passing cloud.
    (This is fine line. The one before is made for this,)
        (The cloud itself moves, the music, rising with the air,
        are heard as if they were whistling twisted in the clouds
        as it were echoing to the clouds)

this   time   pleasure   making   hard   again   meet
That time

of this period the pleasures cannot be met again

54

west   travel   therefore   offer   long   willow   poetry(to be sung)
song

So I have travelled westward and offered the Choyo song.
    (refers to historical fact in late Kan was a scholar called
    Layu who presented on occassion of imperial hunting a fine poem
    describing scene, the Emperor admiring, admitted him. So, to
    present this poem was called Choyofu—R's poem [i.e. Rihaku's—Li
    Po's] was not so called, but means any poem for examination)

north   lit. = gate   blue   cloud   not   possible   determine
promotion   (the time)
waited

At the court the promotions could not be expected (was not obtainable
    as one expected) (he was unsuccessful) (he had employment, but
    did not get ahead as fast as or in the way he wanted).

east   mountain   white   head   return   return   away
So I had to return to the Eastern Mt with my head already become white.

4   bridge   south   head   once   meet   you
(On my returning to Tojan) I passed over the 4 bridge (again)
    and at the Southern end I once again meet you

San   palace   's   north   again   separate from   crowd
(But this meeting is not of long duration) because you are to go to
    the North of the San terrace, so that (we) the group must
    separate.

ask   me   separation   sadness   know   much   few
(If you) ask me how much I regret the parting (much or little)

falling   flowers   spring   end   compete   in   (dawn)
with   turmoil   in confusion
(mixed)

I would avow that my sorrow is as much as struggling with one another
    in a tangle.

words   also   not   possible   ^(to express)   all = (lit.)exhaust
Words cannot be exhausted

55

emotion	also	not	possible	ˆto fathom	ultimate = end
					(lit.)depletes

Nor can the feeling be fathomed.

Calling	child	sitting on	seal	this	words
	boy	one's knees			letter

So calling upon my son, I make him sit on the ground for a long time,
and write to my dictation these words (letter sealed is
used for letter written)

send to	you	thousand	miles	far	mutually	think of =
						recollect

And, sending them to you over 1000 miles, we think of each other
in (at a) distance.

Appendix 2

A List of the Poems of Li Po in Fenollosa's Two "Rihaku" Notebooks.
(YC 20 and 21)

On the inside covers of the two notebooks, Pound continued his running count of poems from earlier volumes. Therefore, he numbered the first of the Li Po poems not 1 but 104. Against his tabulation he marked seventeen poems for special consideration (my numbers 5, 9, 12, 14, 16, 18, 19, 20, 21, 23, 24, 25, 36, 38, 41, 42, 44). He then made a short list and marked six poems for further consideration (12, 14, 20, 23, 25, 38), all of which he used for *Cathay*. (To these six he would add five more: 4, 43, 44, 45, 48.) Of the eleven poems he considered but did not use, four are Sennin poems (5, 36, 41, 42), one is a satiric antiwar poem (19), and five are in one way or another expressions of alienation and loss (9, 16, 18, 21, 24).

The following provides references to English versions of some but not all of the poems Pound did not translate. (There is no complete English translation of Li Po.) Citations refer to one of the following:

Florence Ayscough and Amy Lowell, *Fir-Flower Tablets* (Boston: Houghton Mifflin, 1921).
Witter Bynner, *The Jade Mountain: A Chinese Anthology* (New York: Knopf, 1960).
Arthur Cooper, *Li Po and Tu Fu* (London: Penguin, 1973).

Wu-Chi Liu and Irving Yucheng Lo, *Sunflower Splendor: Three Thousand Years of Chinese Poetry* (New York: Anchor, 1975).

Shigeyoshi Obata, *The Works of Li Po* (New York: Dutton, 1922).

Arthur Waley, *The Poetry and Career of Li Po* (London: Allen & Unwin, 1950).

In the list that follows the first number is my own number followed by Pound's number in parentheses and the first line of the poem in Fenollosa's translation.

Notebook I (YC 20)

1 (104)   Great elegance longtime not flourish. ("Ancient Airs," in *Liu and Lo*, pp. 113–14).

2 (105)   Shin emperor sweep six together.

3 (106)   The great white mountain, how blue! how blue!

4 (107)   The horses of Dai, though taken to Etsu, care nothing for Etsu. ("South-Folk in Cold Country," in *Cathay*).

5 (108)   Five storks come from the north-west.

6 (109)   It being now February or March in the capital (of Kan).

7 (110)   Shoshu dreamed of being a butterfly. ("Chang Chou and the Butterfly," in Obata, p. 106).

8 (111)   In Sei there are chivalrous youngsters.

9 (112)   The Hoangho [river] always runs to the Eastern ocean.

10 (113)   Pine white . . . solitary straight.

11 (114)   Gen Kunpei forsook the world.

12 (115)   Fortgate against barbarians abounds in wind and sand. ("Lament of the Frontier Guard," in *Cathay*).

13 (116)   *Sho*, King of En, inviting (calls as adviser) Kakkwai.

14 (117)   The thousand gates have peaches + apricots. ("Poem by the Bridge at Ten-shin," in *Cathay*).

15 (118)   In old time there were two daughters named, *Ko* and *Yei*. ("The Parting," in Waley, pp. 36–37).

16 (119)   Yellow cloud is on yonder fortress—crows think of returning to their nests. ("The Crows at Nightfall," in Obata, p. 87).

17 (120)   How high! How dangerous it is! ("The Perils of the Shu Road," in Ayscough and Lowell, pp. 6–8).

[Pound records a 121 which corresponds to no poem.]

18 (122)   In the time the crows nest on the Koso terrace. ("A Song for the Hour when the Crows Roost," in Ayscough and Lowell, p. 78).

19 (123)   Last year we fought at the source of the So Ken River. ("The Nefarious War," in Obata, pp. 141–42).

20 (124)   My hair was at first covering my brows. ("The River-Merchant's Wife: A Letter," in *Cathay*).

21 (125)   The sun rises out of an Eastern corner.

22 (126)   The mud in the water of Dokuroku!

23 (127)   The jewel stairs have already become white with dew. ("The Jewel Stairs' Grievance," in *Cathay*).

24 (128)   The moonlight in front of the raised floor—(bed). ("Quiet Night Thoughts," in Cooper, p. 109).

Notebook II (YC 21)

25 (129)   A (fine) boat of shato wood, with sides of *mokuran*. ("The River Song," in *Cathay*. N.B.: Pound's numbering suggests he did not know he made his "Song" from two different poems).

26 (130)   Oko ferry, looking Westward, the great River impedes one going to Western Shin.

27 (131)   The Shin Mts. and the So Mts.—all have their white clouds. ("A Farewell Song of White Clouds," in Obata, p. 29).

28 (132)   Shu ho's eternally like autumn.

29 (133)   The Shu ho brocade ostrich.

[Pound did not number 30 and 31, probably because he regarded them as parts of 29.]

30   Among the myriad folded peaks of Shu ho.

31   An old man of Shu ho county.

32 (134)   Gabi Mt. rises prominently against the Western extreme heaven. ("Song upon a landscape painting in opaque color by Governor Choyen of Toto").

33 (135)   The autumn when the half moon hangs over Gabisan. ("The Yo-Mei Mountain Moon," in Obata, p. 59).

34 (136)   Seikei purifies my mind. ("Theme of the Rest-House on the Clear Wan River," in Ayscough and Lowell, p. 57).

35 (137)   The Omu island lies . . . along the Kanyo Ferry. ("Parrot Island," in Ayscough and Lowell, p. 61).

36 (138)   Lying in clouds for 30 years.

37 (139)   Going out of my gate and looking toward the Southern Mt.

38 (140, 141)   I now remember that it was To-so Kiu of Rakuyo. ("The Exile's Letter," in *Cathay*).

39 (142)   In the morning I started by the Shujaku gate. ("Passing the Night at the White Heron Island," in Ayscough and Lowell, p. 71).

40 (143)   Buoyant, buoyant the river wind rises.

41 (144)   I am the original madman of *So*. ("The Song of Luh Shan," in Obata, pp. 161–62).

42 (145)   Seafarers speak of Yei island. ("His dream of the Sky-Land: A Farewell Poem," in Obata, pp. 115–17).

43 (146)   An Old acquaintance, starting from the West, takes leave of Ko Kaku Ro. ("Separation on the River Kiang," in *Cathay*).

44 (147)   When blue Mt. peaks are visible toward the Northern suburb. ("Taking Leave of a Friend," in *Cathay*).

45 (148)   We hear it said that Sanso's roads. ("Leave-Taking near Shoku," in *Cathay*).

46 [Pound did not number 46.]   That which forsakes me, namely, the day which was yesterday, cannot be stopped. ("A Farewell to Secretary Shu-Yün at the Hsieh T'iao Villa in Hsüan-Chou," in Bynner, pp. 66–67).

47 (149)   In evening, coming down from a blue Mt. ("Coming down from Chung-Nan Mountain by Hu-Szu's Hermitage, He Gave Me Rest for the Night and Set Out the Wine," in Cooper, p. 151).

48 (150)   Above the *ho* terrace, the hoo used to play. ("The City of Choan," in *Cathay*).

Notes

1. Letter to his parents, 30 November 1914, Collection of American Literature, Beinecke Rare Book and Manuscript Library, Yale University.

The following abbreviations, followed by page number, will be used in citations: *The Cantos of Ezra Pound* (New York: New Directions, 1975), C; *Gaudier-Brzeska* (New York: New Directions, 1970), GB; *Patria Mia and The Treatise on Harmony* (London: Peter Owen, 1962), PM; *Personae: The Collected Shorter Poems of Ezra Pound* (New York: New Directions, 1971), P; Yale University Collection of American Literature, YC.

2. Pound went on: "I began this search for the real in a book called *Personae*, casting off, as it were, complete masks of the self in each poem. I continued in long series of translations, which were but more elaborate masks" (GB 85).

3. From "The Seafarer," P 64.

4. Hugh Kenner, *The Pound Era* (Berkeley and Los Angeles: University of California Press, 1971), p. 202. The present essay follows Kenner in regarding *Cathay* as a mask for Pound's sensibility. For a discussion of how the translations consolidated Pound's technique, see Donald Davie, *Ezra Pound: Poet as Sculptor* (New York: Oxford University Press, 1964), pp. 38–47, and Wai Lim Yip, *Ezra Pound's "Cathay"* (Princeton: Princeton University Press, 1969).

5. According to the running count Pound kept in the inside covers of Fenollosa's notebooks, there were 150 Chinese poems translated in the Fenollosa collection, of which forty-eight were contained in two thick notebooks

on Li Po. By 3 December 1914, when he sent a letter asking Thomas Bird Mosher to publish a selection in the *Bibelot*, Pound had cut the 150 down to eight poems—the seven poems plus a four-poem departure suite that make up the core of *Cathay*. (Letter in the Mosher Collection of the Houghton Library, Harvard University. See also John Espey, "The Inheritance of To Kalon," in Eva Hesse, ed., *New Approaches to Ezra Pound* [Berkeley and Los Angeles: University of California Press, 1969], p. 323.) Of these (seven plus four) poems, nine were by Li Po, and only one was about war ("The Song of the Bowmen of Shu"). Nor could Pound's next arrangement be called a war sequence: his "Cathay" typescript at Yale does not include "Lament of the Frontier Guard" or "South-Folk in Cold Country," but does append four other poems to the original eight. It was sometime after that, perhaps because the war became more oppressive, that he changed his plans. For the 1915 khaki-bound *Cathay*, he suppressed the four appended poems and added "Lament" and "South-Folk." Here the theme of impeded communication indeed suggests the uncertainties of life during the Great War, and the volume ends with what Hugh Kenner has rightly called its most severe and chilling poem, "South-Folk in Cold Country." A year later, though, the pre-1915 grouping resurfaced. In the version of *Cathay* published in *Lustra* (1916) and in subsequent collections, the four poems following "South-Folk" are restored and the suite's military associations resume their place in a larger structure.

Backtracking further, Pound's first selections from the Mori–Fenollosa–Li Po material show him experimenting with various themes. After going through the forty-eight poems quickly, he marked out seventeen for possible translation, a group which entirely overlooked "South-Folk in Cold Country." Besides the ones he finally adopted, this group contained four poems about the Sennin (Chinese holy men, or, in some of Pound's flights, air spirits), one of which, "The Madman of Shu," was a kind of Chinese "Madness of King Goll." He also chose an antiwar poem more bitter but less tragic than the three in *Cathay*. And he picked out five poems all more or less on the theme of alienation or loss. For details, see appendix 2.

6. Ford Madox Ford, "From China to Peru," *Outlook* 35 (19 June 1915): 800–801. I quote from a reprinting in Brita Lindberg-Seyersted, ed., *Pound/Ford: The Story of a Literary Friendship* (New York: New Directions, 1982), p. 25.

7. See Pound's "How I Began" (*T.P.'s Weekly*, 6 June 1913, p. 707); one of the "friends" of the "Victorians" and "Pre-Raphaelites" that Pound met was Ford Madox Ford:

> I have "known many men's manners and seen many cities." Besides knowing living artists I have come in touch with the tradition of the dead. I have had in this the same sort of pleasure that a schoolboy has in hearing of the star plays of former ath-

letes. . . . I have relished this or that about "old Browning," or Shelley sliding down his front banisters "with almost incredible rapidity."

There is more, however, in this sort of Apostolic Succession than a ludicrous anecdote, for people whose minds have been enriched by contact with men of genius retain the effects of it.

I have enjoyed meeting Victorians and Pre-Raphaelites and men of the nineties through their friends. I have seen Keats' proof sheets, I have personal tradition of his time at second-hand.

8. For information about Fenollosa's life and Mary Fenollosa's bequest to Pound, see Lawrence W. Chisolm, *Fenollosa: The Far East and American Culture* (New Haven and London: Yale University Press, 1963). Pound's account is embedded in T. S. Eliot's "Ezra Pound: His Metric and Poetry," *To Criticize the Critic: Eight Essays on Literature and Education* (New York: Farrar, Straus, & Giroux, 1965), p. 177.

9. Shigeyoshi Obata provides three traditional lives in part 3 of *The Works of Li Po* (New York: Dutton, 1922).

10. The first Mori–Li Po notebook (*YC* 20) begins with a lecture on Chinese literary forms as they pertain to Li Po and continues with an account of Li Po's career. This general discussion continues into the first set of translation and commentary, which concerns Li Po's relation to Confucian tradition. Mori's comments on Li Po's skill as an imitator occurs on the first page of the second notebook (*YC* 21).

11. YC notebook 20, p. 25. Pound elaborated the point in his "Chinese Poetry" (*To-Day* 1, April 1918), when he wrote that Li Po was "a great 'compiler'" and that a compiler "does not merely gather together, his chief honour consists in weeding out, and even in revising" (pp. 54–55).

Material from the Fenollosa notebooks quoted by courtesy of the Pound Center, Collection of American Literature, Beinecke Rare Book and Manuscript Library, Yale University, and by permission of the Ezra Pound Literary Property Trust.

12. Ford, "From China to Peru," p. 25. In words World War II was to load with irony, the review continues: "I daresay that if words direct enough could have been found, the fiend who sanctioned the use of poisonous gases in the present war could have been so touched to the heart that he would never have signed that order, calamitous, since it marks a definite retrogression in civilisation such as had not yet happened in the Christian era." Inexplicably, Eric Homberger's Critical Heritage volume on Pound, which reprints the review, elides the sentences I have quoted (*Ezra Pound* [London and Boston: Routledge & Kegan Paul, 1972], pp. 108–9).

13. My reading of *Cathay* and especially of its relation to Pound's early poetry and translations draws heavily on an honors thesis I was privileged to

supervise in 1979–80: "'The Heart Shall Speak Out His Hiddenness': *Cathay* as the Outgrowth of the Play between 'Word' and 'Thing' in Ezra Pound's Early Prose and Poetry," by Wayne Koestenbaum. The thesis is available in the Harvard University Archives and I hope eventually will be published.

14. In his December 1914 letter to Thomas Bird Mosher (see note 5), Pound suggested that Mosher print the Chinese poems together with "The Seafarer," a poem of Bertrans de Born, certain canzoni of Daniel, possibly a version of Catullus' marriage hymn and Pound's translation of the eleventh book of the *Odyssey*. In *Cathay* (1915), Pound printed "The Seafarer" side by side with the "Exile's Letter."

15. *YC*, notebook 20, p. 127 verso.

16. Arthur Cooper, *Li Po and Tu Fu* (London: Penguin, 1973), p. 127.

17. *YC*, notebook 20, p. 130 verso.

18. See the transcription of the notes in Sanehide Kodama, "Cathay and Fenollosa's Notebooks," *Paideuma* 11 (Fall 1982): 225.

19. Ibid., pp. 222–23.

20. Ibid., p. 228.

21. In his 1914 letter to Thomas Bird Mosher.

22. *Umbra: The Early Poems of Ezra Pound* (London: Elkin Mathews, 1920), p. 128.

23. In his 1914 letter to Thomas Bird Mosher.

24. For discussions of Pound's "Seafarer," see Hugh Witemeyer, *The Poetry of Ezra Pound: Forms and Renewal, 1908–1920* (Berkeley and Los Angeles: University of California Press, 1969), pp. 118–21, and Michael Alexander, *The Poetic Achievement of Ezra Pound* (Berkeley and Los Angeles: University of California Press, 1979), pp. 66–79.

25. Significantly, Pound refers to "Poem at the Bridge" at one point in his jottings as "Han-rei."

26. *YC* notebook 21, p. 49 verso.

27. *YC* notebook 21, p. 57 verso.

28. *Literary Essays of Ezra Pound*, ed. T. S. Eliot (New York: New Directions, 1968), pp. 64–65.

DANTEDANTEDANTE

Dreaming a Renaissance
Pound's Dantean Inheritance

Stuart Y. McDougal

In an unpublished student notebook, dated only 19 January, Ezra
Pound entered the following lines:

It befell that wearied with
        much study
My spirit left for a while
        this corporal
house of life. . . &
journeyed I know not whither
through divers ways
      of strange lights
& mingled darknesses,
Untill after much wayfaring
I came unto a ruined
gateway, crumbled &
broken, arches, &
wondering what this
might portend
& why no moss or other
green thing was upon
the ruins, &
When sudenly I fell. &
found beneath me broken
stones, with this much
of inscription:

Upon one stone

Per me,
and on another, Dolente
& upon a third, Dolore
Lascete ogni speranza
Then I knew of a truth
     that
it was none other than
Hell gate, whereby
damned souls entered
into eternal grief,
& wherefrom none passed
in all eternity. –
& abashed & would have
turned back,
when one said to me,
"fear not – for high
             omnipotence
by light hath pierced hell
& cast down the keepers
thereof –
Come & see the place
     where hell hath lain
& I "Who art thou
master that speakest
with such authority" –
& he, 'I am that one
that through the heavens
followed Beatrice –
before it was willed that
I leave for ever my earthly
dwelling,'
Whereat I would have
done him reverence, but
he forbade me, saying –
'I am but as the least
     of them that serve,
– Follow –[1]

And indeed, the speaker of the poem does follow through a spectral landscape for nine numbered pages, after which there is a gap of ninety-

64

one pages in the manuscript and the poem resumes on page 100. This untitled fragment demonstrates the formative influence of Dante on Pound at a very early date. For the young poet, "wearied with much study," dreams that he has found himself at the gate of hell, the fragments of which (with their Italian inscriptions) confirm that it is Dante's inferno long before the speaker addresses him with the very word Dante applied to Virgil: "Master." Dante's counsel to the speaker—"Fear not"— also echoes Virgil's admonition to Dante the pilgrim in Canto 2 of the *Inferno*. The remaining pages suggest that Pound envisaged a journey much like Dante's, although it is clear at the outset that Pound's journey will be a secular one. His choice of fragments from Dante's hellgate emphasizes "woe," "grief," and the absence of "hope" and neglects entirely the Christian inscriptions (e.g., "Divine power," "supreme wisdom," and "primal love"). The sketchy notes beginning on page 100 offer further support that Pound intended to create a secular equivalent for Dante's three worlds. Pound describes his three realms as "A, 'hell in world,' 'body,'" "B, 'good in world,' 'mind,'" and "C, 'spirit,' 'soul.'" Pound had jotted down notes for parts A and B before putting the manuscript aside. No notes exist for part C. Part A opens with the lines cited above and ends rather abruptly. Part B ("good in world, mind") begins at sunrise and includes descriptions of both the "field of pleasure" and the "cliff of study." The fragment concludes with these lines, which signal an abrupt change in point of view:

> "I am she that
> you found not for neither
> of us followed the straight
> way. & while you
> were before the cliff
> I escaped through the
>   flowers:
>   Earthly
> Matilda & Paradise
> one whom in thy youth
> thou calldst Hilda?

The Hilda of Pound's own youth was Hilda Doolittle, whom he met in 1905, later known as Dryad and later still as H.D., Imagiste, the changes in her name reflecting her metamorphosis in Pound's eyes from

young woman to poetic metaphor to imagist poet. By juxtaposing her with Dante's Matilda, Pound interjects a personal note. The situation described in these lines is one to which Pound would return years later in *Hugh Selwyn Mauberley*, where an aesthete, absorbed in his "phantasmagoria" misses an opportunity for love. Although this project remains (in the language of *Mauberley*) "still born," the ambitious outline indicates that from an early age Pound aspired to write a long work modeled upon the *Commedia*. Pound had planned a journey similar to Dante's, with Dante leading him, just as Virgil had guided Dante. His own work begins with the fragments of Dante's poem encountered within a dream.

Hilda Doolittle was the recipient of Pound's first book of poems, *Hilda's Book*, which Pound gave to her with the phrase *Ecco il libro*, signaling his affinity to the youthful efforts of a Tuscan poet six hundred years before his time. Pound aligns himself with the medieval view of poet as maker in the opening poem of the book:

> I strove a little book to make for her,
> Quaint bound, as 'twere in parchment very old,
> That all my dearest words of her should hold.[2]

Although *Hilda's Book* has echoes, allusions, and paraphrases from Dante's works, Pound's "dearest words" evoke the language of Pound's immediate forerunners, the British poets of the fin-de-siècle, rather than the Italian poets of the *dolce stil nuovo*. This is equally true of the long poem quoted above and of Pound's early printed volumes. The creation of a distinctive voice would take Pound years of persistent effort. As we shall see, his steadfast guide in the development of this voice was Dante.

Pound began reading Dante's works at Hamilton College and continued his study at the University of Pennsylvania. He not only read the *Commedia*, but also *La Vita Nuova* and Dante's Latin works, especially *De Vulgari Eloquentia (On Eloquence in the Vernacular)*. The latter work includes a history and theory of the vernacular which assisted Pound in his own efforts to forge a new language.

Dante begins *De Vulgari Eloquentia* with a historical survey of the development of speech in order to "treat systematically the doctrines of

eloquence in vernacular." In the first paragraph Dante offers a metaphor of his method:

> not only drawing upon the waters of my own natural talent to fill this large vessel, but mixing in the best of what I can extract or compile from others, in order to offer for drinking a most sweet honey-water.[3]

In his description of the formation of a work of art as a mixture of "natural talent" and the "best" of what one can "extract or compile from others," Dante at the outset suggests a poet's awareness of his predecessors' craft.

Dante then attempts to define vernacular speech. After a brief survey of the development of language in biblical times, he focuses on Italy, where the profusion of dialectical variants makes the claim of any one city for supremacy problematic. Dante weighs the arguments of each city, before concluding that "the vernacular we have been tracking . . . suffuses its perfume in every city, but has its lair in none."[4] Dante then postulates an ideal language, composed of characteristics taken from a variety of regional dialects: "the illustrious, cardinal, courtly, and curial vernacular of Latium is that which belongs to all Latian cities and seems to belong to none, against which all the Latin municipal vernaculars are measured, weighed, and compared."[5] These adjectives suggest qualities of luminosity and clarity ("illustrious") as well as balance ("cardinal" [from *cardo*, the Latin for pivot] and "curial" [from *curia*, the Latin for highest courts of justice]) which also become central characteristics of Pound's work. Moreover, Dante holds out the possibility of making an "ideal" language by borrowing elements from a number of languages. In the *Cantos* Pound forges such a language, composed of the disparate elements of tongues widely separated in time and space.

De Vulgari Eloquentia offers Pound an example of how to adopt the method of a precursor, as well as a model for the creation of a language. In this instance, Dante's precursor was the Provençal poet Bertran de Born, whom Dante placed in the ninth *bolgia* of hell for "stirring up strife," specifically for dividing the "young English king" (Prince Henry) from his brother, Richard the Lionhearted, and their father, Henry II. Bertran's punishment (*lo contrapasso*) consists of having his head severed from his body:

> Because I parted persons thus united,
> I carry my brain, parted from its source, alas.
> Thus is the retribution [*lo contrapasso*] observed in me.
>
> (*Inferno* 28.139–41)

Bertran, like Dante later, could "extract or compile from others," and in one of his most famous poems he assembles a "borrowed lady" (*una dompna soiseubuda*) by taking attributes from a number of attractive Provençal ladies in the neighborhood (an activity which, no doubt, stirred up a different sort of strife). Dante knew this poem well, as did Ezra Pound, who interpreted it as a metaphor for a type of poetic activity (the creation of a work of beauty from "borrowed" elements).[6] Dante applies the same method to the making of a language which, like Bertran's lady, is both "borrowed" and "ideal." Dante has "borrowed" his method from Bertran, just as Pound will "borrow" from them both.

Pound comments on the relationship between a poet and his predecessors at the end of his long chapter on Dante in *The Spirit of Romance* (1910):

> Great poets seldom make bricks without straw. They pile up all the excellences they can beg, borrow or steal from their predecessors and contemporaries, and then set their own inimitable light atop of the mountain.[7]

This passage, which evokes the topography of Dante's *Purgatorio*, describes a model of poetic influence which could be applied to Pound as well as Dante. As we have already seen, Dante provides Pound with the example of a great poet who can build upon the achievements of his forerunners, both immediate and remote, and synthesize, modify, and transform their work into new wholes. Although Pound would "beg, borrow or steal" from Dante throughout his career, he did so in a variety of ways, as his own poetic needs continually changed. Pound's relationship to Dante was like the blue of Pound's beloved Lago di Garda, constant but ever changing.

Pound studied *De Vulgari Eloquentia* as a textbook, turning from Dante's brief examples of the poetry of Provençal and Tuscan poets to their complete works for further analysis and, above all, translation. Pound spent nearly a decade translating and retranslating the poems of Arnaut Daniel, and nearly a quarter of a century on the canzoni of Guido Cavalcanti. The intensity and duration of this labor confirm the high esteem in which Pound held Dante as a critic. Pound draws heav-

ily upon this work in *The Spirit of Romance*, both in his selection of Provençal and Tuscan poets and in his methodology, in which carefully chosen examples are "measured, weighed and compared" against an ideal. This ideal is the work of Dante. For Pound, Dante is a "donative author," one who

> seems to draw down into the art something which was not in the art of his predecessors. If he also draws from the air about him, he draws latent forces, or things present but unnoticed, or things perhaps taken for granted but never examined. . . . His forebears may have led up to him; he is never a disconnected phenomenon, but he does take some step further. He discovers, or, better, "he discriminates." We advance by discrimination, by discerning that things hitherto deemed dissimilar, mutually foreign, antagonistic, are similar and harmonic.[8]

Pound applies such qualities of discrimination and discernment in his analysis of the relations between Dante and his precursors in order to demonstrate that Dante was the culmination of a medieval renaissance which began with the development of a vernacular literature in the tenth century. "I am constantly contending," Pound wrote in 1912, "that it took two centuries of Provence and one of Tuscany to develop the media of Dante's masterwork."[9] Pound's analysis of this renaissance has a direct bearing on his own career as a poet and his desire for a similar revival of letters in the twentieth century.

The first chapter of *The Spirit of Romance*, called "The Phantom of Dawn," is devoted to those Latin works which are forerunners of the "spirit" or essence of Romance literature. One of these anonymous lyric poems is what Pound later calls a "Luminous Detail," for it documents the transition from Latin to the vernacular: "Romance literature," Pound writes, "begins with a Provençal 'Alba' supposedly of the Tenth Century. The stanzas of the song have been written down in Latin, but the refrain remains in the tongue of the people" (*SR* 11). Within this single "alba" (or dawn song), a linguistic transformation occurs, as the old language (Latin) gives way to the new (Provençal).[10] But the luminosity of the alba extends further. The moment of metamorphosis within this dawn song bcomes for Pound the dawning of a new age of literature which reaches its zenith in the work of that master of the vernacular, Dante Alighieri.

Pound repeatedly uses the verb "refine" and related chemical and

alchemical terms to describe the development of this vernacular. The troubadour poets, Pound noted, were "melting the common tongue" (*SR* 22) and attempting to "refine . . . the common speech" (*SR* 13). Pound has adopted this metaphor from Dante, in whose works it has a central importance. At the summit of Purgatory, the Provençal poet Arnaut Daniel steps into the Purgatorial fires which "refine" or "purify" him: *Poi s'ascose nel foco che li affine* ("Then he hid himself in the fire that purifies them" [*Purgatorio* 26.148]). In *The Spirit of Romance* Pound comments on the secular use of the verb "refine" by Daniel and Guinicelli. Once again, Dante's usage constitutes the transformation of an element in the works of his precursors from a secular to a spiritual context. In addition, Arnaut Daniel's fate in the *Commedia* can be seen as an example of *lo contrapasso*, "the law of retribution" which we observed in the case of Bertran de Born. In the *Purgatorio* Daniel is designated as *miglior fabbro del parlar materno* ("better craftsman of the mother tongue"): he "refined" the language in life, and so he becomes "refined" in death. Dante's use of the verb "refine" in Canto 26 suggests a connection between the refinement of a language and refinement as a psychological process. Pound employs this image in both senses as well. An early and unreprinted poem in *Hilda's Book*, "Ver Novum," includes the following lines:

> Thou that dost ever make demand for the best I have to give
> Gentle to utmost courteousy bidding only my pure-purged spirits live:
> Thou that spellest ever gold from out my dross
> Mage powerful and subtly sweet
> Gathering fragments that there be no loss
> Behold the brighter gains lie at thy feet.

(*HD* 71)

The phrase "pure-purged spirits" prepares us for the process of refinement which occurs in the next line, where "gold" is separated from "dross," and the "brighter gains" (themselves fragments of his total personality) are laid at the lady's feet. Pound's notion of refinement here is similar to that of Daniel and Guinicelli. In a later uncollected poem, "Histrion," Pound moves closer to Dante's sense of "refinement" in the *Purgatorio*. Here the transformation involves the displacement of the self into another person, or the assumption of the mask of another, processes which become common in Pound's dramatic monologues:

No man hath dared to write this thing as yet,
And yet I know, how that the souls of all men great
At times pass through us,
And we are melted into them, and are not
Save reflexions of their souls.
Thus am I Dante for a space and am
One François Villon, ballad-lord and thief

. . . .

'Tis as in midmost us there glows a sphere
Translucent, molten gold, that is the "I"
And into this some form projects itself:
Christus, or John, or eke the Florentine.[11]

Here the spirits of the young poet's great precursors "pass through" him, as he opens himself to their influence. This, too, is a form of refinement.

If the Provençal poets refined the language, then the Tuscans, in Pound's view, added something new to the matter of the verse: "The art of the troubadours," Pound states, "meets with philosophy at Bologna and a new era of lyric poetry is begun" (SR 101). Several years later Pound suggested that "there is no reason why Cavalcanti and Riquier [Giraut Riquier, the last of the Provençal poets] should not have met while the former was on his journey to Campostella" (LE 103), and in the poem "Provincia Deserta" (1915) Pound juxtaposes their names ("Riquier! Guido") to document this transmission of culture. Such acts of transmission prepared for the fusion of "language" and "philosophy" in the work of Dante.

For Pound, the union of these two different elements is a process of transformation akin to alchemy. Pound discerned the possibility of such transformation through what he called the "objective imagination" of the Tuscan poets, an imagination capable of transforming sensual experience into intellectual perception:

> The cult of Provence had been a cult of the emotions; and with it there had been some, hardly conscious, study of emotional psychology. In Tuscany the cult is a cult of the harmonies of the mind. If one is in sympathy with this form of *objective imagination*, and this quality of vision, there is no poetry which has such enduring, such, if I may say so, indestructible charm.
>
> The best poetry of this time appeals by its truth, by its subtlety, and by its *refined* exactness. (SR 116; italics mine)

71

In his chapter "Il Maestro" in *The Spirit of Romance* Pound elaborates on Dante's ability to objectify emotional states and to fuse the sensual and the intellectual. When Pound later formulated his definition of the "image" as an "intellectual and emotional complex in an instant of time" (*LE* 4) he was refining a Dantean notion which he began to develop in the pages of this work.

Pound's tendency to secularize Dante (which we observed in his unfinished youthful epic) becomes even more pronounced in *The Spirit of Romance*. Early in his chapter on Dante Pound mentions the "Epistle to Can Grande," a letter written by Dante to accompany the *Purgatorio* as an explanation of the four levels of allegory in that extremely difficult work. These "four senses" as Pound called them, following traditional usage, are the literal, the allegorical, the anagogical, and the ethical. After attempting to explain these distinctions in terms of mathematics Pound states:

> Thus the *Commedia* is, in the literal sense, a description of Dante's vision of a journey through the realms inhabited by the spirits of men after death; in a further sense it is the journey of Dante's intelligence through the states of mind wherein dwell all sorts and conditions of men before death; beyond this, Dante or Dante's intelligence may come to mean "Everyman" or "Mankind," whereat his journey becomes a symbol of mankind's struggle upward out of ignorance into the clear light of philosophy. In the second sense I give here, the journey is Dante's own mental and spiritual development. In a fourth sense, the *Commedia* is an expression of the laws of eternal justice; "*il contrapasso*," the counterpass, as Bertran calls it or the law of Karma, if we are to use an Oriental term. (*SR* 127)

Pound's ascription of "the clear light" to "philosophy" and his second explanation of "the counterpass" as "the law of Karma" underscore the amount of distortion involved in this interpretive gloss. Pound knew the Bible well, and he could just as easily have invoked the phrase *lex talionis* in describing this principle of retribution. But Pound is simply not interested in Dante as a Christian poet. Rather, Dante is seen as the great synthesizer of classical and medieval traditions. Pound stresses this secular reading later in the chapter when he argues that it is "expedient" to view Dante's "descriptions of the actions and shades as descriptions of men's mental states in life, in which they are, after death, compelled to continue: that is to say, men's inner selves stand visibly before the eyes of Dante's intellect" (*SR* 128). Absent from this passage is any notion of

damnation. Pound's comments reveal more about his own dramatic monologues than about Dante's poem.

Pound's reading of the *Paradiso* is equally secular. At three points in his long chapter on Dante, Pound praises a simile in Canto 1 of the *Paradiso*, where Dante has drawn upon an incident which Ovid recounts in book 13 of the *Metamorphoses*:

> Beatrice was standing and held full in view
>> The eternal wheels, and I fixed on her keen
>> My eyes, that from above their gaze withdrew.
> And at her aspect I became within
>> As Glaucus after the herb's tasting, whence
>> To the other sea-gods he was made akin.
> The passing beyond bounds of human sense
>> Words cannot tell; let then the example sate
>> Him for whom grace reserves the experience.[12]

In Ovid's version Glaucus, a fisherman of Boeothia, is seated on a grassy area counting his fish after a day's catch. Suddenly the fish begin working their way along the grass back to the sea. Glaucus observes them and assumes the grass must contain some magical property, so he grasps a handful and begins to chew on it. As he does, he starts to yearn for the sea himself. He plunges into the ocean, where he is changed into a sea-god by Oceanus and Tethys. The story has undergone a transformation in Dante's hands. Just as Glaucus's metamorphosis involves leaving one element (earth) and going to abide in another (water), so too must Dante the pilgrim forsake one element for another, although as Charles Singleton has pointed out, "only Ovid's verses, not Dante's, declare this."[13]

In fact, knowledge of how Dante has changed Ovid is necessary for an understanding of Dante's lines. Dante makes the secular transformation of Glaucus by Ovid spiritual and he characterizes it with a coinage of his own (*transumanar*, "to go beyond the human"). Dante's transformation in the presence of Beatrice is an intensely religious moment in the *Commedia*. Pound avoids a Christian interpretation and describes the experience of Glaucus as an example of "the nature of mystic ecstasy" (*SR* 141) and "the perception of cosmic consciousness" (*SR* 155). Pound values Dante's simile as the "objectification" of a mystic state, but also as the demonstration of a central way in which Dante is able to

73

use the work of a major precursor. Just as Dante changes Virgil's land of the dead into a Christian realm of the damned, so does he transform Ovid's secular incident to his own Christian ends. As we have seen, Pound reverses this process in his own use of Dante. In view of the importance Pound gives to this example, one might expect Glaucus to loom large in Pound's later verse and especially in the *Cantos*. Yet such is not the case. Pound does not *simply* "beg, borrow or steal" from Dante or from any other of his predecessors for that matter. Instead, he observes how Dante transforms the materials of an earlier poet; how an example of metamorphosis is in itself metamorphosed. Pound uses the materials of his own precursors in the same way. Glaucus's sole appearance in the *Cantos* occurs in Canto 39, where the single line "Came here with Glaucus unnoticed" identifies Odysseus, the persona of the canto, with Glaucus and by equating their experiences illuminates the erotic encounter at the core of that canto.

In emphasizing the secular Dante, able to absorb and refine the work of his own precursors and contemporaries, Pound was also creating a Dante who would help him confront his own forerunners in English. With his youthful ambitions to write a long poem, Pound enlisted Dante as ally in his struggle with the epic poets of the Anglo-American tradition. For example, Pound sets Dante against Milton as early as *The Spirit of Romance*: "Dante's god is ineffable divinity. Milton's god is a fussy old man with a hobby. Dante is metaphysical, where Milton is merely sectarian. *Paradise Lost* is conventional melodrama" (*SR* 156–57). Pound would also later rail against what he took to be Milton's distortions of English syntax and diction. Rather than follow the Miltonic epic, and incur the burden of such competition, Pound aligns himself with what he defines as the "lyric" tradition of Dante.

For the young Pound, then, Dante is a great lyric poet whose art represents the culmination of three centuries' development of the vernacular. Pound's emphasis on Dante's technique is very much in keeping with his own interests at the time. In "I Gather the Limbs of Osiris," a series of essays and translations published in the *New Age* in 1911–12, Pound argues that "through [technique] alone has *the art* . . . any chance for resurrection" (*SP* 42). His diction echoes a line from the opening of the *Purgatorio* (*Ma qui la morte poesi risurga*) which he used as the epigraph to his 1910 volume of poems *Provença* and to which he would allude in *Mauberley* ("He strove to resuscitate the dead art of po-

etry"). The title of the series applies this metaphor (from an Egyptian fertility ritual in which Isis collects the dismembered limbs of Osiris as a prelude to his rebirth) to one mode of poetic resurrection: translation.

Pound attempts to promote a renaissance of English letters by defining a new tradition of lyric poetry through his versions of the anonymous seafarer poet, the Provençal poet Arnaut Daniel, and Dante's contemporary, Guido Cavalcanti. A modern renaissance in letters has to begin, Pound asserted, with the creation of a new tongue: "For it is not until poetry lives again 'close to the thing' that it will be a vital part of contemporary life" (SP 41). For each of these poets Pound strives to make a new and different language. Like Dante in De Vulgari Eloquentia, Pound argues here for the creation of a language at once precise and concise: "We must have a simplicity and directness of utterance, which is different from the simplicity and directness of daily speech, which is more 'curial,' more dignified" (SP 41). Only in "The Seafarer" does he achieve this.

Through his close study of the poetry of those Provençal and Tuscan artists whose work culminated with Dante, and especially through his translations of Daniel and Cavalcanti, Pound had trained himself with a rare self-discipline to relive this medieval renaissance. Pound's own modernization, then, came through an immersion in medievalism; he found the modern through the remote and distant. When he turned to a "poem of some length," as he described his work in progress when the first cantos were being published, Pound chose as a model the "pre-Dante" poem of a more recent precursor, Robert Browning. Pound's *Three Cantos* begin in part as a discussion with Browning about *Sordello*. Pound is seeking a new and flexible language as well as a form sufficiently capacious to encompass his own needs. Early in *Three Cantos* (1) Pound tries to distinguish his own diction from that of his nineteenth-century predecessors. He addresses Browning:

What a hodge-podge you have made there!—
Zanze and *swanzig*, of all opprobrious rhymes!
And you turn off whenever it suits your fancy,
Now at Verona, now with the early Christians,
Or now a-gabbling of the "Tyrrhene whelk."
"The lyre should animate but not mislead the pen"—
That's Wordsworth, Mr. Browning. (What a phrase!—
That lyre, that pen, that bleating sheep, Will Wordsworth!)

75

> That should have taught you to avoid speech figurative
> And set out your matter
> As I do, in straight simple phrases:
> Gods float in the azure air,
> Bright gods, and Tuscan, back before the dew was shed.

Pound's description of a language "clinging close to the thing" is enacted in the final lines of this passage, but this lyricism is only one of the many languages of the *Cantos* which strongly evoke Dante. Pound's indebtedness to Dante in these cantos extends beyond the creation of a language, although it includes this.

In the middle of *Three Cantos* (2) Pound introduces a Provençal lyric. The passage begins:

> Dordoigne! When I was there,
> There came a centaur, spying the land,
> And there were nymphs behind him.
> Or going on the road by Salisbury
> Procession on procession—
> For that road was full of peoples,
> Ancient in various days, long years between them.
> Ply over ply of life still wraps the earth here.
> Catch at Dordoigne.

Hugh Witemeyer has discussed the way in which the phrase "ply over ply" becomes an organizing principle in the *Cantos*,[14] compressing illusions and incidents around a single name, incident, or place. An equally suggestive phrase is introduced as part of the Provençal "catch" which is being sung at Dordoigne:

> "As the rose—
> *Si com, si com*"—they all begin *"si com."*
> "For as the rose . . ."

Pound's repetition of *si com* leads, like the phrase "ply over ply," to one of the important structural principles of the *Cantos*. Let us return for a moment to Glaucus. As I indicated above, the passage from the *Paradiso* in which Glaucus appears made a great impression on Pound and yet Glaucus appears only in Canto 39, in the context of Odysseus's relationship with Circe. Pound's line, "Came here with Glaucus unnoticed," is bracketed between two lines from Dante and two lines from a nineteenth-century Latin translation of the *Odyssey*. Dante's original

line had read: *qual si fe Glauco nel gustar de l'erba* ("such as Glaucus became on tasting the grass"). The *si* is gone in Pound's version. Pound has moved toward a paratactic technique in which larger units are juxtaposed without the *"si com,"* and this too is the result of his meditations on medieval poetry.

One more connection will suffice. *Three Cantos* (3) concludes with a rendering of Homer's *Odyssey*, book 11, translated from a Renaissance Latin version by Andreas Divus which Pound had purchased at a Paris quai sometime between 1906 and 1910. Following Divus's *Homer* in the volume Pound acquired were several other works including the *Hymni Deorum* of Georgius Dartona. Pound incorporates his discovery of this work into his own poem in part to demonstrate how Homer was kept alive during the Renaissance and in part to establish a parallel with Browning's *The Ring and the Book*, which was also inspired by a found manuscript:

> Justinopolitan
>
> Uncatalogued Andreas Divus,
> Gave him in Latin, 1538 in my edition, the rest uncertain,
> Caught up his cadence, word and syllable:
> "Down to the ships we went, set mast and sail,
> Black keel and beasts for bloody sacrifice,
> Weeping we went."
> I've strained my ear for -ensa, -ombra, and -ensa
> And cracked my wit on delicate *canzoni*—
>   Here's but rough meaning:
> "And then went down to the ship, set keel to breakers,
> Forth on the godly sea. . . .

The Provençal endings "-ensa, -ombra, -ensa" recall Pound's lengthy preparation for this work. Although apprenticed in Provence and tutored in Tuscany, Pound turned to his own true heritage, the Anglo-Saxon, in the construction of an appropriate language for Homer's Greek. Pound had described Anglo-Saxon as a language "which has transmuted the various qualities of poetry which have drifted up from the south" (*SP* 24) and here Pound himself transmutes ancient Greek, Renaissance Latin, and a contemporary language wrought of Anglo-Saxon rhythms, a diction drawn from Anglo-Saxon, the Scots of Gavin Douglas ("Ingle"), and contemporary English into an "ideal language" for what he conceived to be the oldest part of the *Odyssey* (book

11), the giving of blood to ghosts. When Pound shifted this section, slightly edited, to form the opening of Canto 1, he highlighted the appropriateness of this ritual of resurrection to his endeavors in the *Cantos*. In revising the passage, however, he deleted the allusions to the role of Provençal translation in preparing him for this task. The first version had also underscored the Dantean import of this passage:

> Lie quiet, Divus.
>> In Officina Wechli, Paris,
> M. D. three X's, Eight, With Aldus on the Frogs,
> And a certain Cretin's
>> *Hymni Deorum*:
> (The thin clear Tuscan stuff
>> Gives way before the florid mellow phrase.)

In revision, the parenthetical expression is deleted, but the "thin clear Tuscan stuff" remains, one additional ply in the rich fabric of the canto.

The revised Canto 1 highlights another aspect of the Poundian renaissance which occurred during these years. In Canto 81, written thirty years later amidst the wreckage of Europe, Pound notes, parenthetically, "(To break the pentameter, that was the first heave)." The heave began with Pound's first ocean voyage, "The Seafarer," where he crafted a language and a verse line which would serve him well several years later. "The Seafarer" is the only poem in "I Gather the Limbs of Osiris" which Pound never revised. He reprinted it in *Cathay* (1915) to indicate thematic and technical affinities with the Chinese translations. In the revised version of Canto 1, Pound utilizes this language and verse line. Here the real heave occurs as the speaker is able to "set keel to breakers, / Forth on the godly sea." With that heave the pentameter is broken, and the voyage of the *Cantos* is begun.

In *Three Cantos* (2), one of Pound's personae, a painter, is living in Indiana cut off from the French and Italian cities of his youth and "dreaming his renaissance." So, too, did Pound "dream a renaissance," and the model he took for this was his own interpretation of the literary history of Southern France and Northern Italy in the years from 1100 to 1400. By immersing himself in the works of the period, through study, imitation, and translation, Pound sought to resuscitate the dead art of lyric poetry and bring about a renaissance of English and American letters. His own judgment on that attempt, in *Hugh Selwyn Mauberley*,

was rather severe. His accomplishments, several of which I have drawn from *Three Cantos*, were actually considerable, and they owed much to the example of the guide he had designated "master" in the early un-published poem cited above. As Pound returned to Dante's work in the years that followed, he found the *Commedia* to be more than just a "lyric poem," as he designated it in *The Spirit of Romance*, or an "imag-ist poem," as he called it in *Gaudier-Brzeska: A Memoir*: it was a poem containing history, with a panoply of methods which Pound could con-tinue to study and draw upon in his struggle with his own *Cantos*.[15] Pound never ceased to "refine" the materials of his art in the model of Dante, and that image remains a central one in his verse. One of its most poignant expressions, written in Pisa after the war, evokes two Dantean passages examined above: the lines from *Hilda's Book* of forty years earlier ("thou that spellest ever gold from out my dross") and Pound's description of Dante as a "donative" artist who can "draw from the air about him":

What thou lovest well remains,
                                        the rest is dross
What thou lov'st well shall not be reft from thee
What thou lov'st well is thy true heritage
Whose world, or mine or theirs
                        or is it of none?
.   .   .   .
But to have done instead of not doing
                this is not vanity
To have, with decency, knocked
That a Blunt should open
        To have gathered from the air a live tradition
or from a fine old eye the unconquered flame
This is not vanity.
        Here error is all in the not done,
all in the diffidence that faltered. . . .

                                                                (C 520–22)

Notes

1. This notebook is in the Beinecke Library, Yale University. When Don-ald Hall interviewed Ezra Pound in 1960, Pound suggested that he had begun

the *Cantos* around 1904 or 1905. Although this fragment is probably a year or two later than that, it is the earliest example of a long poem by Pound we have, and it may well have been the work Pound was recalling, although very different from the poem we know as the *Cantos* (which Pound began publishing in 1917).

2. Reprinted in H. D., *End to Torment: A Memoir of Ezra Pound* (New York: New Directions, 1979), p. 69. Hereafter cited as *HD* followed by page number.

3. Dante Alighieri, *De Vulgari Eloquentia*, in *Literary Criticism of Dante Alighieri*, trans. and ed. Robert S. Haller (Lincoln and London: University of Nebraska Press, 1973), p. 3.

4. Ibid., p. 28.

5. Ibid.

6. See Stuart Y. McDougal, *Ezra Pound and the Troubadour Tradition* (Princeton: Princeton University Press, 1973), p. 33.

7. Ezra Pound, *The Spirit of Romance* (New York: New Directions, 1968), p. 162. Hereafter cited as *SR* followed by page number.

8. Ezra Pound, "I Gather the Limbs of Osiris," in *Ezra Pound: Selected Prose, 1909–1965*, ed. William Cookson (New York: New Directions, 1973), p. 25. Hereafter cited as *SP* followed by page number.

9. Ezra Pound, "A Retrospect," in *Literary Essays of Ezra Pound*, ed. T. S. Eliot (London: Faber & Faber, 1954), pp. 9–10. Hereafter cited as *LE* followed by page number.

10. Pound adopted the technique of linguistic metamorphosis to his own verse: In Canto 4, for example, he creates a similar linguistic transformation from Latin to an English version of Provençal, the very language enacting the metamorphosis which is the subject of the incidents being juxtaposed: Ityn . . . It is . . . It is . . . 'Tis . . . 'Tis . . . Ytis.

11. Reprinted in *Collected Early Poems of Ezra Pound*, ed. Michael John King (New York: New Directions, 1976), p. 71.

12. Laurence Binyon, trans., *Dante, The Divine Comedy*, in *The Portable Dante*, ed. Paolo Milano (New York: Viking Press, 1969), pp. 368–69.

13. Charles S. Singleton, *Journey to Beatrice* (Baltimore and London: Johns Hopkins University Press, 1977), p. 28.

14. Hugh Witemeyer, "Pound and the *Cantos* 'Ply over Ply,'" *Paideuma* 8 (Fall 1979): 229–35.

15. For a comparative study of Dante's *Commedia* and Pound's *Cantos*, see James J. Wilhelm, *Dante and Pound: The Epic of Judgement* (Orono: University of Maine Press, 1974).

Clothing the American Adam
Pound's Tailoring of Walt Whitman

Hugh Witemeyer

"The vital part of my message, taken from the sap and fibre of America, is the same as his. Mentally I am a Walt Whitman who has learned to wear a collar and dress shirt (although at times inimical to both)." Thus Ezra Pound, writing in London at the age of twenty-three, sought to clarify his relationship to the only "spiritual father" he acknowledged among preceding American poets.[1] His metaphors echo two of Whitman's favorite tropes—vegetation and nudity—but they are mixed in such a way as to reveal Pound's ambivalence toward their source. The organic figures of vital sap and fiber suggest that Whitman and Pound belong to the same family tree so far as content or "message" is concerned. But the sartorial metaphors of collar and dress shirt imply a disapproval of Whitman au naturel and suggest that, in matters of form at least, Pound has come down from the tree.

In his early London years, from 1909 to 1914, Pound often saw himself as Walt *resartus*, a noble savage dressed for the drawing room. His definition of himself as an American expatriate artist combined Whitman's Adamic nudity with Whistler's dapper dandyism. In later years, when Pound reexamined his poetic identity as a result of his confinement at Pisa and Washington, he again measured himself against Whitman. By then, Pound no longer needed to emphasize the superiority of his tailoring. He needed rather to assert his naked American identity with Whitman.

"Who goes there! hankering, gross, mystical, nude?" Whitman asks in *Song of Myself*.[2] To the young Pound, this persona was at once

81

repulsive, attractive, and quintessentially American. "He *is* America. His crudity is an exceeding great stench, but it *is* America" (*SP* 145). "Whitman is the only American poet of his day who matters," Pound told Floyd Dell in 1911. "The rest tried to be american [sic] hard enough but they never lay naked on the earth. They bathed with their clothes on, & the clothes were 'made abroad.'"[3]

Unsavory though it may be, Whitman's nakedness symbolizes the national *virtù*, according to Pound: the unique and donative sensibility which America can give the world through its art. Whitman sounds "our American keynote," Pound asserts in "Patria Mia" (1913).

> It is, as nearly as I can define it, a certain generosity; a certain carelessness, or looseness, if you will; a hatred of the sordid, an ability to forget the part for the sake of the whole, a desire for largeness, a willingness to stand exposed.
>
> > "Camerado, this is no book;
> > Who touches this touches a man."
>
> The artist is ready to endure personally a strain which his craftsmanship would scarcely endure. . . . [The American people] will undertake nothing in its art for which it will not be in person responsible. (*SP* 123)

This quality of courageous personal generosity is well illustrated by Pound himself in his assistance of other artists during the 1910s. The exposed and vulnerable persona of Whitman never ceased to appeal to Pound; late in his career he chose "I Sing the Body Electric" as one of three selections from *Leaves of Grass* to be included in the anthology *Confucius to Cummings* (1964).

Whitman's evocations of his successors spoke directly to Pound when he first aspired to a place in American poetry. He felt that such salutations as "Camerado, this is no book" in the poem "So Long!" were addressed personally to him. He told Homer Pound, his actual father, to begin the study of Whitman with "So Long!" because the poem "has I suppose nearly all of him in it."[4] Whitman's descriptions of the "great individual" in "So Long!" and of the "divine literatus" in *Democratic Vistas* doubtless confirmed Pound's sense that he, like Stephen Dedalus, had a vocation and a spiritual father, too (*WW* 610–11, 932). "I honor him for he prophesied me," Pound said in 1909, "while I

can only recognise him as a forebear of whom I ought to be proud"
(*SP* 145).

In this apostolic succession or poetic genealogy, the task of the divine literatus is to sing America by singing himself. Pound embraced Whitman's vision of the United States as heir to all the ages and consummate center of civilization. As Charles B. Willard has pointed out, Pound "equated his own hope for an American Risorgimento with Whitman's faith in man's ability to realize his divine potential." Indeed, this sense of America's possible future greatness was precisely the "message" which Pound felt he shared with Whitman.[5] Pound believed as Whitman did in the boundless promise of the American Revolution, the exemplary virtues of many of its leaders, and the American mission to carry the gospel of political liberty and personal liberation throughout the world. "It seems to me I should like to drive Whitman into the old world. I sledge, he drill. . . . 'His message is my message. We will see that men hear it'" (*SP* 146). Even after two world wars and many personal failures dampened this early ardor, Pound never entirely abandoned his Whitmanian role of the bard who sees and articulates an ideal vision of America.

Moreover, Pound learned from Whitman that to sing America is to sing oneself. Instead of the wrath of Achilles or arms and the man, *Leaves of Grass* celebrates Whitman's "own physical, emotional, moral, intellectual, and aesthetic Personality, in the midst of, and tallying, the momentous spirit and facts of its immediate days, and of current America" (*WW* 658). It attempts "to put *a Person*, a human being (myself, in the latter half of the Nineteenth Century, in America) freely, fully and truly on record" (*WW* 671). From Whitman's example Pound learned that a modern American long poem including history could be a cumulative, open-ended, personal record built up over the author's lifetime as a work in progress.[6] It could be such a record even if it did not emulate the egotistical sublimities of Whitman's narrator.

Certainly those sublimities could be tiresome. "It is impossible to read [*Leaves of Grass*] without swearing at the author almost continuously," Pound warned his father (*L* 21). Much as he admired and sometimes craved Whitman's embrace, Pound often found it irritating and embarrassing. Lecturing on Villon to a British audience in the winter of 1909–10, Pound contrasted the French poet's shamelessness with Whit-

man's. "Villon is shameless. Whitman, having decided that it is disgraceful to be ashamed, rejoices in having attained nudity." In other words, whereas Villon has experienced and transcended shame, Whitman has simply bypassed it. Pound speaks of

> that horrible air of rectitude with which Whitman rejoices in being Whitman . . . [and] pretend[s] to be conferring a philanthropic benefit on the race by recording his own self-complacency. . . . Villon is a voice of suffering, of mockery, of irrevoeable fact; Whitman is the voice of one who saith:
>
>> Lo, behold, I eat water-melons. When I eat water-melons the world
>>   eats water-melons through me.
>> When the world eats water-melons, I partake of the world's water-
>>   melons.
>> The bugs,
>> The worms,
>> The negroes, etc.,
>> Eat water-melons; All nature eats water-melons.
>> Those eidolons and particles of the Cosmos
>> Which do not now partake of water-melons
>> Will at some future time partake of water-melons.
>> Praised be Allah or Ramanathanath Khrishna![7]

This parody emphasizes the ease with which Whitman's universalist manner can become a mannerism.

Whitman's cosmic embrace often seemed too facile and too inclusive to suit Pound's taste, which was innately rigorous and selective. Roy Harvey Pearce describes the main difference between the poetic temperaments of Whitman and Pound as follows: "The opposition is between a poet who would infuse his world with a sense of self and then, and only then, accept it, and a poet who would infuse his self with a sense of his world. Where Whitman would include, Pound would discriminate. Where Whitman would energize so as to define, Pound would define so as to energize."[8] Pearce's distinction between Whitman's impulse to include and Pound's impulse to discriminate and exclude illuminates many of Pound's reservations about Whitman.

In one sense, to be sure, Pound believed that Whitman was not inclusive enough. His rejection of European culture, his programmatic provincialism, seemed to Pound a source of Whitman's strength but also

a distinct limitation. "Entirely free from the renaissance humanist ideal of the complete man or from the Greek idealism, he is content to be what he is" (*SP* 145). Pound, on the other hand, like Henry James and T. S. Eliot, cherished a cosmopolitan, internationalist ideal of culture which envisioned not the displacement of European civilization by American but a rapprochement between the two. Thus Pound saw himself as "a strife for a renaissance in America of all the lost or temporarily mislaid beauty, truth, valor, glory of Greece, Italy, England and all the rest of it" (*SP* 146). He wanted not only "to drive Whitman into the old world" but also "to scourge America with all the old beauty" of Europe (*SP* 146). Although Pound sided with Whitman against the Boston Brahmins of his day, Pound's conception of culture descends more from theirs than from Whitman's. One reader who recognized this heritage clearly was William Carlos Williams, who self-consciously aligned himself with Whitman and provincialism against Pound, Eliot, and cosmopolitanism.[9]

Yet Pound sought to unite only the best of Europe with the best of America. In this respect, his cultural program is more exclusive than Whitman's. The difference is clearly articulated in Pound's earliest extended poetic imitation of Whitman, a 1911 poem entitled "Redondillas, or Something of that Sort." Here Pound emphasizes his disagreements with Whitman even as the form of the poem declares their underlying kinship.

> I sing the gaudy to-day and cosmopolite civilization
> Of my hatred of cruelties, of my weariness of banalities,
> I sing of the ways that I love, of Beauty and delicate savours.
> . . . .
> I would sing the American people,
>   God send them some civilization;
> I would sing of the nations of Europe,
>   God grant them some method of cleansing
> The fetid extent of their evils.
> . . . .
> Yet I sing of the diverse moods
>   Of effete modern civilization
> I sing of delicate hues
>   And variations of pattern

85

> I sing of risorgimenti,
>> Of old things found that were hidden,
> I sing of the senses developed,
>> I reach toward perceptions scarce heeded. [10]

This is Whitman refined, a discriminating Jamesian bard who would recover for America the "delicate savours," "moods," "hues," "perceptions," and "old things" which Whitman was prepared to leave behind forever in Europe. Whitman would no doubt have called this singer what he called Matthew Arnold: "one of the dudes of literature." [11]

Insofar as *Leaves of Grass* attempts to represent the totality of American life, the poem contradicts Pound's belief that art—and poetry especially—requires selection and intensity. Because Whitman responded to materials without selecting among them, in Pound's view, he "was not an artist but a reflex, the first honest reflex, in an age of papier-mâché letters" (*SP* 110). Again, Pound calls Whitman "'The Reflex,' who left us a human document, for you cannot call a man an artist until he shows himself in some degree capable of reticence and of restraint, until he shows himself in some degree master of the forces which beat upon him" (*SP* 114). The term "reflex" suggests that Pound is viewing Whitman as a simple organism, capable of responding directly to stimuli but incapable of distinguishing, controlling, or reordering them. Even at the time, Pound suspected that this might be a simplistic misreading of Whitman, for he also wrote: "I think we have not yet paid enough attention to the deliberate artistry of the man" (*SP* 146). Nevertheless, the critique of Whitman as a "reflex" anticipates Pound's later vorticist critique of impressionism as passive and receptive rather than active and creative. [12]

The American artist who best exhibits the "reticence" and "restraint" which Pound admired in his early years is not the nude Whitman but the dapper James McNeill Whistler. The Whistler exhibition of September 1912 at the Tate Gallery gave Pound "more courage for living than I have gathered . . . from any other manifest American energy whatsoever." For Whistler united American energy with European devotion to craft. Judged by the high aesthetic standards of the late-Victorian movement toward art-for-art's-sake, which had influenced Pound's taste profoundly, Whistler's art was not an embarrassment to his compatriots. Rather, it exhibited both "comprehension and reticence."

Here in brief is the work of a man, born American, with all our forces of confusion within him, who has contrived to keep order in his work, who has attained the highest mastery, and this not by a natural facility, but by constant labor and searching. . . . The man's life struggle was set before one. He had tried all means, he had spared himself nothing, he had struggled in one direction until he either achieved or found it inadequate for his expression. After he had achieved a thing, he never repeated. There were many struggles for the ultimate nocturnes.

Whistler's "life struggle," as Pound describes it, is a pursuit of "ultimate" beauty through an arduous, self-conscious series of experimental discriminations and exclusions. By this means, "Whistler has proved once and for all . . . that being born an American does not eternally damn a man or prevent him from the ultimate and highest achievement in the arts." Whitman's achievement, with its apparently "natural facility" and many repetitions, had not proved this to Pound's satisfaction. Fortunately, Whistler, too, had "left his message. . . . It was in substance, that being born an American is no excuse for being content with a parochial standard" (*SP* 116–17, 124).

The Whistler exhibition helped Pound see Whitman in perspective as a genuine but parochial American talent. One month after the exhibition opened, Pound told Harriet Monroe: "The 'Yawp' is respected from Denmark to Bengal, but we can't stop with the 'Yawp.' We have no longer any excuse for not taking up the complete art" (*L* 11). Even before the Whistler exhibition, Pound had suggested in a letter to Floyd Dell that Whitman did not pursue his craft rigorously enough. "He was too lazy to learn his trade i.e. the arranging of his rythmic interpretations into harmony. he was no artist, or a bad one—*but* he matters [*sic*]."[13] What redeemed Whitman, in Pound's eyes, was his honesty: he never pretended to be an artist in Pound's sense of the term. "He knows that he is a beginning and not a classically finished work" (*SP* 145). "He never pretended to have reached the goal. He knew himself and proclaimed himself 'a start in the right direction.' He never said, 'American poetry is to stay where I left it'; he said it was to go on from where he started it."[14]

As late as the *ABC of Reading* (1934), Pound insisted that the form of Whitman's poetry must be ignored if its content is to be appreciated. "The only way to enjoy Whitman thoroughly is to concentrate on his fundamental meaning. If you insist, however, on dissecting his lan-

guage you will probably find that it is wrong." [15] Normally, Pound insisted upon the inseparability of form and content; it is a mark of his passion for Whitman's message that Pound was willing to overlook Whitman's frequent violations of the formal principles of economy, musical phrasing, and colloquial word order that were part of the Imagist program for poetry.

In April 1913, seven months after the opening of the Whistler exhibition, Pound published a poem that summarizes his attitude toward Whitman at that time. The poem employs the same metaphors of tree and sap, father and son that Pound had used in his 1909 essay on "What I Feel about Walt Whitman." Entitled "A Pact," the poem openly acknowledges the oedipal ambivalence that Pound felt toward his predecessor.

> I make a pact with you, Walt Whitman—
> I have detested you long enough.
> I come to you as a grown child
> Who has had a pig-headed father;
> I am old enough now to make friends.
> It was you that broke the new wood,
> Now is a time for carving.
> We have one sap and one root—
> Let there be commerce between us. [16]

The pigheaded father broke the "new wood" of free verse; the citified but no less stubborn son will carve it into a thing of beauty, a poetry with the hardness of sculpture. Such were the Parnassian ambitions of Imagist free verse, with its emphasis upon the "absolute rhythm" of the "musical phrase" (*LE* 3, 9).

Some contemporary critics of Imagist free verse connected it with Whitman's practice. But Amy Lowell denied the connection in a 1927 essay that contains many parallels with Pound's statements about Whitman. According to Lowell, Whitman is unlike "the moderns who are supposed to derive from him, since they are perfectly conscious artists writing in a medium not less carefully ordered because it is based upon cadence and not upon metre. Whitman never had the slightest idea of what cadence is . . . he had very little rhythmical sense." He wrote not *vers libre* but "a highly emotional prose . . . the moderns, with the possible exception of Carl Sandburg, owe very little of their form to Whitman." What they do owe to him, Lowell goes on to say, is an attitude of

pride in the "autochthonous song" of America. "We needed Whitman's message; we need it today. . . . much of it is in our blood, unnoticed but invigorating."[17]

Lowell is both right and wrong in this assessment of Whitman's influence upon the form of early modernist poetry. It is true that few of the Imagists modeled their free verse directly upon Whitman's. (Pound was one of the few who occasionally did.) Lowell correctly says that "the moderns have found their prototype elsewhere than in Whitman."[18] As the term *vers libre* suggests, the most immediate prototype was French free verse of the late nineteenth and early twentieth centuries. But that verse was itself profoundly influenced by Whitman, as Betsy Erkkila has demonstrated. So Whitman's impact upon the form of much twentieth-century poetry in English was indirect rather than direct. It came, as Erkkila says, only when Whitman was "smuggled back into the country via his French connections."[19] These included many writers admired by Pound: for example, Rimbaud, Laforgue, Gourmont, Romains, Duhamel, and Vildrac.

To illustrate the point, here are some Whitmanian lines from Romains's "Ode à la foule qui est ici," which Pound quotes admiringly in his 1913 essay, "The Approach to Paris." Pound translates three lines and leaves three in French.

> Crowd, your whole soul is upright in my flesh.
> A force of steel, whereof I hold the two ends
> Pierces your mass, and bends it.
>
> Ta forme est moi. Tes gradins et tes galeries,
> C'est moi qui les empoigne ensemble et qui les plie,
> Comme un paquet de souples joncs, sur mon genou.
>
> (SP 364)

The rhythm and tones of Romains's *unanimiste* poems in turn contributed to those of Pound's *BLAST* and *Lustra* satires. Perhaps all modern free verse is indebted to Whitman, the main point being the one Pound makes in Canto 81: "To break the pentameter, that was the first heave."[20]

In addition to his French connection, Whitman had a British connection that affected Pound's response to him. According to the account of Whitman's reception and reputation that grew up in his later years, he and his work were largely rejected or ignored by the American audi-

ence of his day, especially by the influential Bostonians. In sharp contrast to this neglect was the enthusiastic reception of Whitman by cultivated readers in England and Ireland. As John Addington Symonds said in 1890: "Hitherto he has won more respect from persons of culture in Great Britain than from the divine average of The States." [21] Many late nineteenth-century British writers whom Pound respected were devotees of Whitman's poetry. William Michael Rossetti edited a selection of it for British publication in 1868. Swinburne discovered Whitman in 1862 and wrote several keen appreciations before souring on him after 1872. Ford Madox Brown, Lionel Johnson, Arthur O'Shaughnessy, and Oscar Wilde were also among Whitman's transatlantic admirers. As Harold Blodgett notes: "The English, tired of a second-rate American literature superficially polished by patterning after Old World models, hailed Whitman's originality as the one refreshing aspect of the American output." [22]

This version of the history of Whitman's reception reinforced Pound's dim view of the Anglo-American literary audience. That view was antithetical to Whitman's own, for Pound believed that a democratic public could appreciate good art only if instructed by the aristocratic few who uphold true aesthetic standards in the civilized capitals of the world. In "Patria Mia" Pound says of America that "if you have any vital interest in art and letters, and happen to like talking about them, you sooner or later leave the country. I don't mean that the American is less sensitive to the love of precision, or to TO KALON, than is the young lady in English society. He is simply so much farther removed from the sources, from the few dynamic people who really know good from bad" (SP 122). Pound could not have agreed less with Whitman's statements in the 1855 preface to *Leaves of Grass* that the great poet "sees health for himself in being one of the mass," and that "his country absorbs him as affectionately as he has absorbed it" (WW 16, 26).

In his charitable moods, to be sure, Pound made historical allowances for the American neglect of Whitman in his own time. "One reason why Whitman's reception in America has been so tardy is that he says so many things which we are accustomed, almost unconsciously, to take for granted. He was so near to the national colour that the nation hardly perceived him against that background. . . . He came before the nation was self-conscious or introspective or subjective; before the nation was interested in being itself (SP 124). Again, in a letter of 1931 to

Lincoln Kirstein: "Danger of Concord school omitting to notice Whitman. Historically, people in rough environment, if they have any sensibility or perception, want 'culture an' refinement.' Whitman embodying nearly everything one disliked, etc. Failure to see the wood for the trees" (*L* 234). The images of wood and trees were never far from Pound's mind when he spoke of Whitman.

Still, the fact remains that the country failed to absorb Whitman as affectionately as he had absorbed it. It seemed to Pound that, like Robert Frost, T. S. Eliot, H.D., and Ezra Pound, Whitman had, figuratively at least, to go to London in order to be recognized. America would listen only if instructed by men of taste in the cultural capital. "It is cheering to reflect," Pound writes in "Patria Mia," "that America accepted Whitman when he was properly introduced by William Michael Rossetti, and not before then" (*SP* 112). In 1913, apparently, Pound still hoped that America might heed a Rossettian figure speaking with authority from the heart of a London coterie.

Four years later, however, he was less optimistic. In a 1917 letter to Margaret Anderson, Pound took issue with the motto of *Poetry* magazine, a quotation from Whitman's "Notes Left Over": "To have great poets, there must be great audiences, too" (*WW* 1058). Pound grumbles against "that infamous remark of Whitman's about poets needing an audience" (*L* 107). By this time, Pound seemed resigned to the idea that poets in the English-speaking world neither have nor need an audience beyond themselves. Whitman's vision of the great poet speaking directly to a nation of enlightened equals seemed almost ludicrously remote from the realities which faced Pound and his fellow writers. On no other point do Pound and Whitman differ so strikingly as on the question of audience.

Pound's reservations about Whitman's persona and the modern audience enter into his best-known early poetic imitations of Whitman, a group of satires first published in *Poetry* magazine during 1913 and 1914 and gathered in *Lustra* in 1916. Pound had said, in his 1909 essay "What I Feel about Walt Whitman," that "when I write of certain things I find myself using his rhythms" (*SP* 145). Those rhythms are present in several *Lustra* poems written in imitation of Whitman's addresses, some of them in a form that I have elsewhere called "the Whitmanian envoi." [23] This curious hybrid form combines the democratic openness of Whitman with the *trobar clus* sophistication of the medieval trouba-

dours, the vagabondism of the American open road with the vagabond-ism of the Provençal byways, Whitman's democracy of the spirit with Arnaut Daniel's (and Whistler's) aristocracy of craftsmanship. Pound raises the medieval envoi to a satiric form by infusing it with Whitman's scope and inclusiveness. In this form, the poet addresses his songs and books instead of speaking directly to his readers. He commiserates with them on the abuse they have received or sends them forth to stir up prudes and liberate the spiritually oppressed. The songs so addressed are delicate, light-footed, and impudent—a race of fauns and cupids. *They* are naked rather than the poet.

In "Further Instructions," for example, the songs are "insolent little beasts, shameless, devoid of clothing." They are distinctly urban; whereas Whitman could lean and loaf at his ease, observing a blade of summer grass, Pound's songs "stand about in the streets" and "loiter at the corners and bus-stops." Amusingly, Pound promises to conceal the nakedness of his latest song in a green Chinese coat and "the scarlet silk trousers / From the statue of the infant Christ in Santa Maria Novella," so that this newest of American Adams may move in polite company (*P* 94). The metaphor closely parallels Pound's picture of himself as a Whitman in collar and dress shirt.

In "Salutation the Second," Pound addresses both his earlier books—those published before 1913—and his current songs—the Im-agist lyrics and satires of *Lustra*. The earlier books "found an audience ready" only because "I had just come from the country; I was twenty years behind the times." In other words, their old-fashioned style was what people expected. But the current songs, in the spare and colloquial modern style, baffle the public.

> Here they stand without quaint devices,
> Here they are with nothing archaic about them.
> Observe the irritation in general:
>
> "Is this," they say, "the nonsense
>   that we expect of poets?"
> "Where is the Picturesque?"
>   "Where is the vertigo of emotion?"

Pound commands his "little naked and impudent songs" to "go forth with a light foot" and "dance shamelessly," to "ruffle the skirts of prudes"

and "speak of their knees and ankles" (*P* 85–86). The nudity of the per-
sonified songs differs from that of Whitman's persona in form but not in
function; both are meant to provoke and liberate the shocked reader.

In "Salutation" the nudity belongs to liberated natural creatures, as
the speaker posits a hierarchy of happiness inversely proportioned to the
hierarchy of established social classes.

> O Generation of the thoroughly smug
>   and thoroughly uncomfortable,
> I have seen fishermen picknicking in the sun,
> I have seen them with untidy families,
> I have seen their smiles full of teeth
>   and heard ungainly laughter.
> And I am happier than you are,
> And they were happier than I am;
> And the fish swim in the lake
>   and do not even own clothing.
>
> (*P* 85)

Although this poem is not an envoi, its direct address, anaphora, and
universalist stance all show the influence of Whitman.

The same influence is evident in "From Chebar," a poem that was
written in 1913 although it remained in manuscript until 1976. The title
alludes to the Book of Ezekiel, and the poem, as Louis L. Martz observes, "mingles a Biblical rhythm with the prophetic strain of Walt
Whitman" (*CEP* xii). Addressing America, the prophet projects a vision
of cultural excellence that transcends America.

> Before you were, America!
>
> I did not begin with you,
> I do not end with you, America.
>
> . . . .
>
> Oh I can see you,
> I with the maps to aid me,
> I can see the coast and the forest
> And the corn-yellow plains and the hills,
> The domed sky and the jagged,
> The plainsmen and men of the cities.
>
> . . . .
>
> I am "He who demands the perfect,"

I am he who will not be put off,
I came with the earliest comers,
I will not go till the last.

. . . .

There is only the best that matters.
Have done with the rest. Have done with
    easy contentments.
Have done with the encouragement
    of mediocre production.

I have not forgotten the birthright.
I am not content that you should be
    always a province
The will is not enough,
The pretence is not enough,
The satisfaction-in-ignorance is insufficient.

There is no use your quoting Whitman against me,
His time is not our time, his day and hour
    were different.

                              (CEP 269–71)

No one is "quoting Whitman" more than the narrator himself. Ezekiel/
Ezra uses Whitman's cadences and rhetorical devices to present his
characteristic modifications of Whitman's message.

    Pound sometimes addresses his readers directly not to challenge or
satirize them but to declare a Whitmanian spiritual kinship with them.
But this is an aristocratic kinship rather than Whitman's democratic
embrace, because Pound is addressing fellow artists. In "Dum Capi-
tolium Scandet" he addresses his posterity in the manner of Whitman,
but he means his literary descendants rather than Everyman.

How many will come after me
    singing as well as I sing, none better;
Telling the heart of their truth
    as I have taught them to tell it;
Fruit of my seed.
    O my unnameable children.
Know then that I loved you from afore-time,
Clear speakers, naked in the sun, untrammeled.

                                (P 96)

Again we notice the metaphors of vegetation ("Fruit of my seed") and nudity which are habitual to Pound when he is in his Whitman vein. In "The Rest," Pound addresses the "helpless few" in America who are "artists" and "lovers of beauty," urging them to consider his example of self-exile. The poem offers no hope of artistic liberation for those "of the finer sense" who stay in Whitman's homeland (P 92–93).

The envois which bear the greatest formal resemblance to Whitman's poetry are "Pax Saturni" and "Commission." In the former, the poet sends his songs to flatter American vices; the flatteries are arranged in long Whitmanian catalogs and punctuated by an ironic refrain (CEP 277–78). In the latter, the poet "commissions" his songs to liberate the spiritually oppressed. As Charles B. Willard says: "In this poem Pound attempts to recapture not only Whitman's peculiar metric—initial repetition, balanced lines, the catalogue, loose cadences—but his very spirit and tone, his sympathy for the oppressed and suffering."[24] Again, however, there is a significant difference between Whitman's emphasis and Pound's. Pound stresses not physical bondage and pain but the subtler forms of spiritual tyranny. His songs are sent to speak against "unconscious oppression" and to liberate "the women in suburbs," the "bought wife," and the "adolescent who are smothered in family." It is Whitman refined in the direction of John Updike. Nevertheless, the presence of the familiar organic tropes recalls Pound's conviction that "the vital part of my message, taken from the sap and fibre of America, is the same as his" (SP 145). Pound compares a stifling family to "an old tree with shoots, / And with some branches rotted and falling." He commissions his songs to "Go against this vegetable bondage of the blood" (P 88–89).

After Lustra Pound had little need of Whitman for nearly three decades. Whitman is not a presence in either Homage to Sextus Propertius or Hugh Selwyn Mauberley, Pound's first major sequence-poems in the modern style. Nor does Whitman figure directly in the early Cantos, although the precedent of Leaves of Grass doubtless both challenged and heartened him in his epic endeavor. In 1909 he had written, somewhat enviously: "Whitman is to my fatherland . . . what Dante is to Italy. . . . Like Dante, he wrote in the 'vulgar tongue,' in a new metric. The first great man to write in the language of his people" (SP 146). Perhaps because he envied Whitman this distinction, Pound avoided him as a model in the early stages of his own long poem. In 1934 Pound

95

said that he had examined the work of Whitman twelve years before, carrying away "the impression that there are thirty well-written pages" in it, although he was "now unable to find them" (*ABCR* 192). If Pound's recollection is accurate, this examination would have taken place about 1922, the year in which he recast the early *Cantos* into the form they now have.[25] But if Whitman assisted in the revision, the poem shows no obvious traces of his influence.

Edwin Fussell and James E. Miller, Jr., argue that the first direct echoes of Whitman in the *Cantos* mingle with the Greek and Elizabethan resonances of Canto 47,[26] the great fertility-ritual song, first published in 1937:

> By prong have I entered these hills:
> That the grass grow from my body,
> That I hear the roots speaking together,
> The air is new on my leaf,
> The forked boughs shake with the wind.
>
> (C 238)

Then, in *The Pisan Cantos* of 1948, Whitman becomes a major presence in Pound's long poem.

Pound began *The Pisan Cantos* during his six-month detention in the U.S. Army training center at Pisa in 1945 and completed them during the early years of his incarceration at St. Elizabeths Hospital in Washington. The sequence draws upon the rich resources of his memory to affirm the continuation of his vision of a civilized cultural tradition amidst the defeat of Mussolini's Italy and the wreckage of many of the poet's most cherished hopes. At Pisa Pound had not only his memories of Whitman but also a selection of his poems in *The Pocket Book of Verse*, edited by Morris Edmund Speare (1940), which Pound says he found lying on the seat of a camp privy. Whitman, then, enters *The Pisan Cantos* as an exemplar of the endangered tradition that Pound wishes to affirm. He refers to Whitman three times in Canto 80 and once in Canto 82. Taken together, the references constitute an important ideogram within the sequence. They imply Pound's strong personal identification with the good grey poet of the Camden years, an American voice unheeded by America, an aging voice whose utterance must come to terms with infirmity and death. Pound no longer needs to stress

the superiority of his cultural tailoring; he needs, rather, to assert his essential American identity with Whitman.

Pound's first reference to Whitman in Canto 80 aligns him with other worthy American writers whose achievements are in danger of being lost or forgotten by the American audience. These writers include Sadakichi Hartmann, Richard Hovey, Trumbull Stickney, Frederick Wadsworth Loring, and Bliss Carman:

> and as for the vagaries of our friend
> > Mr Hartmann,
> Sadakichi a few more of him,
> were that conceivable, would have enriched
> > the life of Manhattan
> > or any other town or metropolis
> the texts of his early stuff are probably lost
> with the loss of fly-by-night periodicals
> > and our knowledge of Hovey,
> > > Stickney, Loring,
> the lost legion or as Santayana has said:
> They just died   They died because they
> > just couldn't stand it
> and Carman "looked like a withered berry"
> > 20 years after
> Whitman liked oysters
> at least I think it was oysters
> > and the clouds have made a pseudo-Vesuvius
> > > this side of Taishan
> Nenni, Nenni, who will have the succession?

(C 495)

The vaguely remembered anecdote about Whitman's taste for oysters stands at a great remove from the watermelon parody of 1910. Whitman's appetite is now modest and reasonable instead of cosmic and risible. At issue in the question of who will have the succession is not only the political succession to Mussolini but the literary succession to Whitman and his descendants, including Pound himself. Who will carry on the American poetic tradition?

Pound's second reference to Whitman in Canto 80 continues the tone of nostalgia and loss. Here Pound recalls a trip he made to New York in 1910–11. During this visit he went to Coney Island with John

97

Butler Yeats and John Quinn (*L* 52), and he met e. e. cummings and the painter Warren Dahler in Greenwich Village. These men, too, represent a cultural tradition which may, Pound believes, survive after two world wars only in his memory. Again, he associates Whitman with this tradition:

> or his, William's, old "da" at Coney Island perched on an elephant
> beaming like the prophet Isaiah
>   and J. Q. as it were aged 8 (Mr John Quinn)
> at the target.
>
>   "Liquids and fluids!"
>   said the palmist. "A painter?
> well ain't that liquids and fluids?" [To the venerable J. B.
>   bearded Yeats]
>
>   "a friend," sd/ mr cummings, "I knew it 'cause he
> never tried to sell *me* any insurance"
>
> (with memorial to Warren Dahler the Chris Columbus of
>   Patchin)
>
> Hier wohnt the tradition, as per Whitman in Camden.
>
> (C 507–8)

And as per Ezra Pound in Pisa and St. Elizabeths: like Whitman, limited in his mobility, visited by disciples and pilgrims to whom he holds forth, and still adding new clusters to his long poem.

Pound had no Horace Traubel to record his conversation at St. Elizabeths, but he certainly considered memoirs, anecdotes, and reports of good talk to be an essential component of a living cultural tradition, no less important than books or statues or paintings. It must have seemed natural to Pound that our knowledge of the later Whitman derives as much from biographical anecdotes as from the poet's writings. As early as 1913, Pound had said: "With the real artist there is always a residue, there is always something in the man which does not get into his work. There is always some reason why the man is always more worth knowing than his books are" (*SP* 111). Indeed, *The Pisan Cantos* themselves represent Pound's effort to record for posterity as much of this intangible artist-lore as he can recall from his own early life and contacts.

Pound's third reference to Whitman in Canto 80 differs markedly in

tone and effect from the first two. The tone is desperate and helpless rather than controlled and nostalgic. Confronting the prospect of imprisonment and possible execution brought about by his own rash actions, the speaker identifies himself with Odysseus on the sinking raft in book 5 of the *Odyssey*:

> care and craft in forming leagues and alliances
>   that avail nothing against the decree
> the folly of attacking that island
>   and of the force ὑπὲρ μόρου
>
> with a mind like that he is one of us
>   Favonus, vento benigno
>   Je suis au bout de mes forces/
> That from the gates of death,
>   that from the gates of death: Whitman or Lovelace
>   found on the jo-house seat at that
> in a cheap edition! [and thanks to Professor Speare]
> hast'ou swum in a sea of air strip
>   through an aeon of nothingness,
> when the raft broke and waters went over me.

(C 512–13)

Here Whitman's poems come providentially to Pound in his dark night of the soul, as Leucothea's veil comes to Odysseus, sustaining the naked swimmer against the flux of the elements. The details of Homer's narrative are distantly echoed in "avail" and "strip." For a change, Pound is clothed with Whitman's help, not in Whitman's despite. There is no more callow talk about Whitman's not being "master of the forces which beat upon him" (*SP* 114). The poem in Speare's *Pocket Book of Verse* that best helps Pound to confront the relationship between poetic utterance and death is "Out of the Cradle Endlessly Rocking," to which he alludes directly two cantos later.[27] This, then, is a more personal evocation of Whitman than the cultural salutes proffered earlier in the same canto. Yet even here Pound does not lose sight of general contexts, pausing to thank Professor Speare for making a selection of Whitman available to the public in an inexpensive edition.

Cultural commentary combines again with intense personal response in Pound's final Pisan reference to Whitman late in Canto 82. At the beginning of the passage, Pound is commenting upon the transmis-

sion of culture in the modern world. The process is slow and uneven, never reaching some locations at all. He illustrates the point with an anecdote from his college days at the University of Pennsylvania in Philadelphia, not far from Whitman's Camden. Pound's German instructor, Richard Henri Riethmuller, author of the 1906 study, *Walt Whitman and the Germans*, apparently told his students that Whitman's work was better known in Denmark than in Philadelphia.[28] Pound recalls the occasion as follows:

> and the news is a long time moving
> a long time in arriving
> thru the impenetrable
> crystalline, indestructible
> ignorance of locality
> The news was quicker in Troy's time
> a match on Cnidos, a glow worm on Mitylene,
> Till forty years since, Reithmuller indignant:
> "Fvy! in Tdaenmarck efen dh'beasantz gnow him,"
> meaning Whitman, exotic, still suspect
> four miles from Camden.
>
> (C 525–26)

In part, this is a riposte to William Carlos Williams's celebration of New Jersey localism as a possible basis for culture. But on a more personal level Pound must have been struck by the parallel between his own career and Whitman's. Like Whitman, Pound had lived near Philadelphia (not in Camden but in Wyncote); he had a foreign following (not in Denmark but in Italy); and in his later years he was still perceived in America as "exotic" and "suspect." Little did he imagine, when he told Harriet Monroe in 1912 that "The 'Yawp' is respected from Denmark to Bengal," that Riethmuller's remark would come to have this meaning for him (L 11).

This bitterly humorous commentary upon the American audience is immediately followed by a poignant two-line allusion to "Out of the Cradle Endlessly Rocking" and by a passage which recapitulates one of Whitman's favorite themes: the dissolution of the poet into the fertile cycles of the earth:

> "O troubled reflection
> "O Throat, O throbbing heart"

100

How drawn, O GEA TERRA,
> what draws as thou drawest
>> till one sink into thee by an arm's width
> embracing thee. Drawest
>> truly thou drawest.
> Wisdom lies next thee,
>> simply, past metaphor.
Where I lie let the thyme rise
>> and basilicum
>> let the herbs rise in April abundant.

(C 526)

The explicit conjunction between Whitman and the fertility-ritual theme in this passage supports the claim of Miller and Fussell that Whitman is an implicit presence in Canto 47. The metamorphosis of human into vegetable life always seemed to Pound to be at the heart of Whitman's vision. Not only did he habitually speak of Whitman in terms of sap and fiber, wood and trees, but in *The Spirit of Romance* he related Whitmanian "cosmic consciousness" to a passage in Dante in which Glaucus is transformed into a god by eating magical leaves of grass (*SR* 155).

In Canto 82 the caged Pound is not only identifying himself with the bereaved mockingbird of Whitman's poem, from whose aria the quoted lines are taken; he is also identifying himself with the speaker of the poem. When the mockingbird sings

O brown halo in the sky near the moon, drooping upon the sea!
O troubled reflection in the sea!
O throat! O throbbing heart!
And I singing uselessly, uselessly all the night

he is taken by the eavesdropping Whitman as an emblem of the poet: "O you singer solitary, singing by yourself, projecting me, / O solitary me listening, never more shall I cease perpetuating you" (WW 392–93). On this model, the American bard, having lost his soul mate and ideal auditor, sings "uselessly all the night" to no one in particular. His consolation and liberation is the chthonic lullaby of death whispered to him by the sea as it breaks upon the land. Pound at Pisa readily identifies himself with this bard, as also with the speaker of Lovelace's "To Althea, from Prison." Pound, too, finds solace for the loss of his beloved

101

in the thought of his union with mother earth, his "connubium terrae" (*C* 526). And to this union he, like Whitman, will go unclothed: "By Ferrara was buried naked, fu Nicolo / . . . lie into earth to the breast bone, to the left shoulder" (*C* 526). By the end of Canto 82 Pound's personal identification with Whitman, *sans* collar, *sans* dress shirt, is immediate and moving, with none of the self-conscious distancing that he felt obliged to insist upon when he was younger.

Whitman, then, was a vivid presence in Pound's thought and work during both the early and the late stages of his career. Pound's ambivalence about Whitman's achievement reveals much about Pound's own aspirations as an American poet and about his sense of the American audience. On the one hand, Pound admired the large-spirited, hopeful, and distinctively American "message" of Whitman's poetry. Pound also envied Whitman his reputation as the unofficial epic poet of the nation. Pound's own epic aspirations in the *Cantos* were shaped in part by the precedent of *Leaves of Grass*. On the other hand, Pound deplored Whitman's lack of formal craftsmanship and his provincial conception of culture. Whitman's poetic persona—hankering, gross, and nude— and his inclusive sense of a popular, democratic audience for poetry ran against the grain of Pound's educated ventriloquism and his exclusive sense of an elite, aristocratic audience whose taste should set aesthetic standards for the rest of society. Out of this ambivalence came an illuminating series of comments upon and creative imitations of Whitman, in which Pound defined his poetic identity by measuring it against that of his "spiritual father" (*SP* 145). During the London years, he clothed the American Adam in the collar and dress shirt of his cosmopolitan sophistication; but at the end of the Second World War he asserted his naked American identity with the good grey poet of Camden. The model of Whitman was indispensable to Pound in his tailoring of an American poetic self.

Notes

1. Ezra Pound, *Selected Prose, 1909–1965*, ed. William Cookson (New York: New Directions, 1973), p. 145; hereafter cited as *SP* followed by page number.

2. *Walt Whitman: Complete Poetry and Collected Prose*, ed. Justin Kaplan

(New York: Library of America, 1982), p. 45; hereafter cited as WW followed by page number.

3. G. Thomas Tanselle, "Two Early Letters of Ezra Pound," *American Literature* 34 (1962): 115.

4. *The Selected Letters of Ezra Pound, 1907–1941*, ed. D. D. Paige (New York: New Directions, 1971), p. 21; hereafter cited as *L* followed by page number.

5. Charles B. Willard, "Ezra Pound and the Whitman 'Message,'" *Revue de littérature comparée* 31 (1957): 94–98.

6. See James E. Miller, Jr., *The American Quest for a Supreme Fiction* (Chicago and London: University of Chicago Press, 1979), pp. 69–95 passim, and M. L. Rosenthal and Sally M. Gall, *The Modern Poetic Sequence* (New York and Oxford: Oxford University Press, 1983), chaps. 2 and 9. See also Allen Ginsberg, *Allen Verbatim: Lectures on Poetry, Politics, Consciousness*, ed. Gordon Ball (New York: McGraw-Hill, 1974), pp. 180–81.

7. Ezra Pound, *The Spirit of Romance* (New York: New Directions, 1968), pp. 168–69; hereafter cited as SR followed by page numbers.

8. Roy Harvey Pearce, *The Continuity of American Poetry* (Princeton: Princeton University Press, 1961), p. 90. Pearce concludes that "Whitman's and Pound's means to making an American epic are thus diametrically opposed" (p. 100). A different conclusion is reached by Samuel Hynes, "Whitman, Pound, and the Prose Tradition," in *The Presence of Walt Whitman: Selected Papers from the English Institute*, ed. R. W. B. Lewis (New York and London: Columbia University Press, 1962), pp. 110–36, and by Ian F. A. Bell, *Critic as Scientist: The Modernist Poetics of Ezra Pound* (London and New York: Methuen, 1981), pp. 128–29. See also Bell, "Pound's SILET," *Explicator* 38 (1980): 14–16.

9. William Carlos Williams, "An Essay on *Leaves of Grass*," in *Whitman: A Collection of Critical Essays*, ed. Roy Harvey Pearce (Englewood Cliffs: Prentice-Hall, 1962), pp. 146–54. On Whitman and Williams, see James E. Breslin, "Whitman and the Early Development of William Carlos Williams," *PMLA* 82 (1967): 613–21, and "William Carlos Williams and the Whitman Tradition," in *Literary Criticism and Historical Understanding: Selected Papers from the English Institute*, ed. Phillip Damon (New York: Columbia University Press, 1967), pp. 151–79.

10. *Collected Early Poems of Ezra Pound*, ed. Michael John King (New York: New Directions, 1976), pp. 215–18; hereafter cited as *CEP* followed by page number.

11. Horace Traubel, *With Walt Whitman in Camden*, 3 vols. (New York: Rowman & Littlefield, 1961), 1:45.

12. See Hugh Witemeyer, *The Poetry of Ezra Pound: Forms and Renewal, 1908–1920* (Berkeley: University of California Press, 1969), pp. 176–81.

13. Tanselle, "Two Early Letters," p. 115.

14. *Literary Essays of Ezra Pound*, ed. T. S. Eliot (New York: New Directions, 1968), p. 218; hereafter cited as *LE* followed by page number.

15. Ezra Pound, *ABC of Reading* (New York: New Directions, 1960), p. 192; hereafter cited as *ABCR* followed by page number.

16. *Personae: The Collected Shorter Poems of Ezra Pound* (New York: New Directions, 1971), p. 89; hereafter cited as *P* followed by page number.

17. Amy Lowell, "Walt Whitman and the New Poetry," *Yale Review* 16 (1927): 503, 508, 510–11.

18. Ibid., p. 516.

19. Betsy Erkkila, *Walt Whitman among the French: Poet and Myth* (Princeton: Princeton University Press, 1980), p. 231.

20. *The Cantos of Ezra Pound* (New York: New Directions, 1970), p. 518; hereafter cited as *C* followed by page number. For a discussion of metric innovations in Whitman and Pound, see Edwin Fussell, *Lucifer in Harness: American Meter, Metaphor, and Diction* (Princeton: Princeton University Press, 1973).

21. John Addington Symonds, "Democratic Art, with Special Reference to Walt Whitman," in *Essays Speculative and Suggestive* (1890; 3d ed., London: Smith, Elder, 1907); reprint, *Walt Whitman: A Study* (London: John C. Nimmo, 1893), p. 124.

22. Harold Blodgett, *Walt Whitman in England* (Ithaca: Cornell University Press, 1934), p. viii. On W. B. Yeats and Whitman, see Terence Diggory, *Yeats and American Poetry* (Princeton: Princeton University Press, 1983), pp. 17–30.

23. Witemeyer, *Poetry of Ezra Pound*, pp. 234–38.

24. Charles B. Willard, "Ezra Pound's Debt to Walt Whitman," *Studies in Philology* 54 (1957): 579. See also Willard, "Ezra Pound's Appraisal of Walt Whitman," *Modern Language Notes* 72 (1957): 19–26.

25. See Myles Slatin, "A History of Pound's Cantos I–XVI, 1915–1925," *American Literature* 35 (1963): 188–89.

26. Fussell, *Lucifer in Harness*, p. 140, and Miller, *American Quest*, p. 90.

27. Morris Edmund Speare, ed., *The Pocket Book of Verse: Great English and American Poems* (New York: Pocket Books, 1940). Speare includes "When Lilacs Last in the Dooryard Bloom'd," "Mannahatta," "When I Heard the Learn'd Astronomer," "O Captain! My Captain!" and "Out of the Cradle Endlessly Rocking." Basil Bunting told James Laughlin that Pound knew "Out of the Cradle" by heart; see "For the Record: James Laughlin on New Directions and Others," in *American Poetry* 1 (Spring 1984): 51.

28. Richard Henri Riethmuller, *Walt Whitman and the Germans: A Study* (Philadelphia: Americana Germanica Press, 1906). The anecdote related by Pound (with Riethmuller's name misspelled) does not appear in this book; as Roy Harvey Pearce says, it is "presumably oral." See Pearce, "Ezra Pound's Appraisal of Walt Whitman: Addendum," *Modern Language Notes* 74 (1959): 23–28, and Forrest Read, '76: *One World and the Cantos of Ezra Pound* (Chapel Hill: University of North Carolina Press, 1981), pp. 338–39.

Pound's Parleyings with Robert Browning

George Bornstein

In the summer of 1907 a young graduate student at the University of Pennsylvania recorded in a journal a conversation at once traumatic and comic with Professor Felix Schelling over his future. Schelling had told him that because of his writing "I 'was wasting both my own time and that of my instructors by continuing longer at any institution of learning.' He didn't intend it as a compliment. 'You are either a genius or somewhat of a humbug. When you prove that you are a genius I will apologize.'" In the same unpublished journal the young student recorded his devotion not to academia as represented by Schelling but to poetry as represented by Browning. "As grass blade in its sheathe, so are we like in tendency, thou Robert Browning and myself. And so I take no shame to grow from thee."[1] The student was the iconoclastic Ezra Pound, and over the next two decades he would prove that he was more genius than humbug and would exchange friendly letters with his former professor. He would also make clear his devotion to Robert Browning, both in published work and in letters to others. For example, he used two foreign languages to tell the French critic René Taupin in 1928 that "überhaupt ich stamm aus Browning. Pourquoi nier son père?" ("Above all I derive from Browning. Why deny one's father?")[2]

Pound avowed the importance of Browning to him over his entire career, especially during the crucial decade or so stretching from composition of the *A Lume Spento* poems (published 1908) to the appearance of *Three Cantos* in 1917. Other poets, of course, affected Pound deeply—Homer, Ovid, and Dante among them—but Browning held a

106

special place as Pound's immediate major English predecessor. Each was the leading figure of his generation to develop a postromantic substitution of history—particularly the written documents of both social and cultural achievement—for nature as prime stimulus to the poet's internal powers. Each interacts with past figures both by the direct creation of quasi-historical masks (like Browning's Pictor Ignotus or Pound's Bertrans de Born) and by a more complex process of creating a persona which then struggles to recreate a predecessor (as in Browning's *Balaustion's Adventure* and *Sordello* or Pound's "Near Perigord" and *Three Cantos*). Tracing Pound's complex parleyings with Browning requires three departures from contemporary models of influence study. First, I shall make extensive use of unpublished manuscript materials which display the dynamics of influence more clearly than do the final products in the collected works.[3] Second, in contrast to the disappearance of the author in current theories of intertextuality, Pound insists not only that his texts answer to Browning's but that he himself speaks directly to Browning himself (as when he titles a poem "To R.B.," addresses "Master Bob Browning," or exclaims in vexation, "Hang it all, Robert Browning"). And third, by way of conclusion I shall suggest why the anxiety model of literary influence applies less well to poets like Pound than to those more directly in the Romantic tradition.

I begin not with the customary starting point of *A Lume Spento* but with Pound's unpublished prose speculations on Browning and the related poem "To R.B.," itself only recently published in a problematic transcription. The prose speculations occupy eight pages of a typescript made with a blue ribbon and currently in a folder at the Pound Archive of the Beinecke Library. The account seems to alternate between being a diary and a letter, with occasional verse patched in; for lack of a better term, I refer to it as a journal and have already quoted its account of the conversation with Schelling and oath of allegiance to Browning. In meditating on literature and on young Pound's own literary predicament, the remainder of the eight pages utilize Browning in three major ways: to indicate the kind of misapprehension of Browning against which Pound reacted, to focus a theory of literary influence on Browning, and to identify the unexpected source of Browning's early impact on Pound through the long poems *Balaustion's Adventure* and *Aristophanes' Apology*.

Throughout his career Pound loved to contrast his own enthusi-

107

asms with the denseness of a more orthodox voice, and in the early journal Edmund Clarence Stedman plays a role that would later feature Lascelles Abercrombie, Palgrave's *Golden Treasury,* or the hapless Hermann Hagedorn. Pound writes:

> When Stedman talks of some of Browning as "impertinent verses" and again of "poetry that neither gods nor man can understand," he out of his banking house presumes to judge all other divine and human intellect by his own—for which presuming I question, to say the least, his tact. Even tho these phrases be slung in with some [of] what is intended as praise of Browning's poetry, we must quietly remember that it is only Mr. Stedman trying to squeeze infinity into an oyster shell, To bound creation by the borough of Bronx.
> E.C.S. is here objecting to the "prose run mad" stanzas ending
>
> > Who fished the murex up
> > What porridge had John Keats.
>
> I hope he begins to comprehend it by this time although I feel pretty sure that it was not (it the porridge was not) the Battle Creek health food that much contemporary verse seems to be written on.

Although Pound does not say so, he is reacting to Stedman's influential study *Victorian Poets,* first published in 1875, which went through thirteen editions by 1887 and was revised in 1893.[4] Stedman there saw Tennyson as showing "every aspect of poetry as an art, and the best average representation of the modern time," while he took a more mixed view of Landor and Browning. Pound customarily reversed this distinction, seeing Browning as the greatest poet of his age and Landor as the most complete man of Victorian letters. More important, he would later insist on Browning's clarity and would interpret hostile charges of incomprehension as indicating only the critic's failure to grasp Browning's aims.

In contrast to Stedman's criticism and verse, Pound set up as a wholehearted admirer of Browning in prose and hoped to imitate him in poetry. On the page after berating Stedman, Pound wrote:

> If one is continuously filled with burnings of admiration for the great past masters so that he runs from sweet flame to sweeter flame and then above it all finds his own proper rapture from within, surely his telling this must have on it the tang and taint of theirs who
>
> > Enter in and take their place there sure enough
> > Though they come back and can not tell the world

(for today all roads find Browning.) I think I am beginning to appreciate
him with some germ of intelligence.

The lines cited come from Browning's "Andrea del Sarto," where they
apply to Raphael and others whose reach exceeds their grasp. But Pound
here is not so much a self-critical Andrea as an acolyte who hopes to
follow his beloved masters from afar. The "germ of intelligence" in his
appreciation would help engender a whole career.

Pound began the journal by declaring his allegiance to past poets,
particularly Dante and Browning, in a combination of bravado and almost embarrassing adoration. Their great discoveries meant that a later
poet had either to follow them or else to condemn himself to minor
status:

> Are our riming and our essays to be confined only to such secondary
> things as missed the eyes of our fore-goers? Dante, Browning, and a half
> hundred others are not known in detail to a dozen men, and when one
> stumbles of a flaming blade that pierces him to extacy is he to hide it for
> some rabbit fear of "copyist" "blind follower" or alley taunt "He hath not
> thought's originality"? Is it, tell me whether, is it more original to cry some
> great truth higher and more keen, to add a candle to the daylight that none
> see, or to reverse some million proverbs that the mob may laugh to see the
> worthies butt-end up displayed to common view?

That exclamation captures several hallmarks of Pound's later thought—
the numbering of Dante and Browning among his major influences,
the sense of a small minority of cultured men continuing and advancing
civilization, the notion of ecstasy as the ideal response to great art, and
scorn for those who disagree. At this stage identification with the earlier
poets is nearly total, and Pound will shortly find ways to strive for his
own independence. But in so doing he will follow the model not of an
anxious agon with his predecessors but rather of a masked dialogue with
them; the early identification here will yield to a sense of fellow-
craftsmanship in a literary history governed by an ideogrammic rather
than a linear conception.

The focus of speculation on literary influence in the journal swiftly
narrows to just Browning, and in particular to his long, late, and now-
neglected poems *Balaustion's Adventure* and *Aristophanes' Apology*,
both of which use the persona of the Greek maid Balaustion as a mask
for Browning to work out his own relationship to his admired Euripides.

109

Pound follows the simile of his resemblance to Browning being like that of a grass blade to its sheathe with the admission that he himself may be "less near may hap to life and rooted things, less 'human with' my 'droppings of warm tears.'" The allusion is to the description of Euripides in line 2412 and again in 2671 of *Balaustion's Adventure* and already exemplifies Pound's early skill in the art of making it new. For Browning not only has Balaustion apply the title "The Human with his droppings of warm tears"[5] to Euripides but also borrows that line from his wife Elizabeth's *Wine of Cyprus* and uses it for the motto of his own poem. In citing the phrase, Pound aligns himself with Browning in using a previous poet's words to describe his own relation to an admired forerunner. Similarly, at the bottom of the same page Pound notes Browning's debt to Shakespeare in the passage of the sequel poem *Aristophanes' Apology* ending "Philemon, thou shalt see Euripides / Clearer than mortal sense perceived the man." Paradoxically, masks and literary tradition could lead to seeing a poet plain.

After developing his own thoughts on literary influence in a page of Keatsian doggerel ("And sith our keener beauties sooth may be / The half known strains of older balladry / . . . crouching deep / Within the caverns that old verses keep / I bear the waters of more shadowed springs"), Pound arrives at the formulation most helpful for understanding his intense relation to Browning over the next decade. He writes, "Just my luck, confounded and delightful, that after I had threshed these things out for myself I find 'Balaustion's Adventure' holds them better said, and said some sooner. As my Browning has not lines numbered I can not refer other than to Macmillan edit. p. 661." Turning to page 661 of the two-volume Macmillan edition of *The Poetical Works of Robert Browning* published in 1902, the year in which Pound began to study Browning seriously,[6] we find Balaustion refusing to worry over Sophokles' intention to write a new play on the Alcestis story just dramatized by Euripides: "no good supplants a good, / Nor beauty undoes beauty." She continues,

> Still, since one thing may have so many sides,
> I think I see how,—far from Sophokles,—
> You, I, or anyone might mould a new
> Admetos, new Alkestis. Ah, that brave
> Bounty of poets, the one royal race

110

That ever was, or will be, in this world!
They give no gift that bounds itself and ends
I' the giving and the taking: theirs so breeds
I' the heart and soul o' the taker, so transmutes
The man who only was a man before,
That he grows godlike in his turn, can give—
He also: share the poets' privilege,
Bring forth new good, new beauty, from the old.
As though the cup that gave the wine, gave, too,
The God's prolific giver of the grape,
That vine, was wont to find out, fawn around
His footstep, springing still to bless the dearth,
At bidding of a Mainad. So with me:
For I have drunk this poem, quenched my thirst,
Satisfied heart and soul—yet more remains!
Could we too make a poem? Try at least,
Inside the head, what shape the rose-mists take!

Balaustion's speech amounts to a theory of literary influence. She sees the process not as an anxious contest but as a transmission of power. Far from intimidating future efforts, the force of a great work actually engenders them; it "breeds" and "transmutes" the later poet into a creative divinity of his own to "bring forth new good, new beauty from the old." Her obscure simile of the grape, appropriate to the Dionysiac festival at which Greek tragedies were performed, implies a transmission not simply of the work but of the power that produced the work in the first place. Having "drunk this poem," she now thinks to make one: "Could we too make a poem?" The new work does not threaten the old but rather, since things have many sides, helps make up a part of an ideal order of poetry.

The obvious connection of Balaustion's ideas to Pound not only in 1907 but also throughout his career becomes clearer in context of the work from which they come. Set at the time of the Athenian defeat in the Peloponnesian War, *Balaustion's Adventure* dramatizes the saving of a group of Athenian loyalists from the island of Kameiros. In an adaptation of historical accounts of the Syracusans' willingness to free Athenian captives who could recite passages of Greek tragedy, Browning has Balaustion earn the Kameireans' safety by timely recital of Euripides' tragedy *Alcestis*. Using Balaustion as a mask, Browning presents a

narrative account framing a free translation of the entire *Alcestis* and concluding with an original, alternate telling of the story. The poem itself thus enacts the premises of Balaustion's notion of literary influence, in which a later poet both takes power from an earlier one and simultaneously revivifies his work. We have only to think of Pound's *Cantos* to ponder another long poem which depends on masks, both draws power from and actually translates a Greek work, and insists on the social efficacy of literature. Further, like the *Cantos* with their retelling of Homer's Nekyia, *Balaustion's Adventure* chooses for retelling a Greek work involving a hero's descent to Hades. Browning's full impact on the *Cantos* involves *Sordello*, *Balaustion's Adventure*, and the sequel *Aristophanes' Apology* (which this time translates the *Heracles* of Euripides). But in 1907 that work was nearly a decade away. Browning's ability to "transmute" Pound's own powers would first breed a series of shorter monologues.

Among the early monologues, the recently discovered "To R.B." bears the closest relation to *Balaustion's Adventure* and Pound's responses to it. The R.B. of the title is, of course, Robert Browning, but the speaker is not yet the "E.P." by which the author would later mask himself. Rather, he is a minor poet of the 1870s. Because the only published transcription of the poem lacks Pound's introductory note on the speaker, I quote that note here by way of clarification: "In the early 'seventies' one John Cowper of the 'Minores' met Browning and talked with him concerning a new poem containing a transcript from Euripides. As the others, seeing them talking earnestly drew aside, Cowper's talk became more animated."[7] Lest the point be missed, Pound scrawled by hand on the typescript, "See Browning's 'Balaustion's Apology,'" a title which conflates *Balaustion's Adventure* (1871) with the later *Aristophanes' Apology* (1875). *Balaustion's Adventure* is dedicated to Countess Cowper, and the Cowper of Pound's poem stands in the same relation to Browning that the Balaustion of Browning's does to Euripides and, later, Aristophanes. Both function as masks for the author's wrestling with his relation to an admired forerunner; both poems take that relation as their true subjects.

Pound's Cowper mask shares suspiciously many traits with Pound himself. For example, both admire Cavalcanti and hope to use him as Browning used Sordello, as Cowper makes clear in prose before shifting

to verse. His first metaphor employs the image of breaking wood, which Pound would later apply to himself and Whitman: "Lo thou one branch, and I / A smaller stem have broken, / Both of one tree. . . ." More important, Pound's poem follows the same view of literary influence upheld in Browning's. After describing Balaustion's devotion to Euripides in words borrowed from Browning himself ("thy words I borrow / Being best man's words I know"), Cowper responds to the charge that Balaustion sings with others' music: "Nay we all sing others music, / Would we, would we not." Nonetheless, he and Browning both strive to imitate Balaustion. Following the extended metaphor of the poet as providing not all truth but simply enough to pay an innkeeper on a journey, Cowper berates himself for confusion (as more than one of Pound's later speakers would do) and claims an important though lesser role than Browning:

> But I ramble as ever,
> Thought half-cut from next thought—
> Two radii ill seen are blurred to one.
>
> . . . .
> Thou swing'st the texts great line
> For the full synagogue, too high
> —we use not millions for the children's sum—
> Thou singst the text. I in my lesser place
> Make plain the meaning to some dozen nearest me.

Like Balaustion, Cowper insists that the relation of successive poets is cooperative rather than antagonistic: "One fellow broke the path. / I blaze the trees—So piecemeal make we road." Pound's sophistication clearly outruns Cowper's, just as Browning's outstrips Balaustion's. Both Balaustion and Cowper function as simpler masks for their more complex authors, and for their more complex relation to their forerunners. But while the Browning of *Balaustion* was a great mature poet able genuinely to revise Euripides even while paying tribute to him, the Pound of "To R.B." had not yet attained that status, nor would he for almost a decade. Not until *Three Cantos* would he be able to equal Browning's dialectics.

In the roughly contemporary "Mesmerism," first published in *A Lume Spento* and retained in the collected *Personae*, Pound again ad-

dressed Browning directly, this time without a mask. The title echoes Browning's own poem "Mesmerism," from which Pound also takes his epigraph:

Mesmerism

"And a cat's in the water-butt."—Robert Browning

Aye you're a man that! ye old mesmerizer
Tyin' your meanin' in seventy swadelin's,
One must of needs be a hang'd early riser
To catch you at worm turning. Holy Odd's bodykins!

"Cat's i' the water butt!" Thought's in your verse-barrel,
Tell us this thing rather, then we'll believe you,
You, Master Bob Browning, spite your apparel
Jump to your sense and give praise as we'd lief do.

You wheeze as a head-cold long-tonsilled Calliope,
But God! what a sight you ha' got o' our in'ards,
Mad as a hatter but surely no Myope,
Broad as all ocean and leanin' man-kin'ards.

Heart that was big as the bowels of Vesuvius,
Words that were wing'd as her sparks in eruption,
Eagled and thundered as Jupiter Pluvius,
Sound in your wind past all signs o' corruption.

Here's to you, Old Hippety-Hop o' the accents,
True to the Truth's sake and crafty dissector,
You grabbed at the gold sure; had no need to pack cents
Into your versicles.
                    Clear sight's elector![8]

Couched in the form, language, and meters of Browning, the poem identifies those characteristics of Browning's poetry which Pound admired and sought to adapt for his own verses. First came apparent difficulty—"tyin' your meanin' in seventy swadelin's"—which signals not arbitrary obscurity but a complex and compressed mode of presentation which draws the reader into its unravelling. A decade later Pound would associate such qualities with his enthusiasms for Chinese and Provençal poetry: "The first great distinction between Chinese taste and our own is that the Chinese *like* poetry that they have to think about, and even poetry that they have to puzzle over. This latter taste has occasionally

114

broken out in Europe, notably in twelfth-century Provence and thirteenth-century Tuscany."[9] Second, the poem admires Browning's expansion of poetic diction to include "unpoetic" phrases like "cat's in the
water-butt," which Pound liked enough to use twice in the poem and
again as title for an unpublished early story.[10] So, too, did he admire
Browning's profundity ("Thought's in your verse-barrel"), psychological
insight ("But God! what a sight you ha' got o' our in'ards"), and breadth
("broad as all ocean"). The playful phrase "Old Hippety-Hop o' the accents" suggests by a pun both Browning's innovative metrics (he could
break the pentameter nearly as well as Pound) and his use of foreign
languages or accents (as in "Soliloquy of the Spanish Cloister") in a way
that prefigures Pound's own usage. And finally, Pound praises Browning
as "Clear sight's elector." The final phrase gave him trouble: in one
manuscript, he first wrote "Lordly as Hector" (which didn't fit the previous characterization), then cancelled that and tried "Minerva's direc-
tor" (which associated Browning with the goddess of wisdom), and finally made better sense if not much better poetry by choosing "clear
sight's elector" (which rightly identified Browning with the process of
perception).[11]

Two things which "Mesmerism" does not say are as interesting as
those it does articulate. First, the poem remains silent on its own distortion of Browning. Nowhere, for example, does Pound mention Browning's philosophizing and ratiocination or his troubled allegiance to
Christianity. Rather, Pound presents a selective sketch which stresses
poetic craft and psychological perception. This selectivity results in as
much a portrait of Pound as he would like to become as it is of Browning and provides an early ground for Pound's later departure from his
sometime model. Second, the poem does not mention masks or the dramatic monologue. But it does create a mask and constitute a monologue. To see that, we need to appreciate the subject of Browning's own
poem entitled "Mesmerism," which presents a mesmerist in the act of
conjuring up the spirit and form of an absent woman. Browning's mesmerist stands as paradigm for the poet of personae, both creating a character mask and pondering his relation to his own activity. Pound's poem
continues the process, in that the author both calls up Browning and
suggests his own relation to him. Pound has carried over the preoccupation with a precursor of Browning's Balaustion poems and his own "To
R.B.," but this time with a speaker closer to himself.

115

Other poems from Pound's early period reflect parts of his dialogue with Browning. While Browning wrote *Fifine at the Fair*, Pound responded with "Fifine Answers," a dramatic monologue in which Pound invents a reply for the carnival dancer to a question in Browning's poem; significantly, Pound's Fifine stresses "the work shop where each mask is wrought." [12] To Browning's "Pictor Ignotus" Pound responds with "Scriptor Ignotus," a particularly Browningesque monologue complete with epigraph specifying place and date ("Ferrara 1715"), which concerns a minor English poet's effort to construct an epic rivaling Dante's (*CEP* 24). Pound liked Browning's poem well enough to borrow a line from it ("These sell our pictures") for "In Durance," in which a Pound-like persona laments his isolation from all save the masks of beauty that swirl around his soul (*P* 20). Pound's "Paracelsus in Excelsis" forms a mystical consummation of Browning's *Paracelsus*, and Pound's sonnet "To E.B.B." (Elizabeth Barrett Browning) complements the longer "To R.B." Pound also experimented with Browning's adaption of dramatic monologue to the verse epistle. His "Capilupus Sends Greeting to Grotus (Mantua 1500)," for example, echoes the techniques of Browning's "Cleon," "Karshish," and "A Death in the Desert." Less innovative than "Mesmerism" or "To R.B.," these early poems stay closer to imitation than to the originality to which Pound would shortly bring the form.

Taking over the dramatic monologue for his own work, Pound happily acknowledged its immediate source for him in Browning and ultimate origin in classical verse, particularly Ovid. Two weeks before sending her "To R.B.," he wrote to Viola Baxter:

> What part of Browning do or don't you like? People usually begin at [the] wrong end. Try the "Men and Women" in which Cleon, Karshish (The Epistle of), One Word More, Pictor Ignotus—there are several very nice ones. Ovid began that particular sort of subjective personality analysis in his "Heroides" & Browning is after 2000 years about the first person to do anything more with it. I follow—humbly of course? doing by far the best job of any of them? not quite. [13]

The poems Pound recommends constitute a special subset within Browning's dramatic monologues, for they all highlight the speaker's relation to his discourse as much as the discourse itself. With Cleon and Kar-

shish the epistle form and special historical relation to Christianity create such interest, with "One Word More" a poet identified as "R.B." discusses his relation to his own work, and in "Pictor Ignotus" the course of the speaker's utterance reenacts that of his career.[14] The list further indicates that Pound has in mind not the original *Men and Women* volume published in 1855, which includes poems that are not dramatic monologues and lacks the earlier "Pictor Ignotus," but rather the *Men and Women* grouping that Browning devised for the 1863 rearrangement of his poems, where it contains only dramatic monologues and includes "Pictor." Pound would have found that arrangement in the 1902 Macmillan edition containing the passage from *Balaustion's Adventure* cited in the unpublished journal.[15] He likely had the same grouping in mind a decade later, when he commended Eliot's achievement in the dramatic monologue: "The most interesting poems in Victorian English are in Browning's *Men and Women*, or, if that statement is too absolute, let me contend that the form of these poems is the most vital form of that period of English. . . . Since Browning there have been very few good poems of this sort. Mr. Eliot has made two notable additions to the list" (*LE* 419–20). Like "The Love Song of J. Alfred Prufrock," some of Pound's own mature dramatic monologues would constitute "notable additions" to the genre.

Pound's own definition of his aims parallels Browning's. Stung by the criticism of the confessional *Pauline* and difficult *Sordello*, Browning had explained in a note to *Dramatic Lyrics*, his first volume to contain dramatic monologues: "Such Poems as the majority in this volume might also come properly enough, I suppose, under the head of 'Dramatic Pieces'; being, though often Lyric in expression, always Dramatic in principle, and so many utterances of so many imaginary persons, not mine.—R.B." (1:347). In explaining his own aims to William Carlos Williams in 1908, Pound took over the term which Browning had used as title: "To me the short so-called dramatic lyric—at any rate the sort of thing I do—is the poetic part of a drama the rest of which (to me the prose part) is left to the reader's imagination or implied or set in a short note. I catch the character I happen to be interested in at the moment he interests me, usually a moment of song, self-analysis, or sudden understanding or revelation. . . . I paint my man as I *conceive* him" (*L* 3–4). The two avowals share emphasis on creation of a charac-

117

ter and on drama revealed through discourse; Pound further carries over Browning's stress elsewhere on the cult of the moment. The avowals are also incomplete. For in painting his man as he conceived him, Pound often would make the act of conception his true subject, as in "Near Perigord" or *Three Cantos*; so, too, had Browning, as in *Sordello* or *The Ring and the Book*, which Pound later commended as "serious experimentation" (*LE* 33). Nor was the separation between poet and persona so distinct from biography as Pound and Browning liked to maintain.

Pound continually emphasized Browning's exile from England to Italy in a way that paralleled his own expatriation from America. "The decline of England began on the day when Landor packed his trunks and departed to Tuscany," he wrote in "How to Read." "Up till then England had been able to contain her best authors; after that we see Shelley, Keats, Byron, Beddoes on the Continent, and still later observe the edifying spectacle of Browning in Italy and Tennyson in Buckingham Palace" (*LE* 32). Omitting to mention Browning's composition of most of *Sordello* in England before 1840 or his lionization by Victorian London for the last three decades of his life, Pound focused instead on Browning's self-imposed exile, opposition to Victorian literary norms, and long battle against obscurity, in all of which he resembled Pound himself struggling against contemporary America.[16] Pound would later settle in Italy before returning to his native country. But before he did so, he hoped to recover Provençal culture for his own time as Browning had revivified Italian for his. Writing in 1922 to Professor Felix Schelling, who by then had presumably decided that Pound was a genius and not a humbug after all, Pound said of his earlier career: "My assaults on Provence: 1st: using it as subject matter, trying to do as R.B. had with Renaissance Italy. 2, Diagrammatic translations" (*L* 179).

Doing for Provence what Browning had done for Italy proceeded by creation of a series of dramatic monologues and masks. These had an intimate relation to the poet's self. As Pound explained in a famous passage from *Gaudier-Brzeska*:

> In the "search for oneself," in the search for "sincere self-expression," one gropes, one finds some seeming verity. One says "I am" this, that, or the other, and with the words scarcely uttered one ceases to be that thing.
>
> I began this search for the real in a book called *Personae*, casting off, as it were, complete masks of the self in each poem. I continued in a long series of translations, which were but more elaborate masks.[17]

118

These masks comprise a great deal of Pound's work in the decade between A *Lume Spento* and the *Cantos*, including the Troubadour dramatic monologues, the translations in *Cathay* and *Homage to Sextus
Propertius*, and the linked series of monologues that comprises the
Mauberley sequence. Like Browning's, these monologues (except for
the Chinese ones) often involve artists or connoisseurs, posit a linkage
between artistic and sexual harmony, mix their diction and rhythms,
and claim specific historical settings. They also recall Browning explicitly: for example, where Browning's monk begins "Gr-r-r," Pound's Cino
begins "Bah!"; Pound thought that "The River-Merchant's Wife: A
Letter" might "have been slipped into Browning's work without causing
any surprise save by its simplicity and its naive beauty";[18] and the young
writer in "Mr. Nixon" invokes Browning's Bishop Blougram. Using
masks of poets where Browning more often used those of artists, Pound
executes his search for the real by creating a series of personae who ex-
ternalize various problems in the career of their creator, who also happens to be an innovative but insufficiently appreciated poet. In E.P. and
Mauberley, for example, Pound exorcises two threats to his own development—one a projection of what he feared he had been, the other an
embodiment of what he feared he might become.[19] Because these monologues form the one aspect of Pound's relationship to Browning that previously has received careful study,[20] I should like to pass on here to
Pound's resumption of his direct parleyings with Browning in *Three
Cantos*, with its extended response to *Sordello*.

During the decade culminating in *Three Cantos*, Pound's interest
in *Sordello* increasingly stressed its dialectics of masking as an explora-
tion of the poet's relation both to his own creations and to his literary
predecessors. As early as "To R.B." Pound had his Cowper persona med-
itate making Cavalcanti into his own analogue for the troubadour Sordello. In the 1913 essay "Troubadours—Their Sorts and Conditions" he
naturally coupled Dante and Browning as two poets interested in rendering Sordello in their own work (*LE* 97). The next year, Pound saw a
distinction: "Browning's 'Sordello' is one of the finest *masks* ever presented. Dante's 'Paradiso' is the most wonderful *image*" (*GB* 86). And
the year after that, 1915, he confessed to his father the crucial importance of Browning's work to the *Cantos*, which he was then beginning:

> If you like the "Perigord" you would probably like Browning's
> "Sordello". . . .

119

It is a great work and worth the trouble of hacking it out.

I began to get it on about the 6th reading—though individual passages come up all right on the first reading.

It is probably the greatest poem in English. Certainly the best long poem in English since Chaucer.

You'll have to read it sometime as my big long endless poem that I am now struggling with starts out with a barrel full of allusions to "Sordello."[21]

Appearing in *Poetry* magazine for June, July, and August 1917, the first published version of the opening *Three Cantos* did indeed commence with a "barrel full" of allusions to Sordello. These survive in the final form of the poem as the famous apostrophe beginning Canto 2 ("Hang it all, Robert Browning, / there can be but the one 'Sordello'") and the echoing of Browning's description of Venice opening Canto 3 ("I sat on the Dogana's steps / For the gondolas cost too much that year. / And there were not 'those girls,' there was one face"). But where the final poem devotes Canto 1 to the problems and implications of rendering Divus' Homer and alludes only briefly to Browning in Cantos 2 and 3, the original one devoted the first canto to the problems of continuing from Browning, referred to the Victorian writer in Canto 2, and only arrived at Homer in Canto 3. I focus here on the original *Three Cantos* as Pound's last major poetic parleying with Browning.

They opened with a more extended version of the address to Browning, in which the more decorous "Hang it all" replaces the earthier "Damn it all" of the manuscript draft:

Hang it all, there can be but one *Sordello*!
But say I want to, say I take your whole bag of tricks,
Let in your quirks and tweeks, and say the thing's an art-form,
Your *Sordello*, and that the modern world
Needs such a rag-bag to stuff all its thought in:
Say that I dump my catch, shiny and silvery
As fresh sardines flapping and slipping on the marginal cobbles?
(I stand before the booth, the speech; but the truth
Is inside this discourse—this booth is full of the marrow of wisdom.)[22]

That passage both identifies *Sordello* as starting point for *Three Cantos* and salutes Browning in his own language of quirks, tweeks, and outrageous metaphor. Two points relate particularly to Pound's style of parleying with Browning. First, he takes over Browning's habit of portray-

ing his relation to a key precursor. In "To R.B." he had created a persona in Cowper whose relation to Browning resembled that of Balaustion to Euripides in *Balaustion's Adventure*. Here, Pound acts more directly and seizes on a poem where Browning had done likewise. For just as *Three Cantos* opens with a Pound-like poet meditating on his relation to Browning, so had *Sordello* begun with a Browning-like figure working out his relation to his own precursor, Shelley, whom the poem exorcises implicitly through its historical ground and explicitly as the early "spirit."[23] Pound's parleying with Browning thus stands in the tradition of Browning's parleying with Shelley. Further, the celebrated word "rag-bag" here derives from Browning, who used it in his other Balaustion poem, *Aristophanes' Apology*, as part of Aristophanes' gibes at Euripides:

> . . . why trifle time with toys and skits
> When he could stuff four ragbags sausage-wise
> With sophistry, with bookish odds and ends,
> Sokrates, meteors, moonshine, "Life's not Life,"
> "The tongue swore, but unsworn the mind remains,"
> And fifty such concoctions, crab-tree-fruit. (2:212)

Aristophanes' accusations obviously fit Browning himself—and Pound—as well as they do Euripides. Yet in taking over the "rag-bag" charge, Pound subtly shifts the tone from abuse to raillery: his address to "Robert Browning," as to "Bob Browning" and "Mr. Browning" (117, 118), contains affection and respect as well as exasperation. The opening of *Three Cantos* both states and enacts Pound's continuing insistence on literary influence as a positive process of remaking tradition.

As *Three Cantos* proceeds to appropriate Browning's paratactic presentation of events, use of the narrator as character, and device of the diorama booth,[24] it arrives at a crucial difference. An early draft includes the bold avowal "I'll have up not one man but a crowd of them / Living, & breathing, gouzling & swearing real as Sordello" as well as the more tentative query "You had one whole man? / And I have many fragments, less worth?" retained in *Three Cantos*. These provide the answer to the poem's own question, "What's left for me to do? Whom shall I conjure up; who's my Sordello . . . ?" (115, 117). Creating a host of heroes—Sigismundo, Confucius, Adams, and others—in place of Browning's sole protagonist did help Pound to get beyond Browning's poem. He related them and others partly in a manner which

121

Three Cantos 2 describes as "ply over ply," a phrase which survives in the final Cantos 4 and 40, and which Hugh Witemeyer has suggestively explored as a pervasive technique in the *Cantos*.[25] We may add that the phrase itself is Browning's and comes from one of the numerous discussions of poetic art in *Sordello* (5.163).

One trait of Browning's troubled Pound in *Three Cantos*—his looseness with historical fact, which Pound continually excused but just as continually mentioned. Even before starting the poem Pound had noticed but condoned Browning's drastic alteration of Sordello's long and happy life to an early and frustrated death (*LE* 97). In *Three Cantos* he arraigns and then acquits Browning's great description of the font at Goito so central to the whole of *Sordello*:

> And half your dates are out, you mix your eras;
> For that great font Sordello sat beside—
> 'Tis an immortal passage, but the font?—
> Is some two centuries outside the picture.
> Does it matter?
> > Not in the least.
>
> > > > > (114)

Yet to Pound it did matter. The *Cantos* involved painstaking research and made insistent claims of accurate referentiality. In elevating the previously vilified Sigismundo to hero, Pound carefully bases his case on actual documents to refute the hostile accounts deriving from Sigismundo's great enemy, Pope Pius II.[26] Whatever the vagaries of the *Cantos* during the middle, Fascist years, the stronger earlier and later ones cling stubbornly to a verifiable scaffold. Pound and Browning both substitute history for nature as stimulus to imagination, but Pound's greater devotion to historical accuracy joined his multiple heroes, his diverse cultures, and his commitment to ideogrammic method in enabling the *Cantos* to take their own shape.

Not surprisingly, Pound's few caustic critiques of Browning cluster around the period when he was revising *Three Cantos* and needed to distance himself from his sometime model. As he explained to Iris Barry in 1916, "The hell is that one catches Browning's manner and mannerisms. At least I've suffered the disease" (*L* 90). Centering on diction, word order, and a substitution of thought for perception, his various aversions peaked in a 1919 essay objecting to Browning's translation

of Aeschylus. There Pound holds that Browning sometimes stooped to "unsayable jargon," failed to realize that inversions suitable to an inflected language violate an uninflected one, and yielded to the seduction of "ideas" (*LE* 267–68). These criticisms fit the early Pound as well as they do Browning, of course, and did not last long. Pound soon returned to praising Browning's monologues and to associating him with Landor, with musicality, and with serious technical experiment. By the 1930s he recommended reading Browning to Laurence Binyon and to Sarah Perkins Cope, just as he had in 1907 and 1909 to Viola Baxter and William Carlos Williams.[27] And in the *ABC of Reading* he quoted the long passage on the font in *Sordello* against "Victorian half-wits" who missed Browning's limpidity of narration, lucidity of sound, and variety of rhymes (*ABCR* 188–91).

In the crucial decade culminating in *Three Cantos*, as well as later in his career, Pound's relation to Browning does not follow the anxiety model so pervasive in contemporary notions of literary influence.[28] Though his allegiance wobbled at the time when he needed to cast off *Sordello* from the *Cantos*, the rejection never had that violence or obsessive distortion symptomatic of anxiety. Competitive Pound certainly was, but not anxious in the current sense of that term. Instead, his career exemplified the beneficent conception of literary influence recorded in his student journal and in Browning's Balaustion poems. Three reasons for this present themselves. First, while anxiety theories emphasize the poetic imagination, Pound instead stressed poetic craft. As T. S. Eliot remarked, "Pound's great contribution to the work of other poets is his insistence upon the immensity of the amount of *conscious* labor to be performed by the poet; and his invaluable suggestions for the kind of training the poet should give himself."[29] This concern with technique obviates the anxiety induced by fixation on the act of inspiring or imagining itself; it returns to the notion of the poet as maker. Second, while Pound conceived of literary history as in some ways linear in terms of technique, he thought of the products as arranged in an ideogrammic rather than linear or even cyclic order: major works did not compete with each other but rather built up a field charging each other with energy, as the *Odyssey* did for the *Cantos*. And finally, Pound's firmly comparative stance took him outside his own language to Homer, Ovid, Dante, or Li Po as well as to Whitman, Browning, or Yeats. In contrast, anxiety theories seem to posit a postromantic

123

endgame in English poetry deriving from the blocking figure of Milton. Pound's different conception of poetic art, literary history, and frame of reference enabled him instead to honor and to enlarge the early insights of his graduate days. For him, "the tradition" was always "a beauty which we preserve, and not a set of fetters to bind us" (*LE* 91).

Notes

1. The manuscript is in a file marked "College" at the Pound Archive of the Collection of American Literature, the Beinecke Rare Book and Manuscript Library, Yale University. It consists of eight unpaginated sheets typed with a blue ribbon. In quotation of this and other manuscripts, I have made minor alterations of spelling and punctuation to clarify the sense.

2. *The Selected Letters of Ezra Pound*, ed. D. D. Paige (New York: New Directions, 1971), p. 218. Hereafter cited as *L* followed by page number.

3. For a more general discussion of the strange neglect of manuscript materials in influence studies, see my "Victorians and Volumes, Foreigners and First Drafts: Four Gaps in Postromantic Influence Study," *Romanticism Past and Present* 6, no. 2 (1982): 1–9.

4. Not knowing which edition Pound used, I cite that published in Boston by Houghton Mifflin and Company in 1881. The remarks on "impertinent verses" and "prose-run-mad" occur on page 329 in a discussion of Browning's poem on poetic "Popularity." I have discussed Pound's poetic use of the lines about the murex in "'What Porridge Had John Keats?': Pound's 'L'Art' and Browning's 'Popularity,'" *Paideuma* 10 (Fall 1981): 303–6. The quotation about Tennyson, below, comes from the preface, p. x.

5. For the reader's convenience, all quotations from Browning will be from *Robert Browning: The Poems*, 2 vols., ed. John Pettigrew and Thomas J. Collins (New Haven: Yale University Press, 1981), except where there is special reason to do otherwise. Browning quoted four lines of his wife's description of Euripides as epigraph to *Balaustion's Adventure*: "Our Euripides, the human, / With his droppings of warm tears, / And his touches of things common / Till they rose to touch the spheres."

6. In the "Translations of Aeschylus" section of the essay "Translators of Greek" Pound states, "I have read Browning off and on for seventeen years with no small pleasure and admiration." See *Literary Essays of Ezra Pound* (New York: New Directions, 1968), p. 269; hereafter cited as *LE* followed by page number. Since that section of the essay was first published in *The Egoist* during 1919, 1902 seems the appropriate date for commencement of Pound's serious

reading of Browning. The following quotation comes from *The Poetical Works of Robert Browning*, 2 vols. (New York: Macmillan, 1902) 1:661. The lines, of course, are not numbered.

7. The manuscript of "To R.B." is in the Beinecke Library as part of Pound's correspondence with Viola Baxter Jordan, where it forms one of a series of poems which he sent her from Crawfordsville, Indiana, in a letter of 24 October 1907. The following quotations in this article are taken from the manuscript, which was published without Pound's introductory note as Appendix E of Forrest Read, *'76: One World and the Cantos of Ezra Pound* (Chapel Hill: University of North Carolina Press, 1981), pp. 448–52. Because that transcript is the only published one, I note here two flaws which affect interpretation: on page 448, the second to last line should begin "Thy lyric maid" rather than "The lyric maid" (Cowper is addressing Browning directly), and on page 449 the seventh line should have an "of" before "Kameiros" (which denotes a place of origin). Read's commentary on pp. 65–66 taking the poem as verification of Pound's interest in the Great Seal and other arcana seems eccentric. Donald Gallup has a helpful account of the Pound-Baxter correspondence in "Ezra Pound: Letters to Viola Baxter Jordan," *Paideuma* 1 (Spring and Summer 1972): 107–11; in addition, I am grateful to him for several suggestions about pertinent manuscript materials and for help in securing copies.

8. *Personae: The Collected Shorter Poems of Ezra Pound* (New York: New Directions, 1971), p. 13. Hereafter cited as *P* followed by page number.

9. See Pound's essay "Chinese Poetry," *To-Day* 3 (April–May 1918): 54–57 and 93–95; the quotation is from p. 55.

10. The manuscript is in a folder marked "College: In the Water-Butt" in the Pound Archive at the Beinecke Library.

11. The manuscript is in a folder marked "A Lume Spento: Mesmerism" in the Pound Archive at the Beinecke Library.

12. *Collected Early Poems of Ezra Pound*, ed. Michael John King (New York: New Directions, 1976), pp. 18–19. Hereafter cited as *CEP* followed by page number.

13. Gallup, p. 107; the manuscript is in the Beinecke Library. In *The Spirit of Romance* (New York: New Directions, 1968), p. 16, Pound wrote, "Ovid, before Browning, raises the dead and dissects their mental processes"; hereafter cited as *SR* followed by page number. For a later, similar comment on the derivation of the dramatic monologue, see *ABC of Reading* (New York: New Directions, 1960), p. 78; hereafter cited as *ABCR* followed by page number.

14. For an elaboration of this view of "Pictor Ignotus" see my "Structure of Browning's 'Pictor Ignotus,'" *Victorian Poetry* 19 (1981): 65–72.

15. For a listing of the revised headings see the Pettigrew and Collins edi-

tion, appendix 2. The best discussion is Lawrence Poston III, "Browning Rearranges Browning," *Studies in Browning and His Circle* 2 (1974): 39–54.

16. Pound particularly stressed Browning's Italian exile during his own domicile in Rapallo. Two examples occur in ABCR (132–33) and "The Jefferson-Adams Letters," reprinted in *Selected Prose, 1909–1965*, ed. William Cookson (New York: New Directions, 1973), p. 158.

17. *Gaudier-Brzeska: A Memoir* (New York: New Directions, 1970), p. 85; hereafter cited as *GB*.

18. "Chinese Poetry," p. 94.

19. I have discussed these views of Pound's masks during this period in *The Postromantic Consciousness of Ezra Pound*, ELS Monograph Series (Victoria, B.C.: University of Victoria, 1977).

20. Among discussions of the relation of Pound's dramatic monologues to Browning's, the two most helpful are N. Christoph de Nagy, *The Poetry of Ezra Pound: The Pre-Imagist Stage*, rev. ed. (Bern: Francke Verlag, 1968), chap. 5, reprinted in shortened form as "Pound and Browning" in *New Approaches to Ezra Pound*, ed. Eva Hesse (Berkeley and Los Angeles: University of California Press, 1969), and Hugh Witemeyer, *The Poetry of Ezra Pound: Forms and Renewal, 1908–1920* (Berkeley and Los Angeles: University of California Press, 1969), pp. 60–86.

21. The manuscript of this unpublished letter is in the Pound Archive of the Beinecke Library. It has been quoted from by Myles Slatin both in "A History of Pound's Cantos I–XVI, 1915–1925," *American Literature* 35 (1963–64): 183–95 and in his fine, unpublished dissertation "'Mesmerism': A Study of Ezra Pound's Use of the Poetry of Robert Browning" (Yale, 1957), and by Ronald Bush in the helpful third chapter of *The Genesis of Ezra Pound's Cantos* (Princeton: Princeton University Press, 1976); I am indebted to all three works.

22. *Poetry: A Magazine of Verse* 10 (1917): 113–21, 180–88, and 248–54. Further quotations from *Three Cantos* will be identified by their page number in *Poetry* enclosed in parentheses within the text. The manuscript drafts of *Three Cantos* cited in this essay are in the Pound Archive at the Beinecke Library.

23. Pettigrew and Collins, 1:152.

24. The best discussion of these three points is in Bush, *Genesis*, chap. 3.

25. "Pound and the *Cantos*: 'Ply over Ply,'" *Paideuma* 8 (Fall 1979): 229–35.

26. See Michael F. Harper, "Truth and Calliope: Ezra Pound's Malatesta," *PMLA* 96 (1981): 86–103, and Peter D'Epiro, *A Touch of Rhetoric: Ezra Pound's Malatesta Cantos* (Ann Arbor: UMI Research Press, 1983).

27. *L* 257, 308, 313, 8; for the letter to Viola Baxter, see above, note 7.

28. Here I am thinking of the work of Harold Bloom and his followers

from *The Anxiety of Influence* (New York: Oxford University Press, 1973) onward, as well as some of my own suggestions in *Transformations of Romanticism in Yeats, Eliot, and Stevens* (Chicago: University of Chicago Press, 1976). Not surprisingly, Bloom has little use for Pound.

29. "Ezra Pound," in *Poetry: A Magazine of Verse* 68 (1946): 337–38.

Pound and Yeats
The Road to Stone Cottage

A. Walton Litz

In *The Pisan Cantos,* written at the close of the Second World War when he was held in solitary confinement at a United States Army prison camp near Pisa, Ezra Pound recalled again and again the years just before the First World War, as if the London of 1909–14 was the only stable point left in a disintegrating personal universe. Most of all he remembered his early associations with Ford Madox Hueffer and William Butler Yeats, who are given pride of place in the famous elegiac passage in Canto 74 that begins with a line from "The Seafarer," itself a memorial to Pound's first great achievement as a poet-critic.[1]

> Lordly men are to earth o'ergiven
> these the companions:
> Fordie that wrote of giants
> and William who dreamed of nobility
>
> (C 432–33)

The story of Pound and Yeats, like that of Pound and Ford Madox (Hueffer) Ford, has been told many times, most comprehensively by Richard Ellmann in *Eminent Domain* and Terence Diggory in *Yeats and American Poetry,*[2] and I do not intend to review the entire literary friendship once again. This essay is a more detailed narrative, based on new evidence, of the interactions between Pound and Yeats in the years that preceded the three winters they spent together at Stone Cottage in Sussex in 1913–16. Ellmann and Diggory have done a fine job in tracing the general contours of a relationship that stretched over three dec-

128

ades, but I would like to stress one thing that often gets lost in discussions of influence and counterinfluence: it was from the beginning a personal as well as a literary friendship, and in the years after 1917 the personal element dominated. Although each poet remained sensitive to the other's criticisms, their poetic practices diverged widely in the years after the First World War, and the often troubled relationship was sustained by memories of the London years and by the strong ties between the two families. Ezra Pound's wife Dorothy was the daughter of Olivia Shakespear, with whom Yeats had a brief love affair in the 1890s and who remained the center of his London life until her death in 1938, while Dorothy's closest friend in the years before the war had been Georgie Hyde-Lees, who married Yeats in 1917. We should remember that literary friendships are not solely "literary."

When Ezra Pound arrived in London in the autumn of 1908, it was natural that his greatest ambition should have been to meet William Butler Yeats, since he considered Yeats the greatest living poet. In his preface to the *Poetical Works of Lionel Johnson* (1915) Pound recalled that in "America ten or twelve years ago one . . . was drunk with 'Celticism'" and the poetry of the nineties,[3] and his early poetry through *Exultations* (October 1909) is saturated with the Yeats of *The Wind among the Reeds*. The Yeatsian echoes have often been identified, but the influence reached far beyond the pastiche effect that such identifications suggest. As Pound remarked in the "Note Precedent to 'La Fraisne'" in *A Lume Spento*, the "mood" of the Yeats of the nineties had become part of his temperament;[4] and it seems clear that his developing notion of "personae" owed nearly as much to *The Wind among the Reeds* as to the example of Browning. In the first edition of *The Wind among the Reeds* (1899) Yeats assigned many of his poems to shadowy speakers drawn from his own earlier works, such as "Hanrahan" and "Michael Robartes," speakers who are—as he said in a note to the volume—more "principles of the mind" than actual personages;[5] and although by 1906 the speakers had been generalized into "The Poet" or "The Lover" or simply "He," a structure remained that Pound could adapt to dramatize his own moods. But perhaps the most enduring testimony to Pound's early infatuation with Yeats is his poem "The Tree," first published in *A Lume Spento* and often reprinted. In 1926 Pound made it the program piece for *Personae: The Collected Poems*, as if to indicate "How I Began." In Yeatsian cadences "The Tree" announces

129

Pound's lifelong ambition to transform personal perceptions into something like myth.

Evidently Pound sent a copy of A *Lume Spento* to Yeats, since he could write to William Carlos Williams on 21 October 1908: "W. B. Yeats applies the adjective 'charming.'"[6] This sounds like the perfunctory response of a busy man of letters, and we now know that Pound did not actually meet Yeats (who had been out of London most of the time) until May 1909, when Olivia and Dorothy Shakespear took him to 18 Woburn Buildings. Meanwhile he had firmly established himself in Olivia Shakespear's literary circle, which included the Australian poets Frederic Manning and James G. Fairfax, and had delivered his first course of lectures at the Regent Street Polytechnic, "The Development of Literature in Southern Europe." In the introductory lecture, devoted to the "essential qualities" of literature, Pound reviewed "Dicta of the great critics," beginning with Aristotle and ending with Yeats, a conclusion that must have startled even Yeats's greatest admirers.[7] Meanwhile, during an early visit to the Shakespears in February, he sat—as he proudly told Mary Moore of Trenton—on the same hearth rug where Yeats had sat, and "talked of Yeats, as one of the Twenty of the world who have added to the World's poetical matter—He read a short piece of Yeats, in a voice dropping with emotion, in a voice like Yeats's own," although he had not heard the voice at that time.[8] This intense reverence must have made Yeats well disposed toward their first meeting, which probably occurred before Pound told Williams on 21 May 1909 that he had been "praised by the greatest living poet" (*L* 7–8). Soon Pound was a regular at Yeats's "Monday evenings," and we can gauge the nature of their relationship at the end of the year from these remarks in Yeats's letter to Lady Gregory of 10 December:

> Which reminds me that this queer creature Ezra Pound, who has become really a great authority on the troubadours, has I think got closer to the right sort of music for poetry than Mrs. Emery [Florence Farr]—it is more definitely music with strongly marked time and yet it is effective speech. However he can't sing as he has no voice. It is like something on a very bad phonograph.[9]

On New Year's Day of 1910 Pound wrote to his mother that Yeats was "the only living man whose work has more than a most temporary interest,"[10] a remark which prefigures his extravagant call in the preface to

The Spirit of Romance (June 1910) for "a literary scholarship, which will weigh Theocritus and Yeats with one balance, and which will judge dull dead men as inexorably as dull writers of today, and will, with equity, give praise to beauty before referring to an almanack." [11] This is a major theme developed in Pound's later criticism and Eliot's "Tradition and the Individual Talent," the need (in Eliot's words) for a sense of tradition in which all literature has "a simultaneous existence and composes a simultaneous order." As Pound puts it more succinctly in his 1910 preface: "All ages are contemporaneous" (*SR* 8). I think we must conclude that Pound could not have reached this critical position, which was to become one of the foundations of literary modernism, without an overwhelming belief in Yeats's greatness. Unlike Joyce, whose strategy when he met Yeats was to hide his admiration and clear a space for himself through an arrogant response, Pound needed to celebrate an older contemporary. The readjustments and "anxiety" would come later. No wonder Yeats took such a liking to this "strange creature": there was no cause for self-doubt in the friendship, no need to ruminate painfully on the distance between himself and the young as he had in the retracted preface to *Ideas of Good and Evil* (1903) that recorded his encounter with Joyce. [12]

I doubt if this uncritical praise of Yeats would have continued for so long if Pound had not become aware of a major change in Yeats's art. The Yeats that Pound celebrated in 1909 and early 1910 was still the poet of the nineties (the "phantom poet" behind A *Lume Spento* and *Exultations*), and already Pound was feeling restive about the effects of this style on his own poetry. The opening lines of "Revolt," first published in *Personae* (April 1909), reflect this uneasiness and desire for change. The poem is subtitled "Against the Crepuscular Spirit in Modern Poetry."

I would shake off the lethargy of this our time,
    and give
For shadows—shapes of power
For dreams—men.

"It is better to dream than do"?
                Aye! and, No!

Aye! if we dream great deeds, strong men,
Hearts hot, thoughts mighty.

131

No! if we dream pale flowers,
Slow-moving pageantry of hours that languidly
Drop as o'er-ripened fruit from sallow trees.
If so we live and die not life but dreams,
Great God, grant life in dreams,
Not dalliance, but life!

(*CEP* 96)

Like Yeats at this time, Pound sought to leave behind the "shadows" of nineties verse, and it is curious that he never talks of Yeats's more recent and "harder" poems, such as "In the Seven Woods" or "Adam's Curse," which could have helped him on his way—he may never have read them. But sometime before midsummer 1910 he saw or heard some of Yeats's newest work that would appear in *The Green Helmet and Other Poems* (September 1910), including "Reconciliation" and "No Second Troy," a poem that would become his touchstone to the "new Yeats."

Why should I blame her that she filled my days
With misery, or that she would of late
Have taught to ignorant men most violent ways,
Or hurled the little streets upon the great,
Had they but courage equal to desire?
What could have made her peaceful with a mind
That nobleness made simple as a fire,
With beauty like a tightened bow, a kind
That is not natural in an age like this,
Being high and solitary and most stern?
Why, what could she have done, being what she is?
Was there another Troy for her to burn? [13]

On 27 November 1910 he wrote to a friend in Paris, quoting "No Second Troy" with this comment: "That is the spirit of the new things as I saw them in London. The note of personal defeat which one finds in the earlier work has gone out of it." [14] Five months earlier he had written to the same friend:

Yeats has been doing some new lyrics—he has come out of the shadows & has declared for life—of course there is in that a tremendous uplift for me—for he and I are now as it were in one movement with *aims* very nearly identical. That is to say the movement of the "90"ies (nineties) for drugs & the shadows has worn itself out. There has been no "influence"—

132

Yeats has found within himself spirit of the new air which I by accident had touched before him.

He is in transit I think from the *"dolce stile"* to the *"stile grande"*— and he looks to his new work & *l'avenir* rather than playing cenotaph to [the] memory of the dead "rhymers" and their period.

His art can of course be no greater—but there is in it now a new note of personal & human triumph that will carry him to more people. At least—one senses great things approaching and this belief in the *l'avenir* is the thing, the one thing that uplifts us—it makes no difference whether one sees the thing in ones own time.[15]

During 1910–11 Pound was deeply immersed in his translations and imitations of those thirteenth-century Italian poets who wrote in the *dolce stil nuovo*; but he also hankered after a more contemporary style and took heart from Yeats's advance in that direction. This feeling that the two poets were in "one movement with aims very nearly identical" seems to have continued into 1911, with Pound writing to his father in May that Yeats "is as I have said once before, a very great man, and he improves on acquaintance."[16] The poems of *Canzoni* (July 1911) do not seem inconsistent with this sense of shared purpose, in spite of the twelfth section of "Und Drang" ("Au Jardin"), which twice quotes the opening line from Yeats's "The Cap and Bells" (in *The Wind among the Reeds*) and inverts its meaning. Whereas Yeats's poet/jester dies when his love is unrequited, leaving only his cap and bells behind, Pound takes a more "modern" view:

> And I loved a love once,
> Over beyond the moon there,
>> I loved a love once,
> And, may be, more times,
>
> But she danced like a pink moth in the shrubbery.
>
> Oh, I know you women from the "other folk,"
> And it'll all come right,
> O' Sundays.
>
> "The jester walked in the garden."
>> Did he so?

(CEP 174)

Terence Diggory believes that "Au Jardin" is a reaction against Yeats, "containing" the material from the early Yeats that had threatened to

133

flood the "Und Drang" sequence at an earlier point: "The distance Pound gains from Yeats's tale of romance parallels the estrangement between the lover and the lady in Pound's poem." [17] But "Au Jardin" and its predecessor "Au Salon," the last two poems in both "Und Drang" and *Canzoni*, are really attempts in a more modern, conversational style to expose the ironies that arise when the ideals of the *dolce stil nuovo* are tested against the realities of contemporary life. Any satire of Yeats is incidental to Pound's ironic reflections on his own "medievalism."

"Au Jardin" and "Au Salon" would not seem so different from the other poems in *Canzoni* (some of which reach back to 1909) if Pound had not lost his nerve at the last moment and cut some of the poems in proof. He had originally intended the volume to be a "chronological table of emotions: Provence; Tuscany, the Renaissance, the XVIII, the XIX, centuries, external modernity (cut out) subjective modernity." [18] Among the cancelled poems were "To Hulme (T.E.) and Fitzgerald (A Certain)" and "Redondillas" (*CEP* 214–22), and their inclusion— along with the "subjective modernity" of "Au Salon" and "Au Jardin"— would have tipped the balance of the volume more toward satire and realism. Five years later, when Elkin Mathews asked him to make some cuts in *Lustra*, Pound recalled the harm he had done to the structure of *Canzoni*, even though the deleted poems were not "good enough": "I was affected by hyper-aesthesia or over squeamishness and cut out the rougher poems." [19]

Another "rough" poem, "The Fault of It," was published in the *Forum* for July 1911 but never reprinted in Pound's lifetime. The epigraph, "Some may have blamed you—," comes from the opening line of Yeats's "Reconciliation," and is followed by:

> Some may have blamed us that we cease to speak
> Of things we spoke of in our verses early,
> Saying: a lovely voice is such and such;
> Saying: that lady's eyes were sad last week,
> Wherein the world's whole joy is born and dies;
> Saying: she hath this way or that, this much
> Of grace, this little misericorde;
> Ask us no further word;
> If we were proud, then proud to be so wise
> Ask us no more of all the things ye heard;
> We may not speak of them, they touch us nearly.

(CEP 207)

134

Pound's poem might be taken as a critique of Yeats, but it is not so much a reversal of Yeats's "Reconciliation" as an extension or interpretation, and is in harmony with the tougher pieces in *The Green Helmet*. I think it would be a mistake to read any of Pound's poems of 1911 as "attacks" on Yeats or attempts to distance himself from the older poet. Nothing he wrote at that time could be thought of as an advance over Yeats's "All things can tempt me," which was included in *The Green Helmet* but had first been published in the *English Review* for February 1909 in this slightly different form.

> All things can tempt me from this craft of verse;
> One time it was a woman's face, or worse
> The seeming needs of my fool-driven land,
> Now nothing but comes readier to the hand
> Than this accustomed toil. When I was young
> I had not given a penny for a song
> Did not the poet carry him with an air
> As though to say "It is the sword elsewhere,"
> I would be now, could I but have my wish,
> Colder and dumber and deafer than a fish.

In December 1911 Pound could still write, in "Credo": "Mr Yeats has once and for all stripped English poetry of its perdamnable rhetoric. He has boiled away all that is not poetic—and a good deal that is. He has become a classic in his own lifetime and *nel mezzo del cammin*. He has made our poetic idiom a thing pliable, a speech without inversions" (*LE* 11–12).[20]

Meanwhile, in August 1911, Pound had visited Ford Madox Hueffer in Giessen, Germany, where—as he remembered in his 1939 memorial tribute—he showed *Canzoni* to his host (actually his sixth volume of verse) and was treated to the now famous, therapeutic "roll on the floor."

> He inveighed against Yeats' lack of emotion as, for him, proved by Yeats' so great competence in making literary use of emotion.
>
> And he felt the errors of contemporary style to the point of rolling (physically, and if you look at it as mere superficial snob, ridiculously) on the floor of his temporary quarters in Giessen when my third volume displayed me trapped, fly-papered, gummed and strapped down in a jejune provincial effort to learn, *mehercule*, the stilted language that then passed for "good English" in the arthritic milieu that held control of the respected British critical circles. . . .

135

> And that roll saved me at least two years, perhaps more. It sent me back to my own proper effort, namely, toward using the living tongue (with younger men after me), though none of us has found a more natural language than Ford did.[21]

In the mythology of his literary life that Pound later constructed, this moment became a turning point in his art and his relationship with Yeats. In 1936 he told Henry Swabey that Yeats had been uninterested in Hueffer and the achievement of the *English Review* under Hueffer's direction, and in a 1937 letter to William Carlos Williams he coined an explanatory slogan: "Yeats for symbolism Hueffer for clarity."[22] This distinction was then canonized in Canto 83:

> Le Paradis n'est pas artificiel
> and Uncle William dawdling around Notre Dame
> in search of whatever
> paused to admire the symbol
> with Notre Dame standing inside it
> Whereas in St Etienne
> or why not Dei Miracoli:
> mermaids, that carving . . .
>
> (C 528–29)

Here the contrast is between diffuse symbolism and the clarity of Pound's favorite quattrocento church in Venice, Santa Maria dei Miracoli; or, as he puts it in Canto 82, between *verba* and *res*.

> even I can remember
> at 18 Woburn Buildings
> Said Mr Tancred
> of the Jerusalem and Sicily Tancreds, to Yeats,
> "If you would read us one of your own choice
> and
> perfect
> lyrics"
> and more's the pity that Dickens died twice
> with the disappearance of Tancred
> and for all that old Ford's conversation was better,
> consisting in *res* non *verba*,
> despite William's anecdotes, in that Fordie
> never dented an idea for a phrase's sake
>
> (C 524–25)

136

This schematic reconstruction of Pound's early career was partly conditioned by the growing artistic estrangement between Yeats and Pound in the 1920s and 1930s; the pattern becomes more complicated when one looks closely at the actual events of 1911–16. After his visit with Hueffer in Germany, Pound told his mother that Yeats's close friend Eva Fowler and her husband did not belong in his "new and rearranged cosmos,"[23] and at times it seemed the same thing could be said of Yeats. Although Pound remained in close touch with Yeats and joined enthusiastically with him in "booming" the Bengali poet Rabindranath Tagore, the distance between the two poets widened. Imagism was conceived as a reaction against "symbolism," and Yeats was the most prominent reminder of a symbolist past. Pound's complex attitude toward Yeats at this time is summed up in the nickname he and Dorothy Shakespear frequently used in their letters, "the Eagle." In part it referred to Yeats's growing aristocratic pretensions and his favorite image of isolated nobility, but it also referred to the telegraphic address of the Royal Societies Club, "Aquilae, London," and was an ironic comment on Yeats's newfound responsibilities as a man of letters, since in 1910 he had been a founding member of the Academic Committee of the Royal Society of Literature.

Pound's more critical attitude toward Yeats is clear in the poem "In Exitum Cuiusdam: On a certain one's departure," first published in *Ripostes* (October 1912), which opens with a tag from Yeats's "The Poet Pleads with His Friend for Old Friends" (in *The Wind among the Reeds*). Yeats had urged his friend to "think about old friends the most," but Pound will have none of that in his reference to Yeats's literary "circle":

"Time's bitter flood"! Oh, that's all very well,
But where's the old friend hasn't fallen off,
Or slacked his hand-grip when you first gripped fame?

I know your circle and can fairly tell
What you have kept and what you've left behind:
I know my circle and know very well
How many faces I'd have out of mind.

(CEP 182)

At this time when Pound was feeling most assertive and rambunctious, Yeats was undergoing the crises of middle age reflected in some of the poems of *Responsibilities*. The result was a temporary reversal of

roles, with Pound acting as confident adviser and representative of the "modern." When Yeats agreed to contribute five new poems to *Poetry* (Chicago)—the November 1912 issue announced that "Mr. Ezra Pound has consented to act as foreign correspondent"—he asked Pound to check the punctuation, but Pound went far beyond that to make substantive changes. In "Fallen Majesty," for example, he tightened up the last line, altering "Once walked a thing that seemed, as it were, a burning cloud" to "Once walked a thing that seemed a burning cloud." Yeats protested, and on 2 November 1912 Pound asked Harriet Monroe, the editor of *Poetry*, to reverse some of his "emendations and changes": "Oh *la la*, ce que le roi désire!" But Yeats did accept a few of Pound's revisions and eventually responded to most of them: the final versions of the poems are substantially what Pound wanted. In the fall of 1913, when Yeats was preparing his next volume, *Responsibilities*, Pound told Miss Monroe that "he is still revising the poems we've printed . . . they look more like the versions I sent first, at least it suits me to believe so." [24]

Pound obviously felt in late 1912–early 1913 that Yeats was wavering between two poetic worlds, and needed a shove in the right direction. Writing to Harriet Monroe about the five poems published in the December 1912 issue of *Poetry*, he said: "I don't think this is precisely W.B.Y. at his best . . . but it shows a little of the new Yeats—as in the 'Child Dancing.' 'Fallen Majesty' is just where he was two years ago. 'The Realists' is also tending toward the new phase." At a time when he was formulating the principles of Imagism, Pound needed to separate himself as much as possible from the "old Yeats," and to redefine the "new Yeats" in his own terms of hardness and clarity. I do not think it has been generally noted that one of the most famous passages in "A Few Don'ts by an Imagiste" (*Poetry*, March 1913) deliberately plays against the style of the "old Yeats": "Don't use such an expression as 'dim lands *of peace*.' It dulls the image. It mixes an abstraction with the concrete. It comes from the writer's not realizing that the natural object is always the *adequate* symbol" (*LE* 5). "Dim lands of peace" appears in Hueffer's early poem "On a Marsh Road: Winter Nightfall," first published in 1904; presumably Hueffer had cited it in one of his conversations with Pound as an example of his own early sins against the prose tradition in poetry. But it is also quintessential early Yeats (the adjective "dim" occurs twenty-six times in *The Wanderings of Oisin*). We can see the profound impact of Pound's criticisms in Yeats's letter to Lady Greg-

ory of 3 January 1913, where the uncertain older poet has adopted the exact language of Pound's evolving Imagist doctrine:

> My digestion has got rather queer again—a result I think of sitting up late with Ezra and Sturge Moore and some light wine while the talk ran. However the criticism I have got from them has given me new life and I have made that Tara poem ["The Two Kings"] a new thing and am writing with a new confidence having got Milton off my back. Ezra is the best critic of the two. He is full of the middle ages and helps me to get back to the definite and the concrete away from modern abstractions. To talk over a poem with him is like getting you to put a sentence into dialect. All becomes clear and natural.[25]

It is a sign of Yeats's vulnerability and Pound's new strength that Yeats was asking for help and criticism. "I have had a fortnight of gloom over my work," he wrote to Lady Gregory on 1 January 1913, "I felt something wrong with it. However on Monday night I got Sturge Moore in and last night Ezra Pound and we went at it line by line and now I know what is wrong and am in good spirits again. I am starting the poem about the King of Tara and his wife ["The Two Kings"] again, to get rid of Miltonic generalizations."[26] Since Pound had just spent the Christmas holidays at Milton's cottage with Ford Madox Hueffer, Violet Hunt, and Compton Mackenzie and his wife, the epithet "Miltonic" had a special force for him at that moment. "Beastly dark low-ceilinged hole," he had written to Dorothy Shakespear over the holidays. "I suppose IF one had always lived in such a place—in an unenlightened age one might have writ rhetorical epics about original sin."[27]

The balance of power was reversed most decisively in the early months of 1913, when Pound was preparing his Imagist manifestos. Yeats showed him two poems written to the dying Mabel Beardsley (poems 4 and 5 of "Upon a Dying Lady"), and when Pound objected to weak rhymes such as "mother" and "brother" in the following passage from poem 5, Yeats obediently cut the entire section:

> Although she has turned away
> The pretty waxen faces
> And hid their silk and laces
> For Mass was said to-day
> She has not begun denying
> Now that she is but dying

139

The pleasures she loved well
The strong milk of her mother
The valour of her brother
Are in her body still
She will not die weeping
May God be with her sleeping.[28]

In *The Spirit of Romance* (1910) Pound had said: "Yeats gives me to understand that there comes a time in the career of a great poet when he ceases to take pleasure in riming 'mountain' with 'fountain' and 'beauty' with 'duty'" (*SR* 50). Now Pound was returning the lesson. "*One* of [the] lyrics is rather nice," he told Dorothy Shakespear, "but he cant expect me to like stale riming, even if he does say its an imitation of an Elizabethan form. Elizifbeefan. . . . Its just moulting eagle."[29] And a few days later Dorothy sent Ezra a sketch of a rather wan eagle perched on a mountaintop, with the inscription: "The Eagle has been inspired."[30]

Writing to Dorothy Shakespear in September 1912 about his appointment as "'foreign correspondent' or 'foreign edtr.' or something of that sort" for *Poetry* magazine, Pound had said that he was sending "a denunciation of everybody except Yeats & [Padraic] Colum for their next number."[31] But if Yeats read "Status Rerum" when it appeared in the January 1913 issue, he probably did not realize that he had been given special consideration:

> Mr. Yeats has been subjective; believes in the glamour and associations which hang near the words. "Works of art beget works of art." He has much in common with the French symbolists. Mr. Hueffer believes in an exact rendering of things. He would strip words of all "association" for the sake of getting a precise meaning. He professes to prefer prose to verse. You would find his origins in Gautier or in Flaubert. He is objective. This school tends to lapse into description. The other tends to lapse into sentiment.
>
> Mr. Yeats' method is, to my way of thinking, very dangerous, for although he is the greatest of living poets who use English, and though he has sung some of the moods of life immortally, his art has not broadened much in scope during the past decade. His gifts to English art are mostly negative; i.e., he has stripped English poetry of many of its faults. His "followers" have come to nothing.[32]

This theme was repeated in a letter to Harriet Monroe of 13 August 1913: "F.M.H. happens to be a serious artist. . . . He and Yeats are the

two men in London. And Yeats is already a sort of great dim figure with its associations set in the past" (*L* 21).

Given this sense of Yeats as a fading giant, it is not surprising that Pound approached their first winter together at Stone Cottage with some trepidation. "My stay in Stone Cottage will not be in the least profitable," he wrote to his mother in November 1913. "Yeats will amuse me part of the time and bore me to death with psychical research the rest. I regard the visit as a duty to posterity" (*L* 25). But once settled in Stone Cottage he became absorbed in long conversations with Yeats and found that he "improves on acquaintance."[33] Yeats admired Pound's first attempts to mine a Noh drama from Ernest Fenollosa's notes,[34] and their joint work on the Noh gave a sense of common purpose to this and the succeeding two winters. In turn, Yeats's investigations into magic and the occult rekindled Pound's earlier interest in the esoteric, and he even wrote home for the copy of *Demoniality; or, Incubi and Succubi* that he had mentioned in 1908 in his headnote to "La Fraisne."[35] Like Yeats, Pound really preferred "Ennemoser on Witches" to Wordsworth,[36] and when Dorothy Shakespear asked him for help in understanding "symbolism," he made a sharp distinction between the literary and esoteric traditions:

> What *do* you mean by symbolism? Do you mean real symbolism, Cabala, genesis of symbols, rise of picture language, etc. or the aesthetic symbolism of Villiers de l'Isle Adam, & that Arthur Symons wrote a book about—the literwary movement? At any rate begin on the "*Comte de Gabalis*", anonymous & should be in catalogue under "Comte de Gabalis". Then you might try the Grimoire of Pope Honorius (IIIrd I think).
>
> There's a dictionary of symbols, but I think it immoral. I mean that I think a superficial acquaintance with the sort of shallow, conventional, or attributed meaning of a lot of symbols *weakens*—damnably, the power of receiving an energized symbol. I mean a symbol appearing in a vision has a certain richness & power of energizing joy—whereas if the supposed meaning of a symbol is familiar it has no more force, or interest of power of suggestion than any other word, or than a synonym in some other language.
>
> Then there are those Egyptian language books, but O.S. [Olivia Shakespear] has 'em so they're no use. De Gabalis (first part only) is amusing. Ennemoser's History of Magic may have something in it—Then there are "Les Symbolistes"—french from Mallarmé, de l'Isle Adam, etc. to [Remy] De Gourmont, which is another story.[37]

141

Pound thought the "symbolism" documented by Arthur Symons in his *Symbolist Movement in Literature* had run its course in England, and was the opposite of Imagism: hence the constant attacks on the symbolists and their use of "association" in the various Imagist and Vorticist essays. On the other hand, the "symbolism" of vision and the esoteric remained a powerful source of poetic inspiration, and Pound had nothing but admiration for this aspect of Yeats's work.

Most of all Pound was impressed during that first winter at Stone Cottage by Yeats's generosity and nobility. George Moore, who had attacked Yeats in the earlier two volumes of his trilogy *Hail and Farewell*, got closer to the bone in a chapter of his third volume, *Vale*, that was published in the *English Review* for January 1914. Moore was especially caustic in his comments on Yeats's hatred for the "middle classes" and pretensions to an aristocratic ancestry. Yeats replied with the two poems that frame *Responsibilities*: "Pardon, old fathers" and "While I, from that reed-throated whisperer," which was originally titled "Notoriety (*Suggested by a recent magazine article*)." Pound could see the comic side to Yeats's "lofty poems to his ancestors,"[38] but he was also touched by the heroic gesture. Reading the letters written during that first winter, one senses that the term "the Eagle" has lost much of its irony. When Pound gave an interview on Imagism to a reporter from the London *Daily News and Leader* in March, he could say: "Next to Mr. Yeats, I regard Mr. Hueffer as one of our strongest forces to-day," a statement which delicately readjusts his judgment of a few months before.[39]

Yeats's tone of sad distinction emerges clearly in the remarks he made in Chicago on 1 March 1914 at a banquet given for him by *Poetry* magazine. Pound had badgered Miss Monroe into awarding Yeats the $250 prize for the best poem published during the magazine's first year; Yeats had responded by keeping $50 for a bookplate and insisting that the rest go to a younger writer, who turned out to be Ezra Pound.[40] In his graceful speech Yeats showed how far he had assimilated Pound's ideas and critical language. After reading a poem by Mary Coleridge as an example of "poetry as simple as daily speech," he recalled his own earlier attempts to purge his language of rhetoric, and the more recent criticism and support given by Pound:

> We rebelled against rhetoric, and now there is a group of younger poets who dare to call us rhetorical. When I returned to London from Ireland, I had a young man go over all my work with me to eliminate the

142

abstract. This was an American poet, Ezra Pound. Much of his work is experimental; his work will come slowly, he will make many an experiment before he comes into his own. I should like to read to you two poems of permanent value, "The Ballad of the Goodly Fere" and "The Return." This last is, I think, the most beautiful poem that has been written in the free form, one of the few in which I find real organic rhythm. A great many poets use *vers libre* because they think it is easier to write than rhymed verse, but it is much more difficult.

The whole movement of poetry is toward pictures, sensuous images, away from rhetoric, from the abstract, toward humility. But I fear I am now becoming rhetorical. I have been driven into Irish public life—how can I avoid rhetoric?[41]

At the same time Yeats was giving this speech, Pound was writing the review of *Responsibilities* that appeared in the May 1914 issue of *Poetry* under the title "The Later Yeats" (*LE* 378–81). Like so many of his clipped, elliptical early reviews, "The Later Yeats" not only evaluates a body of poetry but tells the initiated reader how Pound arrived at that evaluation. When read against the complicated history of his relationship with Yeats as it developed from 1909 to 1914, "The Later Yeats" becomes a kind of artistic autobiography. It opens with the questions Pound himself was asking a year or so before: "Will Mr Yeats do anything more?" "Is Yeats in the movement?" "How *can* the chap go on writing this sort of thing?" The reply is unequivocal: Yeats's "vitality is quite unimpaired," he remains "the best poet in England," and although not of "the movement" he has paralleled it in the best of his later work. Pound declares that "Mr Yeats is so assuredly an immortal that there is no need for him to recast his style to suit our winds of doctrine," but that "there is nevertheless a manifestly new note in his later work."

In reply to the question "Is Mr Yeats an Imagiste?" Pound says "No, Mr Yeats is a symbolist, but he has written *des Images* as have many good poets before him." Here "symbolist" is not used pejoratively, as it is in most of Pound's criticism of the time, and one feels that it has a larger meaning apart from the specific literary tradition. It is not incompatible with Yeats's "prose directness" in his best poems, among them "No Second Troy," which Pound singles out once again as striking the "new note—you could hardly call it a change of style—[that] was apparent four years ago" in *The Green Helmet and Other Poems*, a volume which found Yeats at "such a cross roads as we find in *Voi che intendendo il*

143

terzo ciel movete." Pound is quoting the first line of Dante's Canzone 15 (in the Temple Classics edition), the poem that Dante used in the second book of the *Convivio* to mark his transition from praise of Beatrice to praise of Lady Philosophy. As in his earlier letter of June 1910, Pound seems to be tracking Yeats's career against Dante's.

Since *The Green Helmet* "one has felt his work becoming gaunter, seeking greater hardness of outline." Pound finds this "quality of hard light" most obvious in "The Magi," but it informs many other poems. The only sign that he may have attributed this "hardness" to his own influence lies in the comment on "To a Child Dancing in the Wind," where he directs the reader to the earlier version ("To a Child Dancing upon the Shore," *Poetry*, December 1912) that had undergone his "emendations and changes." Throughout the review he is at pains to be generous, and in commenting on the "passage of imagisme" that opens "The Magi" he makes a distinction that reflects not only on Yeats but on his own later work, especially the poems that end the two parts of *Hugh Selwyn Mauberley*, "Envoi" and "Medallion."

> There have always been two sorts of poetry which are, for me at least, the most "poetic"; they are firstly, the sort of poetry which seems to be music just forcing itself into articulate speech, and secondly, that sort of poetry which seems as if sculpture or painting were just forced or forcing itself into words. The gulf between evocation and description, in this latter case, is the unbridgeable difference between genius and talent. It is perhaps the highest function of art that it should fill the mind with a noble profusion of sounds and images, that it should furnish the life of the mind with such accompaniment and surrounding. At any rate Mr Yeats' work has done this in the past and still continues to do so. (*LE* 380)

In the end Pound's assessment of *Responsibilities* rises above the techniques of particular poems, and comes to rest on phrases like "noble profusion" and "life of the mind." This is why he could take no interest in "The Two Kings," which remained dead on the page even after heavy revision, and why he consistently praised "The Grey Rock" in spite of a syntax "obscurer than Browning's." [42] In "The Later Yeats" Pound admits that "The Grey Rock" is "obscure, but it outweighs this by a curious nobility, a nobility which is, to me at least, the very core of Mr Yeats' production, the constant element of his writing" (*LE* 379).

Looking back now from the perspective of seventy years, "The Grey Rock" seems to anticipate the methods of later modernism in its

144

interlacing, without specific commentary, of two narratives that the reader must compare and interpret. Used like the *Odyssey* in *Hugh Selwyn Mauberley* or *Ulysses*, the obscure tale from Irish legend illuminates Yeats's account of the Rhymers and their tragic fate; but Yeats leaves us to draw the moral. Significantly, Pound does not focus on this "superimposition" of one narrative on another; he is more interested in the idea of "nobility," a reminder that it is the general tone of *Responsibilities*, more than the techniques of individual poems, that gives the volume its central place in early literary modernism. It established a role for the poet and an attitude toward the social and literary values of the "middle class" that would dominate avant-garde writing for the next decade.

Rounding back to where we began, with the tribute in Canto 74 to lordly men who "are to earth o'ergiven," we realize that Pound—the most occasional of poets—is quite specific in his praise. "Fordie that wrote of giants" may well recall Ford Madox Hueffer's tireless efforts to preserve a tradition, but it is also (as Hugh Kenner has pointed out) a precise reference to Hueffer's story "Riesenberg," first published in the *English Review* for April 1911, a brilliant allegory foreshadowing the coming war which tells of a "forbidden valley" in Germany inhabited by two giants. And in "William who dreamed of nobility" Pound is equally exact, remembering Yeats's replies to George Moore and the aristocratic defiance of "The Grey Rock." *The Pisan Cantos* themselves are a dream of nobility lost, nobility wasted, and it seems only fitting that the broken poet at Pisa should have cast his mind back to those winters when he shared Yeats's heroic dream "at Stone Cottage in Sussex by the waste moor" (*C* 534).

Notes

1. "The Seafarer" was first published in the *New Age* 10 (30 Nov. 1911) as the opening section of "I Gather the Limbs of Osiris," a series of "expositions and translations in illustration of 'The New Method' in scholarship."

Quotations from the cantos are from *The Cantos of Ezra Pound* (New York: New Directions, 1970), hereafter cited as *C* followed by page number.

2. Richard Ellmann, *Eminent Domain: Yeats among Wilde, Joyce, Pound, Eliot, and Auden* (New York: Oxford University Press, 1967), pp. 57–87, and Terence Diggory, *Yeats and American Poetry: The Tradition of the Self* (Princeton: Princeton University Press, 1983), pp. 31–58. See also Thomas Parkinson,

"Yeats and Pound: The Illusion of Influence," *Comparative Literature* 6 (Summer 1954): 256–64; K. L. Goodwin, *The Influence of Ezra Pound* (London: Oxford University Press, 1966); and Thomas Rees, "Ezra Pound and the Modernization of W. B. Yeats," *Journal of Modern Literature* 4 (Feb. 1975): 574–92.

3. *Literary Essays of Ezra Pound*, ed. T. S. Eliot (New York: New Directions, 1968), p. 367; hereafter cited as *LE* followed by page number.

4. *Collected Early Poems of Ezra Pound*, ed. Michael John King (New York: New Directions, 1976), p. 8; hereafter cited as *CEP* followed by page number.

5. See *The Variorum Edition of the Poems of W. B. Yeats*, ed. Peter Allt and Russell K. Alspach (New York: Macmillan, 1957), p. 803.

6. *The Selected Letters of Ezra Pound, 1907–1941*, ed. D. D. Paige (New York: New Directions, 1971), p. 4; hereafter cited as *L* followed by page number.

7. Noel Stock, *The Life of Ezra Pound* (New York: Pantheon Books, 1970), pp. 58–59.

8 From Dorothy Shakespear's notebook, 16 Feb. 1909. See *Ezra Pound and Dorothy Shakespear: Their Letters, 1909–1914*, ed. Omar Pound and A. Walton Litz (New York: New Directions, 1984), p. 3; hereafter cited as *EP/DS* followed by page number.

9. *The Letters of W. B. Yeats*, ed. Allan Wade (London: Rupert Hart-Davis, 1954), p. 543. Reprinted with permission of Michael B. Yeats and Macmillan Publishing Company. Copyright 1953, 1954 by Anne Butler Yeats, renewed 1982 by Anne Butler Yeats.

10. Parkinson, "Yeats and Pound," p. 258.

11. *The Spirit of Romance* (New York: New Directions, 1968), p. 8; hereafter cited as *SR* followed by page number.

12. The preface is printed in Richard Ellmann, *The Identity of Yeats* (New York: Oxford University Press, 1964), pp. 86–88.

13. Yeats, *Variorum Edition*, pp. 256–57. "No Second Troy" and "All Things Can Tempt Me" are reprinted with permission of Michael B. Yeats and Macmillan Publishing Company from *The Poems*, by W. B. Yeats, edited by Richard J. Finneran. Copyright 1912 by Macmillan Publishing Co., Inc., renewed 1940 by Bertha Georgie Yeats.

14. Unpublished letter in a private collection.

15. Letter of 30 June 1910, in a private collection.

16. Parkinson, "Yeats and Pound," p. 257.

17. Diggory, *Yeats and American Poetry*, p. 42.

18. Pound to Dorothy Shakespear, 16 July 1911 (*EP/DS* 37–38).

19. Pound to Elkin Mathews, 30 May 1916, in *Pound/Joyce*, ed. Forrest Read (New York: New Directions, 1967), p. 285.

20. Written in December 1911, "Credo" was first published in the *Poetry Review* 1 (Feb. 1912) as part of "Prologomena [*sic*]."

21. *Ezra Pound: Selected Prose, 1909–1965*, ed. William Cookson (New York: New Directions, 1973), pp. 461–62.

22. Parkinson, "Yeats and Pound," p. 259.

23. Letter of 29 Aug. 1911, from D. D. Paige's typed copies of the Pound letters in the Pound Archive, Beinecke Rare Book and Manuscript Library, Yale University.

24. The five poems published in *Poetry* (Dec. 1912) were: "The Mountain Tomb," "To a Child Dancing upon the Shore" (later "To a Child Dancing in the Wind"), "Fallen Majesty," "Love and the Bird" (later "A Memory of Youth"), and "The Realists." The information and quotations in this and the following paragraph are drawn from the accounts in Ellmann, *Eminent Domain*, pp. 64–65, and Ellen Williams, *Harriet Monroe and the Poetry Renaissance* (Urbana: University of Illinois Press, 1977), pp. 62–63.

25. Quoted in A. Norman Jeffares, *W. B. Yeats: Man and Poet* (London: Routledge & Kegan Paul, 1949), p. 167.

26. Ellmann, *Eminent Domain*, p. 66.

27. Pound to Dorothy Shakespear, 28 Dec. 1912 (*EP/DS* 170).

28. The cancelled passage is quoted in A. Norman Jeffares, *A Commentary on the Collected Poems of W. B. Yeats* (Stanford: Stanford University Press, 1968), p. 194. Reprinted with permission of Michael B. Yeats and Macmillan Publishing Company from *The Poems*, by W. B. Yeats, edited by Richard J. Finneran. Copyright 1919 by Macmillan Publishing Co., Inc., renewed 1947 by Bertha Georgie Yeats.

29. Pound to Dorothy Shakespear, 21 Jan. 1913 (*EP/DS* 183).

30. Letter of 30 Jan. 1913 (*EP/DS* 186–87).

31. Letter of 23 Sept. 1912 (*EP/DS* 161).

32. "Status Rerum," *Poetry* 1 (Jan. 1913): 125.

33. Pound to Dorothy Shakespear, 21 Nov. 1913 (*EP/DS* 276).

34. Pound to Dorothy Shakespear, 16 Dec. 1913 (*EP/DS* 287).

35. *De Daemonialitate, et Incubis et Succubis*, by the seventeenth-century Franciscan theologian Lodovico Maria Sinistrari. The manuscript was discovered in 1872 and first published, with a French translation, in 1875. Pound owned the 1879 edition, which contained an English translation.

36. See Pound's reminiscences of life at Stone Cottage in Canto 83.

37. Pound to Dorothy Shakespear from "Stone Cold Cottage," 14 Jan. 1914 (*EP/DS* 302). The esoteric works mentioned are *Le Comte de Gabalis, ou entretiens sur les sciences secrètes*, by the Abbé de Montfaucon de Villars (1670), a work frequently augmented and reprinted in the seventeenth and eighteenth

centuries which provided Pope with some of his machinery for *The Rape of the Lock*; *Le Grimoire du Pape Honorius*, falsely attributed to Pope Honorius III, first published in 1629; and Joseph Ennemoser's *The History of Magic*, first translated from the German in 1854.

38. Pound to Dorothy Shakespear, 14 Jan. 1914 (*EP/DS* 302).

39. "'The Imagistes': A Talk with Mr. Ezra Pound, Their Editor," *Daily News and Leader*, 18 March 1914, p. 14.

40. For an account of the prize and the banquet, see Williams, *Harriet Monroe*, pp. 77–78 and 102–4.

41. *Poetry* 4 (April 1914): 27.

42. Pound to Dorothy Shakespear, 8 May 1913 (*EP/DS* 224).

Pound and Williams

Thomas Parkinson

Relations between poets are never simple, but the relations between Pound and Williams have a rich complexity that gives them symbolic importance in the history of American poetry. They were friends from their university days until the death of Williams. In the world of contemporary poetry they remain among the greatest resources available to the young writer; what they have given to the American tradition has not been exhausted and probably never will be. They were among our great liberators, and they are among the great contrasts in the American legacy, equivalent to Whitman and James in their achievements and in the charge that their testaments leave to their godchildren.

Pound once wrote to Williams that it was "possibly lamentable that the two halves of what might have made a fairly decent poet should be sequestered and divided by the . . . buttocks of the arse-wide Atlantic Ocean." [1] Pound is responding to the appearance of *Kora in Hell* in 1920 and to Williams's using their relationship in his "Prologue" as symbolic of problems in poetics for American writers. That is a good starting point for a consideration of the special nexus of poetic agreement and tension that distinguishes the art and affection of Dear Bill, Deer Bull, My dear William, My Dear Old Sawbukk von Grump and Dear Ezra, Dear Ez, Liebes Ezrachen, Dear Esq, Dear Editor, You poor dumb cluck, No Ezekiel, Dea Rez—those are some of the salutations used in their correspondence.

The salutations are playful, and even when the correspondence treats questions of treason and imprisonment, the tone is that of two

young men, in one of the above instances ("You poor dumb cluck") young men in their sixties. They were always amazingly youthful, and in reading their special conspiratorial works, I sometimes feel that they were in a deep sense emotionally arrested at the age of twenty, which in part accounts for the attraction they exert for the young even after their deaths, and for their willingness to pay so much time and attention to those young who came knocking at their doors.

Eventually, however, this impression dwindles and the abiding seriousness of their positions becomes clear. Their youthfulness is one of their limitations, but it is not crippling. The bouncy tone of puppy conduct and language dwindles when they approach the center of their agreements and dissensions, that is, the life of the imagination.

In spite of the steady creative tension that bound them together, their professional relations were happy and productive. Pound dedicated *Ripostes* (1912) "To William Carlos Williams" and a year later arranged with Elkin Mathews the publication of Williams's first mature book *The Tempers* and reviewed it with praise and prophecies of future distinguished work. When Pound conceived of the Bel Esprit project in 1921 to relieve Eliot of economic troubles, he thought of Williams as another poet to be liberated from irrelevant labors. Williams's A *Voyage to Pagany* (1928) was prefaced by the dedication "To the first of us all / my old friend / EZRA POUND / this book is affectionately dedicated." In spite of some breaks, an especially long one after the outbreak of World War II from 1939 to 1946, they were cheerful conspirators, acting as each other's agents, reviewing each other's work, praising one another's work to editors, critics, and other poets, and jointly promoting Major Douglas's theories of Social Credit.

They shared common ground, memories of youth, disenchantment with the dominant economic system of capitalism, the urge to invent and the sense of ordering art, and a continuous tradition that transcended mere convention because it was the fundamental life of the imagination. They were remarkably free with each other, engaging in the frankness of equals. There were occasional outbursts, especially when Williams wearied of Pound's more dogmatic instigations and replied brusquely and truculently. Their affectionate long association inevitably won out over such moments. For long periods of Williams's life, Pound was a life-line, and it was more than professional respect that led him to call Pound "the first of us all"; Ezrachen was "my old

friend," and whatever stresses that friendship underwent, it remained unbreakable.

Pound was emotionally tied to Williams, but for both of them their affections were qualified and enriched by their symbolic relationship as "two halves of what might have been a fairly decent poet." Pound cast Williams, very properly, in the role of the American friend who, unlike Eliot and H.D., remained tied to the American continent, thus evoking for Pound a sense of doubt and a figure complementary to himself. And Williams accepted the role. In fact he leaped to it. When *Al Que Quiere* was published in 1917, he turned his attention toward the improvisations that would ultimately form *Kora in Hell* (1920). Those poems were the occasion for bringing his entire relation to poetry into focus, and the ultimate prologue defined a distinctive poetics. In the prologue he uses Pound as the means to distinguish his work from that of the expatriates Pound and Eliot. Williams provoked Pound into writing him a letter that he quotes selectively, a very funny intimate letter that Williams edits so that Pound seems like a bumptious elitist. But Williams's main fire is reserved for Edgar Jepson, a tool of Pound's in his cheerful vendetta against Harriet Monroe. Williams simply borrowed a page from Pound's book on how to run literary conspiracies.

In fact, Williams added a paragraph to the effect that if one cannot find a fellow conspirator, it is proper to use an intimate personal letter by an adversary, written in the innocent belief that personal letters are not public material. In the correspondence that followed the publication of *Kora in Hell*, after citing the judgment of *Hugh Selwyn Mauberley* by an ungrateful protégé, Pound wrote, "I must cross the proper names out of this, as you're such a devil for printin' one's private affairs" (*L* 160). Obviously Pound thought Williams an admirable rogue, but he did take seriously the argument posed by *Kora in Hell* and its ancillary material.

The prologue to *Kora in Hell* is a complex document, but one important point is that it is the first public statement by Williams critical of Eliot and, by implication, of certain facets of Pound. Basically, the differences are established in the anecdote of their argument in their early days: "I contended for bread, he for caviar. I became hot. He, with fine discretion, exclaimed: 'Let us drop it. We will never agree, or come to an agreement.' He spoke then like a Frenchman, which is one who discerns."[2] This was the base for their continued mutual aid; the differ-

151

ences that appear when Williams treats Jepson's admiration for Eliot's "La Figlia che Piange" are differences of principle. When Pound uses Jepson as his "bolus" to purge Harriet Monroe, then Williams can say of him "E.P. is the best enemy United States verse has. He is interested, passionately interested—even if he doesn't know what he is talking about. But of course he does know what he is talking about. He does not, however, know everything, not by more than half."[3] The issue can be summarized very clearly and on one point, that of residence, which in turn means cultural identity:

> I praise those who have the wit and courage, and the conventionality, to go direct toward their vision of perfection in an objective world where the signposts are clearly marked, viz., to London. But confine them in hell for their paretic assumption that there is no alternative but their own groove.[4]

Kora in Hell was a programmatic work that asserted the supremacy of the innovative imagination over received associations, but the primary target was the conventional view of poetry in English, with its local habitation in London and its embodiment in the poetry of Eliot and the attitudes of H.D. and Pound. Williams was not one bit troubled by the fact that the improvisations of *Kora* had an earlier parallel in the *Illuminations* of Rimbaud and Baudelaire's *Le Spleen de Paris*; Williams accepted his affiliations with French culture, both its experimental literature and its inventive painting. What he could not endure was the conventionality and the remove from experience that he saw in Edgar Jepson's admiration for Eliot's "La Figlia che Piange," surely an odd choice for a poem that vindicated a specifically American poetic achievement.

The programmatic aspect of *Kora in Hell* was important but at the same time intentionally humorous. Williams made use of Pound wittily and amicably, and Pound reacted accordingly. When *Kora in Hell* was published in full in 1920, Pound wrote three friendly analytical letters to Williams. He knew that there was, as they say in the Mafia, nothing personal involved, just business. What annoyed him most, oddly, was Williams's sly statement that he was "the best enemy of American verse." His defense in his letter to Williams of 11 September 1920 shows the rightness of Williams's argument, affirming his enmity to the faults of American verse and confessing the inadequacy of Jepson's mind: "there was no one else whose time wasn't too valuable to waste on trying to

penetrate Harriet [Monroe]'s crust. That silly old she-ass with her paeons for bilge . . ." (L 157). Pound's irritation with her was endless and far too often justified, but more important than such political literary judgment was Pound's definition of his relation to America.

Pound's reactions to American poetry were not merely aesthetic but in the fullest sense cultural, and his reaction to Williams as a person differentiates him from Williams in a strange and troubling manner. It probably troubles people of this epoch more than it would the contemporaries of Pound and Williams, who were more naturally concerned with immigration and the question of national connection. Pound's argument seems to be that the longer one's family inhabits the American continent, the worse the virus that infests the blood. Hence, Williams, coming from stock only recently introduced to the continent, has a greater richness because a greater freedom from the plague that is Americanism.

> There is a blood poison in America; you can idealize the place (easier now that Europe is so damd shaky) all you like, but you haven't a drop of the cursed blood in you, and you don't need to fight the disease day and night; you never have had to. Eliot has it perhaps worse than I have—poor devil.
>
> You have the advantage of arriving in the milieu with a fresh flood of Europe in your veins, Spanish, French, English, Danish. You had not the thin milk of New York and New England from the pap; and you can therefore keep the environment outside you, and decently objective.
>
> With your slower mental processes, your later development, you are very likely, really of a younger generation; at least of a younger couche. . . .
>
> Different from my thin logical faculty. (L 158)

The metaphor shifts from blood poison to blood thinning—perhaps a kind of cultural leukemia?—that comes with several generations of residence in America. Williams as the son of immigrants had an ambiguous advantage. He was an American, newly arrived, mixed in blood. Pound manages to express an emotion new to me, that is, snobbish self-derision. He really does admire Williams, and he really believes that Williams's position is more advantageous than his own or Eliot's. His own mind moved too quickly: it had no checks to restrain it with hesitations, doubts, no natural density that derives from lingering over the strangeness of experience. Williams had opaqueness, the density that comes from original perception, while Pound's mind moved unchecked from abstraction to abstraction, logic aborting perception. It is common

153

wisdom that we tend to accuse others of the sins we find potential in ourselves and that they are the cause of the gravest guilt: here, in a rare self-critical moment, Pound reveals one reason for his hatred and distrust of abstraction: it was a tempting and inevitable personal vice.

Pound's responses to *Kora in Hell* and its prologue came at a time when he was in serious doubt. The magnificent collaboration of the arts that he had looked forward to in 1913, that miraculous year when all seemed possible, had been destroyed by the war, so that London no longer seemed habitable. Yeats admired *Mauberley*, but Pound was no longer satisfied with the praise of the greatest living poet; he wanted understanding responses from a respected contemporary, and he asked Williams for just that. Williams was a testing point, both in his work and as representative of the American culture that at once intrigued and appalled Pound. He thought vaguely of returning to the United States but ultimately chose Paris, where his presence would evoke more trouble in Williams's truculent urgencies. Williams became a focal point where Pound's interests and doubts could coalesce.

By 1921 Pound was in the process of abandoning London for Paris, and Williams, tired to death by his work as physician and as midwife to *Contact* and mortician for *Others*, yearned for some escape. His judgments and feelings focused on Pound. He urged him to come to America and lecture. Pound, with eminent practicality, asked what the economic benefits would be and, evidently, did not find them attractive. Williams wrote to Pound in an attempt, as he said, "to normalize myself by addressing you":

> It is growing bitter to think of you there far off where I cannot see you or talk to you. It would be as if— It would be the sun coming up to see you again. . . . I wish I were in Paris with you tonight. I am a damned fool who sees only the light through a knothole. I resist, it's about the most I can say for myself. Yet I remember moments of intense happiness—no it wasn't happiness.[5]

Williams's position seems a variation of Descartes's: I resist, therefore I am. His depression with the state of America grew deeper. Pound was committed to Europe. McAlmon emigrated into his dreadful marriage, and the practice of medicine became more demanding and irritating and preempted attention and energy that might better have gone into his quest for an indigenous American culture. Hence his ambivalence

toward his life increased, and when Pound spoke of Europe the invitation became ever more seductive. His inclination to travel depended upon the quality of life in America and the attractiveness of the exchange rate.

Williams was not alone in having troubles. Pound could resolve his doubts and escape his disappointment with the artistic life of England by yet another emigration. T. S. Eliot had no such escape, and the strains of his life led to a serious breakdown, which Pound diagnosed as the result of overwork. Pound responded by organizing support for artists, especially poets, with Eliot being the first beneficiary of that *Bel Esprit*. Williams was to act not only as a donor and possible organizer of an American system of donorship but as a potential candidate for at least enough support to grant him a summer of leisure in Paris. Pound had in mind a long-range conspiracy: "the struggle is to get the first man released" (*L* 173).

Williams was not impressed and responded with amiable irreverence: "Oh why don't you go get yourself crucified on the Montmartre and will the proceeds to art? I'll come to Paris and pass the hat among the crowd. What the hell do I care about Eliot?"[6] In the body of his next letter, Williams carried on his battle with Pound and asked whether he should trade his illusions for Pound's. Pound had taunted Williams with the offer of freedom as successor to Eliot:

> I wd. back you for the second, if you wished. But I don't really believe you want to leave the U.S. permanently. I think you are suffering from nerve; that you are really afraid to leave Rutherford. I think you ought to have a year off or a six months' vacation in Europe. I think you are afraid to take it, for fear of destroying some illusions which you think necessary to your illusions. I don't think you ought to leave permanently, your job gives you too real a contact, too valuable to give up. But you ought to see a human being now and then. (*L* 173)

This passage shows Pound's relationship with Williams in much of its complexity, for Pound is genuinely fond of Williams and at the same time enjoys pushing him toward a violent reaction. He can show an understanding of what Williams's medical practice meant to him, something more than a source of income, while renewing the conflict between them that Williams had already made public in the prologue in *Kora in Hell*. This paragraph affected Williams deeply, and after his ini-

tial annoyance, he wrote a postscript that committed him to a European venture, and, although it would not occur until over two years later, it might never have occurred without this challenge. He ultimately responded with a sense of liberation to Pound's letter with its statement that the aim of Bel Esprit was the "release of energy for invention and design." Pound's generous offer of housing for a summer was itself a release of energy.

The first extended postscript of five hundred words (the original letter was about half that length) was followed by another equally long, Pound's description of Bel Esprit evoked thought after thought. Williams was deeply grateful to Pound for recognizing that his medical practice had value for him. Pound had had the beneficent effect of leading him to a definition of his life and his future.

> My pace is a slow one but as I am gifted by nature with an inflexible stubbornness and an excessively adherent youthfulness I have not worried about that. If I am to succeed in any kind of valuable work I shall succeed in spite of advancing years.
>
> If I am defeated by sickness or accident I shall always know that I have kept company with my imagination through thick and thin.[7]

He could, now and thanks to Pound's suggestion, realize that he must, even so, go abroad, and soon.

> Now the time has come when I want to go abroad; I do not say that I feel starved for a trip or cramped in any way. I simply feel a strong desire to move in among a few others more or less like myself. I suppose it is really ridiculous to imagine they are any more in the sun than I am. They cannot be so, not today. But they are more used to it. I like good manners and good company. In fact—if life had been more amenable to reason and more luxurient [sic] where I have happened to be in the world reality might have found me—I would have enjoyed the happiest existence [sic] conceivable.[8]

Williams included with this letter twenty-five dollars as his first semiannual contribution to Bel Esprit. The contribution comes with a special irony, for Eliot with help from Pound had just completed *The Waste Land*, which Williams much later would describe as "the greatest catastrophe to our letters." Pound's project continued until early 1923 when Eliot declined to participate and took over the editorship of the *Criterion*. Williams, whether through self-interest or not, maintained his support of the project even after the publication of *The Waste Land*.

In December of 1922 Williams wrote a spirited defense of Pound after the *New York Tribune* published a particularly nasty editorial attacking Pound's project. Williams's answer was not published and it is just as well, for it was ill-tempered, impatient, and not very effective. The real impact of the project did not come in any direct effect on Eliot or Williams but because it awakened both a sense of community and affection among writers and, for Williams, acted as an opening to an expanded set of possibilities, beyond Rutherford. Pound was the seminal focus, not so much causing but revealing Williams's true feeling and motives. Williams, in time, would go to France, but it seems reasonably certain that without the instigations of Pound and without his affectionate generosity, that time might never have come.

In July of 1922 Williams had to give up the idea of a summer in Paris: "It's no use. Can't be done. One hundred and seven dollars to Paris. THIRD class plus the same for return trip. At least fifty dollars in the city—AT LEAST. And I'd only be there ten days."[9] He promised Pound that he would be there in 1923, but in July of 1923 he wrote from Rutherford that he would positively see Pound in Paris or Italy in the spring. And so, during his sabbatical year of release from the practice of medicine, he would.

Williams found himself in the awkward position of being published, largely through the agency of his expatriate friends McAlmon and Pound, in France, and France became increasingly his second homeland, much more than it ever was for Pound. *The Great American Novel* and *Spring and All* preceded Williams's stay in France, the first published under Pound's editorship as part of a series printed in Paris by William Bird, the second edited and published by Robert McAlmon and printed in Dijon. Two products came from the stay in France, showing the two sides of Williams, the first being the completion of his American recording *In the American Grain* and the second his first novel, *Voyage to Pagany*, very rightly dedicated to Ezra Pound when it appeared in 1928. I say rightly dedicated because without the urging of Pound and without the questioning stirred in Williams by that urging, he might never have made the move to Europe that provided the material and the impetus for the book.

It is paradoxical, however, that Pound's instigations of Williams to travel to Europe gave them very little time together. Pound could not see Williams at Rapallo and arrived in Paris a bare ten days before Wil-

157

liams's departure. Although Williams spent six months on the Continent, they saw little of each other, and on Williams's final day of 12 June 1924 he could call on Pound only in the very early morning; Pound was sleeping, and it was fifteen years before the two would meet again. Pound would shortly establish himself in Rapallo with his complicated domestic life and his dedication to the *Cantos*. Williams after his sabbatical year had a fresh body of experience to bring home with him, but home was Rutherford.[10]

Williams and Pound were then fixed in their geographically defined cultural positions. They continued their transatlantic collaboration, Williams dedicating a book to Pound in 1928 and writing laudatory reviews of the *Cantos* in 1931 and 1935. Pound edited twenty-one poems and eighteen prose pieces by Williams under the title "The Descent of Winter" to form the bulk of the Autumn 1928 issue of *Exile*, thus complementing Williams's dedication to Pound of *A Voyage to Pagany*. In the same year Pound wrote an appreciation of Williams for *The Dial*. In 1933 Pound included a generous selection from Williams's poetry in his *Active Anthology*.

Through the 1920s and well into the 1930s Pound and Williams were allies, but as Pound became more rigidly fascist in his attitudes, especially during the Spanish Civil War, Williams drew back from him, so that in 1939, when Pound came to the United States to avert any possible conflict between his native country and Italy, they had very little to say to one another. Their friendship would eventually survive their differences, but from 1939 to 1946 Williams lost patience with Pound.

The relations between Williams and Pound were tripartite: first, they were friends, loyal to their past associations; second, they were culturally divided and represented for each other opposing sets of possibility; and finally, they were politically united in their espousal of social credit and its attendant simplified labor theory of value and politically divided by Pound's admiration for Mussolini and Williams's hatred of authoritarian brutality. Even after the bombing of Guernica (and Williams, because of his family connections, identified his well-being with that of Republican Spain), he defended Pound, but his patience was running very thin, and he became more assertive about the rightness of his cultural commitment. In March of 1938 he affirmed the superiority of his life, as a full unit, to that of the merely literary:

What the hell have you done that I haven't done? I've stayed here, haven't I, and I've continued to exist. I haven't died and I haven't been licked. In spite of a touch schedule I've gone on keeping my mind on the job of doing the work there is to do without a day of missing my turn. Maybe I haven't piled up a bin of superior work but I've hit right into the center of the target first and last, piling up some work and keeping it right under their noses. I've interpreted what I could find out of the best about me, I've talked and hammered at individuals, I've read their stuff and passed judgment on it. I've met a hell of a lot more of all kinds of people than you'll even get your eyes on and I've known them inside and outside in ways you'll never know. I've fought it out on an obscure front but I haven't wasted any time.[11]

Such a letter practically sets aside friendship for a superior cultural reality, as if Williams's larger identity superseded the personal life. Increasingly Williams came to speak and think as a distinct being who represented a complex of realities that were antipathetic to those that Pound represented. He found it increasingly difficult to separate Pound as fascist from Pound the generous and inventive contributor to the modern arts. The disconnection between Pound's art and his politics sickened Williams, so that by the collapse of Republican Spain in 1939 Williams had effectively broken off his connections with Pound.

When Pound did come to the United States in 1939, he and Williams spent very little time together. Williams at first greeted him with a hearty hug after their fifteen years of separation, but he saw him only once again before his return to Italy. At that time he saw in Pound the lunatic of a set of fixed ideas, moving toward a kind of logical and abstract insanity, or so he wrote to James Laughlin:

The logicality of fascist rationalization is soon going to kill him. You can't argue away wanton slaughter of innocent women and children by the neoscholasticism of a controlled economy program. To hell with Hitler who lauds the work of his airmen in Spain and so to hell with Pound if he can't stand up and face his questioners on this point.[12]

The questioner, about Guernica, was Williams himself. A final wedge was being driven between Williams and the two always forgivable aspects of Pound, the old friend and the poet:

He's an old friend and an able poet, perhaps the best of us all, but his youthful faults are creeping up on him fast and—you can't avoid issues

159

forever by ignoring them or attempting to change the topic of conversation. Even the lion finally gets a horn through the guts.[13]

The wedge was politics, expressed in the greatest war of human history. It would be, except for a few brief exchanges, the cause of their separation from 1939 until Pound's incarceration at St. Elizabeths. Williams had no sympathy for Pound—old friendship and poetic achievement became irrelevant.

When the United States entered the war after the bombing of Pearl Harbor, Williams was to see his two sons inducted into the Navy and undergo the anxiety of their absence in the Pacific. He had his medical practice and he worked on his long poem. The relations between Pound and Williams took on symbolic weight, so that *Paterson* became an effective act of war. Of the larger works by Pound, Williams, and Eliot written during and immediately after the war, *Four Quartets* taken as a whole, and especially the last three quartets, affirms Eliot's ultimate identification with the culture of England; *The Pisan Cantos* define Pound as the last remnant of the broken anthill of Europe; *Paterson* embodies Williams's commitment to the culture of the American Locale.

> "Paterson," I know, is crying to be written; the time demands it; it has to do just with all the peace movements, the plans for international infiltration into the dry mass of those principles of knowledge and culture which the universities and their cripples have cloistered and made a cult. It is the debasing, the keg-cracking assault upon the cults and the kind of thought that destroyed Pound and made what it has made of Eliot. To let it into "the city," culture, the benefits of culture, into the mass as an "act," as a thing. "Paterson" is coming along—this book is a personal finger-practicing to assist me in that: but that isn't all it is.[14]

The book in question was ultimately published not by Laughlin but by Cummington Press as *The Wedge*.

Williams saw two wars before him, the terrible political war and, obliquely related to it, the second and long-term cultural war that came between him and Pound, the war between received convention and innovative tradition, between the socially acceptable and the imaginative. Even personal affection dwindled in importance, not because of the social embarrassment caused Williams by Pound's broadcasts from Rome and the subsequent visits from the F.B.I. questioning Williams about his political views and his relation to the Second World War after Pound

mentioned Williams by name during one broadcast—the annoyance was real, and three visits from the F.B.I. would unsettle even a patriotic doctor with two sons in the service. But when Pound was returned to the United States for trial and incarcerated at St. Elizabeths, Williams had simply let friendship go, and the cultural war continued, trailing with it elements from the political war. His indifference to Pound is clear in the letter he wrote on 1 February 1946 to Dorothy Pound:

> Dear Dorothy:
> Your letter of December 10th received, there is nothing I can do for Ezra who, as you may know, is now confined at St. Elizabeth's Hospital, Washington, D.C. as insane. Laughlin, who spent a day with him there recently seems to feel that this represents the true situation.
> I have no desire to write to Ezra. I don't think he'd want to hear from me in the first place and in the second I don't think anything I could say would do him any good. Laughlin is trying to get some money together, I understand, for medical care to be administered to Ezra in the hospital. That's all I know.
> If Ezra wants me to do anything for him as an old friend and you communicate his wishes to me yourself, I'll write and even go to Washington to see the man, not until then.
>
> Sincerely
Bill[15]

The coolness of the letter becomes even more evident when one realizes that Pound had been in St. Elizabeths for over a month, that Laughlin had been kept in touch with events through the lawyer that he had procured for Pound, and that in spite of his knowledge of Pound's situation, Williams had remained silent. When the correspondence resumed, the tone and subject matter briefly returned to the old question of their separation, Williams wishing that Pound could have been with him in the United States while recognizing his necessity, however tragic the outcome, for following another course. At first it seemed that they would work back toward their old relationship, but some new stubborn independence in Williams, some truculence, made him unwilling to gloss over their troubles. Even the recognition of Pound's terrible problems at St. Elizabeths and the mollifying influence of his wife did not keep him from brusqueness and self-assertion. Rather than seeing Pound as a comrade he saw him as an opponent. What seemed to irritate him most was Pound's constant curiosity about what he was reading. This

reaction came not from any sense that he was simply not reading enough but that much more important was the quality of perception. On 8 July 1946 he wrote Pound two letters, the first vetoed by his wife and genuinely rude, moving toward the break that would eventually occur in the correspondence later that year. He included that letter along with one written the same day and more carefully phrased: "Flossie vetoed the enclosed letter—but I send it anyway but in a different mood from that in which it was written—for your amusement." [16]

Pound could hardly have been amused that his oldest friend should tell him that he really was "cracked," that he was sick of him, that he could not learn anything or even ask an intelligent question, that he was a bully who constantly imposed his ideas on others without any concern for their needs or interests. Flossie's veto forced Williams to phrase his concerns more gently and more positively. When he did so, he was still defining the difference between the cultures that he and Pound embodied.

Before satisfying Pound's curiosity about his reading, he cited a sentence from John Dewey's "Democracy and America": "Vital and thorough attachments are bred only in an intimacy of intercourse which is of necessity restricted in range." [17] The sentence meant a great deal to Williams, and my construction of it is that he took it to mean that the fullest direct perceptions and hence meanings came from the immediate and local, not the abstract. It was not reading that mattered to Williams, though he dutifully went on to indicate his reading at the time. He read and translated Eluard, kept up with the surrealists who edited *View*, read the avant-garde works of Anaïs Nin and Henry Miller and Parker Tyler, and, occasionally, he read one of the plays of Shakespeare.

> So, naturally, you conclude "Poor Bill he ain't interested in ideas." 'S all right with me. But it does seem a waste of time to argue with you bastards. Yet, I must be patient—and work. Work! produce. Better stuff. If only I could do it faster. Too many things block me—you are one of them. If only your intelligence was what it was when you were younger! You were, at heart, more generous then. More alert to others. [18]

To those of us who know what Pound's general condition was at the time, this passage may seem heartless, and in extenuation it must be said that Williams had not been in Pound's presence, and, contrary to

his own principles, was acting on merely verbal knowledge. He simply could not get out of the habit of treating Pound as a healthy equal.

> And if I grow angry with you it is just that I do not have your help in my work, you a man with what used to be extraordinary perceptions. Now all you do is ask me, "What are you reading?" What kind of an intellect does that present to me? But, as I say, I must be patient.[19]

His patience was tried even more in succeeding months by Pound's insistence that Williams, along with his entire culture, was living in a twenty-five year time lag. For Williams, Pound simply demanded too much from friendship: "I am half ashamed when I abuse you, knowing your unquestioned abilities, your genius even. But you assume too much. How will you ever be enlightened unless you give the other fellow at least the chance to prove that he is a man also?"[20] Finally, on 17 November, Williams simply closed the correspondence, and they did not communicate for about six months.

After that point, they kept their friendship alive in the face of heart attacks, operations, madness, and public neglect and abuse. Williams resigned himself to Pound's reading lists, followed some of his suggestions, and even incorporated a section of a letter from Pound in book 3 of *Paterson*, a section denying that he had told Williams to read Artaud, and urging that he read the Loeb versions of the Greek tragedies as well as Frobenius, Gesell, Brooks Adams, and the Golding Ovid: "& nif you want a readin' / list ask papa. . . ."

Williams was very busy with the completion of *Paterson* and the increasing demands on his time from universities and writers' conferences, and he was working against time to bring his work to a satisfying form. But to bring his life into focus meant placing in perspective his relations with Pound. *The Autobiography* and the *Selected Essays* gave a perspective on the past, but for the remainder of this essay I will consider what Williams saw in the *Cantos* in the crucial period from 1947 to 1950. Williams wrote the following essay for Dallam Simpson's *Four Pages*, but it was never published in that very little magazine from Galveston, Texas.

> E. P.'s Cantos:
> One thing you must say of E.P., he convinces us of the presence of history. Or convinces us, at once and over all as we read him, uniquely—

163

as no one else writing today, prose or verse, has done—that we are in the presence of history. That we stand continually in the presence of history.

His verses are expert, made up of devices of many sorts to convince us of the simultaneity of the historical present. That 6 billion or 60 billion men and women of all qualities, colors and attainments have preceded us but that through all there struck the same light—or darkness. Many were simple, elemental if you like, but exquisitely accurate and just in their perceptions and performances. But some befouled their senses, the common liars—then as today: liars, as carrion is a lie to flesh, smelling of rot. No one willingly smells rot but the just man—and is moved thereby to action by it, toward the living. E.P. insists that we whiff of it—to find many "great".

He discloses history by its odor, by the feel of it—in the words; fuses it with the words, present and past in whatever "language" (all one) to MAKE his Cantos. *Make* them. Why shall we insist that he be "right"? He is not right, he *is*. First of all he is; second, he is eyes, nose, mouth, touch and a perfume—of history: smitten by a stench of liars.

E.P. at his best seems to realize whole areas of the art which no one else more than touches. He has come to represent for me a preeminence of the work of art itself, over against philosophy book or a steel mill or a political pie, which has not been conceived of in the world for many centuries. His grasp (weak as he may be) is for the world, a world of thought and feeling—and action. There is a magnificent unity or attempt at unity, a seeking to pull the world together into something distinguished and true in his great poem. Something just and worth having.

The breadth of Pound's grasp is not sufficiently realized by those who would evaluate him—how he makes you feel the details as part of a whole. The details as he uses them all contribute toward a whole—even prosaic or fragmentary catalogues, just men's names perhaps but heavily weighted with feeling, seem to gather the strength together to *make* the poem. Somehow there is a magic in them. They do NOT fall into grit and rubble but seem to hang together to make a world, an actual world—not "of the imagination" but a world imagined, which is another thing.

It is sad to think of a man so gifted falling into such bad ways. But whatever his condition may be he is yet something for us to treasure in our day as among our greatest possessions.[21]

This essay represents a simple clear act of generosity and affection by Williams, but it is plainly deeply considered. The key point of praise is that the *Cantos* hang together "to make a world, an actual world—not 'of the imagination' but a world imagined, which is another thing."

Praise of that sort at that time meant the world to Pound, and Williams sent him a copy of it.

Pound also saw and appreciated "The Fistula of the Law," Williams's review of *The Pisan Cantos*, written at the request of Thomas Coles for his little magazine *Imagi*. This review is not completely enthusiastic in its praise and seems more ambiguous, but there is no question about its commitment to Pound's work. What he stresses is "a sense of reality in the words." There is "trash" in *The Pisan Cantos*, but that trash is not in the ideas but in "incommunicable personal recollections—names, words without color." The failure is technical but is more than compensated for by "a new hygiene of the words, cleanliness." In the review Williams affirms his affiliation with Pound on the question of usury. When one tries to condense the common set of ideas that unite, for all their differences, Pound and Williams, it might be simplest and clearest to say, "Art is the basis of reality, not the expression of it," and "In the exact dance of language that is true poetry, the basis of truth is most authentically sounded." Or, in the words of Williams's review, *The Pisan Cantos* derive their truth from being written in "the most authentically sounding language . . . of our present day speech."[22]

Williams would make one more attempt to come to terms with *The Pisan Cantos*, in January 1950. These notes were intended for his own use, and they were not published until ten years after his death. Essentially, they affirm the integrity of the language of the *Cantos* that renders clear the greatness of Pound:

> The greatness of Ezra Pound lies not, as he grows older, in his esteemed "romantic passages," but in the common text of his *Cantos*—the excellence of the fabric, the language of woof and warp, all through. It is the fineness, the subtlety, the warmth and strength of the *material* that gives the distinction. . . .
>
> It is the time, the way the words are joined in the common line, common in the sense that the tissues of music are joined or, as one might speak of the book of common prayer, the general text.[23]

There was no separation between the line, the idea, and the man. The language that Pound developed could change the world, but the world would not accept the language for fear of the change:

> Pound was born with a superb ear. He also had a brain. It is the conjunction of these two which is important. In youth the art dominated, as

165

he has grown older the intelligence (no matter how faultily coordinated) is primary. He has struck not at the branch but at the root. It is the structure, the time structure, of the poem that has been his major field. In the *Pisan Cantos* this time structure is the basic importance.[24]

Williams concedes, as he must with his impatience with anti-Semitism and fascism, the faulty coordination of the ideas in Pound, but he remains the literary comrade and personal friend. In basic ways he could conjoin his sense of the dance of language with Pound's, and though they remained always, as Pound early described them, incomplete in opposed ways, Williams could never deny Pound. He could not forgive what Pound had done but he forgave what Pound was.

Williams beyond this point made no further effort to come to terms with Pound, for in the most important sense, that of basic affection, the terms were fixed. They leave us, their godchildren, the special double legacy of the local American and the cosmopolitan American, a reminder of the great hope that we may yet some day in this troubled country develop a culture that is at once local in its origins and international in its resonance and validity. Pound and Williams shared a belief in the power of the poem that Williams in his last extended meditation on Pound's work expressed:

> The poem should be read. It isn't even necessary to understand every nuance; no one can do that. Read! Read the best and the thing will come out in a cleaner, more timely, more economically adjusted business world and in better statesmen.[25]

In that faith, Williams and Pound lived and died. We have their works, and we have their quarrels and their affections. They have enriched the national life.

Notes

1. *The Selected Letters of Ezra Pound, 1907–41*, ed. D. D. Paige (New York: New Directions, 1971), p. 160; hereafter cited as *L*, followed by page number.

2. William Carlos Williams, *Imaginations*, ed. Webster Schott (New York: New Directions, 1970), p. 26.

3. Ibid., pp. 26–27.

4. Ibid., p. 27.

166

5. Letter of 4 January 1921, quoted with permission of Manuscripts Department, Lilly Library, Indiana University, Bloomington, Indiana. Previously unpublished material by William Carlos Williams copyright © 1984 by William E. Williams and Paul H. Williams. Published by permission of New Directions, agents of the estate of William Eric Williams and Paul Williams. Hereafter cited as Lilly.

6. Lilly, letter of 29 March 1922.

7. Ibid.

8. Ibid.

9. Lilly, letter of 13 July 1922.

10. Lilly, letter of 29 March 1922.

11. Paul Mariani, *William Carlos Williams: A New World Naked* (New York: McGraw-Hill Book Co., 1982), pp. 413–14.

12. Ibid., p. 428.

13. Ibid.

14. *The Selected Letters of William Carlos Williams*, John C. Thirlwall (New York: McDowell, Obolensky, 1951), p. 214.

15. Lilly.

16. Lilly, letter of 8 July 1946.

17. Ibid.

18. Ibid.

19. Ibid.

20. Ibid.

21. Lilly, appended to letter to Pound of 21 February 1949.

22. William Carlos Williams, "The Fistula of the Law," *Imagi* 4 (Spring 1949): 10–11.

23. William Carlos Williams, "The Later Pound," ed. Paul Mariani, in *Massachusetts Review* 14 (Winter 1973): 124.

24. Ibid., pp. 128–29.

25. Ibid., p. 129.

Pound and Eliot

Robert Langbaum

Pound and Eliot. One of the great friendships and collaborations of Anglo-American literary history. We are tempted to find an analogy in the famous friendship and collaboration of Wordsworth and Coleridge.

But there are important differences. First of all, no two friends can have been more opposite in personality than Pound and Eliot. Pound was the more "American" of the two—the more democratic, individualistic, spontaneous, sincere, a radical at heart. Even as a famous old man Pound remained a bohemian, dressed as he had been all his life in odd and striking ways. Hugh Kenner describes him as adorned in 1912 with earring, red beard, and a green velvet jacket. Eliot was at heart conservative, armored with Boston and English reserve. With his addiction to conservative English tailoring, Tom Eliot projected even as a young man the image of a stuffed shirt whom the upper class but bohemian Bloomsbury group found faintly comic. "Come to lunch," Virginia Woolf wrote to Clive Bell in the early 1920s, "Tom is coming . . . with a four piece suit."[1] Eliot's sly form of rebellion was to look like a banker rather than a poet.

In philosophical orientation, Pound and Eliot came to occupy opposite poles, whereas Wordsworth and Coleridge came to argue over matters of degree in what was essentially the same Burkean position. Pound remained all his life vociferously and belligerently anti-Christian and pagan. His later anti-Semitism derived partly from his hatred of the Hebraic element in Christianity and partly from his hatred of banking.

168

Eliot, instead, was religious by nature and began, soon after the publication of *The Waste Land* (1922), the movement toward Anglo-Catholicism which culminated in his conversion and adoption of British citizenship in 1927.

The transitional poem is *The Hollow Men* (1925) with its echoing of church liturgy. After that all Eliot's major poems and plays are overtly Christian. Only once does Pound in a *published* source mention a non-dramatic poem of Eliot's after *The Waste Land* (my observation is confirmed by Donald Gallup's 1983 Pound bibliography). The exception is Pound's little-known response, published anonymously in *Edge* (May 1957), to Eliot's little-known *The Cultivation of Christmas Trees* (1954). "Let us lament," Pound concludes, "the psychosis / Of all those who abandon the Muses for Moses." Pound, does, however, comment in his letters on Eliot's later poems. For example, in a still unpublished letter of 17 December 1934, he writes: "the Possum what onct used to rite a POEN now and then / when I wuz near enough to annoy him / and he not thinking he was a bishop and rife fer ecclesiastikle preferment."[2] In a since published letter from Rapallo dated 30 January 1935, he makes a similar attack on Eliot's Anglo-Catholicism: "A couple of bawdy songs from father Eliot wdn't go bad with the electorate. I see he has written a play." Of the play he wrote from Rapallo a year later: "Waal, I heerd the *Murder in the Cafedrawl* on the radio lass' night. . . . Mzzr Shakzpeer *still* retains his posishun. I stuck it fer a while, wot whiff the weepin and wailin."[3] Pound objected not only to the Christian content but also to the liturgical style that went with it. The only play of Eliot's he admired was the unfinished *Sweeney Agonistes* (1926–27), especially the part called "Fragment of an Agon," where the style is disconnected, ironic, and modern in idiom with jazz as the musical model.

On the other side, Eliot, while still a student at Harvard, was not impressed by Pound's early poems, which he considered "old-fashioned romantic" and "touchingly incompetent."[4] Eliot changed his mind in 1914 when, as a shy novice, he looked up Pound in London and was so overwhelmed by Pound's enthusiastic recognition of the modernity of "Prufrock" and so impressed by Pound's technical mastery, that he cast himself in the role of disciple though only three years younger than Pound.

No poet can ever have done more for another than Pound did for

Eliot in those early years. As London correspondent for the Chicago magazine *Poetry,* he spent six months bludgeoning its editor Harriet Monroe into publishing "Prufrock." Pound arranged the poems for Eliot's first volume, *Prufrock and Other Observations* (1917), and without Eliot's knowledge personally borrowed the money to pay for printing the volume. But the price Eliot paid was discipleship. This explains Eliot's almost total acquiescence in Pound's revisions of *The Waste Land* manuscript, revisions which are the most spectacular example of Pound's influence on Eliot's career. In two of the 1922 letters exchanged on the revisions (Pound had by then moved to Paris), Eliot addresses Pound as "Cher maître," while Pound replies, "Filio dilecto mihi" (*L* 170–71). This was of course a joke, but a significant one. Their whole relation was carried on humorously, which is how Eliot came by Pound's fond nickname for him, Possum.

Eliot later recalled that Pound "was so passionately concerned about the works of art which he expected his protegés to produce that he sometimes tended to regard them almost impersonally, as art or literature machines to be carefully tended and oiled for the sake of their potential output."[5] Eliot's biographer Lyndall Gordon writes that

> One observer said [Pound] treated Eliot as a kind of collector's piece. With his prize beneath his eye, he would recline in an American posture of aggressive ease, and squint sideways up at the visitor, over the rims of his pince-nez, to see how impressed he was with Eliot's apt answers.[6]

It does not detract from Pound's unprecedented generosity in acting as unpaid literary agent for Eliot, Joyce, Hemingway, and other young writers to detect in Pound the impresario's desire (he displayed the American talent for publicity) to run the avant-garde literary world, which he did for a time to the benefit of us all. It was when he later desired to run the political and economic world as well that he ran into trouble. Pound's biographer Noel Stock tells us that in 1922 Pound, working from astrological data, "decided that the Christian Era had ended at midnight on 29–30 October 1921: the world was now living in the first year of a new pagan age called the Pound Era."[7] There is doubtless an element of humor in this, but the humor does not negate the element of prophecy as confirmed by the title of Hugh Kenner's excellent book, *The Pound Era.*

*   *   *

On 12 November 1917 Knopf issued, in connection with the American edition of Pound's *Lustra*, a small anonymous pamphlet called "Ezra Pound: His Metric and Poetry." The pamphlet was written by T. S. Eliot and is disciple's work. Pound arranged for Eliot to write it, edited the text by making three small deletions, and gave the pamphlet its title. Eliot defends Pound's poetry against the attacks that had been made on it. In answer to the reviewer who wrote that Pound "baffles us by archaic words and unfamiliar metres . . . breaking out into any sort of expression which suits itself to his mood," Eliot replies: "It is, in fact, just this adaptability of metre to mood, an adaptability due to an intensive study of metre, that constitutes an important element in Pound's technique." Against the charge of excessive erudition, Eliot replies equivocally: "to display knowledge is not the same thing as to expect it on the part of the reader; and of this sort of pedantry Pound is quite free." And against the charge that Pound's example has fathered a lot of sloppy free verse, Eliot replies soundly: "Pound's vers libre is such as is only possible for a poet who has worked tirelessly with rigid forms and different systems of metrics. . . . Pound was the first writer in English to use five Provençal forms." [8]

After the publication of *The Waste Land* in 1922, Eliot began breaking the bonds of discipleship. He began mixing praise of Pound with a certain amount of critical reservation. In reviewing *Personae*, Pound's collected shorter poems, in *The Dial* of January 1928, Eliot praises Pound as the greatest living "master of verse form." But the review ends with "the question (which the unfinished Cantos make more pointed) what does Mr. Pound believe?" [9] This question became the subject of lifelong contention between the two poets, a contention ranging from friendly to hostile: it is not always easy to determine the proportions of the mixture. The very praise—the greatest living "master of verse form"—implies a reservation that Eliot more or less maintains. Pound is the greatest living *craftsman*, but pointedly not the greatest living *poet* because of Eliot's doubts about Pound's content. The dedication of *The Waste Land* to Pound as "il miglior fabbro" ("the best craftsman") may contain the same reservation. [10]

For all its air of praise, Eliot's review of *Personae* is partly an attack on Pound's content. Eliot begins by saying that Pound has had "an immense influence, but no disciples," for "influence can be exerted through form, whereas one makes disciples only among those who sym-

171

pathize with the content." He describes Pound's influence on his own verse, but then confesses, "I am seldom interested in what he is saying, but only in the way he says it." "In form," Pound "is still in advance of our own generation and even the literary generation after us; whereas his ideas are often those of the generation which preceded him." His ideas are compounded of "the Nineties," "some medieval mysticism, without belief," and "Mr. Yeats's spooks." Having said that in the *Cantos*, "Pound's auditory sense is perhaps superior to his visual sense," Eliot realizes that he has made Pound sound like Swinburne, so he hastily differentiates them: "Swinburne's form is uninteresting, because he is literally saying next to nothing, and unless you mean something with your words they will do nothing for you." [11] Pound, he continues lamely, intends a meaning even if the meaning is unclear or uninteresting to the reader. Eliot, nevertheless, may have had Pound in mind when he wrote in his subtle 1920 essay "Swinburne as Poet," "The bad poet dwells partly in a world of objects and partly in a world of words, and he never can get them to fit. Only a man of genius could dwell so exclusively and consistently among words as Swinburne." [12] In my opinion Pound's ear is so much finer than Swinburne's that as a poet of sound he can be compared only with the Milton he so much berates.

In his review of *Personae* and elsewhere, Eliot raises what remains the crucial issue in evaluating Pound—the question of content. In his 1919 review of Pound's volume *Quia Pauper Amavi* and more elaborately in the Introduction to his 1928 selection of Pound's poems, Eliot suggests that in his shorter poems Pound has little of his own to say, since his best poems are translations or adaptations from Provençal troubadours, classic Chinese poets, and the Latin poet Sextus Propertius. The poems on contemporary life, in which Pound broaches his own ideas, are less successful. "Pound," writes Eliot in his Introduction, "is much more modern, in my opinion, when he deals with Italy and Provence, than when he deals with modern life." "If one can really penetrate the life of another age, one is penetrating the life of one's own." [13] Eliot is applying the paradoxes he worked out in "Tradition and the Individual Talent" (1919), an essay for which he must have had in mind so backward-looking and erudite a poet as Pound, who nevertheless organized the modernist movement in Anglo-American poetry.

Eliot, in his Introduction, finds in Pound a dissociation between his "personal feeling" (which includes his ideas) and his technique:

"there is the aspect of deeper personal feeling, which is not invariably, so far, found in the poems of most important technical accomplishment. . . . it is not until we reach *Mauberley* (much the finest poem, I believe, before the *Cantos*) that some definite fusion takes place."[14]

Most readers will agree that in *Mauberley* Pound's ideas are as interesting as his technique. But the fusion Eliot was hoping for has proved disappointing in the *Cantos*. If Pound had little of his own to express in the shorter poems, the ideas he advances in the *Cantos* are often an embarrassment that spoils the poetry; while the poetry itself, where it is good, is better than anything he had written earlier. But the poetry is good as fragments not as a whole. For writing a long poem, Pound shows himself deficient in organizing ability.

In 1918 Pound adopted the Social Credit theory of Major C. H. Douglas. This is a monetary theory which takes a medieval view of banking and interest. Pound uses the word *usura* for excessive interest not tied to production, and in the medieval manner uses the word as a talisman of all evil. Pound took Social Credit in a direction of his own when he combined it with fascism; Douglas was antifascist. Pound latched on to Douglas's theory with an eagerness that suggests his need to find something to *say*. Social Credit and Confucianism, with Confucianism's western counterpart the Enlightenment, were to constitute a "system" analogous to Yeats's A *Vision* and Dante's Aquinian theology, a system which hopefully would give form and meaning to the *Cantos*. "As to the *form* of The *Cantos*," Pound replied to an inquirer as late as February 1939, "All I can say or pray is: *wait* till it's there. I mean wait till I get 'em written and then if it don't show, I will start exegesis." He did not, like Dante, he added, have an "Aquinas-map" to guide him: "Aquinas *not* valid now."[15]

According to Hugh Kenner, "it was in the first glare of the Douglas revelation that Pound wrote *Mauberley*" (1920), which bids farewell to his aesthetical retreat from society because Pound now had a key by which to make society conform to the artist's imagination. The *Cantos* were now reconceived as "nothing less than a vast historical demonstration, enlightened by Douglas's insight."[16] Pound shows good periods in history when culture flourished, presumably because money represented productivity, and periods which were bad, presumably because money merely chased after money. But the monetary explanation is not always evident, as for example in the first Confucius canto (13).

In the Rapallo letter of 11 April 1927, Pound outlines for his father the "main scheme" of his "rather obscure," fragmented poem:

A.	A.	Live man goes down into world of Dead
C.	B.	The "repeat in history"
B.	C.	The "magic moment" or moment of metamorphosis, bust thru from quotidien into "divine or permanent world." Gods, etc. (*L* 210)

We can easily recognize these motifs in the *Cantos* without understanding how they cohere. Pound tells his father they are arranged contrapuntally as in a fugue (hence the double set of letters). This is more confusing than clarifying, as is Pound's attempt in the rest of the letter to show connections among details in the *Cantos*.

Even the famous Canto 45 on *usura* is no exception to what I have been saying about the lack of fusion between the poetry and the ideas, especially the ideas about money. We are so overwhelmed by the biblical cadences and rhetoric (the repetitions and parallel constructions) as to forget that the content will not bear investigation:

> WITH USURA
> wool comes not to market
> sheep bringeth no gain with usura.

Yet modern banking coincides with unprecedented European prosperity. We are inclined to agree with Pound that at least in modern times the arts and sexuality have suffered:

> Usura rusteth the chisel
> It rusteth the craft and the craftsman
>
> . . . .
> Usura slayeth the child in the womb
> It stayeth the young man's courting
> It hath brought palsey to bed, lyeth
> between the young bride and her bridegroom
> CONTRA NATURAM. [17]

Yet population increased enormously during the nineteenth century, and while the handicrafts declined, literature, music, painting, philosophy and science flourished. Ruskin railed against much the same social symptoms, but attributed them to an unprecedented complex of causes brought on by the Industrial Revolution and not to a single cause recur-

174

ring throughout the past. Ruskin and Pound, like all romantic thinkers, like Eliot, too, in his social thought, longed nostalgically for the organic society of the past.

Pound does better with the journey-to-the-dead motif in the superb Canto 1, where he returns to translating and deals with myth rather than ideas. Pound translates Andreas Divus's sixteenth-century Latin translation of Homer's chapter on Ulysses' journey to Hades. By translating a Renaissance Latin translation of an ancient Greek poem into a modern English that recalls Anglo-Saxon verse ("Men many, mauled with bronze lance heads, / Battle spoil, bearing yet dreory arms" (C 4]), by layering the language, Pound shows how myth endures through changes of language and how the memory of myth and the memory in language of its own changes sustain cultural continuity.

In accordance with his antinarrative "ideogrammic" method, Pound fragments the narrative in order to lyricize it, to give it lyric intensity. "The *Divina Commedia* must not be considered as an epic," he wrote in 1910. "It is in a sense lyric, the tremendous lyric of the subjective Dante." [18] In Canto 1 Pound translates the beginning of Homer's book 4, yet the first line indicates that, as in a fragment, something has preceded: "And then went down to the ship" (C 3); similarly in the last line the canto breaks off abruptly, suggesting something to follow, "So that:" (C 5). A few lines earlier the *Odyssey* itself breaks off, as Pound switches without explanation to a Homeric Hymn in praise of golden Aphrodite. The movement from underworld to golden Aphrodite may be a ritualistic movement, as described by Frazer in *The Golden Bough* (the last line names "the golden bough of Argicida")—a movement from death to renewed sexuality and fertility. [19]

The journey-to-the-dead motif is taken up again in the "hell cantos" (14, 15), which Pound in a letter of 1932 describes as "specifically LONDON, the state of English mind in 1919 and 1920" (L 239). In contrast to Canto 1, these cantos are ideological and full of abstract hatred. Although the first line sets the cantos in Dante's Inferno, the sinners wallow in a swamp of excrement ("Profiteers drinking blood sweetened with sh-t" [C 61]) for which there is only slight precedent in Dante's end of Canto XVIII and last line of Canto XXI. Like Dante, Pound puts whole classes of people into hell. The difference is that Dante's are moral classes as determined by the Church, while Pound's classes are determined by eccentricities like Social Credit theory and his

175

own notions. There can be no consensus that such occupational groups as "financiers" and "the press gang" belong in hell, or that the politicians identifiable as Lloyd George and Woodrow Wilson (C 61) belong there. The hell cantos are powerful in that they horrify us, but we are less horrified by the sinners than by the unbridled violence of Pound's bias and hatred. "An intellectual hatred is the worst," as Yeats wrote.

So little did Eliot, after his conversion, approve of Pound's ideas that he placed his good friend among the modern heretical writers—Lawrence, Yeats, Hardy—whom he attacks in *After Strange Gods* (1934), not for their literary quality but for their content. Pound's Confucianism, says Eliot, is typical of "the rebellious Protestant." Pound finds Guido Cavalcanti "much more sympathetic than Dante," because "Guido was very likely a heretic." "With the disappearance of the idea of Original Sin . . . of intense moral struggle, the human beings presented to us both in poetry and in prose fiction today . . . become less and less real." Thus the sinners "Mr. Pound puts in Hell" are unreal. One finds "politicians, profiteers, financiers, newspaper proprietors and their hired men, . . . those who do not believe in Social Credit, . . . and all 'those who have set money-lust before the pleasures of the senses.'" It is a hell, to quote Pound, "'without dignity, without tragedy,' . . . I find," Eliot continues,

> one considerable objection to a Hell of this sort: that a Hell altogether without dignity implies a Heaven without dignity also. If you do not distinguish between individual responsibility and circumstances in Hell, between essential Evil and social accidents, then the Heaven (if any) implied will be equally trivial and accidental. Mr. Pound's Hell, for all its horrors, is a perfectly comfortable one for the modern mind to contemplate, and disturbing to no one's complacency: it is a Hell for the *other people*, . . . not for oneself.[20]

The last sentence makes one realize that in his poetry Pound seldom struggles with his own deficiencies; he lashes out against other people. The exception, until *The Pisan Cantos*, is the masterly sequence *Hugh Selwyn Mauberley*, where Pound satirizes his own aestheticism: "His true Penelope was Flaubert." But he satirizes himself mainly as poet not as man, and in the second poem of the sequence begins blaming the age as incompatible with poetry: "The age demanded an image / Of its accelerated grimace." In poem 5 of the sequence, he attacks the age, in memorable lines, for having produced World War I:

There died a myriad,
And of the best, among them,
For an old bitch gone in the teeth,
For a botched civilization.[21]

If we compare *Mauberley* with "Prufrock," in which the persona is also a projection of the author, we see that Eliot's self-examination is unforgiving though he mixes self-satire with pathos:

But though I have wept and fasted, wept and prayed,
Though I have seen my head [grown slightly bald]
   brought in upon a platter,
I am no prophet—and here's no great matter.[22]

The difference can also be accounted for by Pound's singular lack of interest in *psychological* characterization, which is what distinguishes his Browningesque dramatic monologues from Browning's dramatic monologues.[23] Almost all Eliot's major poems are self-examining: when we read about the neurotic apathy or aboulie of Eliot's youth, we realize that *he* is the walking dead of *The Waste Land*. The exceptions are the satirical quatrain poems of 1920, written under Pound's influence, in which Eliot mercilessly satirizes members of other ethnic groups— Sweeney, Bleistein, Grishkin—who are obviously external to himself.

After all Pound's suffering during the immediate post–World War II years, when he was arrested by the American army in Italy for his wartime profascist broadcasts, exposed in a cage in the American army prison camp outside Pisa, and committed to a mental hospital in Washington, D.C., after all this suffering Pound seems in certain passages of *The Pisan Cantos* to be at last examining himself critically:

"Master thyself, then others shall thee beare"
   Pull down thy vanity
Thou art a beaten dog beneath the hail.

                      (C 521)

Even here Hugh Kenner sees a restatement of Social Credit theory: "*vanus*" is "the false accounting" that makes money out of nothing.[24] If Kenner is right, Pound would again be accusing others and the lines would lose their beauty; but given the moral imperative of these lines and the lovely lines above them:

177

The ant's a centaur in his dragon world.
Pull down thy vanity, it is not man
Made courage, or made order, or made grace,

(C 521)

I think Kenner must be wrong. Even so Pound remains politically unrepentant in *The Pisan Cantos* and concludes the above passage of self-criticism with a self-defense:

But to have done instead of not doing
      this is not vanity

. . . .
      To have gathered from the air a live tradition
or from a fine old eye the unconquered flame
This is not vanity.

(C 521–22)

In a September 1946 article in *Poetry* Eliot writes: "If I am doubtful about some of the [recent] *Cantos*, it is not that I find any poetic decline in them, but an increasing defect of communication."[25] F. R. Leavis, in the *Times Literary Supplement* of 11 September 1970, quotes from a letter Eliot, toward the end of his life, sent him after reading the "Retrospect 1950" in a new edition of Leavis's influential *New Bearings in English Poetry* (1932). Eliot expresses his agreement with Leavis's remark about

the aridity of the *Cantos*, with the exception of at least one item & a few lines from one of the so-called *Pisan Cantos* where it seems to me also that a touch of humanity breaks through: I mean the lovely verse of "Bow [*sic*] down thy vanity" and the reference to the Negro who knocked him up a table when he was in the cage at Pisa. And of course Pound's incomparable sense of rhythm carries a lot over. But I do find the *Cantos*, apart from that exceptional moment, quite arid and depressing.[26]

Pound, on his side, kept up after Eliot's conversion a teasing criticism of his Anglo-Catholicism—in the opening of Canto 46, for example, which follows the *usura* canto:

And if you will say that this tale teaches…
      a lesson, or that the Reverend Eliot
      has found a more natural language.

(C 231)

Pound seems to be criticizing the religiosity and the language of Eliot's later poems. "Curious, is it not," says Pound in Canto 80,

> that Mr Eliot
> has not given more time to Mr Beddoes
> (T.L.) prince of morticians.

(C 498)

The reference to the author of *Death's Jest-Book* (1850) recalls Pound's often expressed wonderment that Christians are so preoccupied with death and his account in Canto 29 of the young Eliot's confession to him (the speaker's name was later changed to Arnaut Daniel): "I am afraid of the life after death" (C 145). The Beddoes passage continues with an address, as Kenner suggests, to Eliot, lover of cats, as a cat: "Prowling night-puss leave my hard squares alone / they are in no case cat food." Leave my tough, indigestible poetry alone, he says, continuing with an intricately syncopated passage that begins by naming the "Battle Hymn of the Republic":

> "mi-hine eyes hev"
> > well yes they *have*
> seen a good deal of it
> > there is a good deal to be seen
> fairly tough and unblastable
> > and the hymn...
> well in contrast to the *god*-damned crooning
> > put me down for temporis acti [the old days].

(C 498–99)

I have seen too much tough reality, Pound seems to be saying, to tolerate the Tennysonian crooning of *Four Quartets*.

Pound also reproves Eliot for disagreeing with him politically: "(at which point Mr Eliot left us)," he says in the midst of a political passage in Canto 65 (p. 378). "Yeats, Possum and Wyndham," he says in Canto 98, "had no ground beneath 'em" because they did not believe in Social Credit; "Orage," who did believe, "had" (C 685). In Canto 74, the first of *The Pisan Cantos*, Pound adapts the famous last lines of Eliot's *The Hollow Men* ("*This is the way the world ends / Not with a bang but a whimper*") to admonish the loyal British subject Eliot (called Possum) that the deaths of Benito Mussolini (called Ben) and his mistress Clara Petacci, who in 1945 were shot by Italian partisans and ex-

179

hibited strung up by the heels in Milan, restored heroism to the modern world: "yet say this to the Possum: a bang, not a whimper, / with a bang not with a whimper" (*C* 425).

I have said that with one exception Pound never names in published sources any nondramatic poem of Eliot's after *The Waste Land*. He does, however, openly attack Eliot's criticism—in "Credo" (1930), for example: "Mr. Eliot who is at times an excellent poet and who has arrived at the supreme Eminence among English critics largely through disguising himself as a corpse." Note the implied criticism of the later poetry (we know Pound liked the early poetry) in "at times." The criticism is corpselike because of Eliot's impersonal, academic tone contrasting to Pound's personal tone in criticism. "I believe," Pound continues, "that postwar 'returns to christianity' . . . have been merely the gran' rifiuto and, in general, signs of fatigue." [27]

The attack on Eliot's criticism is even stronger in a Rapallo letter of 1932: "I dunno how you feel about Eliot's evil influence. Not that his crit. is *bad* but that he hasn't seen *where* it leads. What it leads TO. Attention on lesser rather than greater." Pound was probably thinking of Eliot's arguments for minor Metaphysical poets and Jacobean dramatists; Eliot was later to defend minor poetry in an essay on Kipling (1941). Pound probably has Eliot in mind when he goes on in this letter to describe the lowest class of critic: "The pestilence masking itself as a critic distracts attention *from* the best work, either to secondary work that is more or less 'good' or to tosh, to detrimental work, dead or living snobisms, or to indefinite essays on criticism" (*L* 240–41).

*   *   *

Amazingly Pound and Eliot remained good friends, perhaps even best friends, through all this disagreement. When Eliot died on 4 January 1965, Pound, old, sick, and poor, flew from Italy to attend the memorial service at Westminster Abbey. "Who is there now for me to share a joke with?" he wrote in the Eliot memorial issue of the *Sewanee Review*. "His was the true Dantescan voice—not honoured enough, and deserving more than ever I gave him." [28] At the Abbey the contrast between the two poet friends must have been striking. One had reaped all the honors the Establishment has to bestow, including the Nobel Prize. The other, for all his fame, was still poor and an outcast, shadowed by imputations of treason and insanity.

Now Pound began to admit that he might have erred. We see the admission in the above suggestion that he had not sufficiently honored Eliot's later poetry, which in being Christian was "Dantescan." We see it in the "Pull down thy vanity" passage in Pisan Canto 81. We see it in his confession to a friend that the *Cantos* were "a botch. . . . I picked out this and that thing that interested me, and then jumbled them into a bag. But that's not the way to make a *work of art*."[29] "I cannot make it cohere," he admits in the late Canto 116. And in the beautifully moving lines, which in the 1975 New Directions *Cantos* are printed last as Canto 120 (1969), he expresses disappointment that he has not completed Dante's scheme, which was one of his models, by failing to write a *Paradise* to follow upon the hell and purgatory cantos. Here is the whole canto:

> I have tried to write Paradise
>
> Do not move
>   Let the wind speak
>   that is paradise.
>
> Let the Gods forgive what I
>   have made
> Let those I love try to forgive
>   what I have made.

(C 803)

Late in life Eliot remarked, as often before, that he owed Pound everything. He repaid the debt handsomely, first by using his editorial connections with *The Criterion* and Faber and Faber to publish Pound's work (Pound disapproved of both the magazine and the publishing house). In his letter of 4 October 1923 Eliot complained to John Quinn of how difficult it was to help Pound now that their roles were reversed: "Apart from the fact that he is very sensitive and proud and that I have to keep an attitude of discipleship (as indeed I ought) every time I print anything of his it nearly sinks the paper."[30]

Furthermore, after Pound's arrest for treason and his commitment to the Washington, D.C., mental hospital, St. Elizabeths, Eliot, according to Pound's lawyer, was "the most faithful and concerned" of Pound's friends.[31] Eliot worked out business trips to the United States so he could visit Pound yearly, even though he had to endure lectures at-

tacking his religion and his publishing house. He persuaded the authorities to give Pound more comfortable quarters along with special privileges, and led the campaign to secure Pound's release and to have the treason charge dropped. In addition Tom did, as Mrs. Eliot told me, many things for Ezra that people do not know about. Eliot was on the Library of Congress committee that awarded Pound the Bollingen Poetry Prize of 1949 for *The Pisan Cantos*, in which Mussolini is conspicuously praised. The award raised a storm of controversy. If we had lost the war, we would not have forgiven Pound. But since we won, certain people could afford to understand that politics should not influence literary judgment.

Actually Pound was never so widely appreciated as during his years at St. Elizabeths (1945–58). It became the fashion for young writers to visit him there. He was by now a legendary figure, a survivor of that dwindling generation of early modernists who were already considered classics. Always on the lookout for disciples, Pound was surprisingly accessible; and the contrast between his fame, on the one hand, and his accessibility and pitiable incarceration, on the other, presented an example of the informality appropriate to a poet and of the poet's oppression by society. Thus Pound—like Coleridge when he lived during his last years under surveillance near London—exerted yet another round of influence on a new generation.

What about mutual influence between Pound and Eliot? The influence seems to run one way, from Pound to Eliot. The exception seems to be the confirmation Pound found in "Gerontion" and *The Waste Land* for the "mythical method" that he and Eliot discovered in the manuscripts and *The Little Review* serialization of Joyce's *Ulysses* (March 1918–December 1920). We are told that Pound wrote the *Cantos* with a copy of "Gerontion" and *Ulysses* on his table. Nevertheless, Pound does not in the *Cantos* use the "mythical method" as it is described by Eliot in his review of *Ulysses* and as we find it in *Ulysses* and *The Waste Land*. Pound lays historical periods side by side; he does not, aside from occasional injections of modern language into ancient situations, fuse antiquity and modernity as they are fused in the Stetson passage of *The Waste Land* (1), where the same words describe an ordinary conversation about gardening between two modern Englishmen and the mutual recognition between two Phoenician sailors who fought with Carthage against Rome. In the same way, the splendid metamor-

phoses in the *Cantos* are epiphanies in the Greek sense—manifestations of gods in ancient situations (as for example the epiphany of Dionysus in Canto 2). They are not Joycean epiphanies in that they do not transform commonplace modern situations.

Pound's editing of *The Waste Land* manuscript is the most famous example of his influence on Eliot. Pound cut out three long narrative passages leading, but with a big leap, to the intense lyrical passages that remain. In other words, Pound changed *The Waste Land* from a poem mixing passages of low and high intensity to a poem of continuously high lyric intensity. "The test of a writer," he said in a letter of 1915, "is his ability for . . . concentration AND for his power to stay concentrated till he gets to the end of his poem, whether it is two lines or two hundred" (*L* 49). Pound wanted the long poem to yield the same high intensity as the short poem. Eliot, instead, was working toward a different theory, one which would permit him to write verse drama. "In a poem of any length," he said in 1942,

> there must be transitions between passages of greater and less intensity, to give a rhythm of fluctuating emotion essential to the musical structure of the whole; . . . no poet can write a poem of amplitude unless he is a master of the prosaic.[32]

Eliot uses deliberately prosaic passages even in a nondramatic poem like *Four Quartets*. Pound had no use for drama, and appreciated only the lyric effect—which is why he cut *The Waste Land* down in size, and why in the *Cantos* he uses a sequence of only moderately long poems. Even the cantos that quote prose letters are, I think, intended to give a lyric effect through presentation of the prose in fragments intended to set up poetic vibrations.

Pound turned *The Waste Land* into a Poundian poem of juxtaposed images, of those jumps and disconnections that he called his "ideogrammic method" as an acknowledgment of his debt to Fenollosa's essay, "The Chinese Written Character as a Medium for Poetry." Fenollosa, who argues that ideograms give Chinese poetry an imagistic concreteness, merely confirmed a method that grew out of Imagism which in turn grew out of the nineteenth-century romantic replacement of rhetoric by immediate sensuous presentation.

Although Pound made *The Waste Land* incoherent in one sense, he insisted on its unity in another sense at a time when Eliot thought of

183

The Waste Land as a sequence of poems. He would not let Eliot publish it in magazines in installments, but insisted that it be printed all together. When Eliot in a 1922 letter suggested omitting the beautiful lyric on Phlebas's drowning, since Pound had cut the rest of part 4 when he cut out the narrative about a shipwreck leading to the lyric, Pound replied from Paris: "I DO advise keeping Phlebas. In fact I more'n advise. Phlebas is an integral part of the poem; the card pack introduces him, the drowned phoen[ician]. sailor" (*L* 171). Pound understood, better than Eliot at that point, the replacement of narrative continuity by continuity of the mythical pattern. How sad that in an earlier letter in which he organizes Eliot's poem for him, he speaks of "never getting an outline" for the *Cantos*, "my deformative secretions" (*L* 169).

Nevertheless Pound's influence on Eliot was not fundamental; for Eliot had already arrived at his own style in "Prufrock," written during 1910–12, well before he met Pound. "Prufrock" is full of jumps and disconnections:

> Shall I say, I have gone at dusk through narrow streets
> And watched the smoke that rises from the pipes
> Of lonely men in shirt-sleeves, leaning out of windows?...
>
> I should have been a pair of ragged claws
> Scuttling across the floors of silent seas.
>
> And the afternoon, the evening, sleeps so peacefully!

Where did Eliot get this style, since it is not in his principal influences at the time—the late nineteenth-century French poet Laforgue and the seventeenth-century English Metaphysical poets (Laforguian and Metaphysical poems move logically, even if the logic is ingeniously stretched). Eliot, I think, got the style of jumps and disconnections from the same source as Pound, from the romantic poetic tradition. Both poets got the style from poems like Wordsworth's "Tintern Abbey," Coleridge's "Frost at Midnight" and Keats's "Ode to a Nightingale," which move by leaps of psychological association. The poetry, Browning wrote to Ruskin in answer to his charge of obscurity, lies in the leaps.[33] Browning asks us to make formidable leaps between stanzas in "By the Fireside," as does Yeats in the great poems beginning with his middle period, in "Among School Children," for example. The poetry of jumps between what Pound called "luminous details" derives from the epi-

phanic mode of much romantic poetry—the mode according to which the poetry exists in the epiphany or spot of time or privileged moment.[34] Pound tried to write the first long poem which would employ not narrative but conjunctions of "luminous details."

Pound and Eliot collaborated most closely between 1917 and 1920, when they were determined to improve their poetry through a discipline that would check the sloppiness free verse was falling into. Pound suggested as model Gautier's strict tetrameter quatrains in *Émaux et Camées,* and Eliot suggested adding Laforgue's satirical rhyming. The experiment resulted in Eliot's *Poems, 1920* and Pound's *Hugh Selwyn Mauberley* (1920), volumes in which both poets use Gautier's straitjacket in order to break out of it. Eliot breaks out through the ruggedness of satire:

> Apeneck Sweeney spreads his knees
> Letting his arms hang down to laugh,
> The zebra stripes along his jaw
> Swelling to maculate giraffe

and through subject matter. In the last two stanzas of this poem, "Sweeney Among the Nightingales," he makes the little quatrain express Frazer's gigantic scheme in *The Golden Bough,* the scheme used in *The Waste Land,* by assimilating the failed plot against Sweeney to the murder of Agamemnon as type of the murders in the sacred wood at Nemi of god-kings (the line, "The Convent of the Sacred Heart," includes in the scheme the sacrifice of Christ) in order to renew the fertility of the land:

> The nightingales are singing near
> The Convent of the Sacred Heart,
>
>   And sang within the bloody wood
> When Agamemnon cried aloud,
> And let their liquid siftings fall
> To stain the stiff dishonoured shroud.

In all his quatrain poems, Eliot adheres to Gautier's meter; but he modifies, except in one poem, the rhyme scheme from *abab* to *abcb.* Pound, instead, in poem 1 of *Mauberly* immediately plays a syncopated variation on the iambic, thus moving toward free verse while, as I hear it, trying to maintain Gautier's tetrameters:

For three years, out of key with his time,
He strove to resuscitate the dead art
Of poetry;

The need to forego, in order to maintain the tetrameter, the expected accent on "dead" creates an exciting syncopated pause between "art" and "Of." All hell breaks loose in the transition from the fourth line to the first line of the next stanza:

Of poetry; to maintain "the sublime"
In the old sense. Wrong from the start—

No, hardly,

The iambic tetrameter is almost abandoned with the long pause and syntactical ellipsis between "start" and "No," and with the sequence of three accented syllables. It is only a step to the syncopated free verse of poem 4 on the war:

These fought ‖ in any case,
and some ‖ believing,
pro domo, ‖ in any case . . .

In poem 5, also on the war, Pound returns to quatrains, but they are unrhymed and the tetrameter is only approximated; the second quatrain is separated into two-line units. In the poems that follow, the quatrain is more or less maintained but with abcb and other variations, with variable meters, and with sometimes a longer stanza.

Pound shows himself a subtler metrist than Eliot. Both poets achieve triumphs of diction in these volumes. Most spectacular is Pound's line, "walked eye-deep in hell" (4) about soldiers in the trenches. Best of all is his line about the war dead, "Quick eyes gone under / earth's lid" (5), where the combination of motion with stasis produces a noble serenity worthy of Homer.

Pound's most sustained triumph of diction is *Cathay* (1915, reprinted in *Personae*), his translations of classic Chinese poetry. Hugh Kenner in *The Pound Era* says that *Cathay* is about World War I, and he is right in that the volume contains several poems about ancient Chinese wars which are treated antiheroically—"Our mind is full of sor-

row, who will know of our grief?" ("Song of the Bowmen of Shu")—in the manner of literature about World War I. Even more important, Pound perfects in these translations the modernist style of the war and immediate postwar years, the style we associate with early Hemingway. Eliot wrote in 1919 that the style of *Cathay* "owes nothing to the Chinese inspiration; it is a development—in fact, the development—of Mr. Pound's style.[35]

The style of *Cathay* is plaintively modern in its understatement, its avoidance of general or value-laden words, its reliance on concrete details but with the poignant admission that the speaker has no ordering principle by which to indicate that one detail is more important than another. Emotions are not named, they are projected through objective correlatives. All this is illustrated in my favorite poem of the volume, "The River-Merchant's Wife: A Letter," in which the wife expresses her sorrow over her husband's long absence:

> The leaves fall early this autumn, in wind.
> The paired butterflies are already yellow with August
> Over the grass in the West garden;
> They hurt me. I grow older.

The poem ends:

> If you are coming down through the narrows of the
>   river Kiang,
> Please let me know beforehand,
> And I will come out to meet you
>   As far as Chō-fū-Sa.

That last line is the key to the poem's style in that the detail is exquisitely precise and yet, for us who do not know where Chō-fū-Sa is, irrelevant; so that the line vibrates.

Eliot does not in his prewar poems employ this style, except in the question of the blank young man in "Portrait of a Lady": "Are these ideas right or wrong?" But the style comes to fruition in *The Waste Land*—in the plaintive opening, "April is the cruellest month," in the snatches of conversation that follow, "In the mountains, there you feel free. / I read, much of the night, and go south in the winter" (1, ll. 17–18), in the lament of the seduced girl in part 3, "I can connect / Noth-

ing with nothing" (ll. 301–2), and in the desperate question addressed to the protagonist by the neurotic lady of part 2:

> "Do
> "You know nothing? Do you see nothing? Do you remember
> "Nothing?" (ll. 121–23)

Cathay may have helped Eliot develop the war and postwar style.

As for influence from Eliot to Pound, Pound in a letter of 21 August 1917 wrote of *Three Cantos* just after their first publication in *Poetry* (June, July, August 1917): "Eliot is the only person who proffered criticism instead of general objection" (*L* 115). But looking back in 1939, Pound wrote: "I have had five, and only five, useful criticisms of my writing in my lifetime, one from Yeats, one from Bridges, one from Thomas Hardy, a recent one from a Roman Archbishop and one from Ford." [36] Eliot is conspicuously absent from the list.

Perhaps the best proofs of mutual influence are the echoes of each other in their writing. Here are a few examples. The opening line of Canto 8 (1925), "These fragments you have shelved (shored)" (*C* 28), echoes *The Waste Land* (1922), "These fragments I have shored against my ruins" (5, l. 430). The lines in Eliot's "Journey of the Magi" (1927), "A hard time we had of it" and "The summer palaces on slopes, the terraces, / And the silken girls bringing sherbet" echo Pound's lines in "Exile's Letter" (*Cathay*, 1915): "And what with broken wheels and so on, I won't say it wasn't hard going / . . . And the vermilioned girls getting drunk about sunset." In Canto 20 (1928), the line "Give! What were they given?" (*C* 94) echoes *The Waste Land* (1922), "*Datta* [Give]: what have we given?" (5, l. 400). The lines in Canto 7,

> And the old voice lifts itself
>   weaving an endless sentence.
> We also made ghostly visits, and the stair
> That knew us, found us again on the turn of it,
> Knocking at empty rooms, seeking for buried beauty
>
> (*C* 24–25)

sound like "Gerontion," the utterance of an old man, in the lines where the old man says that what were once religious rituals have been taken over by aesthetes and occultists: by Mr. Silvero, caressing porcelain, "Who walked all night in the next room" and

188

By Madame de Tornquist, in the dark room
Shifting the candles; Fräulein von Kulp
Who turned in the hall, one hand on the door.
    Vacant shuttles
Weave the wind. I have no ghosts.

"Gerontion" was written in May–June 1919; Canto 7 was written in November–December 1919; Ronald Bush, in *The Genesis of Ezra Pound's Cantos*, speaks of Pound's debt in Canto 7 to "Gerontion," citing different lines than I do.[37] A sentence in Eliot's famous passage on "dissociation of sensibility" in "The Metaphysical Poets" (1921) resembles a sentence in Pound's essay "Cavalcanti" (1934). "The difference," Eliot says, between Tennyson and Browning, on the one hand, and Donne on the other, "is not a simple difference of degree between poets. It is something which had happened to the mind of England." Pound writes: "The difference between Guido [Cavalcanti] and Petrarch is not a mere difference of degree, it is a difference in kind"—the context suggests that the difference is something which had happened to the mind of Europe.[38] We cannot be sure who echoes whom, because "Cavalcanti" was written between 1910 and 1931 and the two poets read each other's work in manuscript.

    *   *   *

Where then do the two poets stand in relation to each other now? Eliot seems to rate higher than Pound among academics (he is certainly taught more than Pound), for Eliot's oeuvre is complete and consistent, displaying an easily discernible line of development. His output is remarkably small but remarkably even. Although his verse ranges from the nonsense of *Old Possum's Book of Practical Cats* (Eliot would have enjoyed its current success as a musical comedy since he always wanted to make it in the commercial theater), through plays designed to hold the stage, to the solemnity of *Four Quartets*: although Eliot worked in so many genres, his work in each is distinguished in its own kind. Pound, instead, wanted poetry to be always at the highest pitch; so when it falls short, it seems a failure.

Eliot established himself as the most authoritative critic of his time, and there is for the academic mind a satisfying consistency between his criticism and his verse. The great early essays, "Tradition and the Individual Talent," with its argument for a learned, impersonal poetry;

189

"Hamlet," with its imagist theory of the "objective correlative" for emotion; and "The Metaphysical Poets," with its praise of a witty poetry that does not dissociate sensibility from thought—these essays account for his early triumphs in poetry, for "Prufrock," "Portrait of a Lady," "Gerontion," *The Waste Land*. When with his conversion Eliot changed poetic style, he wrote the essays on Dante (1929) and Lancelot Andrewes (1926) to explain the change from an imagist poetry of jumps and disconnections to a poetry of vision and statement as in *Ash Wednesday*, "Journey of the Magi," and *Four Quartets*.

Eliot stands even higher in the English academy than in ours, because as an outsider who enthusiastically embraced English citizenship, religion, literature, and gentlemanliness, he renewed for the English their faltering confidence in their own institutions. American academics are more restless, since there are those who claim Eliot's niche for Wallace Stevens or William Carlos Williams.

Pound seems to appeal to poets more than Eliot, especially young poets now. Eliot's oeuvre arrives too signed, buttoned up, and delivered; it leaves no point of entry for young poets. Pound, who was remarkably prolific and remarkably uneven, offers young poets fruitful starting points as they mine the *Cantos* for passages of great poetry that appeal to them. Pound's obscurity enables them to take over a style, a cadence, a kind of music and pour into it their own ideas and feelings. His Social Credit and fascist ideas can easily be ignored. A well-known contemporary poet told me that he picked up a copy of the *Cantos* while a soldier in Italy just after World War II, that he did not understand them but that the rapturous experience of reading them made him want to be a poet. He also said that Pound's criticism provides practical tips for writing that a young poet can find nowhere else.

Pound's published criticism never achieved the authority of Eliot's, because it is often undisciplined in thought and style, and personal to the point of quirkiness. But he was as influential as Eliot if we take into account his conversations and correspondence with other writers, his editing of their manuscripts, and his choice of works to be published in the magazines that employed him. (His letters, humorous and full of pregnant insights, are a delight to read.) Both critics did the important job of revising the literary canon, but Eliot's revisions have been more influential since few readers know enough foreign languages to follow Pound's recommendations.

One might argue that, despite his unevenness, Pound was so prolific that he actually wrote more lines of great verse than did Eliot with his small output. Certainly Eliot never wrote lines so free-flowing musically as these from Canto 20:

> Sandro, and Boccata, and Jacopo Sellaio;
> The ranunculae, and almond,
> Boughs set in espalier,
> Duccio, Agostino; *e l'olors*—
> The smell of that place—
>
> (C 90)

or these from the first Pisan canto:

> yet say this to the Possum: a bang, not a whimper,
>   with a bang not with a whimper,
> To build the city of Dioce whose terraces are the colour of stars.
> The suave eyes, quiet, not scornful,
>   rain also is of the process.
> What you depart from is not the way
> and olive tree blown white in the wind
> washed in the Kiang and Han
> what whiteness will you add to this whiteness,
>   what candor?
>
> (C 425)

One almost feels that the obscurity is necessary, that meaning would weigh down the words. Yet the obscurity is annoying in those places where the verse is less successful. And the lines preceding the above Pisan canto passage extol the "heroic" deaths of Mussolini and his mistress, so that content again becomes an issue.

Even if we cannot, because of Pound's deficiency in the *Cantos* of valid content, communicativeness, and organizational ability, even if we cannot all agree to call him the greatest English-speaking poet of the first half of the twentieth century (I myself place Eliot above him and Yeats above them both), we can, I think, all agree that he is the greatest single *personal* force in the poetry of that time.

Notes

1. Quoted in Clive Bell, "Encounters with T. S. Eliot," *Old Friends: Personal Recollections* (New York: Harcourt, Brace, 1957), p. 120.

191

2. The quotation from Ezra Pound's typed letter to F. V. Morley, 17 December 1934 (Beinecke no. 1421), is published by permission of the Collection of American Literature, Beinecke Rare Book and Manuscript Library, Yale University.

3. *The Selected Letters of Ezra Pound, 1907–1941*, ed. D. D. Paige (New York: New Directions, 1971), pp. 266, 277; hereafter cited as *L* followed by page number. See also Christina C. Stough, "The Literary Relationship of T. S. Eliot and Ezra Pound after 'The Waste Land'" (Ph.D. diss., University of Southern California, 1980).

4. Quoted in Donald Gallup, *T. S. Eliot and Ezra Pound: Collaborators in Letters* (New Haven: Wenning/Stonehill, 1970), pp. 4, 9.

5. T. S. Eliot, "Ezra Pound," *Poetry*, September 1946; reprinted in *Ezra Pound: A Collection of Critical Essays*, ed. Walter Sutton (Englewood Cliffs, N.J.: Prentice-Hall, 1963), p. 18.

6. Lyndall Gordon, *Eliot's Early Years* (Oxford and New York: Oxford University Press, 1977), p. 67.

7. Noel Stock, *The Life of Ezra Pound*, expanded edition (San Francisco: North Point Press, 1982), pp. 246–47.

8. T. S. Eliot, "Ezra Pound: His Metric and Poetry," reprinted in *To Criticize the Critic* (New York: Farrar, Straus & Giroux, 1965), pp. 165–68.

9. T. S. Eliot, review of Ezra Pound's *Personae, The Dial*, January 1928, pp. 4–7.

10. Pound himself translates this phrase of Dante's (*Purg.* XXVI, 117) as the "best craftsman" in "Near Perigord" (2), *Personae*.

11. Eliot, review, pp. 4–7.

12. T. S. Eliot, *Selected Essays*, new ed. (New York: Harcourt, Brace, 1950), p. 285.

13. T. S. Eliot, Introduction to Ezra Pound, *Selected Poems*, ed. T. S. Eliot (London: Faber & Gwyer, 1928), pp. xiii, xii.

14. Ibid., pp. xiv–xv.

15. Quoted in Stock, *Life of Pound*, p. 359.

16. Hugh Kenner, *The Pound Era* (Berkeley and Los Angeles: University of California Press, 1971), p. 408.

17. *The Cantos of Ezra Pound* (New York: New Directions, 1975), pp. 229–30; hereafter cited as *C* followed by page number.

18. Ezra Pound, "Dante," *The Spirit of Romance* (1910), reprinted (New York: New Directions, 1968), p. 153.

19. Hugh Kenner sees here the beginning of the monetary theme in that gold is still "innocent stuff . . . ornamenting Aphrodite" (*Pound Era*, p. 425). If Kenner is right, this would be an example of fusion between the poetry and the

monetary theme. But I wonder how many readers find the monetary theme here, even after having read Kenner.

20. T. S. Eliot, *After Strange Gods: A Primer of Modern Heresy* (New York: Harcourt, Brace, 1934), pp. 44–47.

21. Pound's shorter poems will be quoted from Ezra Pound, *Personae: The Collected Shorter Poems* (New York: New Directions, 1971).

22. Excerpts from Eliot's poems are quoted from T. S. Eliot, *Collected Poems, 1909–1962* (London: Faber & Faber; New York: Harcourt Brace Jovanovich, 1963); copyright 1963 by Harcourt Brace Jovanovich, Inc.; copyright © 1963, 1964 by T. S. Eliot. Reprinted by permission of the publishers. *Poems and Plays, 1909–1950* (New York: Harcourt, Brace, 1952).

23. In the early dramatic monologues, like "Cino" and "Sestina Altaforte," Pound triumphs in Browning's style, but unlike Browning presents in each only one emotion without complication or suggestion of psychological motives. "Near Perigord," not a dramatic monologue though like one, is more enigmatic, but not psychologically. The question is whether Bertrans de Born was *politically* motivated in loving Maent.

24. Kenner, *Pound Era*, p. 308.

25. Eliot, "Ezra Pound," reprinted in *Pound: Critical Essays*, ed. Sutton, p. 23.

26. F. R. Leavis, letter in *Times Literary Supplement*, 11 September 1970, p. 998.

27. *Ezra Pound: Selected Prose, 1909–1965* (New York: New Directions, 1973), p. 53.

28. Ezra Pound, "For T.S.E.," in *Sewanee Review*, A Special Issue for T. S. Eliot (1888–1965), January–March 1966, p. 109.

29. Quoted in Stock, *Life of Pound*, pp. 457–58.

30. Quoted in Gallup, *Eliot and Pound*, p. 30.

31. Quoted in Stock, *Life of Pound*, p. 422.

32. "The Music of Poetry," a 1942 lecture reprinted in T. S. Eliot, *On Poetry and Poets* (New York: Farrar, Straus & Cudahy, 1957), pp. 24–25.

33. Browning's letter to Ruskin is quoted in W. G. Collingwood, *The Life of John Ruskin* (Boston and New York: Houghton Mifflin, 1902), pp. 164–65.

34. "Pound," writes George Bornstein, "separates the image [or epiphany] from the quest for it . . . traces product rather than 'process'" (*The Postromantic Consciousness of Ezra Pound* [Victoria, B.C.: University of Victoria, 1977], pp. 51–52). The "process" is the action of poems like "Tintern Abbey" that dramatize the evolution of an epiphany, poems which in *The Poetry of Experience* (1957) I call "dramatic lyrics."

35. T. S. Eliot, review of Pound's *Quia Pauper Amavi*, in *The Atheneum*, 24 October 1919, p. 1065.

36. Ezra Pound, "Ford Madox (Hueffer) Ford; Obit," in *Nineteenth Century and After*, August 1939, pp. 178–79.

37. Ronald Bush, *The Genesis of Ezra Pound's Cantos* (Princeton: Princeton University Press, 1976), pp. 220–21. See also Gordon, *Eliot's Early Years*, p. 100; and Myles Slatin, "A History of Pound's Cantos I–XVI, 1915–1925," in *American Literature*, May 1963, p. 188.

38. Eliot, *Selected Essays*, p. 247. Ezra Pound, *Literary Essays*, ed. T. S. Eliot (New York: New Directions, 1968), p. 153.

The Contemporary of Our Grandchildren
Pound's Influence

Marjorie Perloff

Pound has provided a box of tools, as abundant for this generation as those Spenser provided for the Elizabethans, and a man who is not influenced by Pound in this sense of trying to use at least some of those tools, is simply not living in his own century. (Basil Bunting)[1]

When I was living in Verona [at age twenty-three] . . . I was told to go out to Sirmione on Lake Garda, where the Latin poet, Catullus, supposedly had a villa. . . . It's still one of the most beautiful places I have ever been to, or expect to go to. Lake Garda in front of you, the Italian Alps on three sides of you, the ruined and beautiful villa around you, and I read a poem that Pound had written about the place, about Sirmione being more beautiful than Paradise, and my life was changed forever. (Charles Wright)[2]

He was born the year of Brahms' Fourth and of *Diana of the Crossways*; of the *Mikado* and the second volume of *Das Kapital*; in the reigns of Grover Cleveland and Victoria. At his death every school of poets writing in English was under his influence. . . . I have seen students learn Chinese because of him, or take up medieval studies, learn Greek, Latin, music; the power of his instigation has not flagged. (Guy Davenport)[3]

Question: What do you think about giving an award to somebody who held all the positions that Pound held?

Answer: It's irrelevant! If the award is lucky enough to find him, God bless the award. The award needs him—he doesn't need the award. Certainly, give him *all* the awards. It's a shame he didn't get the Nobel and all the other awards at once—he was the greatest poet of his age! (Allen Ginsberg)[4]

195

If these words, spoken by four very different poets, sound extravagant—as they will to certain readers—we might substitute for Ginsberg's nebulous "greatest" a phrase like "most influential" and then there can barely be room for disagreement. For what poet writing in England or America since World War II has *not* learned from Pound? In casting about for suspects, I have come up with a few, but even those few have not escaped the anxiety of what must be the largest poetic influence of our century. Ted Hughes, for instance, is a poet no one seems to have claimed for the Pound tradition,[5] and yet when we read the lines

Fifteenth of May. ‖ Cherry blossom. ‖ The swifts
Materialize at the top of a long scream
Of needle—[6]

we hear, despite the un-Poundian enjambment, the rhythms and inflections of *Cathay*—inflections guided by the Imagist credo of "Direct treatment of the thing" as well as by the recognition that "To break the pentameter, that was the first heave."

Or what about James Merrill, a poet who once declared that in the *Cantos*, "We find precious little unity except of the contents of a single, very brilliant and erratic mind," and who pronounced Pound's and Eliot's a poetry "only to react against"?[7] Merrill's own epic *The Changing Light at Sandover* (1983) incorporates into the text of a poem almost as long (560 pages) as the entire *Cantos*, patches of narrative and of dramatic dialogue, allusions to historical and mythological figures, scientific documentation, personal letters, foreign phrases, and typographical play (capital letters for messages from the dead received via the Ouija board, phonetic spelling as in "U" for "you," "4" for "four" and "V" for "vie"). The resulting sequence, centrally different as it is from Pound's own "rag-bag," could hardly have come into being without the example of the *Cantos*. As Hugh Kenner predicted more than a decade ago in *The Pound Era*: "we can hardly distinguish what Pound instigated from what he simply saw before it was obvious. . . . He is very likely in ways controversy still hides, the contemporary of our grandchildren."[8]

Contemporary in what sense? It is usual, when talking of the Pound tradition, to draw a family tree that goes, by way of Williams, to Black Mountain, the Objectivists, and the Confessional poets. Pound and Olson, Pound and Zukofsky, Pound and Lowell—these connections

196

have been made often enough and I shall not rehearse, in the short space available to me here, these individual and well-known cases.[9] Rather, I want to take up the larger question: What is it in Pound's oeuvre that has made such a difference in the poetry of the later twentieth century, a difference that transcends, in curious ways, the local differences between individual poets?

The obvious place to begin is surely with Pound's poetic, the famous obiter dicta of the critical prose. Denise Levertov probably speaks for many poets when she remarks, in her homage to Pound for the 1972 *L'Herne* (Paris) symposium:

> Reading *The Cantos* was for me until quite recently an experience which seemed to have little direct connection with the experience of studying the *ABC* and other prose. Though there was much that I responded to in *The Cantos*, all that appeared unclear and even chaotic in them seemed to me disturbingly at variance with Pound the critic's emphasis on clarity, on communication, and at the same time on music.[10]

Here Levertov may well be echoing Robert Creeley:

> For my own part I came first to the earlier poems, *Personae*, and to the various critical works, *Make It New*, *Pavannes and Divisions*, *ABC of Reading*, *Guide to Kulchur*, and *Polite Essays*. It was at that time the critical writing I could most clearly use, simply that my own limits made the *Cantos* a form intimidating to me.[11]

Again, Carl Rakosi, a poet who has gone so far as to declare the *Cantos* "disastrous as a model," declares that Pound's critical writing—particularly the famous "Don'ts" essay—is an absolute foundation stone of contemporary American writing."[12] And when Donald Davie, a very different poet from the three above, writes his first book on Pound, he devotes the central chapters to the aesthetic as formulated in *Gaudier-Brzeska* and in the writings on Gourmont and Fenollosa.[13]

Whatever poets have made of the actual texture of the *Cantos*, it seems that Pound's poetic, as articulated in the famous essays, has become synonymous with modernism itself. Such axioms as "Use no superfluous word, no adjective which does not reveal something" ("A Retrospect"); "The image is not an idea. It is a radiant node or cluster from which, and through which, and into which ideas are constantly rushing" (*Gaudier-Brzeska*); "Good writers are those who keep the language

197

efficient"; and "Poetry . . . is the most concentrated form of verbal expression" (*ABC of Reading*)[14]—these aphorisms are now embedded in our critical vocabulary. We talk of *melopoeia, phanopoeia, and logopoeia* as if this triad had been used by Aristotle in the *Poetics*; again, we refer to "ideogram," "vortex," and "luminous detail" as if these terms had always been applied to poetry. For Donald Davie as for Denise Levertov, for Charles Tomlinson as for Charles Wright, for Thom Gunn as for Theodore Weiss,[15] the thrust of the Poundian poetic is that poetry *matters*, that it is *important*, that if "a nation's literature declines, the nation atrophies and decays" (*ABCR* 32). Which of us does not believe or want to believe this inspired doctrine? POETRY IS NEWS THAT STAYS NEWS. In the self-conscious eighties, when voices from all sides are expressing doubts about the future of poetry, Pound's message is the one poets want to hear.

But when we turn from the explosive poetic to the poetry itself, the question of influence becomes more complicated. There are three areas, I would suggest, in which Pound's legacy has been indisputable: (1) the drive toward precision, particularity, immediacy—*le mot juste*; (2) the "break[ing of] the pentameter" in favor of the "musical" free verse line; and (3) the use of translation as the invention of a desired other. I shall discuss these three legacies briefly before turning to what seems to me the deeper, more lasting influence—and one that we have begun to witness only in recent years—namely, the example of the *Cantos* as "a poem including history," the new conception of the poem as "the tale of the tribe" that no longer privileges lyric over narrative (or even drama), that can incorporate the contemporary and the archaic, economics and myth, the everyday and the elevated.

1. Pound's insistence on precision, the luminous detail, the phalanx of particulars has become a rallying cry for poets as diverse otherwise as George Oppen and Frank O'Hara, poets who have wanted to avoid what John Ashbery has called the disease of "objective correlativitis."[16] Here is Basil Bunting writing to Louis Zukofsky in 1932:

> The value of Pound's preaching of Confucius does not lie in Confucius, whose wisdom seems to me to be mixed with the usual quantity of bunk, some of it quite as unpleasant as anything in St. Paul: but in the fact that Pound has not isolated a set of precepts but developed a pervading stress on the immediate, the particular, the concrete; distrust of abstractions; shrinking from even the suspicion of verbalism; from the puns and

polyvalencies in which mystics delight. It is not unspeculative but skeptical. It will build with facts, but declines to soar with inevitably unsteady
words.[17]

Distrust of abstractions, shrinking from even the suspicion of ver-
balism—here Bunting seems to be speaking for a whole generation.
Allen Ginsberg, calling on Pound in 1967, explains to the (nearly silent)
old poet that he has been able to find certain works of art in Venice, say,
a fountain or a fresco or "the casa que fue de Don Carlos," merely by
following the "descriptions—of exact language composed"—the "tin
flash in the sun dazzle" and "soap-smooth stone posts" of the *Cantos*.
When Pound demurs, declaring that "any good [in the *Cantos*] has
been spoiled by my intentions—the preoccupation with irrelevant and
stupid things," Ginsberg replies: "Ah well, what I'm trying to tell you—
what I came here for all this time—was to give you my blessing then,
because despite your disillusion . . . my perceptions have been strength-
ened by a series of practical exact language models which are scattered
throughout the *Cantos* like stepping stones."[18] And the next evening,
sitting behind Pound in Santa Maria del Carmelo, Ginsberg tries his
own hand at an "exact language model":

> Carmini, organ, apse brilliant yellow
> > gilt angels, violincello,
> > > Byzance cross hung silhouette,
> > > Flowers on altar, Pillars wrapped in red velvet—
> old man sat before me,
> > brown canvas shoes, one heel raised alter,
> > > hat and cane in hand
> > Smooth woodslab resting
> > > under a fold in his coatback.[19]

Ginsberg's cataloging of items, his notion, one by one, of things seen is,
of course, only superficially Poundian; the passage in question—and
this would be true of *Howl* or *Kaddish* or A *Supermarket in California*
as well—does not exhibit Pound's principle of juxtaposition, of intercut,
of cultural overlayering, one image or ideogram jostling another. Nevertheless, the emphasis is on the *particular*, not as metaphor but as embodiment of a specific perception. Whitman would be the more plausible model, but Whitman was no longer alive in 1967 and Ginsberg
needed Pound, even as he needed Williams, as intermediary.

The case of Zukofsky presents another variation on the fate of Pound's presentational methods. Overtly, the Objectivist creed grew out of Pound's Imagism and Vorticism: "*Impossible* to communicate anything but particulars—historic and contemporary—things, human beings as things their instrumentalities of capillaries and veins binding up and bound up with events and contingencies. The revolutionary word if it must revolve cannot escape having a reference. It is not infinite. Even the infinite is a term." [20]

But although Zukofsky makes much of "presentation in detail: the isolation of each noun so that in itself it is an image," [21] the fact is that his poetry, like Bunting's or Oppen's or Creeley's or H.D.'s later work, abjures "direct presentation" in favor of a lyric mode that looks like this:

> Whatever makes this happening
>   Is unheard
>   To a third.

> Two. Where two should
>   Stand. One. One.
>   With the sun. In a wood.

> Tomorrow is unsought.
>   No oasis of ivy to inurn
>   Either foot or fern. [22]

This is, as Burton Hatlen has recently said about a related poem, a long way from the Poundian "phalanx of particulars": "Zukofsky doesn't *want* us to pass through the words of his poem, to engage directly with 'things.' . . . Rather, he wants the words themselves to become presences within the poem, simply because language is the only presence we can know. . . . the poem (deliberately I think) evokes the gap that separates words from things." [23]

Why then the repeated appeal on Zukofsky's part to Pound as the poet of precision, of "presentation in detail"? I think we must understand Objectivist doctrine—whether in Zukofsky or in Oppen or even in Creeley—less as the continuation of Imagist precision or of the "Ideogrammic Method" than as the repudiation of the Symbolist model that had dominated Anglo-American poetry at least until the Second World War. [24] "Like Williams and Pound," writes Hatlen, Zukofsky "refuses the transcendental temptation, the impulse to look beyond the given world (either 'up' to God or 'within' to the human spirit) for a source of mean-

ing." [25] Indeed, Pound's declaration in *Gaudier-Brzeska* that "the image is the poet's pigment," that "one does not want to be called a symbolist, because symbolism has usually been associated with mushy technique" (GB 84–85), provides the impetus for the stress on precision that we meet in contemporary poetics. Asked by Charles Tomlinson whether "Pound provided a sound inoculation against the New Critics," Robert Creeley replies: "Yes . . . he warned against the muzziness that can come of a too conscious fuddling of symbolism. . . . Pound has always been intent to make a clear demarcation between a symbol which in effect exhausts references as opposed to a sign or mark of something which constantly renews its references." [26] Donald Davie similarly remarks, "Pound's repeated assertion [in *The Pisan Cantos*] that the paradisal is *real*, out there in the real world, is a conscious challenge to the whole symbolist aesthetic." [27] And the same year that he publishes his Pound book, Davie writes a poem called "In California," that begins:

> At Ventucopa, elevation
> Two-eight-nine-six the water hydrant frozen,
> Deserted or broken settlements,
> Gasoline stations closed and boarded, [28]

lines that Poundians will immediately connect to the opening of "Provincia Deserta":

> At Rochecoart,
> Where the hills part
> > in three ways
> Are three valleys, full of winding roads. [29]

Imagism as a challenge to Symbolist aesthetic—this, rather than the actual *Poundspeech* with its abrupt collage cuts and startling juxtapositions, is what comes down to so many of our poets. Indeed, the cult of exactitude, of a stubborn literalness, is likely to turn up in such unexpected places as James Merrill's *Mirabell: Book of Numbers*.

> Between our dining room and stairs
> Leading to the future studio
> From long before our time, was this ill-lit
> Shoebox of a parlor where we'd sit
> Faute de mieux, when not asleep or eating.
> It had been papered by the original people—

> Blue-on-eggshell foliage touchingly
> Mottled or torn in places.[30]

"Blue-on-eggshell foliage . . . / Mottled or torn"—the phrasing is Poundian although Pound would have omitted the word "touchingly." Tell it straight, he would have argued, and the reader will be touched, alright.

2. "I scarcely know," John Berryman wrote in 1949, "what to say of Pound's ear. Fifteen years of listening has not taught me that it is inferior to the ear of *Twelfth Night*."[31] High praise indeed, if a bit stilted. But compare it to the response of a British poet who had barely heard of Pound when he went up to Cambridge in 1945. In his memoir *Some Americans*, Charles Tomlinson recalls:

> While still at grammar school, I had invested half a crown . . . in a copy of the Sesame Books selection of Ezra Pound. . . . Puzzled, I read it through many times, tried to scan the opening lines of "E.P. Ode Pour L'Election de Son Sepulchre"; tried the same with "The River-Merchant's Wife." Evidently it couldn't be done. This was a naive discovery, no doubt. Scansion had figured prominently in one's education—in English, French, and Latin, I am grateful that it did. But here its only use was to point the difference, to suggest, with the Mauberley extract, that perhaps some type of syncopation was at work. . . . It was a sense of cleanliness of the phrasing that drew me, still puzzled, to Canto 2, toward the end of the book. I returned many times to
>
>> Lithe turning of water,
>>> sinews of Poseidon,
>> Black azure and hyaline,
>>> glass wave over Tyro. . . .
>
> The canto closed on the word "And. . . ." That was also something to think about.[32]

What was it that made Pound's prosody seem so revolutionary? Writing of the breaking of the pentameter that first occurs in the *Cathay* poems, Donald Davie explains:

> It is important to understand what is involved. From Edmund Spenser onwards in English verse the finest art was employed in running over the verse line so as to build up larger units of movement such as the strophe, the Miltonic verse paragraph, or, in Shakespearean and other theatrical poetry, the sustained dramatic speech. . . . the grammatical unit, the sen-

tence, is draped over the metrical unit, the line. . . . This is not to "break" the pentameter (or more generally the verse-line of whatever length), but rather to submerge it, by incorporating the line into the building of larger and more intricate rhythmical units. . . . It was only when the line was considered as the unit of composition, as it was by Pound in *Cathay*, that there emerged the possibility of "breaking" the line, of disrupting it from within.[33]

Here Davie perceives, quite rightly, I think, that Pound's great contribution to modern prosody was his focus on the line, rather than the larger stanzaic block, "as the unit of composition." Whitman, one might object, had already done the same thing, but the Whitman free-verse line is still inherently iambic (or anapestic):

I believe a leaf of grass is no less than the journey-work of the stars, ‖
And the pismire is equally perfect, | and a grain of sand, and the
    egg of the wren, ‖
And the tree-toad is a chef-d'oeuvre for the highest, ‖
And the running blackberry would adorn the parlors of heaven ‖[34]

In contrast, Pound's line repeatedly violates the iambic norm, which is to say that it goes counter to the stress pattern inherent in English:

Torches melt in the glare‖
    set flame of the corner cook-stall‖
Blue agate casing the sky (as at Gourdon that time)‖
    the sputter of resin, ‖
Saffron sandal so petals the narrow foot: |Hymenaeus Io! ‖
    Hymen, |Io Hymenaee! ‖ Arunculeia! ‖
One scarlet flower is cast on the blanch-white stone. ‖[35]

This particular habit of lineating, with its heavy stressing, its spondaic, amphibracic, and cretic feet, its long sonorous vowels in assonantal patterns, was taken over by a score of poets, for example: Bunting:

Swirl sleeping in the waterfall!‖
On motionless pools scum appearing‖
    disappearing! ‖

Eáves fórmal on the zénith, ‖
lófty cíty Kyótò, ‖
weálthy, withoút antíquitìes! ‖ [36]

H.D. in her early poetry:

Crásh on crásh of the seá, ‖
stráining to wréck mén, seá-boàrds, cóntinènts, ‖
ráging agaínst the wórld, ‖ fúrioùs, ‖
stáy at lást, | for agaínst your fúry ‖
and yoúr mád flíght, ‖
the líne of héroes stánds, gód-lìke ‖ [37]

And in her late:

Ô ébony ísland, | Ô táll cýprèss-trées, ‖
nòw I am bléssed anéw as my dárk veíls →
clíng clóse and clóse and máke an imáge of mé ‖ [38]

Charles Wright:

Caráfe, | còmpotiér, | seá shêll, | váse: ‖
Blánk spáces, | white óbjects; ‖
Lúminoùs knóts alóng the bláck rópe. ‖ [39]

Larry Eigner:

fláke diámond of →
                    the seá ‖
the shimmering sánd ‖
    dilátion | shádow in raín ‖ [40]

Interestingly, many poets who have praised Pound's music, like Robert Duncan or Allen Ginsberg, do not follow his two cardinal rules: (1) use the end-stopped line as a unit, and (2) avoid conventional iambic rhythm. Duncan's "A Poem Beginning with a Line by Pindar," for example, begins with a line one might find in Pound—"The light foot hears you and the brightness begins"—and follows Pindar's line with the Poundian "God-step at the margins of thought, / Quick adulterous tread at the heart." But these Poundian inflections soon give way to Duncan's own characteristic rhythm:

In Goya's canvas Cupid and Psyche →
have a hurt voluptuous grace →
bruised by redemption. ‖ The copper light →
falling upon the brown boy's slight body →
is carnal fate that sends the soul wailing →
up from blind innocence, ǀ ensnared →
    by dimness   into the deprivations of desiring sight. ‖ [41]

Here the consistent enjambment coupled with light, irregular stressing (chiefly anapestic) creates what is almost a prose rhythm, although alliteration and assonance are marked. The effect is carried even further in Zukofsky's "A":

When we dream that we speak ‖
We think we speak →
From free decision of the mind; ‖
Yet we do not speak, or if we do, ‖
This decision thought to be free →
is imagination ǀ —or memory; ‖
Is nothing but the accord →
An idea involves. ‖
A suspension of judgement →
Apprehends, is not free. ‖
In dreams also we dream that we dream ‖
I grant no one is deceived →
In so far as he perceives. ‖
The imaginations of the mind →
        in themselves →
Involve no error, ‖
But I deny that a man →
      affirms nothing →
In so far as he perceives. [42]

Zukofsky's predominantly three-stress lines, sometimes run over, sometimes pausing, are visual rather than auditory units; the rhythm pushes us forward from line to line, sound structure depending upon the very subtle pattern of word repetition—*dream, speak, free, perceives*—all

with the same vowel sound and occasionally rhyming ("deceived"/"perceives"), but recurring in different contexts.

It is interesting that Allen Ginsberg, who has written extensively on Pound's "lovely stress syncopation," his "lines that could be chanted rhythmically without violating human common sense," his breaking of the pentameter as "no less than the whole alteration of human consciousness,"[43] himself uses the repetitive, bardic, oracular, loosely iambic free-verse line of Whitman rather than Pound's more classically "musical" one; in *Howl*, for that matter, the linear unit is often stretched out into small paragraphs:

> who jumped off the Brooklyn Bridge this actually happened and walked away unknown and forgotten into the ghostly daze of Chinatown soup alleyways & firetrucks, not even one free beer,
> who sang out of their windows in despair, fell out of the subway window, jumped in the filthy Passaic, leaped on negroes, cried all over the street, danced on broken wineglasses barefoot smashed phonograph records of nostalgic European 1930's German jazz finished the whiskey and threw up groaning into the bloody toilet, moans in their ears and the blast of colossal steamwhistles[44]

Indeed, to talk about the legacy of Pound's rhythm is to realize that there is finally as much metrical difference as likeness. For who can really imitate this sort of thing?

> "Búk!"| said the Sécond Báronèt, | "éh . . .
> "Tháss a fúnny loókin' búk"| saíd the Báronèt
> Loóking at Báyle,| folío,| 4 vóls. |in gílt leáther,| "Áh . . .

(C 139)

Here the language is alternately slangy and formal—"Buk" and "Thass" side by side with "Looking at Bayle" and "in gilt leather." Few poets writing today move as easily between these two poles; few would invent a line like the third, with its 14 syllables carrying 8 stresses and its 3 caesurae, the slow and broken rhythm appearing to be "free" until we realize that it can be scanned as follows:

/ x x /	/ x /	/ /	x / / x	/
choriambus	cretic	spondee	antispast	monosyllable

In its intricacy, Pound's is a rhythm that has given *les jeunes* a goal to aim toward, the "musical phrase," *not* the sequence of the metronome.

3. "In my opinion," wrote Basil Bunting in 1932, "'Propertius' was the most important poem of our times, surpassing alike 'Mauberley' and 'The Waste Land.'" And he explains:

> The question of the relation of Pound's poem with the book of Propertius' elegies does not arise, except for the literary historian. There is no claim that this is a translation. The correspondence, the interpenetration of ancient and modern is Pound's, not Propertius's. . . .
>
> The beautiful step of the verse, the cogent movement of thought and feeling throughout, the sensitive perception of the little balanced in the great and their mutual dependence, the extraordinary directness, here and there quite naked, achieved in spite of the complexity of the whole conception; a poem that is a society and an age, that of Rome as well as that of London. (*BBMP* 254)

What Bunting, like so many other twentieth-century poets, learned from Pound was that "translation" should not suffer from what Peter Quartermain nicely calls "the archeological fallacy that the experience the original audience had of the poem can be replicated"[40] (*BBMP* 150). In the same year that he praised *Propertius*, Bunting published his version of Horace's Ode 13 from book 1, compressing the original twenty lines into twelve, remarkable for their curious—and quite un-Horatian—conjunction of guttural north Umbrian monosyllables, archaisms, and modern slang:

> Please stop gushing about his pink
> neck smooth arms and so forth, Dulcie; it makes me sick,
> badtempered, silly: makes me blush.
> Dribbling sweat on my chops proves I'm on tenterhooks.
> —White skin bruised in a boozing bout,
> ungovernable cub certain to bite out a
> permanent memorandum on
> those lips. Take my advice, better not count on your
> tough guy's mumbling your pretty mouth
> always. Only the thrice blest are in love for life,
> we others are divorced at heart
> soon, soon torn apart by wretched bickerings.[45]

Horace with an Anglo-Saxon overlay—the mode is identifiably Poundian. Think, for that matter, of Canto 1, whose mode Guy Davenport characterizes as follows:

207

It is a translation of the most archaic part of the *Odyssey*: the descent of Odysseus into Hades, a motif that goes all the way back to the Gilgamesh epic. And how does Pound translate it? Not from the Greek, but from the Latin of Andreas Divus, the first Renaissance translator of Homer, thereby working another archaic fact into his symbol. And into what kind of English does he translate it? Into the rhythms and diction of *The Seafarer* and *The Wanderer*: archaic English.[46]

Such "daedalian art"[47] sets the stage for all those twentieth-century "translations," like Bunting's version of Horace, that use the "archaic," the "classical," the historically or geographically remote culture as a source of invention. Pound's influence in this sphere has been so enormous that there is no measuring it, and one would have to discuss at some length the poetry of Olson and Duncan, of H.D. and Zukofsky, to understand even its rudiments. Pick up any poetry magazine today— say, the eclectic *American Poetry Review*—and you will find scores of "translations" that are in fact free versions of this or that Persian or Indian or Hungarian poet. Again, the movement called Ethnopoetics has made what its founder Jerome Rothenberg calls Pound's "pivotal breakthrough in translation"[48] the cornerstone of its recreation of tribal and sacred texts from "primitive" and ancient cultures: a journal like *Alcheringa* carries into new realms (the Mayan, the Somali, the Polynesian) Pound's "invention of China," as Eliot called it, or his invention of Rome and Provence.

This is not to say that the results of the modern translation-as-invention fever have always been happy. In the Introduction to his *Imitations* (1961), Robert Lowell writes:

> This book is partly self-sufficient and separate from its sources, and should be first read as a sequence, one voice running through many personalities, contrasts, and repetitions. . . . I have been reckless with literal meaning, and labored hard to get the tone. Most often this has been *a* tone, for *the* tone is something that will always more or less escape transference to another language and cultural moment. I have tried to write alive English and to do what my authors might have done if they were writing their poems now and in America.[49]

It sounds, for all the world, like Pound declaring in 1931 that *Propertius* "presents certain emotions as vital to me in 1917, faced with the infinite and ineffable imbecility of the British Empire, as they were to Proper-

tius some centuries earlier, when faced with the infinite and ineffable imbecility of the Roman Empire."[50] Indeed, asked by Frederick Seidel about his own adaptation of a Propertius poem (see "The Ghost [After Sextus Propertius]" in *Lord Weary's Castle*), Lowell replies:

> I got him through Pound. When I read him in Latin I found a kind of Propertius you don't get in Pound at all. Pound's Propertius is a rather Ovidian figure with a great deal of Pound's fluency and humor and irony. The actual Propertius is a very excited, tense poet, rather desperate; his line is much more like parts of Marlowe's *Faustus*. And he's of all the Roman poets the most like a desperate Christian. His experiences, his love affair with Cynthia, are absolutely rending, destroying.[51]

Propertius, that is to say, becomes a mirror image of Robert Lowell.

But the transference cannot always be willed. In a stinging review of *Imitations*, John Simon argues:

> The begetter of Lowell's imitations is, without question, Pound, and particularly the Pound of the versions of Propertius. . . . But it is precisely because Pound was able to ignore his original so sublimely, and because Pound is a great enough poet in his own right, that the damage to Sextus Propertius becomes an homage to Ezra Pound and English free verse. Lowell, however, is not that free from his models, nor has his free verse the energy and variety of Pound's. It is the neither-fish-nor-fowlness of Lowell's imitations, plus all the red herring they contain, that makes them perverse as translation and unpalatable as poetry.[52]

We need not agree with this harsh judgment in order to see the problems a "free" or "creative" translation à la Pound may raise. Take, for example, Lowell's "imitation" of the late Heine lyric, "Mein Tag war Heiter":

> Mein Tag war heiter, glücklich meine Nacht.
> Mir jauchzte stets mein Volk, wenn ich die Leier
> Der Dicktkunst schlug. Mein Lied war Lust und Feuer,
> Hat manche schöne Gluten angefacht.[53]

In literal English:

> My day was merry, happy was my night.
> The people cheered me on whenever I smote
> The lyre of poetry. My song was joy and fire,
> It kindled many a lovely blaze.[54]

209

And in Lowell's version:

> My zenith was luckily happier than my night:
> whenever I touched the lyre of inspiration, I smote
> the Chosen People. Often—all sex and thunder—
> I pierced those overblown and summer clouds.[55]

Heine, suffering on his "mattress-grave," remembers a time when both his days *and* his nights were happy; he remembers how his poetry moved the people ("Mein Volk"), what fiery power his song could have. Lowell changes all this: "Mein Tag" is now equated with the poet's youth, "Meine Nacht" with his old age. The poet's song "smote" not "mein Volk" but, in an allusion to the Jewish poet's radicalism and youthful atheism, "the Chosen People." "Lust" is mistranslated as "sex" (i.e., "lust"), and the poet recalls himself as quintessential rebel, "piercing those overblown and summer clouds" of ordinary life with his sexual anger.[56] Heine's concern for the lyric imagination is thus reduced to a set of references to the poet's youthful rebellion; it can be related to Lowell's own poem by that name.

But suppose we forget about the Heine original and read Lowell's poem as his own version of German Romanticism even as we read the *Homage* as Pound's invention of Propertius. In this case, we have Lowell-Heine solemnly announcing that his youth ("zenith") was happier than his "night." Not a very arresting statement. Again, the "lyre of inspiration" is now viewed as some sort of irritant, a way of shaking up Lowell's own "Chosen People," which is to say the Lowells and Winslows of Boston. We know from *Life Studies* that Lowell as a young man was "all sex and thunder," but in what sense could he pierce the "overblown and summer clouds" (of New England?) with his angry sexuality? Are we to assume that New England responded to his clarion call? And, if so, what is his role now that his "zenith" has passed?

It is hard to take these questions seriously and indeed the poem only treats its material as gesture. Heine's particular sense of loss—the loss experienced by one who was once the poet of the people—evaporates and there is nothing that quite fills the gap. It is a problem by no means unique to Lowell, the point being that Poundian "translation" is a very difficult process, depending finally upon the poet's ability to make the past present. As Guy Davenport has put it:

What is most modern in our time frequently turns out to be the most archaic. The sculpture of Brancusi belongs to the art of the Cyclades in the ninth century B.C. Corbusier's buildings in their cubist phase look like the white clay houses of Anatolia and Malta. . . . in *Finnegans Wake* [Joyce] writes across the fact of the Indo-European origin of European languages, seeing in the kinship of tongues the great archeological midden of history, the tragic incomprehensibility of which provides him with a picture of the funeral of Western culture. (*GOI* 21)

4. I turn now to what seems to me the most interesting side of the Pound legacy: namely, the poet's canto structure. In a review of Stanley Burnshaw's *The Seamless Web* (1970), Davenport remarks:

for all his careful inspection of the kinds of voice with which poems speak, Mr. Burnshaw sees *the poem* as a particular kind of poetry to the exclusion of other kinds. Poetry for him is lyric or elegiac almost wholly, and I think what moves him is *song*, the rich surge of emotion, the radiant glory of speech in flight. This is splendid, of course, but it tends toward a puritanism that diminishes our taste for the comic, the satiric, the grotesque, the narrative poem, the wholesome and drab. (*GOI* 213)

An epic is a poem including history. Perhaps Pound's chief gift to the contemporary poet, we are now beginning to see, is his recovery for poetry of "the comic, the satiric, the grotesque, the narrative," his move beyond the isolated lyric poem (*poema*) valorized by New Critics like Stanley Burnshaw, the poem as embodiment of "the radiant glory of speech in flight," of crystallized emotion, toward a larger, more capacious poetic form (*poesis*) that could once again accommodate various levels of discourse.

This is the point made in the opening chapters of Michael A. Bernstein's *The Tale of the Tribe*. One of Pound's main motives in the *Cantos*, Bernstein argues, is to challenge the dominance the novel had achieved by the end of the nineteenth century as *the* genre that could engage political, economic, historical, and social realities. The *Cantos* attempt to reappropriate these "realities" and to absorb them into the lyric fabric; the "Inductive or Ideogrammic Method" is combined with "Confucian Historiography":

The seemingly unobtrusive moment in Canto VIII, when the first series of historical letters is introduced into *The Cantos* and the personality of Sigis-

211

mundo is shown by juxtaposing his prose instruction concerning a painter he wishes to engage with a lyric poem he writes for Isotta degli Atti *without privileging either medium*, represents one of the decisive turning-points in modern poetics, opening for verse the capacity to include domains of experience long since considered alien territory.[57]

The recovery of such "alien territory" occurs most obviously, among Pound's heirs, in Williams's *Paterson* and Olson's *Maximus*. The connections between these poems and the *Cantos* have been made frequently, not least by Bernstein himself, who takes up the knotty problem of the relationship between the historical and mythological codes, between symbol and rupture in these works. Other critics have traced a lineage from the *Cantos* via *Paterson* to the long poetic sequences of Lowell and Berryman. *The Dream Songs*, for example, has been called "Poundian" in its range and allusiveness, its shifting from humor to pathos, from high style to black slang.[58] But neither Berryman nor Lowell, nor for that matter Ginsberg or Bunting, violate the lyric frame as do such other Poundian poets as Zukofsky and, in their different ways, Guy Davenport and Jerome Rothenberg. A few examples must suffice here.

Zukofsky's "A"-12 (1950–51) takes up 138 of the 800-odd pages that constitute "A," the long poem written over the half century between 1928 and 1974, when "A"-23 was completed. Following hard upon the two-page "A"-11, which is a formal love song for the poet's wife Celia and his son Paul, "A"-12 begins on a musical note that takes us back to the opening line of "A"-1, "A / Round of fiddles playing Bach," with the lines:

> *Out of deep need*
> Four trombones and the organ in the nave
> A torch surged—
> Timed the theme Bach's name
> Dark larch and ridge, night.
>
> ("A," p. 126)

Not only is the subject here music, but the lines have an intricate sound pattern: ti*med*—the*me*—na*me*; d*ar*k—l*ar*ch; lar*ch*—rid*ge*. The musical motif comes back again and again, in references to Paul's violin playing, to "H— playing / The Turkish Concerto / By Mozart" ("A," p. 161), and so on. But Bach is also viewed as a father and throughout "A"-12 we find interwoven stories of fathers and sons: Odysseus and

212

Telemachus, the physician Nichomaeus and Aristotle ("A," p. 236), the groaning old father of Gertrude Stein's *The Making of Americans*, who protests to his son, who is dragging him through his own orchard, "Stop! I did not drag my father beyond this tree" ("A," p. 168), and, centrally, Zukofsky's own father and grandfather in their relationships to him and his own relationship to Paul as well as to the "Poor Pay Pfc. Jackie," neighborhood kid and surrogate son, who is sent off to fight in the Korean War and writes a series of letters (in slangy, nonorthographic prose) to the poet.

Reading fragment after fragment about the poet's childhood on the Lower East Side and then about Paul's childhood, one realizes that the germ of a whole novel is contained in the pages of "A"-12. But the narrative cannot be linear because for Zukofsky, as for Pound in less extreme form, experience is regarded as unfinished, indeed always only potential—moving toward something that never quite happens. There is no unifying principle in "A"-12, no Supreme Fiction that will bring all the fragments together, because, in Don Byrd's words, "the structure of history is not to be found in logic or mythologic . . . but in language and the complex web by which language is involved with perception." [59] And because language is so central, straight prose—the medium of the novel, however alogical its structure—cannot be sufficient. Rather, the literary pastiches and borrowings (for example, the dialogue between Titania and Bottom on pages 133–34, the speech of Stephen Dedalus on Aristotle on page 142, or the condensed version of a Reznikoff narrative on pages 208–10) [60] are arranged in a verbal-visual structure that accords with Zukofsky's declaration:

I'll tell you.
About my *poetics*—

$$\int \genfrac{}{}{0pt}{}{\text{music}}{\text{speech}}$$

An integral
Lower limit speech
Upper limit music

("A," p. 138)

213

Between these "limits" we find pictograms like the valentine on page 129:

Paul   Louis
from
his
nice best best
friend of Louis

or the playful graph on pages 163–64, that begins

MAN ⟶ EARTH ⟶ WORLDS

Thus the discourses of commerce (the greeting card) or of science (the graph) are absorbed into the fabric of the poem. Again, "A"-12 follows the example of the *Cantos* in juxtaposing the found object to the moment of metamorphosis; Zukofsky's father, for example, becomes for the boy Paul, the image of Aristotle:

> P.Z. remembers the day "Aristotle" died,
> Still owns his snowshoes
> Indispensable in Macedonia.
> I bought him two balloons:
> "Plato" and "Aristotle".
> Filled with air they had faces
> Mounted on snowshoes
> As expected
> "Plato" and "Aristotle."
> "Aristotle"—
> Carus, to Paul, it was sad.
>
> ("A," p. 164)

Such moments occur against the backdrop of historical events: "the first John Jacob Astor / Landing in Baltimore / With $25 and seven

flutes to sell" ("A," p. 190), within ever shifting political and geographic frames. The "upper limit / Music" appears in odal hymns, chants, and sonnets; the "lower limit / Speech" in the conversations of the poet with Paul or with his father or with the poet Lorine Niedecker.

To what voice can we attribute all this heterogeneous material? Of Pound's voice in the *Cantos*, Michael A. Bernstein writes:

> Pound's authorial "voice," I think, is often implicitly and theoretically definable as that unspoken "marginal presence" which silently articulates (makes sense out of) the gaps in the printed text, a voice we only really discover in the process of "speaking it" ourselves. . . . He wanted the text to give the impression of the tribe's own heritage narrating itself, of the different historical voices addressing us as if without the mediation of one unique narrator or controlling author. It is almost as though the texture of *The Cantos* were designed to illustrate Karl Popper's idea of an "epistemology without a knowing subject," of information objectively existing and available for communal use without necessarily being fully realized in any single individual's competence.[61]

This abandonment of the "speaking subject" is carried a step further in Zukofsky's "A." In the *Cantos*, after all, the "ideogrammic method" allows us to move from image to image, following a particular thread (mythological, historical, economic, etc.), whereas in "A" such binding devices are rare and accordingly the reader must tease out, even more extensively than in Pound, the "repeat in history." Indeed, the status of history in these poems is curious. As Guy Davenport, himself a great inventor of collage-texts,[62] puts it:

> To say that *The Cantos* is "a voyage in time" is to be blind to the poem altogether. We miss immediately the achievement upon which the success of the poem depends, its rendering time transparent and negligible, its dismissing the supposed corridors and perspectives *down* which the historian invites us to look. . . . In Pound's spatial sense of time, the past is here, now; its invisibility is our blindness, not its absence.[63]

This is also true of a poem like "A"-12, in which the time of Roosevelt and Wilkie coexists with "1313. Rabbi Hacen Ben Salomo— / (Great One Singer Son of Peace)— / Taught Spanish Christians / To dance in a church" ("A," p. 186). But in "A," as in a work like John Ashbery's *Litany*, these "events" are not only spatialized; they are, as such "language" poets as Ron Silliman have argued, subordinated to the play

215

of language itself: "Each line &/or stanza a study in balance, silence (peace) proposed as maximum stress in all directions, thus active. This never-to-be resolved equilibrium of the spoken within the written within the spoken etc. is for him the motivating center of craft." [64]

Zukofsky thus carries further Pound's program for a poem including history, a poem that no longer privileges the lyric over, say, the found object (actual letter received, newspaper passage, document), a poem in which the single startling epiphany gives way to collage, which is to say to the juxtaposition of disparate materials without commitment to explicit syntactical relations between elements and without a consistent authorial voice as ordering principle. This notion of collage is taken even further in the work of Jerome Rothenberg, not so much in his lyric poems as in the unique anthologies that began to appear in 1968 with the publication of *Technicians of the Sacred.*

Rothenberg has regularly praised what he calls "the collage composition of the *Cantos*" and is fond of quoting Pound's statement that "*all* ages are contemporaneous *in the mind.*" [65] In the "Pre-Face" to *Revolution of the Word: The Avant-Garde, 1914–45,* in which he presents us with an alternative tradition to the accepted modernist canon, Rothenberg writes:

> When Pound writes (1915) of a basic poetic process that involves "a rush of experience into the vortex" (i.e., the mind), he is talking about a condition that has become newly critical. . . . where the ideas truly "rush," the process no longer links event to event in good straight lines. In the face of multiple chronologies, many poets turn to synchronicity (the simultaneous existence of all places & times) as a basic organizing principle. As a method, a process of making the poem, this becomes "collage." [66]

How does this purpose work in a Rothenberg anthology? In an essay called "On Anthologies" (1978), Rothenberg begins:

> It seems to me that I've been making anthologies for as long as I've been making poems *per se.* . . . As a kid I inherited a large desk with a sheet of glass on top, beneath which I would slip in pages of poems—my own & others'—& pictures, etc. that I had been coming across in the stuff I was reading. I used to arrange them to form "shows" of works that seemed, by juxtaposition, to inform each other. I also typed up poems from different places & times & kept them in a series of folders marked *anthology.* That was from high school days & stopped sometime in college, when I started to *buy* books & be deceived by other people's arrangements. [67]

216

What the poet recognizes here is that it is by *juxtaposition* that works "inform each other." Or, as Pound points out in the ABC *of Reading*, the word "red" can only be defined by putting together such words as

ROSE   CHERRY
IRON RUST   FLAMINGO

(ABCR 22)

To put an anthology together thus means to assemble seemingly diverse particulars: "I've felt," says Rothenberg, "a sense of the book as poem, a large composition operating by assemblage or collage: my own voice emerging sometimes as translator, sometimes as commentator, but still obedient to the other voices, whether 'out there' or 'in here.'"[68] Notice that this takes us back to Michael Bernstein's account of voice in the *Cantos* as "unspoken marginal presence," as "information objectively existing and available for communal use without necessarily being fully realized in any single individual's competence."[69]

America A Prophecy, assembled in 1973 with the collaboration of George Quasha, begins with Pound's dictum that poetry is "language charged with meaning to the utmost degree" and outlines four sources upon which the anthology draws: (1) "the aboriginal poetry of the American continent"; (2) "other traditions, usually relegated to the status of 'folklore,' notably Afro-American oral poetry"; (3) "an ongoing meditative and visionary tradition, European in origin"; and (4) a "metapoetry" or "expansion of verbal possibilities" that includes diaries, letters, notebooks, scientific writing, visual and ritual media, modern experimental poetry, and so on.[70] In arranging texts from these four sources, the emphasis is to be on "the interplay of myth and history," following the injunctions of Emerson, Thoreau, and Whitman and especially those of Pound.

Let us look at a particular unit: the section called "Image-Making" under the category of "Map Four: Renewals" (pp. 403–52). Image-making, so the editors' headnote tells us, "includes such concepts as hieroglyphics, emblem poems, symbol, visualization, image, imagism, ideogram, phanopoeia, vortex, cubism, surrealism, frottage, hypnologues, photoheliograph, metaphor, objectivism, dialectic, concrete poetry, projectivism, deep image, chance imagery, and mudra" (p. 401). This dizzying catalog of nonparallel items (some refer to trope, others to genre or mode or movement; some, like cubism, are familiar terms;

217

others, like *hypnologues*, are coinages; still others, like *mudra*, refer to a specific religious practice)[71] interestingly includes a number of Poundian items (imagism, ideogram, vortex, phanopoeia) and indeed Pound's presence provides a point of reference for the entire text. Thus the section opens with a statement about the thaumaturgic power of the written word, taken from Boris de Rachewiltz's (then Pound's son-in-law) essay "Pagan and Magic Elements in Ezra Pound's Works." This passage is followed on later pages by such Pound items as an italicized section from "A Retrospect" (p. 409); an extract from Fenollosa's *Chinese Written Character*, prefaced by Hugh Kenner's biographical note on Fenollosa in *The Pound Era* (p. 415); Rothenberg's own account of the Vortex, again quoting Kenner (pp. 417–18); the entire "Seven Lakes Canto" (Canto 49 on pp. 418–20); a passage about "ideogrammic structure" quoting *Guide to Kulchur* (p. 420); and a note on Pound and the Objectivists (p. 430).

These Pound references function, so to speak, as metapoetic signposts. The "poem" itself begins with (1) ten lines from Longfellow's *Hiawatha*; (2) a frame from the Dresden Codex, one of the Mayan books containing history, prophecy, song, science, and genealogy, "written on long strips of bark paper, folded like screens and covered with gesso" (p. 404); (3) a pictograph from the mural of Tlalocan at Teotihuacan, which depicts a Toltec paradise; "the sexual motif," according to the end note, "appears to inform the imagery of the ritual, reminding us of the Tibetan Tantric link between sexuality and higher consciousness"; (4) the image of the "torsion-form" which is, according to Wilhelm Reich, the "basic form" of the "sexual embrace"; (5) two emblem poems written by the Shakers between 1844 and 1859, "visionary drawings . . . really spiritual message in pictorial form," felt to be controlled by supernatural agencies. The drawings, according to Edward Deming Andrews (*The Gift to Be Simple*), "often contained poems inscribed in a circle, heart or perhaps a scroll carried by a dove or angel" (p. 407). Since these ink drawings are hard to decipher, the editors helpfully transcribe the poems written around and within the leaf: "Ho ho ho (Shout) / Now while my love is flowing / You are not forgotten," and so on. This transcription is followed by the italicized sentence:

> *"It is wonderful how a handwriting which is illegible can be read, oh yes it can."* (Gertrude Stein, from *The Geographical History of America* [1936])

218

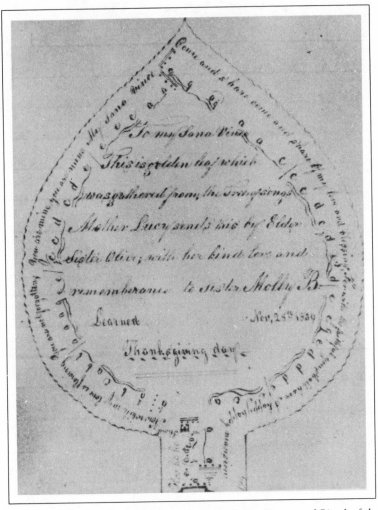

From Edward D. Andrews, *The Gift to Be Simple: Songs, Dances, and Rituals of the American Shakers* (New York: Dover Publications, 1940), p. 36.

Here the conjunction of Shaker emblem poem and Stein aphorism seems to me precisely the sort of thing we find in the *Cantos*, for we suddenly realize that the "illegible" (to us) handwriting on the left can be read, oh yes it can, since the editors have supplied us with the printed version on the right and a commentary beneath it. If a text is illegible, the collaging of writing and print implies, wait and before long it will reveal its secret.

A few pages later, under the heading "The Standard of Clarity," Rothenberg introduces us to a text by Louis Agassiz, "acknowledged as a master of the art of scientific description by Emerson, Thoreau, and William James. Ezra Pound claimed him as a model" (p. 411). "The art of Agassiz," says Rothenberg, "consists in revealing the Minute Particular as Luminous Detail; or, in Pound's phrase, the natural object is always the adequate symbol." What follows is a minute description of *Cyanea Arctica* that begins, "Seen floating in the water Cyanea Arctica exhibits a large circular disk, of a substance not unlike jelly, thick in the centre, and suddenly thinning out towards the edge, which presents several indentations" (p. 411). As Agassiz continues, he introduces a series of metaphors—tentacles as "floating tresses of hair," organs as "bunches of grapes," "four masses of folds, hanging like rich curtains, loosely waving to and fro," the "disk" of the animal opening and closing like an umbrella (p. 412). Ironically, the "scientific" description by Agassiz is more heavily metaphoric than the poem to which it is juxtaposed, Emily Dickinson's "Banish Air from Air," which takes its terms—the notion of "banish[ing] Air from Air," of dividing light—quite literally. Moreover, the "Three Definitions from *Sharp Eyes*" by the naturalist William Hamilton Gibson that are printed directly beneath Dickinson's lyric, look like perfect haiku:

Poppies

Flowers closed like two clam-shells;
inner petals coiled.

Lupine

The wheel-like leaf closes
downward against the stem
at its center,
like a closed umbrella,

or rises
in the form of a goblet.

And Rothenberg concludes: the texts "combine accurate observation
and sharp descriptive language with a post-Transcendentalist sense of
immanent power in all living things. [Gibson's] illustrations of his own
text suggest both Blake's illuminations and later uses of photo-montage"
(p. 413). Thus a strong case is made for the proximity of scientific and
poetic discourse: the collage suggests that Gibson is a poet, the author of
delicate haiku-like utterance, even as Dickinson, wedged between Agassiz and Gibson, turns into something of a scientist: "While Cubes in a
Drop / Or Pellets of Shape / Fit / Films cannot annul. . . ."

To find, at the center of "Image-Making," Pound's "Seven Lakes
Canto" is to see the collage principle of the *Cantos* at work. For Canto
49 is itself a collage, consisting, so Hugh Kenner tells us, of (1) [eight]
anonymous poems much rearranged; (2) the Emperor's poem; (3) a folk
song; (4) a terminal Poundian distich and four interpolated Poundian
lines."[72] Sanehide Kodama has identified the source of the poems as
"eight famous paintings of scenes along a river in China which pours
into Lake Dotei. Ezra Pound's parents owned an old Japanese manuscript book which contained the eight Chinese and eight Japanese poems
illustrated by the paintings. The book is entitled *Sho-Sho* [the river]
Hakkei."[73] So the first six lines of the canto, evidently based on the sixth
painting or scene, go like this:

> For the seven lakes, and by no man these verses:
> Rain; empty river; a voyage,
> Fire from frozen cloud, heavy rain in the twilight
> Under the cabin roof was one lantern.
> The reeds are heavy; bent;
> and the bamboos speak as if weeping.
>
> (p. 418)

We read this passage quite differently in *America A Prophecy* than
we would if we met it in the normal sequence of the *Cantos*. For one
thing, lines like "Fire from frozen cloud, heavy rain in the twilight,"
and later, "sharp long spikes of the cinnamon" remind us of William
Hamilton Gibson's "the wheel-like leaf closes / downward against the
stem / at its center, / like a closed umbrella." For another, Rothenberg's

"framing"—the account of Vortex preceding the canto and of ideo-grammic structure following, the latter leading into Wylie Sypher's dis-cussion of the synchronization of time-sense in modern art, "corre-sponding to cinematic montage or juxtaposition of elements"—such framing foregrounds the imagistic, perceptual quality of Pound's col-lage, itself made up of so many fragments, rather than its references to money and banking ("State by creating riches shd. thereby get into debt?"), which connect it to the neighboring cantos in the Adams se-quence. The metatexts, in other words, "inform" one another even as the analogies to Agassiz or to Gibson or to Gertrude Stein provide a sense of ongoing process, of beginning again and again. To cut up and rearrange texts, the anthology implies, is to see familiar works in quite a new way. How seriously, for example, can we take Pound's "Sun up; work / sundown, to rest / dig well and drink of the water," when we read it against Stein's "Question and butter. / I find the butter very good / Lifting belly is so kind. / Lifting belly fattily" (p. 422)?

As we make our way through "Image-Making," Pound's canto is fur-ther "informed" by texts written by the poet's followers—Williams, Op-pen, Zukofsky—and by contemporary analogues—for example, to Dada and Surrealist works—as well as by later texts, partially belonging to the Pound tradition but also standing apart from it—a John Cage par-able, of which more in a moment, a Jackson MacLow "Light Poem" (1962), a series of concrete poems, and finally Bernadette Mayer's "Fic-tion," which deploys Steinian language, syntax, and "naive" story-telling devices to invent a kind of antipoem including history.

"Image-Making" can thus be read as a poetic sequence about differ-ent solutions to the question of the thaumaturgic power of the image, the point being that, as different as Stein's *Tender Buttons* is from the mural of Tlalocan, as different as Emmet Williams's concrete poem "Like Attacks Like" (p. 43) is from the Shaker emblem poems, these works are addressing themselves to related questions: (1) How do we per-ceive? (2) How do we record our perceptions? And (3) what do we take these perceptions to mean? Since it is often difficult to know where a given text ends and the editors' commentary begins, or again, at what point that commentary blurs into a commentary by some other critic or scholar, the collage anthology becomes, in an ironic sense, the "seam-less web" Stanley Burnshaw describes. Consider the place, in the larger

scheme of things, of the following anecdote told by John Cage, which is printed just a few pages after the "Seven Lakes Canto":

Translating Basho's Haiku

Text: Japanese	English transliteration
Matasutake ya	Mushroom;
shiranu ko-no-ha no	ignorance; leaf of tree
hebaritsuku	adhesiveness

Basho, 1644–1694

Versions:

R. B. Blythe translates Basho's haiku as follows:

The leaf of some unknown tree sticking on the mushroom.

I showed this translation to a Japanese composer friend. He said he did not find it very interesting. I said, "How would you translate it?" Two days later he brought me the following:

Mushroom does not know that leaf is sticking on it.

Getting the idea, I made during the next three years, the following:

That that's unknown brings mushroom and leaf together.

And the one I prefer?

What leaf? What mushroom?

(p. 437)

What leaf, what mushroom? Pound is not likely to have posed this Zen question: he is too assertive, too passionately didactic to allow for an "opening of the field" quite as self-surrendering as this one. But Rothenberg, standing apart from both, can see the obvious connections between Cage's anecdote and the sequence of Japanese "stills" in the "Seven Lakes Canto." Or again, between the Basho haiku and the William Hamilton Gibson naturalist descriptions of flora and fauna.

"To know the season," Guy Davenport observes, "we must understand metamorphosis, for things are never still, and never wear the same mask from age to age. The contemporary is without meaning while it is happening: it is a vortex, a whirlpool of action. It is a labyrinth. . . . The Cantos . . . are labyrinthine in structure, a zigzag of subject, modifying and illuminating each other by proximity, treating time as if it were a space over which one can move in any direction" (GOI 56). As the lessons of Pound's "poem including history" come home to us, we will witness more such "labyrinthine structures." Anthologies like America A Prophecy, "short stories" like Davenport's Tatlin!, performance

223

works like David Antin's *Tuning,* and long poems like Zukofsky's "A," or, in its very different way, James Merrill's "Ouija Board" trilogy—these give testimony to the vitality of the "daedalian art" of the *Cantos.*

Notes

1. Basil Bunting in conversation with Eric Mottram, 1975; see William S. Milne, "Basil Bunting's Prose and Criticism," in *Basil Bunting, Man and Poet,* ed. Carroll F. Terrell (Orono, Maine: National Poetry Foundation, 1980), p. 286; hereafter cited as *BBMP* followed by page number.

2. Charles Wright in conversation with Stuart Friebert and David Young, 1976, "Charles Wright at Oberlin," *Field, Contemporary Poetry and Poetics* 17 (Fall 1977): 48.

3. Guy Davenport, "Ezra Pound, 1885–1972," in *The Geography of the Imagination: Forty Essays* (San Francisco: North Point Press, 1981), pp. 175–76; hereafter cited as *GOI* followed by page number.

4. Allen Ginsberg, "The Death of Ezra Pound" (radio interview, 1972), *Allen Verbatim: Lectures on Poetry, Politics, Consciousness,* ed. Gordon Hall (New York: McGraw-Hill Book Co., 1974), p. 179.

5. In Keith Sagar's standard work *The Art of Ted Hughes* (Cambridge: Cambridge University Press, 1975), for example, Pound's name does not so much as appear in the index.

6. Ted Hughes, "The Swifts," *Season's Songs* (1975); reprinted in *New Selected Poems* (New York: Harper & Row, 1982), p. 144.

7. See Donald Sheehan, "An Interview with James Merrill," *Contemporary Literature* 9 (Winter 1967): 3.

8. Hugh Kenner, *The Pound Era* (Berkeley and Los Angeles: University of California Press, 1971), pp. 557–58.

9. Under the editorship of Carroll F. Terrell and Burton Hatlen, the National Poetry Foundation at the University of Maine, Orono, has brought out a series of volumes that contain seminal materials, both critical and bibliographical on Louis Zukofsky, Basil Bunting, and George Oppen. The Pound relationship is central to all three: *Louis Zukofsky, Man and Poet,* ed. Carroll F. Terrell (1979); *Basil Bunting, Man and Poet,* ed. Carroll F. Terrell (1981); *George Oppen, Man and Poet,* ed. Burton Hatlen (1981). See especially, in the last volume, Rachel Blau du Plessis, "Objectivist Poetics and Political Vision: A Study of Oppen and Pound," pp. 123–48.

On Pound and Olson, see especially Catherine Seelye (ed.), *Charles Olson and Ezra Pound: An Encounter at St. Elizabeths* (New York: Grossman Publishers, 1975); Robert von Hallberg, *Charles Olson: The Scholar's Art* (Cambridge, Mass.: Harvard University Press, 1978), pp. 44–63. On Pound and

Duncan, see esp. Don Byrd, "The Question of Wisdom as Such," in *Robert Duncan: Scales of the Marvelous* (New York: New Directions, 1979), pp. 38–55; Ekbert Gaas, "An Interview with Robert Duncan," *Boundary* 2 8, (Winter 1980): 1–20. On Pound and Creeley, see two special Creeley issues: *Boundary* 2 6–7 (Spring–Fall 1978); *Sagetrieb* 1 (Winter 1982).

In *The Influence of Ezra Pound* (London: Oxford University Press, 1966), K. L. Goodwin is mainly concerned with Pound's relationship to his contemporaries, especially Yeats and Eliot. The influence on Olson, Bunting, and H.D. is minimized because Goodwin considers them only minor poets. Conversely, the influence on such Pound contemporaries as Archibald MacLeish and Hart Crane now seems curiously exaggerated.

10. Denise Levertov, "Grass Seed and Cherry Stones," in *The Poet in the World* (New York: New Directions, 1973), pp. 251–52.

11. Robert Creeley, "A Note on Ezra Pound" (1965), in *A Quick Graph* (San Francisco: Four Seasons Foundation, 1970), p. 196. See also "I'm given to write poems," *A Quick Graph*, pp. 68–69; David Ossman, "Interview with Robert Creeley" (1961), in *Contexts of Poetry: Interviews, 1961–1971* (Bolinas: Four Seasons Foundation, 1973), pp. 3–12; "Robert Creeley in Conversation with Charles Tomlinson," *Contexts of Poetry*, pp. 15, 19.

12. L. S. Dembo, "An Interview with Carl Rakosi," *Contemporary Literature* 10 (Spring 1969): 180.

13. Donald Davie, *Ezra Pound: Poet as Sculptor* (New York: Oxford University Press, 1964), chaps. 3 and 4, and cf. Davie, *Pound* (London: Fontana/Collins, 1975), chap. 2.

14. "A Retrospect" (1918), *The Literary Essays of Ezra Pound* (New York: New Directions, 1968), pp. 4–5; *Gaudier-Brzeska* (New York: New Directions, 1970), p. 92; hereafter cited as GB followed by page number; *ABC of Reading* (New York: New Directions, 1960), pp. 30, 32; hereafter cited as ABCR followed by page number.

15. Theodore Weiss's fascinating love-hate essay on Pound, "E.P.: The Man Who Cared Too Much," first appeared in *Parnassus* 5 (Fall–Winter 1976); it is reprinted in *The Man from Porlock: Engagements, 1944–81* (Princeton: Princeton University Press, 1982), pp. 17–57.

16. See "Tradition and Talent" (review essay on Philip Booth, Adrienne Rich, Stanley Moss), *The New York Herald Tribune Book Week*, 4 September 1966, p. 14. In "The Mind's Own Place," *Kulchur* 10 (1963), reprinted in *Montemora* 1 (Fall 1975): 132–33, George Oppen writes: "Modern American poetry begins with the determination to find the image of the thing encountered, the thing seen each day whose meaning has become the meaning and color of our lives." Frank O'Hara's equivalent of this "image of the thing encountered" is "presence"; see Edward Lucie-Smith, "An Interview with Frank O'Hara," *Stu-*

225

dio International (September 1966), reprinted in *Standing Still and Walking in New York,* ed. Donald Allen (Bolinas: Grey Fox Press, 1975); and "Larry Rivers," ibid., p. 96.

17. "Open Letter to Louis Zukofsky" (1932), in *BBMP,* p. 242.

18. Allen Ginsberg, "Encounters with Ezra Pound: Journal Notes," *City Lights Anthology* (1974), reprinted in *Composed on the Tongue* (Bolinas: Grey Fox Press, 1980), pp. 4–5.

19. Ibid., p. 12.

20. Louis Zukofsky, "An Objective," *Prepositions,* expanded edition (Berkeley and Los Angeles: University of California Press, 1981), pp. 16, 13. This section on Louis Zukofsky appeared in slightly different form in "Postmodernism and the Impasse of Lyric," *Formations* 1 (Fall 1984): 51–52.

21. Ibid., p. 13.

22. Louis Zukofsky, *All: The Collected Short Poems, 1923–1964* (New York: W. W. Norton & Co., 1971), p. 52, by permission of W. W. Norton and Company, Inc. Copyright © 1971, 1966, 1965 by Louis Zukofsky.

23. Burton Hatlen, "Zukofsky, Wittgenstein, and the Poetics of Absence," *Sagetrieb* 1, 1 (Spring 1982): 92.

24. On this point, see my *Poetics of Indeterminacy: Rimbaud to Cage* (Princeton: Princeton University Press, 1981), esp. chap. 1.

25. Hatlen, "Zukofsky," p. 73.

26. "Robert Creeley in Conversation with Charles Tomlinson," *Contexts of Poetry,* pp. 15–16.

27. Davie, *Ezra Pound,* p. 181. Davie, *Pound,* p. 43: "It still needs to be stressed that the momentousness of Imagism as Pound conceived of it lies just in its being not a variant of *symbolisme* nor a development out of it, but a radical alternative to it."

28. Donald Davie, *Events and Wisdoms* (Middletown, Conn.: Wesleyan University Press, 1965), p. 26.

29. *Personae: The Collected Shorter Poems of Ezra Pound* (New York: New Directions, 1971), p. 121.

30. James Merrill, *The Changing Light at Sandover* (New York: Atheneum, 1982), p. 97.

31. John Berryman, "The Poetry of Ezra Pound" in *The Freedom of the Poet* (New York: Farrar, Straus & Giroux, 1976), p. 264.

32. Charles Tomlinson, *Some Americans: A Personal Record* (Berkeley and Los Angeles: University of California Press, Quantum Books, 1981), pp. 1–2.

33. Davie, *Ezra Pound,* pp. 44–45.

34. Walt Whitman, "Song of Myself," *Leaves of Grass,* ed. Scully Bradley and Harold W. Blodgett, Norton Critical Edition (New York: W. W. Norton & Co., 1973), p. 59.

The notation used is a modified version of Trager-Smith. A primary stress is marked ('), secondary (^), tertiary (`), caesura with a double bar (‖), a shorter pause with a single bar (|). An arrow at the end of a line means the line is enjambed.

35. *The Cantos of Ezra Pound* (New York: New Directions, 1975), p. 15; hereafter cited as C followed by page number.

36. Basil Bunting, "Chomei at Toyama," *Collected Poems* (Oxford and New York: Oxford University Press, 1978), p. 63. By permission of Oxford University Press, © 1978.

37. H.D., "Sea Heroes," *Selected Poems* (New York: New Directions, 1957), p. 11.

38. H.D., "Winter Love," *Hermetic Definition* (New York: New Directions, 1972), p. 109.

39. Charles Wright, "White," *Hard Freight* (1973), reprinted in *Country Music: Selected Early Poems* (Middletown, Conn.: Wesleyan University Press, 1982), p. 21.

40. Larry Eigner, *Selected Poems*, ed. Samuel Charters and Andrea Wyatt (Berkeley: Oyez, 1972), p. 66.

41. Robert Duncan, *The Opening of the Field* (1960; reprinted, New York: New Directions, 1973), p. 62.

42. Louis Zukovsky, "A" (Berkeley, Los Angeles, and London: University of California Press, 1978), p. 189.

43. Allen Ginsberg, *Allen Verbatim*, pp. 172, 180.

44. Allen Ginsberg, *Howl and Other Poems* (1959; San Francisco: City Lights, 1982), p. 14.

45. Basil Bunting, *Collected Poems*, p. 129.

46. Guy Davenport, "The Symbol of the Archaic," in *GOI* 21.

47. See Guy Davenport, "The House That Jack Built," in *GOI* 57–58. "The essence of daedalian art is that it conceals what it most wishes to show."

48. Jerome Rothenberg, "A Dialogue on Oral Poetry with William Spanos" (1975), in *Pre-Faces and Other Writings* (New York: New Directions, 1981), p. 27.

49. Robert Lowell, *Imitations* (New York: Farrar, Straus & Giroux, 1961), p. xi.

50. Letter to the Editor of the *English Journal*, 24 January 1931, in *The Selected Letters of Ezra Pound, 1907–1941*, ed. D. D. Paige (New York: New Directions, 1971), p. 231.

51. Frederick Seidel, "An Interview with Robert Lowell," in *Robert Lowell: A Portrait of the Artist in His Time*, ed. Michael London and Robert Boyers (New York: David Lewis, 1970), p. 279; hereafter cited as London and Boyers.

52. John Simon, "Abuse of Privilege: Lowell as Translator," *Hudson Review* 20 (1967–68), reprinted in London and Boyers, pp. 143–44.

53. Heinrich Heine, *Sämtliche Werke*, ed. Oskar Walzel et al. (Leipzig: Insel, 1911), 3: 404.

54. The translation is John Simon's in London and Boyers, p. 142. Cf. Hal Draper, *The Complete Poems of Heinrich Heine, a Modern English Version* (Boston: Suhrkamp/Insel, 1982), p. 88.

55. Lowell, *Imitations*, p. 39.

56. John Simon makes a similar point: see London and Boyers, p. 142.

57. Michael A. Bernstein, *The Tale of the Tribe: Ezra Pound and the Modern Verse Epic* (Princeton: Princeton University Press, 1980), pp. 39–40.

58. See, for example, Joel Conarroe, *John Berryman: An Introduction to the Poetry* (New York: Columbia University Press, 1977), p. 97: "*The Dream Songs*, in spite of crucial differences in intention and poetic strategy, resembles the *Cantos* more than any other modern sequence, with the possible exception of Lowell's *Notebooks*. . . . Each is a poem in progress, composed over a long period of time, that develops in concert with the life-in-progress of a protean poet. Each introduces an enormous cast of characters. . . . Each is thickly allusive, and each constantly alludes to itself, building up an elaborate network of cross references, repeated images, recurring motifs, and thematic variations."

59. Don Byrd, "The Shape of Zukofsky's Canon," *Paideuma*, Louis Zukofsky Issue, 7 (Winter 1978): 464.

60. In "The Transfigured Prose," ibid., pp. 447–53, Cid Corman gives an interesting account of the reworking of a passage in Reznikoff's *The Manner Music* into the poetic version found in "A"-12.

61. Bernstein, *Tale of the Tribe*, pp. 170–72.

62. I have discussed Davenport's collage mode in "Between Verse and Prose: Beckett and the New Poetry," *Critical Inquiry* 9, no. 2 (1982): 415–33.

63. Guy Davenport, "Persephone's Ezra," in *GOI*, 150–51.

64. Ron Silliman, "Louis Zukofsky," *Paideuma* 7: 405.

65. Rothenberg, "A Dialogue on Oral Poetry," *Pre-Faces*, p. 27; "Deep Image and Mode: An Exchange with Robert Creeley" (1960), ibid., p. 58.

66. Rothenberg, *Pre-Faces*, p. 105.

67. Ibid., p. 139.

68. Ibid., p. 143.

69. Bernstein, *Tale of the Tribe*, p. 172.

70. *America A Prophecy: A New Reading of American Poetry from Pre-Columbian Times to the Present*, ed. George Quasha and Jerome Rothenberg (New York: Random House, 1973), pp. xxix, xxxiii.

71. *Hypnologue* is Eugene Jolas's term for "a verbal replica of the experiences between waking and sleeping" (p. 428); *mudra* is Chogyam Trungpa's

term for a "a symbol, in the sense of gesture or action. It arises spontaneously as an expression of the inspiring color of phenomena. Also it is a symbol expressed with the hands to state for oneself and others the quality of different moments of meditation" (p. 437). Each term on Rothenberg's list is explained and exemplified somewhere in the section.

72. Hugh Kenner, "More on the 'Seven Lakes Canto,'" Paideuma 2 (1971); reprinted in part in Carroll F. Terrell, ed., A *Companion to the Cantos of Ezra Pound* (Berkeley: Los Angeles, and London: University of California Press, 1980), p. 190.

73. "The Eight Scenes of Sho-Sho," *Paideuma* 6 (1977); reprinted in part in *Companion to the Cantos*, pp. 190–91.

Contributors

GEORGE BORNSTEIN (University of Michigan) is the author of *Transformations of Romanticism in Yeats, Eliot, and Stevens; The Post-romantic Consciousness of Ezra Pound*; and other books.

RONALD BUSH (California Institute of Technology) is the author of *The Genesis of Ezra Pound's Cantos* and *T. S. Eliot: A Study in Character and Style*.

LILLIAN FEDER (Graduate Center, City University of New York) is the author of *Ancient Myth in Modern Poetry; Madness in Literature*; and other works.

HUGH KENNER (Johns Hopkins University) is the author of *The Pound Era; A Homemade World*; and other books.

ROBERT LANGBAUM (University of Virginia) is the author of *The Poetry of Experience; The Mysteries of Identity*; and other books.

A. WALTON LITZ (Princeton University) is the author of *Introspective Voyager: The Poetic Art of Wallace Stevens* and other books, and has recently edited, with Omar Pound, *Ezra Pound and Dorothy Shakespear: Their Letters, 1909–1914*.

STUART Y. MCDOUGAL (University of Michigan) is the author of *Ezra Pound and the Troubadour Tradition* and *Made into Movies: From Literature to Film*.

THOMAS PARKINSON (University of California, Berkeley) is the author of *W. B. Yeats: Self-Critic; W. B. Yeats: The Later Poetry*; and other books.

MARJORIE PERLOFF (University of Southern California) is the author of *The Poetics of Indeterminacy; Frank O'Hara*; and other books.

HUGH WITEMEYER (University of New Mexico) is the author of *The Poetry of Ezra Pound, 1908–1920* and *George Eliot and the Visual Arts*.

Index

233

LEAVE IN POCKET

PEACHTREE

J
KRENSKY

Krensky, Stephen.

Louise, soccer star?